Born in 1961, **FRANK GARDNER** has been the BBC's Security Correspondent since 2002, reporting on issues as diverse as terrorist attacks and hostage-taking to Afghan security and Arctic endurance challenges. He holds a degree in Arabic & Islamic Studies and was previously the BBC's correspondent in Dubai, then Cairo. In 2004, while filming in Saudi Arabia, he and his cameraman were ambushed by terrorists. His cameraman was killed and Frank was left for dead with eleven bullet wounds. He survived his injuries, returning to active news reporting within a year, and he still travels extensively. The author of two bestselling books: *Blood and Sand* and *Far Horizons*, Frank has also written for *GQ*, the *Economist* and the *Sunday Times*. He was awarded an OBE in 2005 for services to journalism. *Crisis* is Frank's first novel, and he is currently working on his second, *Ultimatum*. He lives in London with his family.

www.penguin.co.uk

Praise for *Crisis*:

'Fast, taut, tense, accurate. A terrific read'
FREDERICK FORSYTH

'A nerve-shredding thriller with an intimate knowledge of the world it portrays. This is intelligent, high-voltage story-telling of the very highest order'
TONY PARSONS

'A terrific page-turner'
SUNDAY TIMES

'Written by someone who has been there, done that and knows what it's about, *Crisis* is a thriller you just can't put down'
Sir ROGER MOORE

'Follows the path pioneered by Frederick Forsyth . . . authenticity seeps from every page . . . this is a promising start'
DAILY MAIL

'Gardner knows his subject – and it shows. A rattling good read'
JOHN HUMPHRYS

'Action-packed . . . the book's title scarcely does justice to such a thrilling read'
HUFFINGTON POST

'Gardner has written a fast and exciting story rooted in the present horrifying dangers that surround us. *Crisis* is brimful of an insider's insights and reeks of authority'
GERALD SEYMOUR

'Impressive . . . Gardner's debut begins at speed and scarcely draws breath thereafter'
THE TIMES

'A seriously compulsive page turner'
PETER SNOW

'Combines insider knowledge with heart-in-mouth excitement'
i-NEWSPAPER

'Few thriller debuts possess the confidence and verve of Frank Gardner's *Crisis* . . . a book of exhilarating panache'
SUNDAY TIMES

'Fast moving'
THE SUN

'An absolutely irresistible debut: smart, authentic, and always entertaining . . . intelligent, polished and simply, but effectively, written – high-voltage story-telling at its best and worthy of Frederick Forsyth or John le Carré'
CRIME REVIEW

'Gardner obviously has an up-to-the-minute understanding of contemporary warfare and he is also a very good writer. This is a thrilling adventure that shows brave men doing brave things'
LITERARY REVIEW

'Gardner is a dab hand at ratchetting up the tension . . . a must read'
BUSINESS STANDARD

Also by Frank Gardner

BLOOD AND SAND
FAR HORIZONS

and published by Bantam Books

Crisis

Frank Gardner

BANTAM BOOKS

LONDON • TORONTO • SYDNEY • AUCKLAND • JOHANNESBURG

TRANSWORLD PUBLISHERS
61–63 Uxbridge Road, London W5 5SA
www.penguin.co.uk

Transworld is part of the Penguin Random House group of companies
whose addresses can be found at global.penguinrandomhouse.com

First published in Great Britain in 2016 by Bantam Press
an imprint of Transworld Publishers
Bantam edition published 2017

A CIP catalogue record for this book
is available from the British Library.

ISBNs 9780857503169 (B format)
9780857503725 (A format)

Typeset in 11/13 pt Palatino LT Std by Jouve (UK), Milton Keynes
Printed and bound by Clays Ltd, Bungay, Suffolk.

Penguin Random House is committed to a sustainable
future for our business, our readers and our planet. This book
is made from Forest Stewardship Council® certified paper.

1 3 5 7 9 10 8 6 4 2

Crisis

Prologue

BUTTERFLIES. SUNLIGHT AND butterflies. That was what he remembered. Dappled patterns on tropical foliage, bird calls from high up in the tree canopy, and so many butterflies. Really big ones. As big as a man's hand and blue as a gem. Dazzling, dancing, beckoning him to follow. Come with us, they seemed to say, and you'll be safe.

In convoy they drove out that morning, the families of the oil company senior executives, singing on their way to the annual corporate picnic. Last year, it was a private beach near Cartagena, and this year a country club on the very edge of the jungle. Beside drooping vines there were trestle tables laden with food, baseball for the grown-ups, a makeshift jungle gym for the kids. And Luke Carlton, just turned ten, was bored to tears. Inquisitive and adventurous, the games did nothing for him. He watched, scowling and grumpy, as the CEO stood on an upturned crate. He was American, jowly and gregarious, with a big belly-laugh and a lime-green polo shirt that struggled to contain his ballooning waistline. He was making some sort of speech in slow, halting Spanish with a terrible accent. Luke reckoned he and his classmates could speak better Spanish than that.

Luke picked his moment. Unseen, he slipped away from the group and darted into the forest, following the butterflies. With every step, he expected to hear his name called and the sound of running footsteps followed by a sharp rebuke, but it never came. The path veered left and he took it, arrived at a fork and turned right. The butterflies were everywhere, folding their gossamer wings as they alighted. They were his friends – they had to be: why else would they be showing him the way? More than once he stopped and held up his hands for them to land on. He smiled when one fluttered onto his nose and another onto his blond hair, which his mother had brushed only that morning.

He should probably be heading home, he thought, and began to backtrack down the path. But there, blocking his way, was a large fallen log. He didn't recognize it. At his feet a trail of chestnut-coloured ants swarmed across the track.

Soon the path gave out altogether and there, hanging off his bare leg, was a leech. Slimy, black as a slug, gorging on his blood. He tried to flick it off with his thumb and forefinger but it was stuck fast to his flesh. Luke shrugged. It didn't occur to him that he was lost, just that he'd be in trouble with his parents when he got back.

At that moment he saw that he was not alone. There were three of them, standing silent and watching. Never in his wildest dreams had Luke seen anyone who looked like that. Their faces were painted a vivid purple, their scalps shaven smooth, and each had some black object inserted into his lower lip. Round their necks they wore strings of animal teeth. Or were they bones? He couldn't tell. The men were small and wiry, naked but for the filthy cloths around their waists. Two carried long, curved bows; the third clutched a blowpipe. Their language was strange, all rasps and clicks, definitely not the Spanish they were teaching him at school. One moved, an arm slowly extending. Were they going to shoot him? Rooted to the spot, Luke wondered what it was like to be hit by an arrow. Did you die straight away, or slowly? Would it hurt? Were they – were they going to eat him? But now they were making a sign to him, gesturing – they wanted him to follow them.

They walked for hours. With clicks and grunts they urged him on, offering swigs of brackish water from the gourds at their waists. And then through the tangle of forest vines he could see a clearing, a dozen round thatched huts, smoky fires, barefoot children, the discarded carcass of a monkey. He caught his breath. A jeep from his father's company, with the familiar brown-and-yellow logo, stood between the huts. He ran to the door and yanked it open. 'Dad!' But a woman he didn't know was sitting in the driver's seat, her eyes red and sad. *'Mi chico,'* she said to him and held out her arms.

He stood his ground. 'Where's my mum and dad?' he demanded. 'I want my mum and dad!'

'Your mother and father . . . There has been a terrible, terrible accident on the road. All day they looked for you, and when they tell them you are found they came at once. They were driving so very fast. They could not wait to see you, they did not see the truck. Oh, Luke, we are so, so sorry.'

A butterfly fluttered close to his face. He slapped it away. 'You're lying!' he shouted. 'Where are they? I want to see my mum and dad!' But she shook her head and her eyes welled with tears, though his were still dry. 'They are gone, Luke. Your parents are gone. They are in Heaven now. May God look after you.'

Chapter 1

FIRST CAME THE antennae. Brown, swivelling, twitching. Then the shiny armour-plated body, emerging from the dark recesses of the drains. Jeremy Benton watched with disgust as the first cockroach of the night crawled out from his hotel sink. This place was a dump and he couldn't wait to leave it. Forty-seven years old, hair thinning, mortgage worries mounting. Alone in a Colombian hotel room, trying to focus on the job instead of fretting about his bank balance, while the ceiling fan turned lazy circles and the sweat rolled down his fleshy neck and soaked his fraying collar.

The insect grew bolder, probing the grime-encrusted porcelain, foraging and tasting. In one impulsive movement, Benton launched himself off the bed and struck with a rolled-up magazine. 'Got you!' He missed and the roach shot back into the drains. He sat down heavily, already out of breath. He looked at his watch. It was time. He reached under his jacket and felt the cold, metallic shape of the Browning 9mm automatic. Not the weapon he had asked for – this model had a date stamp on it that was even older than him – but it was all they'd had at short notice in the embassy armoury. They had even made him sign out every single one of the thirteen rounds that had come with it. He had put in his time on the range this year – you had to if you expected to keep your firearms licence in the Service – but he hoped he wouldn't need the pistol. If he was honest with himself, Benton knew he wasn't cut out for the heavy stuff. If he was really honest, he would say he was scared shitless.

Jeremy Benton had been offered the usual 'security envelope' for tonight's job, a close-protection detail of SAS troopers disguised, not always convincingly, as civilians. It was a toss-up between personal safety and raising profile, so Benton had gone for a compromise. The security detail had dropped him off at the hotel, then melted away. This operation, he had told London, was so sensitive, so secret, it had to be kept low profile. He needed to be alone.

Dusk falls quickly on the Pacific coast of Colombia and it was not yet seven o'clock when he slipped out of his hotel in the dark. To Benton, Tumaco by night had an intangible, brooding malevolence. Maybe it was its proximity to the dangerous border with Ecuador, or perhaps the resentful looks cast at him by some of the ninety thousand impoverished townspeople, mostly of African descent, who stared out from darkened doorways with nothing to do and nowhere to go. There were still huge disparities of wealth in this country. In Bogotá you could mix with millionaires and dine in the finest restaurants, but down here on the coast, the Afro-Colombians were close to the bottom of the economic pile.

And always there was the dank, fetid smell that rose from the rotting shanty huts on stilts, perched above the mud banks where crabs competed for space with rats. Only one industry counted down here: the white stuff, in all its stages – paste, powder and leaf – and how to get as much as possible smuggled across the border or out to sea. Gone were the days of the once seemingly invincible cartels, the Montoyas and the Norte del Valle. The world's most infamous drug kingpin, Pablo Escobar, was long dead and buried. In twenty-first-century Colombia the cocaine cartels and traffickers, the *narcotraficantes,* had fragmented into numerous smaller cartels or criminal *bandas,* harder to catch and just as ruthless. But the Colombian government, with help from the Americans and the British, had been steadily taking them down, one by one, going after the structures, the family leaders, the organizers. You didn't stay long at the top in this business – two years at most – before you ended your days bunkered in a flat with six mobile phones in front of you, waiting for the door to come crashing in.

Benton walked briskly away from the hotel security guard on the gate, turned a corner and dropped to his knees behind a wall, pretending to do up his shoelaces while glancing up and around him to see if anyone was following. Old-fashioned tradecraft, tried and tested. He breathed out slowly: yes, he was alone. He moved on, down a potholed back lane, past a row of street stalls where smoke rose from a dozen sizzling barbecues, and onto a string of straw-roofed drinking dens. The soft lilt of salsa played from somewhere behind a bar, reminding him of how much he loved this continent. A boy ran up to him and tugged at his trousers. '*Señor! Señor!* Give me a present!' Benton patted his pockets without breaking his step, produced an old pen and handed it to the child, whose face betrayed his disappointment. Benton smiled and walked on.

As arranged, Fuentes was waiting for him, one hand curled round a perspiring beer, the other drumming nervously on the Formica table. They spoke quietly in Spanish, Fuentes swigging his beer and looking periodically over his shoulder, Benton sipping a lukewarm Sprite.

'You're absolutely sure it's going down tonight?' asked the MI6 officer.

'*Seguro.* You brought the equipment?' said Fuentes.

'*Por supuesto.*' Benton nodded. 'Of course.' He patted the day sack between his knees, feeling through the material for the angular contours of the night-vision goggles and the infrared camera. Fuentes was every bit as jumpy as he was – he could see that, even in the dim light of the solitary bulb that dangled above the bar. In two years of working together they had never undertaken anything quite as risky as this.

'You know what they will do to me and my family,' said Fuentes, 'what they will do to you too, if they catch us?'

Benton didn't reply. He put a handful of damp, curled peso notes on the bar for their drinks and motioned for them to leave. They had been over this before. No one was forcing him to take the risk, Benton reminded him. They had planned the operation together. The two men had built up trust between them, agent and case officer, and mutual respect. Both of them wanted to see it through. Privately, though, Benton drew some reassurance from the knowledge that the agent, Geraldo Fuentes, had been regularly polygraphed, hooked up by wires to several electronic monitors, while a dour security man with thin lips and unblinking eyes had thrown questions at him. He had passed each time with flying colours; his loyalty was not in doubt.

Not far south of Tumaco the track gave out and the jungle took over. Fuentes parked the pickup truck, backing it deep into the undergrowth as Benton had shown him. 'No nosy parking,' the MI6 officer had told him, when they had started to train him. 'You never know when you'll need to get out in a hurry.' He switched off the engine and for a minute the two men sat in silence, adjusting their senses to the tropical night. A whining in their ears announced the first of the mosquitoes and Benton slapped irritably at his neck. 'Bloody mozzies,' he grumbled. 'We don't get them up in Bogotá.'

Fuentes put a hand on his arm, his finger to his lips, and shook his head emphatically. It would be an uncomfortable night for both of them. '*Tranquilo*,' he whispered. 'It is only the ones that bite in the daytime that carry the dengue fever.' He didn't mention the virulent strain of jungle malaria carried by the night-biting variety.

The mission was simple: get in close, get the photos, and get out. It was what the military would call 'a close target recce'. Fuentes had a good idea where the sentries would be posted – after all, he knew most of them by name. At his last meeting with his MI6 case officer he had drawn him a sketch map of the location and they had rehearsed what to do if they were compromised: disperse in opposite directions, then zigzag back through the jungle to the pickup. The practice run had not been a stunning success: Benton had tripped over a root almost immediately and had had to be helped back to his feet.

Twenty minutes after they'd set off they squatted, lathered in sweat. Benton was being driven half insane by the persistent whine of the mosquitoes. Fuentes poked him gently in the ribs and pointed. Down the track ahead and to the right, they could just make out through the foliage a yellow light. Benton reached into his sack, took out the NV goggles and fiddled with the focus. In the humid night air the lenses steamed up immediately and he had to wipe them twice on his shirt. On the third attempt the scene swam into focus.

He was looking at an open-sided thatched hut and a group of men sitting at a table, lit by a hurricane lamp that hung from a hook. He recognized the man in the middle from the files: El Gato. The Cat. A middle-ranking player. Why did these narco types always have to give themselves such stupid names? Benton panned right to the other men at the table and held his breath. Fuentes had been right. They were Asians, not Colombians. Chinese Triads? Japanese Yakuza? Christ knows, he couldn't tell, but some kind of international deal was definitely going down. This would have to go in his next report and he would need the images to send back to London. And tonight was quite possibly the only chance he would get. Less than three months to go before his Colombia posting was up and he was not going to pass up this chance. For the briefest of moments he saw himself being ushered into the Chief's office back at Vauxhall Cross and congratulated. Perhaps even a knighthood on retirement.

He gestured to Fuentes that he needed to move closer, but the agent shook his head and drew his finger across his throat. Benton considered him in the darkness, so close they could hear each other's breathing even above the incessant chorus of frogs and cicadas; the jungle at night is far from quiet. For Benton, this was a fork-in-the-road moment and he knew it.

He rose to his feet, gently shaking off Fuentes' restraining hand. Reaching down, he removed the Browning from its holster, slid back the mechanism and chambered a round. There was a loud metallic click as the gun was cocked and Fuentes winced.

Benton took tentative steps forward through the undergrowth, pausing every few yards. His heart was racing and his throat felt like sandpaper. He wished he had brought the bottle of water from the truck. He looked through the viewfinder and reckoned he was almost in range to get a good enough picture. He let the camera dangle round his neck and felt the comforting weight of the pistol. He took another step forward.

Without warning, a sentry reared up behind him and struck him hard between the shoulder blades with the metal butt of an assault rifle. Benton's pistol fell uselessly from his grasp. He groaned and slumped.

'Oye! Venga!' the sentry called out to the men in the hut, and suddenly there was pandemonium, shadowy figures spilling towards them. Fuentes, unseen, hugged the ground, watching in silent horror as they dragged Benton backwards by his armpits to the hut. Guards were fanning out with torches in all directions.

Fuentes got up and ran, faster than he had ever run in his life, thrashing blindly through the lush foliage that tore at his face and shirt, stumbling like a drunk the last few yards to the truck. He jumped into the cab, dropping the keys at his feet. Scrabbling with his fingers amid the detritus he'd been meaning to clear out, he found them too late to start the engine. Crouched behind the dashboard, half hidden by the surrounding bushes, he could see figures silhouetted on the same dirt track they had driven down only an hour ago. They were calling to each other, their torch-beams probing the night. And then Fuentes heard something that nearly made his heart stop. The distant sound of a man screaming, in intense drawn-out terror and pain.

Chapter 2

'GOD, IT'S RAMMED in here tonight.'

'Sorry, babes?'

'It's a bloody crush!' shouted Luke, cupping his hand to her ear above the thumping music. 'And stop calling me "babes"!'

'But you know I only do it to wind you up!' She slid her hand around his waist and pulled him closer. He caught her scent. Nearly a year together and still it did something for him. Slender and self-assured, Elise was nearly as tall as he was.

They had met at the art gallery where she worked, on the opening night of an exhibition of brightly coloured gouache paintings. His immediate thought had been: This girl is out of my league.

It was true that Elise had no shortage of admirers, but the man who had strolled in intrigued her. He had the loose, easy movements of someone capable of immense speed and power. His face was angular, lightly tanned, beneath short, sandy hair. Grey eyes. Was he a model? God, she hoped not – she wasn't going to make that mistake again. No, the broken nose and weathered look told her otherwise. This was not a man who spent a lot of time in front of the mirror. There was something paradoxical about him: a blend of danger, adventure . . . and security. She felt safe in his presence.

A week later, on their first date, he had nearly blown it. 'Tell me about yourself,' she had said, appraising him watchfully as she sipped her peach Bellini in a bar off Piccadilly.

He'd wondered what he should say. Born in London, brought up in South America, orphaned at ten. Most of his adult life in the Royal Marines and Special Forces. On operations he had killed at least four people and didn't lose any sleep over it. Too much information for a first date? Yes, probably.

'Well,' he had begun, with a half-raised eyebrow, 'I suppose you could say I'm from everywhere.' It was his International Man of Mystery line and had worked wonders on nights out in Plymouth and Poole. Elise had said nothing, just got up and walked away to the bar. You twat, Luke, he thought, you've lost her already.

But Elise had waved him over to join her, a frosty mojito lined up for him on the bar. 'Drink this,' she'd ordered, with a smile. 'It might improve your conversation.' Things had moved quickly: six months on from that night they were sharing a flat. Now they were spending their Thursday evening on a small, sweaty dance floor in a members-only nightclub in Mayfair, waiting for friends who hadn't shown up, surrounded by rich boys in blazers and tasselled loafers, their girlfriends in pearls. You could almost touch the money in the air here, thought Luke, but what on earth made all those people want to dress like their parents when they weren't even out of their twenties? A boy in a canary-yellow cashmere cardigan was dancing backwards and collided with Luke, too busy mouthing the words to 'Get Lucky'. Luke regarded him with pity: he was wearing Ray-Bans in a nightclub.

'OK,' he said to Elise, 'let's get out of here.' She offered no resistance: it was not her kind of place either.

Together they side-slipped through the crowd, emerging into the cool drizzle of the London night. Elise paused to light a cigarette, smiling coyly at him as he cupped his hands around hers to shield her lighter from the breeze, the gap left by his missing middle finger standing out next to her own perfect, shapely hands. Luke had never understood the smoking thing and vowed to have another go at her to stop. Maybe next year. They turned into Curzon Street, almost empty now at past one in the morning, then crossed the road near the palatial Saudi Embassy, nodding at the two armed and bored policemen guarding the gates, then walked up a dimly lit side-street to where they had left the car.

'Excuse, please. You have light?' The man stepped out of the shadow of a parked van.

Seriously? thought Luke. That was such a cliché – it belonged in some dated vigilante film. A Charles Bronson classic, the ones his uncle used to watch. But Luke was instinctively on his guard. He didn't like the look of the man, who had the air of organized crime about him. What was he? Albanian, perhaps. Hard to tell in this light. Elise had caught it too, but her manners got the better of her and she fished in her bag for a lighter.

At that moment Luke felt a pair of huge arms lock

tight around him from behind and immediately his training kicked in. As the first attacker made a lunge for Elise's handbag, Luke dropped his weight to his knees and pitched himself forward, jack-knifing his assailant over his shoulders. The man landed with a smack on the wet pavement, knocking the wind from his lungs and cracking his head on the concrete. 'You fugger!' he wheezed, in pain and surprise.

He was not the only one. What the hell d'you think you're playing at? Luke asked himself, as he straightened up. You think this is a punch-up in Union Street in Plymouth on a Saturday night? Remember who you work for now. It's supposed to be all about discretion, subtlety and hugging the shadows, not crash-banging across the city like Daniel Craig. Next time just give them the bloody money and walk on.

But the action wasn't over. Elise's slim frame was deceptive: she had her own training, honed over long, painful hours in the *dojo*. As the second man lunged for her handbag she stepped back, putting her weight onto her right leg, bending it slightly, then pistoning out a side-thrust kick with her left leg towards the man's jaw. It would have been a technically perfect move, if only the heel of her shoe hadn't snapped. Elise lost her balance and fell sideways onto the pavement. In an instant the man was on top of her, grappling for her handbag. And then he was rising clear, as if pulled by some hidden hand. Luke's fingers were clamped on the man's oily hair as he lifted him up, then slammed him face down onto the ground, where he stayed.

Elise winced, rose quickly to her feet, forgetting the broken heel, and lost her balance again. Luke caught her and, for a moment, they clung to each other, recovering their breath. One assailant lay face down but breathing, the other had already abandoned his friend, slinking off into the night. Before she had time to protest, Luke scooped her up and carried her to the car. Inside, doors locked, seatbelts on, she kissed him forcefully on the lips. 'Thanks, babes,' she whispered.

'No drama,' he replied. 'Lucky only one of us was wearing heels.'

Chapter 3

IN THE DAMP, humid air of the tropical night, the torchbeam reached out like an accusing finger. 'Turn him over,' said the captain. 'Do it now.' Gingerly, with uncharacteristic delicacy, the Colombian police conscripts approached the motionless body. In their confusion they tried to turn it over in opposite directions, pulling against each other, then collapsing backwards into giggles, like over-excited schoolchildren.

'Madre de Dios!' The captain pushed them out of the way. 'Must I do everything myself?' He grabbed the body by the shoulder furthest from him and gave it a heave, jumping back just too late as it settled heavily on his polished black boots. *'Ay, mierda!'* he exclaimed in disgust. The man had soiled himself and a thick rivulet of dried blood had run down his neck from where his ear would have been. It was clear that he had not died peacefully. In their green jungle fatigues the policemen stood in a circle, craning their necks for a better view. 'Search his pockets, find some ID,' ordered the captain, reaching for his mobile phone.

From somewhere behind them in the village a dog barked, and over on the horizon, towards the lights of

Tumaco, a solitary firework arced into the night sky then puttered out, drifting silently to the ground. In this part of Colombia, corpses turned up in all sorts of places. Hell, thought the captain. This was the sixth that month. He turned away, dialling the number for the duty sergeant at the fortified hotel they used as their base in town.

'Capitán!' a conscript called, sounding excited. 'This *muchacho* is not from here. He is a *gringo*! His name is—'

The captain snatched the maroon booklet out of the man's hands. Slowly he read aloud, straining to make out the italic script in the torchlight, 'Her Bree-tannic Ma-jess-ty . . . Sec-re-tary of State . . . requests and requires . . .' One of the younger policemen coughed and turned the first page of the passport for his captain. There was the dead man's face staring up at him above a suit and tie, both ears still attached. Benton, Jeremy Maynard. British citizen. Date of birth: 14 January 1969. Sex: M. Place of birth: Scarborough, UK. *'Mierda!'* The captain swore again. This was going to be complicated.

Just over eight kilometres away in a secluded whitewashed bungalow with peeling paint and a purple neon light above the door, Major Humberto Elerzon was starting to enjoy himself. La Casa de Dreams was one of the few consolations he had found in this godforsaken dump of a town. He hated Tumaco and its lousy climate, its ravenous mosquitoes, and its casual capacity for violence nurtured by its close association with the drugs trade. He hated it and always had done, since the first day of his posting – a punishment posting, no question. Tipped for promotion to colonel, he had been a rising star in the corridors of power at Police Headquarters in Bogotá, until that one stupid mistake. It was National Day, fiesta time and maybe he had drunk a little too much, but how could he resist her? When they'd thought no one was looking they had left the party together, raced down the steps to his car and checked into a nearby hotel. The receptionist had recognized her and made the call once they were up in the 'matrimonial suite'. The major shuddered at the memory. The humiliation, the shame, the embarrassment. All those junior cops standing there, grinning in the doorway, the cameras going off and him in his underpants. How was he supposed to know she was the president's niece, for Christ's sake?

So here he was, past forty, his career torpedoed, sentenced to eke out his posting in this far-flung corner of the country, running a provincial police station in one of the most dangerous parts of Colombia. His wife had long since lost all respect for him. In truth, they had never been close, and when he had told her of his posting to this coastal backwater she had flatly refused to leave the cool comfort of Bogotá. He suspected another man was involved but, frankly, he was past caring. He paid her a portion of his monthly salary and sought what comfort he could in the dingy bars and brothels of Tumaco. There was money to be made here, no question about that. He had known people in Customs to retire to Miami on what they had made in this part of Colombia, simply from looking the other way at the right moment. But the men from Internal Affairs would be keeping close tabs on him – they had told him as much, practically spelled out that even his own subordinates would be watching him. He was trapped. Which was why he was thinking of making alternative arrangements.

Major Elerzon did not like to be disturbed when he was being entertained in La Casa de Dreams so when his mobile rang from his jacket on the chair by the window he chose to ignore it. Of far more interest was the magenta bra of the woman in his arms. Rosalita was not her real name but she had been his favourite since his first, exploratory visit. True, they had had a brief falling-out last year when she'd given him an unwelcome dose of crabs, but they had kissed and made up, and now he was turning his attention to the clasp at her back. Bloody mobile! Why wouldn't it stop ringing? Probably some imbecile checking up on him. With a groan he heaved himself off the bed, catching his reflection in the mirror and reminding himself to get down to the police gym. He snatched up the phone. '*Sí?*'

By the time he had put down the phone Major Elerzon's libido had wilted. What the hell was an Englishman doing dead on his patch? This was no place for tourists. Must be a narco.

Twenty minutes later he was back at the police base in the fortified hotel, just in time to watch the patrol bring in the body. This was a disaster. If he didn't move quickly the press would be all over it before he could file his report, and those *cabrones* in Bogotá would hang him out to dry. He retreated to his office to think, retrieving a half-empty bottle of tequila from beneath a crumpled copy of yesterday's newspaper. Before long there was a knock on the door. The coroner, of whom he had seen far too much in the past year.

'Well?'

'Es complicado,' replied the coroner.

'You mean you don't know what he died of?' snapped the major, lighting a cigarette without offering one to his guest. He had never liked the coroner, a respected local family man who seemed to lead a squeaky-clean life.

'Not yet, no. You see, someone really wanted him dead. I mean, really, really wanted him dead.'

'Go on.' The major breathed smoke up to the ceiling in a thin coil and watched it curl around the motionless blades of the fan. It still wasn't fixed.

'It's as if he was killed several times over. He was stabbed in the ribs. I expect you saw that in the patrol commander's report.' The major looked down at his desk. 'There's the ear, of course, but he didn't die from that, and then there's a needle mark in his neck. He may have been injected with something. I'm sending blood samples up to the toxicology lab on the next flight.'

'Any narcotics on him?'

'Nothing. But they did find this.' The coroner reached into his tunic and handed across a plastic evidence bag.

Reluctantly, the major put down his cigarette, opened the bag, took out a small notebook and flipped through the pages. There were scribblings in some foreign script. Japanese? Chinese? He didn't know. Either way, it probably wasn't important but he decided he should look after it himself.

Chapter 4

THE CALL CAME through on the secure line to Vauxhall Cross at just after 0600. It was the duty officer who took it, bleary with tiredness and nearing the end of his shift. From more than eight thousand kilometres away, the voice spoke, distorted by clicks and pauses on the line from inside the SIS Colombia station, tucked away in a nondescript farmhouse in the wooded hills just north of Bogotá. The DO stifled a yawn and began to jot notes – then nearly broke his pen. This was unbelievable. The CIA were always carving stars into that wall of theirs at Langley, one for every officer killed in the line of duty, but over here, in the Service? Unheard of. He peered across the desk at the emergency numbers taped to the wall, took a deep breath and dialled.

At 0630 Luke Carlton was in the gym in Battersea when his phone lit up beside him. He liked being up early: after twelve years in the forces it was a hard habit to shake, even if it sometimes infuriated his girlfriend. Although he was out now, a civilian, he still put himself through a punishing hour of CrossFit most mornings, the exhausting, all-round fitness programme of choice for those who had served in Special Forces.

Two minutes' intensive strength and endurance exercise, pause, then repeat for fifty minutes. The memory of the attempted mugging in Mayfair was still fresh and he would do his damnedest to keep up his fitness.

Now his phone was flashing insistently. Before answering, his eyes flicked to the TV monitor on the wall. Had something big happened? Some horror committed by Boko Haram in Nigeria? A hostage crisis in Yemen? 'Breaking news' read the subtitled caption. 'House prices surge in London suburbs.' No clues there then. But a phone call at this time of day could mean just one thing: the office. Wiping the sweat out of his eyes with his forearm, he glanced at the number on the small screen and recognized it immediately. The voice at the other end asked how quickly he could get over to Vauxhall Cross. In the few months since he'd started working for MI6, he had fitted in surprisingly quickly. If he chose to stay, and many didn't, he had been told he could go far.

'How soon can I be in?' Luke checked his watch. 'Depends how smartly you need me dressed. I'm in the gym.'

'I don't care what you're wearing,' said his line manager, Angela Scott. 'Come dressed as an astronaut, for all I care. Just get in here now.'

He knew better than to ask what was going on. In any case, he'd be briefed soon enough. 'Roger that.'

'What?'

'Sorry. I haven't quite shaken off the military jargon yet. I'm on my way.'

She hung up.

In sweat pants and trainers, Luke took the lift down from the gym to the underground garage. Elise and he lived in one of those modern steel-and-glass apartment blocks that had sprung up on the south bank of the Thames. Mussels Wharf, it was called – they'd had a few laughs about that. Renting for now, but maybe they'd look to buy something next year – if they were still together, of course. He got a few funny looks as he pulled out into the traffic, but he always did, driving a scratched Land Rover Defender out of a flash Thameside apartment block. His London friends liked to claim that it stank of manure but Luke didn't give a monkey's. This was his way of staying in touch with his country roots. Besides, there was something pleasingly familiar about its blunt, functional lines and its quasi-military practicality.

Past the New Covent Garden fruit-and-veg depot, and the hideous concrete statue at Vauxhall Bridge – what were they thinking, building that? – then his windscreen gradually filled with the imposing green-and-sandstone fortress that now paid his salary, Vauxhall Cross, known to those who worked there as VX. It was the publicly declared headquarters, since 1994, of MI6, the Secret Intelligence Service. What a difference from Century House, the dingy old tower block in Lambeth where his uncle had worked before the move to Vauxhall. What a soulless dump that had been. Once, Luke had gone there with him. He had been just old enough to take it all in: the petrol station at street level, the brown raincoats hanging on pegs, the brown suits, even the brown soup in the canteen. To him it seemed a monochrome world inhabited by chain-smoking men in suits and typing girls with names like Betty who stooped to stroke his cheek. But he remembered his uncle talking about some real characters there. A woman who knew every detail in every file, back in the Stone Age before it was all digitized and encrypted. His uncle had talked, probably more than he should have, about the occasional ripple of excitement when a Soviet defector was reeled in, and the brief, intense feeling of camaraderie as he and his colleagues had stood together and sung Christmas carols. 'Nothing like it,' he had told his nephew, 'all of us working for a common cause. One day you'll understand.'

The lights were changing now and Luke tried to focus on what he was about to walk into. But still his uncle's stories kept flooding back to him. A tea trolley had come round every day at eleven o'clock and four, pushed by an East End lad called Charlie. It was an open secret, said his uncle, that his close relatives were linked to the notorious Kray twins, Ronnie and Reggie, the kings of London's violent underworld in the 1960s. Someone must have decided it was better to have those guys onside. There had been a rough edge to Service employees in those days, thought Luke, unlike the polished smoothies in the Foreign and Commonwealth Office. Charlie had been there so long that he knew everything about everyone's private life. They'd given him an MBE and he'd retired to Margate to bask in his glory. Then, said his uncle, there was the old caretaker who could recognize people by their footsteps. He had come back into Century one day, after years stationed in Warsaw, and this old boy had had his back turned away from him but he said, 'Welcome home, Mr Carlton, nice to have you back.' Amazing. And then there was the Cut, said his uncle, the Lambeth side-street with its Greek-run brothels and tawdry Italian restaurants where well-spoken Service secretaries met their intelligence officer lovers to share their hopes and dreams of postings to distant embassies, far away from SE1 and the dismal clank of trains pulling into Waterloo on a rainy afternoon.

Luke stopped at the large green-painted steel gate. High on a wall, a camera swivelled towards him, the CCTV feeding his image back to the security officers' control room inside. On tiny oiled wheels, the gate slid open and he nudged the Land Rover forward. A man emerged from a sentry box with an inspection mirror, gave the vehicle the once-over, then waved him on. Inside the building he got out of the car and locked it, then pressed his electronic swipe card to a reader, prompting an automatic door to hiss open for him. 'Carrying sensitive material like documents?' read the notice on the wall. 'Then check security procedures.'

Luke strode quickly past the royal coat of arms and the official commemoration plaque. 'The Secret Intelligence Service,' it read. 'Opened by Her Majesty the Queen on July 14th 1994.' Incredible to think that in his uncle's day MI5 and MI6 had officially not existed.

'Shocking, isn't it?'

He turned. Springer, a young intelligence officer he barely knew, was holding open the lift doors for him. 'I mean, what *are* they going to tell his family? Nice bloke, Benton. He was an instructor on my course down at the Base. Useful squash player too.'

The lift pinged open at Luke's floor and Springer nodded a goodbye. 'Hang on,' said Luke, in turn holding open the lift door. 'What do you mean, telling his family? What's happened to Benton?'

Springer's face showed that he knew he had said too much, even within those secure walls. 'Oh, right,' he said. 'Well, you'll know soon enough.' Then the lift door closed on him.

For a minute Luke stood on the landing, people rushing past him. He was shocked. He had never met Benton but they had spoken many times on the phone and Luke had seen his reports, always carefully nuanced and caveated. Now he had become a casualty and Luke had no idea how MI6 would handle a man killed in the course of duty. What would they put on his tombstone? 'Benton. Career spook. Useful squash player. RIP.' Maybe not.

'Coffee's on the sideboard. Grab a cup. You've got a few minutes to prep before we go in to see the Chief.' Angela Scott was a woman of few words. Petite and short, her auburn hair was tied back, her clothes neat, stylish but simple, a tiny gold crucifix just visible on her pale, freckled chest. As line managers go, Luke reckoned he could do a lot worse than Angela.

A former station chief in Mexico City, she had been at the sharp end of agent running. Yet from the first day he had been assigned to her team in the Latin America division she had taken him under her wing, never once patronizing. She had recognized that he needed time to adjust to his new life after twelve years in the Forces, but in the few months they had been working together he had shown her that he was a fast learner. And his Spanish was better than hers. Way better. Angela had done six months at a cosy language institute for British students in Guatemala, while Luke had spent his early childhood in Colombia and returned often, absorbing the language, perfecting his slang.

'All I can tell you for now,' she said, 'is that we've

lost our station chief in Bogotá. Of course, you knew Jerry Benton from his reports. He's been killed on a deniable op, which we hadn't even told the Colombians about. And we've lost contact with Synapse.'

'Synapse?' said Luke. 'Christ. He was Benton's primary agent. The intel he was feeding us was pure gold.'

'Yes. It's bad.' Angela let out a small sigh. 'The Colombians are seriously peeved. Our ambassador will have to go into the Foreign Ministry to explain what the hell our man was doing in a coke-infested jungle six hundred and fifty kilometres from the capital. Benton was declared and it's supposed to be a friendly nation.' She glanced down at her watch and frowned. 'Look, here's the thing. C's called us up to his office. He wants to be put fully in the picture before he addresses the whole staff.'

'C' was the first abbreviation Luke had learned on his induction. It was what they called the Chief of SIS. It was not an abbreviation for 'Chief' but the first letter of 'Cumming', from the founder of the Service in 1909, Sir George Mansfield Smith-Cumming, a monocled and medalled character in cocked hat and braid. He had always signed his letters 'C' and somehow the tradition had stuck, one of the few that had.

'Director of Ops will be there,' continued Angela.

'Don't you mean controller of Ops?' replied Luke.

'That's a sore point for some people here. No, Sir John Sawers changed that title when he was Chief. Part of his drive to bring us more into line with the rest of Whitehall. We don't have controllers any more, we have directors. Anyway, you're about to meet most of them: Operations, Counter-terrorism, the Americas, Legal Affairs. Basically, the big guns. Luke, you grew up in Colombia and you've spent the last three months on the Latin America counter-narcotics file, so I'm expecting you to deliver a situational brief. Do you need more time?'

'Ideally.'

'Well, I'm afraid you haven't got it. See you upstairs at half past.' She glanced at his trainers and sweat-soaked tracksuit. 'Oh, and you'd better get changed. There's a locker down the end of the corridor. Lorimer from our Brussels station keeps a shirt and suit in it for whenever he pops over.' She appraised him. 'You're about the same size. Best put it on. He'll get over it.'

In the space of twenty-eight minutes Luke found the locker, changed into the suit – a little tight in places but it would do – splashed some water over his face, then cast a last-minute eye over his recent case notes. Not much he could do about the shoes. It would just have to be trainers and a suit.

He was met on the sixth floor and escorted through to the outer office, past framed photographs of David Cameron, Prince Charles and other pillars of the Establishment, past and present. The carpet up there was thicker, he noticed. Then it was into the boardroom, which looked to Luke like any other boardroom he had ever seen in countless films. Long, polished table, expensive finish, a row of framed abstracts on the wall and around fifteen or so seats all filling fast. He recognized most of the faces from his induction briefing, though he doubted any of their owners would know who he was. Quiet, ordinary-looking men and women, they might have been partners in a City law firm or a West End residential estate agency, not spymasters in Britain's most secret of secret agencies.

Luke took almost the last free seat, settling himself with some difficulty beside an overweight man in a cherry-pink polo shirt who offered him a broad smile. Had they met before? Luke didn't think so.

'Sid,' said the man, holding out a fleshy, slightly damp hand in greeting. 'Sid Khan. It's really Syed Khan, but everyone calls me Sid.' Luke took in the gold pendant and the curly chest hair poking out of the neck of the polo shirt: not exactly what he was expecting in an MI6 boardroom. Who was this guy?

'Are you on the tech side?' asked Luke, then kicked himself for making assumptions.

'Used to be. Transferred from Cheltenham. Started out here in Science and Technology. You know, working with all the gizmos and gadgets. Just the place for a bloke from Bradford with a knack for computers.'

'Right,' said Luke, still none the wiser as to what the man was doing in MI6's boardroom at a moment of crisis. 'What do you do now?'

The room went quiet as the Chief walked in. Khan leaned over hurriedly to whisper in Luke's ear: 'I run Counter-terrorism.'

Now he remembered. Of course. Sid was a legend. A first-class degree from Manchester in . . . What was it? Human/computer interaction or something. Fluent in Urdu. Rapid progression up through GCHQ, transfer to SIS, then postings to Dhaka, Islamabad and Riyadh. Apparently he'd thrown a lot of people off-balance in those countries. In a good way. They would have been expecting some clean-cut Oxbridge type in a Jermyn Street suit. Instead they'd got Sid, who ate *roti* and *naan* with his fingers, and disarmed his hosts with his easy charm. Word was that after David Cameron had upset Pakistan with that speech he'd made to Indian business leaders in Bangalore in 2010, saying they couldn't look both ways on terrorism, it was Sid who had salvaged the relationship between the two countries' intelligence agencies. Islamabad had been ready to shut down cooperation and withhold information until Khan had won them round.

The Chief took his place at the head of the table. The room tensed in expectation and Luke found himself involuntarily stiffening in his chair, as if he were back on the parade square at Lympstone. The Chief was now his commanding officer and he'd better make a good impression.

Like Angela, Sir Adam Keeling, the new Chief of MI6, was a man of few words, and many had questioned whether he had the patience to put up with all the process and protocol of Whitehall machinery. He was a career intelligence officer, a veteran of Cold War postings behind the Iron Curtain, some unorthodox assignments in central Asia, then back and forth to the Middle East. He was widely credited within the Service for getting Colonel Gaddafi's entire arsenal of poison gas dismantled.

'OK.' He faced the two lines of sombre faces, then paused while a female Royal Navy rating entered noiselessly through a side door, deposited a fresh pot of coffee in front of him and left the room. 'To state the obvious, this is a tragic day for the Service, for all of us here, and for Britain. Benton was a first-class intelligence officer and I don't wish to hear of another such death on my watch. The PM's already sent condolences to his family, Foreign Secretary's going to see them today. Sid, what have we got on the perps? Who was behind this?'

Khan locked the fingers of both hands together

and cracked his knuckles, causing a few people to wince, then stood up and made his way to the opposite end of the table from the Chief. Luke realized that the director of CT probably had his detractors in the building; probably in this room, in fact. It was a steep pyramid at the top of SIS. One chief, three director-generals and a raft of directors below that, nearly all with an eye on the top job. If they weren't in the running by the time they reached fifty, he'd heard, then a fair few people tended to walk out of the door to seek their fortune in the well-paid world of commercial intelligence. But Sid Khan was younger, unorthodox and, Luke bet, had probably ruffled a few feathers.

'Our initial assessment,' said Khan, 'is that the Colombian coke barons were behind this. The drug traffickers, the *narcotraficantes* or, as everyone calls them, the narcos. Most likely one of the clans. Someone like the Usugas. They've got the hump with what we're doing to their shipments. Twenty per cent chance it could also be dissident rebels from the FARC movement, miffed at the peace talks with the government.'

The Chief said nothing so Khan continued, 'Some of these people are diehard Marxists, still wearing the old Che Guevara T-shirts, still dreaming about a great People's Bolivarian Republic stretching all the way from the Caribbean to Chile. We know there's a crossover, a nexus, between the drug barons and the guerrillas. They're into all sorts of other stuff too over there, illegal mining, extortion, you name it. Looks like Jerry might have got himself a bit too close to one of their deals.'

The Chief made a low humming sound. Those who knew him recognized it as a danger signal. It meant he was far from satisfied. He rubbed his temples with the fingertips of both hands, causing his silvery grey hair to rise and fall before he spoke.

'Right, let's be clear on this,' he said. 'I need two things and I need them fast. I want to know who killed my station chief and, most importantly, I want the full low-down on whatever he was on to. Who's this "third party" he referred to in his last report? What were they cooking up? Are we talking narcotics, terrorism or proliferation? Or all three? We're a national bloody intelligence agency with nearly a billion-pound budget, not a guessing shop. I want to know a lot more than this. What are the Met doing?'

'Counter-terrorism Command are sending two detectives,' said Sid. 'We've requested Spanish speakers but apparently no one's available. They're all in Spain on that trawler from Liverpool.'

'Fabulous,' said the Chief, without a hint of mirth. No one smiled. He turned to Greg Sanderson, the head of Latin America Division, the only person in the room Luke actually knew. 'What have the Latins come up with?'

Sanderson pushed his glasses back to the bridge of his nose. They seemed to Luke to be rather too big for his face. 'Well,' he began, 'the Colombians have already opened their own investigation, as we'd expect. ANIC – their national intelligence agency – are the lead on this. But that's serious bandit country where Jerry was operating and it's really more of a local police operation. I believe their man in charge on the ground is . . .' he glanced at a handwritten note '. . . Major Humberto Elerzon. Don't know him, as yet.'

'OK. Anyone else? Yes, Angela?'

'C, you should hear what Luke Carlton on my team

has to say. With respect to everyone else in the room, he's our in-house Colombia expert.'

'Carlton . . . No relation, I suppose, to Matthew Carlton?'

'My uncle, sir.'

The Chief relaxed briefly. 'No need for the "sir",' he told Luke. 'Casual professionalism is our hallmark here. I remember your uncle. A good man.'

Luke felt a double twinge of satisfaction. He was pleased that his uncle had not been forgotten but, more importantly, a nod from the Chief in a room like this could do him no harm. As a newcomer in their ranks, it gave Luke a certain pedigree.

'So,' continued the Chief, 'you've obviously seen the prelim report put together by Night Duty. Let's hear you put some flesh on the bones.' With that, he settled back in his chair and folded his arms.

As one, all eyes turned to focus on Luke as he got to his feet and strode, self-conscious in his borrowed suit, to the end of the table to take Khan's place. The director of CT gave him a slap on the back as the two men passed each other. For good luck? Did Khan know that Luke had not seen the report? Angela shot him an apologetic look but said nothing. Luke was on his own and he was all too aware that his reputation would be built or destroyed by what he said in the next ten minutes.

'Right,' he began. 'The current situation is that most processed Colombian coke leaves the country by container ship. They call it rip-on, rip-off. At the last minute, just before the container is sealed, someone paid off down at the port chucks in a bunch of holdalls weighing three hundred to four hundred kilograms in all. When it docks in Europe, at Antwerp or Valencia or wherever, someone collects it. Thanks to Jerry Benton and his people, we've had some pretty good interceptions lately.'

Almost everyone had flinched at his mention of the murdered intelligence officer.

'Then there are the light aircraft,' continued Luke. 'They're flying two to three hundred kilos a time up to Honduras or Mexico. There are also the fast boats heading up both sides of Central America, and finally the mini-subs.'

'I'm sorry – the what?' interrupted the Chief.

'Miniature submarines,' replied Luke. 'They've become quite a phenomenon down there. The narcos build the subs themselves to stash drugs and smuggle them up the coast. They tend to be launched out of the swamps south of Buenaventura, then sail just below the surface all the way up to Panama and beyond. But the Colombian Navy's getting good at catching them too. Their chief of Naval Ops says they've caught over a hundred mini-subs to date.'

'Ingenious,' said the Chief. 'Go on.'

Luke noticed that Sanderson was scribbling on a piece of paper, then passing it to Khan, who looked at Luke and nodded slowly. It occurred to Luke that he was either making a really good impression or pissing off half the people in the room.

'Operation Sword of Honour,' he persevered, looking from one to another to make sure he had eye contact with everyone, however fleetingly. 'It's the Colombian campaign to take out the HVTs, the high-value targets. It's huge, it's ongoing, and we're giving them a big boost on the intel side. It's got everyone onboard over there: Special Ops, Marines, Judicial Police, attorneys, intelligence fusion centres, counter-IEDs. There's also our own joint units. They're having a major impact on the BACRIMs and that's hacking them off big-time.'

'Excuse me,' interrupted Khan. 'Am I the only person in this room who doesn't know what a BACRIM is?'

'Sorry,' said Luke. 'It's shorthand for *banda criminal*, the gangs that produce and ship the cocaine.'

'Thought you'd know that, Sid,' remarked the Chief, allowing himself the faintest of smiles on that blackest of days. Luke tried not to smile with him. This was not going to endear him to the man in the pink polo shirt.

'Telephone intercepts,' continued Luke, getting into his stride now. He was on his home turf: this stuff was his bread and butter and he was giving them what they wanted. 'The intercepts form the backbone of a major percentage of all narcotics prosecutions in Colombia and we're helping them. We've got several thousand lines operational at any one time and dozens of listening suites in-country. Signals intelligence – SIGINT – is proving key as well. The Colombians are getting direct feeds from our American counterparts at NSA. And there's the HUMINT side, of course. We've got informants inside every major *banda*, a lot of them reporting direct to us. To Benton, in fact.'

The room was very quiet.

'So, the port of Tumaco, where he was killed, is the major transit point for Colombian coca paste heading south into Ecuador and on to Peru for processing in the jungle labs. It's often more cost-effective for the narcos to smuggle it across unprocessed, less to lose if they get caught. The Colombians are very hot on counter-narcotics, their neighbours rather less so. There are two major gangs down there: Los Rostrojos and Los Chicos. Both very violent. Cutting off ears is the Chicos' trademark.'

He let the words settle, knowing the effect they would have on the room.

'So if I could suggest, C, we need to establish exactly who Benton was in contact with, who he was trailing, and why it was so important he risked his life to discover what they were up to.'

The Chief looked across at Angela and tilted his head ever so slightly. The look said, 'Your boy did OK.' Luke breathed an inward sigh of relief. He had come out unscathed from his first ever directors' summit at Vauxhall Cross.

'Thank you.' The Chief nodded curtly. Then he addressed the room: 'I knew Jerry, and that man was not a time-waster. He was on to something big and I'm making it a Tier One National Security Priority that we find out what it was.' He looked pointedly at Angela. 'I want someone who knows what he's doing at the sharp end on this case, I want a fluent Spanish speaker, and he – or she – had better be someone who can look after themselves.'

The meeting broke up and they filed out, grim-faced. Angela motioned for Luke to stay behind. 'It's you, of course,' she said.

'Say again?'

'Oh, come on, Luke, false modesty doesn't suit you. You know you're the best Spanish speaker in the Service, you know Colombia, and you fit the Chief's last criterion. I want you on the next flight down to Bogotá. Of course you'll have someone from LA tagging along with you.'

'Our Los Angeles station?'

'No!' Angela gave a short, brittle laugh. 'No, LA is

Legal Affairs. You'll get to know them rather well in this place.'

Luke groaned. After four years in Special Forces he tended to give lawyers as wide a berth as possible. 'Please tell me you're joking. Are you saying I've got to take a lawyer with me to the Colombian jungle? Seriously?'

'We don't joke in the Service,' said Angela. 'And, yes, I'm afraid that's just the world we live in now. Oh, and you'll be reporting directly to Sid Khan.' She gave a slight smile. 'Yes, I know, he's not exactly out of Central Casting, is he? And that's just what we like, keeps people guessing. But don't be fooled by his manner, Luke. Khan's done the hard yards, believe me. He likes people to think outside the box, in the way he does. He'll be weighing you up, with his mathematician's brain, so don't disappoint him. He's expecting you now. Fourth floor. Someone will meet you outside the lift. And, Luke?' Her face softened. 'Please don't end up like Benton.'

As the lift pinged open at the fourth floor Luke found himself looking straight into the face of a girl with the most beautiful unblemished skin he had ever seen. Caribbean parentage, he guessed, can't be more than twenty-five. He almost felt old.

'Luke Carlton?' Absolutely no trace of an accent. 'Hi, I'm Shakina. I work for Sid Khan. Would you like to come this way, please?'

Luke followed her, trying hard not to glance at the hips beneath the tight beige skirt. Get a grip, he told himself. You're about to be given your mission, and here you are, perving.

When they reached the door to Sid Khan's office

she knocked twice, then showed him in, closing the door after him. Khan was already back behind his desk, reading something he held in one hand and twirling a teaspoon round a china mug – 'Keep Calm and Carry On Spying' – with the other. 'A present from my late wife.' He gestured at it.

'Right,' said Luke. So Khan was a widower. He felt a pang of sympathy for the man. He wondered if Khan was one of those people who worked long, late hours, trying to put off the loneliness of going home to the bachelor flat and the microwave dinner for one. He made a quick appraisal of the room. A box of Tetley teabags lay open on Khan's desk, there were several papers bordered with red ink and marked 'Strap 2', and on the wall above his desk a group of framed photos of cricket teams.

Khan looked up and smiled before he spoke. 'There are corridors of excellence in this building. I need to know you have what it takes to walk down them.'

'Right.' Luke had no idea where Khan was going with this.

'That's what they said to me on my first day in this place,' continued Khan. 'Agents, young man. They're the beginning, middle and end of everything we do here at SIS. Understand that and you'll go far in the Service.' He turned to gaze out of the window at the traffic on the river below. A cargo barge was emerging from beneath Vauxhall Bridge, emitting a trail of oily smoke from its chimney as it chugged downstream towards Docklands.

Khan turned back to Luke and picked up where he had left off. 'I've been here over twenty years now and that rule hasn't changed. We still persuade people to do difficult and dangerous things for this country,

Luke. Others might disagree, but we are the world's leading HUMINT service. Some people do it for the money, others because they believe in an ideal. I expect they banged on about that at the Base, didn't they?'

'They did,' agreed Luke.

'Now, Synapse was our key agent on this case and he was risking his life on that op. How much do you think we were paying him?'

'I couldn't say. A thousand quid a month?'

'Try half that. Less. Synapse wasn't doing it for the money. He was doing it because he believed it was the right thing to do. Jerry Benton spent two years developing him as an agent; they trusted each other and it was all starting to pay off. As of today, that's all gone down the tube. Unless you can find him. So you need to track him down, fast, and get inside his head.'

'Right.'

For a long moment, Khan said nothing, just looked at him, that mathematician's brain sizing him up, cogs whirring inside his head. Then he levered himself out of his chair and walked over to where Luke was standing. He wondered what was coming next. An embrace? A kiss on both cheeks? Instead Khan placed both hands on Luke's shoulders, gave them a squeeze, then let go. 'I want to tell you a story,' he said. 'I know you've got a flight to catch so I won't take much more of your time, but this is important. Back in my university days I used to go running with a mate at weekends out on the moors.' Khan caught his look. 'I know, I know. You're thinking, How did that fat knacker ever go running? Right?' Luke said nothing. 'Well, that was before I hit the balti curries and put all this on.' He patted his sizeable belly almost affectionately. 'So my mate's old man used to take us out for dinner now and then, and we got talking. He'd been in the Service, stationed in Berlin in the early sixties, about the time the Wall went up. He told us how one Saturday night he was walking down the main drag there, the Ku'damm, minding his own business, when he noticed a crowd starting to form ahead. Turned out there was this middle-ranking East German Army officer, a border guard, drunk as a skunk, having an altercation with a West German policeman. Crowd were getting pretty hostile. They wanted the policeman to arrest him. So tell me, Luke, what would you have done?'

'Intervened?'

'Exactly! It was a golden opportunity. Flash your diplomatic ID, take him under your wing, get him off the hook and he's for ever in your debt. Now you've got a man on the other side of the Wall.'

'So your friend's dad was able to recruit him?' said Luke.

'No!' Khan's voice was almost a shout. 'No, he didn't! And that's just the point. He walked on by and he regretted it to the day he died. So, my point is, young man, don't go missing any opportunities. Take every chance that comes your way. Good luck out there.'

Then Khan embraced him, sending him off with a slap on the back. And a faint feeling of foreboding.

Chapter 5

IN THE LIFT down to the ground-floor car park, Luke was already making a mental checklist of what he needed to do before he headed out to Heathrow. Concurrent activity, they called it in the military. It was a hard habit to shake off. Buckled into his Land Rover once more, he turned left out of the gates into the traffic streaming into Westminster, then crossed Lambeth Bridge into Horseferry Road and pulled over to dial the number he needed to call.

'Jorge? It's me, Luke. *Sí . . . sí . . .* Listen, I can't do squash tonight, something's come up but I need your help.'

'Any time, my friend. So what's up?'

Luke had been introduced to Jorge at a Latin America forum organized by a London think-tank just off the Strand. Like sharks circling their prey, they had eyed each other warily, both convinced the other was not quite what his business card said. Luke's card read, 'Foreign & Commonwealth Office', yet Jorge was looking at a man with broad, load-bearing shoulders, a broken nose and a missing finger. FCO? Sure. And here was this young South American, a naval attaché at just thirty-six? Luke checked him out in the

Diplomatic List and found that Commander Jorge Enríquez was Colombia's youngest naval attaché at any of their embassies anywhere in the world. And for good reason, Luke had discovered, when he dug a little further. The man's résumé spoke for itself.

On his first command in Cartagena Jorge had helped direct an operation that had netted a record haul of 92 per cent pure coke and put several very violent and sadistic people behind bars. After promotion they had moved him to the Pacific Coast, where his enthusiasm for the job, combined with a background in intelligence, had led to several imaginatively planned and successful operations. His achievements had not gone unnoticed by the cartels, and when a contract was taken out on his life, the Defence Ministry in Bogotá had sent him to London, to give him a break. Jorge's arrival at the tall, red-brick Colombian embassy in Knightsbridge had coincided almost exactly with Luke's first month on the job at SIS. After that first introduction Luke had reported the contact to Angela, who had encouraged him to get to know the young prodigy of a naval officer. Colombia was, after all, considered a 'friendly' country by the Service. Their professional friendship had soon turned into a social one, going for beers after fiercely competitive games of squash, and Jorge introducing Luke to a succession of his stunningly beautiful Latina girlfriends. 'I want you to meet Gabriela,' he would say, or Beatriz, or Alejandra. Elise said he was a bit fly, but Luke liked him. More importantly, no one else in London knew more about Colombia's coke cartels than Jorge Enríquez.

Luke pulled up at the Colombian Embassy just behind Harrods and waited while a security guard removed the orange cones that were keeping a space free for his dented and faded Land Rover. He parked behind a spotless yellow Lamborghini with Qatari numberplates. Up the flight of steps, into the embassy, a right turn into a reception area and there was Jorge, in a well-cut charcoal-grey suit, silk tie and brown brogues, a tiny Colombian flag pinned to his lapel. He was holding out a steaming cup of rich *café tinto.* Luke took the coffee, savouring its rich aroma. So much better than the overbrewed stuff they served at VX.

Jorge waited for him to drain his cup, then wagged a finger in feigned admonition.

'So you heard, then?' said Luke, knowing the answer already.

'Bad news travels fast, *amigo mio*,' replied the Colombian. 'What the hell was your guy playing at down there? Tumaco is a shit-hole. No one goes there unless they have to.'

'Which is why I need anything you can give me on the gangs there. I'm on tonight's flight.'

Jorge smiled sympathetically. 'You poor bastard. Why couldn't they send you to my city, Medellín? Man, I don't envy you.'

'Thanks. You're all heart.'

'OK. So, here you go.' He handed Luke a thick manila envelope. 'It's everything we've got on the crims in Tumaco. Faces, names, aliases. I have to tell you, there are some real punks down there on the border. Just don't end up getting caught by them, because I'm not coming to get you!'

'And you know I'd do the same for you, Jorge. Now give me another cup of that coffee, then I'm off.'

*

Back in his car, Luke had one more call to make. He had put it off for long enough. When the phone rang in the Stratford Gallery, just off Piccadilly, they were busier than usual. The gallery had just taken on a promising young artist, George someone. Back from the Middle East with some impressive watercolours.

'Stratford Gallery. Elise Mayhew speaking.' Her tone was polite but brisk. The exhibition was less than two weeks away.

'Lise. It's me. I've got to go away for a spell. Might be a week, might be longer. Sorry, wish I knew.'

There was a pause and he pursed his lips. How many of his mates' marriages and relationships had he watched wither and die while they disappeared for weeks and months on end, serving with Special Forces? The endless uncertainty of always being on call, bracing yourself for the bleeper, then coming home with the dreaded thousand-yard stare, having seen and done things you could never talk about outside the unit. A few had fallen completely by the wayside: he had seen one-time supermen with greying stubble and expanding waistlines, now spending their days on a park bench in Hereford, nursing cans of Special Brew. It wasn't a pretty sight. He hadn't wanted to end up like that so he had left the forces. But with this new job came the problem of secrecy. You were supposed to tell only your nearest and dearest what you really did for a living. He and Elise were not married and there were times when he thought she must be close to giving him the boot and moving on. So he told her the bare minimum. Elise knew where he worked, that was all, and he was grateful that she never asked any questions about what he did.

'You're doing that thing again, aren't you?' she said finally.

'What thing?'

'You're chewing the inside of your cheek.' He knew it bugged her. 'I can hear it. So. You're off again. Will you be back in time for the exhibition?' He could hear the hurt in her voice and it cut him to the core. He hated abandoning her like this. 'I'm so sorry, Lise. You know I can't tell you where I'm going but . . . if I was to say it was somewhere hot and tropical, what could I bring you back?'

'You. Wrapped in banana leaves.'

'That is *so* cheesy!'

'I know. That's why you love me. Be safe.'

Luke wasn't fooled by her breezy farewell. She worried about him when he was away. It was something of an issue between them. The truth was, he thought, she probably had good reason to worry this time.

Chapter 6

THE MORNING AFTER they had found the Englishman's body Major Humberto Elerzon was in a truly foul mood. Short of sleep, and troubled by an inexplicable rash in a sensitive place, he swore at anyone who got close to him. All night long those sons of bitches at Headquarters in Bogotá had been ringing his mobile, asking their dumb questions. How had he let this happen? Why hadn't he caught the culprits yet? Where was his report? Now they were sending someone down from Internal Investigations and some overpaid suit from his country's intelligence service, ANIC, was coming with him on the morning flight. Major Elerzon made a quick calculation. His promotion might have stalled for now but he could still play their games. If he was smart he could even come out of this on top. And if that failed? Well, there was always Plan B.

He picked up the phone and issued arrest orders left, right and centre. Names came into his head and flew out of his mouth. 'Gutierrez! Ramierrez! Almieda!' The list went on and on.

'But, Chief,' protested the sergeant, 'the last two are informants. They work for us!'

'I don't care!' shouted Elerzon. 'Lock them up! And tell them I want more names!'

By mid-morning he was feeling better. Dressed in his pressed uniform, despite the heat, he stood beside the runway as the turboprop from Bogotá taxied to a halt. When the men from the capital alighted, squinting at the sun already directly overhead, he gave them his best, most unctuous smile. Their questions came thick and fast, even as they climbed into the jeep, but he held up a calming hand. The situation was well under control, he assured them. 'I have good news,' he said soothingly. 'We have made many arrests and, yes, they are talking. Soon this will all be resolved and you can return home.' The men from Bogotá looked unimpressed, but the major continued brightly, 'First, some breakfast. We have mango, papaya—'

'We have eaten already,' interrupted the man from ANIC. 'Just take us to our hotel, then show us what you've come up with.'

'As you wish,' replied Major Elerzon, tapping the driver on the shoulder, and they lurched forward over the rutted, potholed road and on into town. He checked his guests into the Paradiso, the hotel next to the police base, making a great play of telling the clerk to give them the best rooms in the house. But his mind was telling him one thing alone, over and over again. You need to get these bastards off your patch and back to Bogotá before they go digging where they shouldn't.

Checking in at Heathrow for the direct 22.40 Avianca flight to Bogotá, Luke spotted him immediately at the departure gate. The lawyer. It had to be him. Who else would carry a briefcase, these days? Luke held out his hand and introduced himself. The man looked up, startled, and dropped his boarding pass. 'Oh! Yes. Hello. I'm John Friend, from Legal Affairs. They told you I was coming, I hope?' A nervous laugh.

This, Luke thought, was going to test him in new ways. Friend was wearing a beige fishing jacket with pockets all over the place, the sort of item worn by actors in American films about city men losing their bearings in the wilderness, and a pair of black-rimmed, functional spectacles.

'So how does this work?' asked Luke, as they waited for their flight to be called. 'Are you a career intelligence officer who happens to have a legal brain?'

'Oh, nothing like that. I'm from DoJ, the Department of Justice. Part of the whole cross-government drive to bring us all into line. My job is to make sure the law is followed, that operations are cleared as legal. I'll be looking into whether Benton took the right precautions and got his actions cleared at the appropriate level. And, um, I suppose keeping an eye on what you're up to. You know, *Laborare pugnare parati sumus*!' Friend chuckled knowingly, expecting him to share the joke.

Luke stared at him as if he'd been speaking fluent Martian. 'Sorry. What?'

'It's Latin for "To work or to fight, we are ready!" Just a little saying we lawyers have.'

After that, they sat in silence.

Somewhere over the mid-Atlantic Luke jolted awake as the Airbus A330 bucked its way through an air pocket. A glass of Rioja just after take-off, a reheated meal, and he had packed in a few good hours' kip. He could see Friend was fast asleep next to him, his spectacles halfway down his face, an open copy of the

Cambridge Law Journal lying on his lap. He was snoring gently.

Luke rubbed his eyes, shifted in his seat and stared at his reflection in the window. Quite a journey his life had been so far: from orphan to bleak, lonely adolescence on his uncle's sheep farm in Northumberland, to the comparative fleshpots of Edinburgh to read politics, a first-class degree with honours. Then throwing himself full tilt into the assault courses and mud beaches of south Devon as a potential Royal Marines officer, every inch of his body screaming with exertion. It had been worth it to pass the commando tests and be rewarded with the treasured 'green lid', the distinctive green beret of the Royal Marines, then get assigned to his first operational tour with 45 Commando in Afghanistan. Eight years in the Corps, then through gruelling, bone-breaking Selection into the elite Special Boat Service, and finally to where he was now: on contract to MI6 and serving his probation to become a fully paid-up intelligence officer.

There was an unopened packet of peanuts on his armrest, left there by the flight attendant as he slept and Luke opened it now, shovelling the contents into his mouth and savouring the sudden hit of salt. If someone had said to him two years ago he would end up working for the spooks he would have laughed in their face. Desk jockeys, he would have called them. A bunch of Johnny English fantasists. Joining the Corps, becoming a bootneck, then the SBS, that was all he had ever dreamed of. Sweating his bollocks off in the jungles of Brunei, shivering rigid on some windswept Scottish island with a half-cooked rabbit for supper, living on the edge behind the lines in Afghanistan:

that was the life he had chosen. He was a bootneck through and through. He told people he would only leave if they carried him out in a box. And that was very nearly what had happened.

On his third tour in Afghanistan, helicoptering in one night with a Special Forces task force for the discreet snatch of an HVT, a known Taliban player and his crew just west of Kandahar, the patrol was ambushed well before reaching its objective. Pinned down in open farmland, with concentrated machine-gun fire raking over their heads from a nearby mud-walled compound, Luke had radioed for air support. No mission was supposed to set off without a stack of escort aircraft ready to race to their rescue if they hit trouble. Sometimes the response would be a pair of Warthogs: squat, ugly US Airforce A10 Thunderbolt jets that came screaming out of nowhere, spitting 30mm shells from a rotating Gatling cannon in their nose, a rate of fire so fast it made a noise like an angry chainsaw. Sometimes it would be a pair of Apache helicopter gunships, under-slung with cannon and Hellfire missiles that could lock onto a target eight kilometres away, and sometimes it would be 'fast air': RAF Tornados or NATO F16 fighter jets or the like, dropping their 500-pound bombs, then disappearing over the horizon. And sometimes it would be a Reaper drone, a UAV, hovering unseen and unheard, controlled and directed by a pair of 'pilots' in a windowless cabin on a base in Nevada. But drones can't see well through a low cloud base and tonight was just one of those nights; there was nothing else available. *Not poss. Poor vis. Civcas risk unacc*, came the response. Shit, thought Luke. Someone in a distant ops room had decided they couldn't have air support because there was an unacceptably high risk of causing civilian casualties. He felt like screaming into the radio, 'There aren't any bloody civilians here, you twats! We're getting outmanoeuvred by the Taliban!' But it was no use: they were on their own.

Luke never saw himself as any kind of hero but at that moment, as the mission commander, he didn't hesitate. With his Diemaco C8 assault rifle in one hand and a high-explosive grenade in the other, he jumped up and zigzagged at a sprint towards the compound. Hard targeting, they called it. But at ten metres from his enemy, at the exact moment when he threw his grenade, Luke was not as hard a target as he would have liked. The first Taliban bullet had hit him just below the shoulder, spinning him around; the next removed a finger at the knuckle.

He shifted uncomfortably in his seat on the plane at the thought of that moment and the white-hot pain that had shot through him. He was not the squeamish type but even the memory of losing his finger caused him instinctively to rub the remaining bare knuckle with the thumb of his other hand. He remembered the instant his grenade had exploded, with him already on the ground, reeling and bleeding. Inside the Taliban compound the half-kilo of RDX high explosive had detonated with lethal force and the firing had ceased abruptly. His team had radioed in for a MERT, a Medical Emergency Response Team, bringing a twin-engined Chinook helicopter thundering in from Kandahar airfield. He remembered looking up at the medics, who told him cheerfully, 'You'll live,' as the morphine kicked in and someone pressed a field dressing on his wound to staunch the bleeding.

Forty-four minutes after being shot, Captain Luke

Carlton was under the surgeon's knife; forty-eight hours after that he was sitting up in bed at Queen Elizabeth Hospital in Birmingham, taking visitors. 'I'm threaders,' he told them. It was bootneck slang for a really, really bad day. Yet six months later, fully recovered, he was marching up to the dais at Buckingham Palace for a lady in her eighties to pin the Queen's Conspicuous Gallantry Cross to his chest.

By the age of thirty-two he had already watched too many of his mates loaded onto helicopters in body bags, the dust and grit of southern Afghanistan following them up into the air in a departing spiral. If he carried on in this game, at this pace, his luck was going to run out, he was in no doubt about that. He needed to find a second career, something that kept him on his toes but with rather less chance of getting slotted. It was the ad in the *Globe & Laurel*, the Corps journal of the Royal Marines, both serving and retired, that caught his attention.

'Missing the action?' it read. 'Bored but fit? Fancy a challenge? Call this number.' So he did, encouraged by Elise, who quietly yearned for him to hang up his boots and hand in his uniform.

It had begun with the interviews. Two days of face-to-face evaluations with unremarkable people in an assessment centre somewhere in the Home Counties. Then there had been psychometric aptitude tests, the developed vetting, which probed into every aspect of his past, searching for weaknesses, anything that could be exploited by a hostile adversary. Then finally the induction course down at the Base on the south coast, where the Service trained all its recruits. Surveillance, counter-surveillance, dead-letter drops, agent handling, how to deal with friendly and not-so-friendly foreign intelligence liaison officers, and personal security, both digital and physical. Days and nights spent treading the rain-splashed streets of some coastal town, learning the tradecraft, meeting supposed 'contacts', coming up with a convincing cover story when challenged to explain what exactly he was doing driving down a dark alleyway at two o'clock in the morning with a bunch of blueprints of the local power station in his glove compartment. Luke had loved it. In Afghanistan he had had only the briefest glimpse of intelligence work, meeting Taliban informants cultivated by the brigade intelligence cell. But this was different: this was close to home; it felt real; he wanted in.

Chapter 7

'SEÑORES Y SEÑORAS . . .' The cabin announcement cut short Luke's reflections. They were coming in to land. He glanced across at Friend, this unwanted chaperone from Legal Affairs. A flight attendant was trying to wake him and get him to put his seat into the upright position. Friend, still submerged in his dream, was waving her away and muttering something about tennis on Saturday being out of the question.

They landed with a screech of wet tyres, taxiing past pools of water that had collected on the runway. It had just gone 0400, Luke noted, probably still another hour till sunrise, but he could imagine the low clouds clinging to the hillsides and the pink-walled tenement blocks crawling up the slopes, like an advancing army. When the aircraft door swung open he took a deep breath of the cool Andean air. It was the smell of his childhood. Just for a second he felt a pang of homesickness, a longing for the life he had known as a boy, in those impossibly distant years before his parents had been lost in that car crash.

'Señor Carlton?' They were almost inside the terminal when an officer in military uniform stepped into their path, a photo of Luke in one hand, a walkie-talkie in the other. He wore a khaki bush hat folded up on one side, like an Aussie soldier from the First World War. A shoulder flash on his uniform said 'DIRAN', the acronym for the Dirección de Antinarcóticos, the police counter-narcotics division. 'I am Lieutenant Lopez from the DIRAN. You are welcome in Colombia. Please,' he gestured down the corridor, 'this way.'

'Well, that's a bit of all right!' exclaimed Friend, as the officer escorted them through the diplomatic channel, to some resentful stares from other passengers. Phone calls had been made, even as they were winging their way westwards through the night. Despite the fiasco of the undeclared MI6 operation that had ended with Benton's murder, Colombia had graciously offered to give Luke and the lawyer every possible assistance. Luke searched his memory but couldn't remember travelling before with someone who had so many pieces of hand luggage: Friend looked as if he had just emerged from the January sales. Yet Luke felt strangely protective towards him and now he relieved him of some of his load. He liked to travel light and had no bags to collect but Friend, unsurprisingly, had checked in a large suitcase, so now they stood, bleary-eyed, at the carousel as it coughed into life. As he waited, trying not to show his impatience, Luke discreetly observed the other passengers and the local Colombian airport staff. Was anyone showing an interest in them? No.

'Luke! Luke Carlton? Is that you?'

Oh, Christ, this was all he needed.

'It *is* you! Oh, my God, I don't believe it. It's Steve! Stevie Monk! Bella, I was at uni with this guy. He was in my politics class.'

Luke cursed himself for not seeing the pair earlier and taking evasive action. Steve Monk was a total arse. He had come up to Luke at the Freshers' Fair in their first week at Edinburgh and said, 'Hey, guess what? I'm already dating someone here and she's the runner-up to Miss England. Beat that!' Luke, nearly a head and shoulders taller, had looked down at him, said, 'Good for you,' and walked on. They had never been friends.

Now Luke forced a smile and reluctantly held out his hand. Monk approached, grinning from ear to ear, a Union Jack T-shirt beneath his fleece. His companion, Bella, was in a pair of uncomfortably tight white jeans above purple-and-mauve striped socks.

'They are with you?' asked the Colombian police officer, looking questioningly from Luke to the backpackers.

'No!' replied Luke, a little too emphatically. 'Absolutely not.' But in the instant that his head was turned towards the policeman Monk had whipped out his phone and snapped a photo. 'Cheers! One for the album when we get back. We're taking a sabbatical,' he gushed. 'Bella's resigned from her job in PR and I'm taking a year out from accountancy. We're going zip-wiring near Cali! But, hey, what about you? Didn't you join the SAS or something? And what brings you to Colombia?' The pair looked expectantly from Luke to the policeman, standing silently in his jungle-green uniform. 'You're not under arrest already, are you? Been indulging in a bit of the old Bolivian marching powder already, have we?' Monk laughed at his own crass joke.

Luke sensed the lawyer watching him, interested to see how he would extract himself from this awkward situation. 'I'm doing a thesis for a think-tank,' he lied. 'Human rights and democracy in Latin America, that sort of thing. Getting some good access here.' He gestured towards his police escort. *Now go away.* He wasn't happy at being ID'd before he was even out of the airport.

Outside the terminal it was getting light. A grey, dank Andean dawn, drained of colour and heavy with the promise of more rain. The bags loaded into the police 4x4, the doors locked, the shaded windows up, Luke relaxed a little. Friend was in the back, fussing with his seatbelt and asking casual questions about the couple they had just encountered. The police lieutenant got behind the wheel and Luke checked the messages on his phone. There was one from Elise, just a simple *x*. Nice. He hit reply and sent her one back. But now his secure phone was flashing with an incoming message from VX. It was from Comms Monitoring, and he didn't like it one little bit.

'ALERT. PLEASE READ. Forwarding from Social Media,' it read. 'Posted on Twitter at 0931GMT.'

> Steve Monk @smonkmeister 17m
> Shout out to Edinb Politics class of '03. Just seen Luke Carlton in Bogotá! Bet he's a spy now! #007 #Bond

And there, blurred but recognizable, was his picture. Fuck. What a knob, thought Luke. I should have taken his phone off him and chucked it into the crowd. A quick check of Monk's Twitter profile revealed he had a reassuringly low number of followers. Less than a hundred, in fact. Maybe he was new to Twitter, but still. There was no Instagram account, as far as he could see; he did find a LinkedIn profile in Monk's name but he hadn't refreshed it in some time. Nevertheless he had to report it to Angela.

They moved off from the airport terminal, inching through the early-morning traffic and swerving round potholes. Luke rang his line manager. 'Don't worry, it's sorted,' she told him. 'We've shaded his Twitter account.'

'Sorry, you've what?'

'It's just a little trick the tech people can do. It means Monk can use his Twitter account to his heart's content but nobody else can see what he's posting. He won't know that, of course. His account is effectively frozen for as long as you're in-country.'

'Nice one, thanks.'

'You're welcome. And, Luke? We can't let this happen again. First thing you're doing when you get back is attending the Stay Secret on the Internet course.'

'Yes, ma'am.'

So that was a relief but, still, operational security had been put at risk. Nothing more he could do about it now, but Luke was uneasy. He swivelled round in his seat to check on Friend, who was staring intently out of the window.

'Rather a lot of yellow taxis here,' remarked the lawyer.

'No take taxi!' interjected the police lieutenant at the wheel.

'He's right,' said Luke. 'It's a gamble over here.'

'I'm not sure I follow you,' said Friend. The policeman shrugged, concentrating on the traffic ahead, so Luke explained.

'Some of the drivers are honest, some are not.

There've been cases of passengers getting locked in, driven to a cash machine and mugged at knifepoint. And then there's burundanga. Ever heard of it?'

'I can't say I have,' replied Friend, now eyeing every yellow taxi with suspicion.

'It's a drug they make from a plant here. They call it devil's breath. Makes you do things you don't want to, like handing over all your valuables. Or one of your kidneys.'

'Strewth!' exclaimed Friend, backing away from the window.

'There are even stories of people having it blown in their faces as a powder, then waking up half naked on a park bench two days later, unable to remember a thing.' Luke turned back to glance ahead. 'It looks like we've arrived.'

A guard was saluting them as a white-painted barrier lifted to let them pass. *'República de Colombia,'* read a green sign in front of a nondescript barracks building. *'Policia Nacional,'* it said. *'Dios y Patria.'*

'God and country.' Luke translated the last bit for Friend's benefit. 'This is the headquarters of the DIRAN, the counter-narcotics division. They have their own air wing so they'll be flying us down to the coast in the morning.'

'Hang on,' protested Friend. 'I thought we were staying at the Hilton?'

'No such luck, John. This is our billet for tonight.'

The police lieutenant parked the vehicle, then ushered them through a glass door and down a hallway. A sign on the wall said: *'No a las drogas, no a la violencia, sí a la vida.'* No to drugs, no to violence, yes to life.

The policeman showed them into a waiting room,

then went off to sort out their accommodation. The room was lined with chairs where just one man sat alone. Now he sprang to his feet, looked as if he were going to salute them, then thought better of it. To Luke, he did not look remotely South American. Ill-fitting jeans, stained white trainers and a limp beige jacket? He had to be British.

'Mr Carlton, sir? Staff Sergeant Coles. From the embassy. I work with the DA – the Defence Attaché. Good flight, I hope? Anyway, all the kit you ordered is stowed in the day sack over here.' He indicated a canvas rucksack at his feet. 'I'm going to need you to sign for it, I'm afraid,' he added.

How quaint, thought Luke. He could fly eight thousand kilometres, cross several time zones, arrive on a different continent yet still, in the timeless tradition of British bureaucracy, there was paperwork to be signed. Friend was standing just behind them, listening to the introductions and grunting with approval, but now he excused himself. 'I'm just going to try to find a Gents,' he said. 'Not feeling too chipper after that flight.'

'Just ask for *el baño*,' Luke called after him.

'Right you are.' Friend quickened his pace down the corridor.

'Nasty business that, in Tumaco,' said the sergeant. 'Best watch your back down there, sir. Haven't had the pleasure of visiting that part of the coast myself but I hear it's a bit tasty. Mind you, from what I've heard, that should suit you fine, sir.'

'No need for "sir". "Luke" will do fine.'

'Righto, sir. Ready to get down to business?' In one swift movement Coles hefted the bag from the floor onto a bare wooden table. 'I'm assuming you'll want to start with the personal weapon. It's right there on the top, beneath the flap.'

Luke had selected the model he wanted for this mission the previous day. It was the last thing he'd done before driving out of Vauxhall Cross. He had opted for a Swiss-made Sig Sauer P229 with built-in infrared, visible laser sight and screw-on suppressor. One mag inserted into the weapon and two spare, all pre-loaded. He stripped it down now, inspected the working parts, ran his finger along the slide and sniffed it, savouring the familiar smell of gun oil, then reassembled it, cocked it, sighted it on an old Dakota transport plane parked outside on the tarmac, then squeezed the trigger with an empty magazine. Now he turned his attention to the rest of the rucksack's contents. Carefully, he went through the small grab-bag of medical essentials: a standard first field dressing, a phial of quick-clot blood coagulant and a lightweight combat application tourniquet. Then he unpacked a neatly folded black parcel: one of the new gel-based body armour vests. Under normal conditions the gel wobbled and rippled as it moved, but when hit with sudden force, such as a 9mm bullet fired at point-blank range, it hardened in a fraction of a second, making it difficult to penetrate.

Luke reached further into the rucksack and pulled out a Garmin GPS, some detailed maps of Tumaco and the border area, a prismatic compass, HF radio comms equipment, a coded log book, nylon hammock, mosquito net, hunting knife, torch, Puritabs, some basic survival kit and enough emergency rations to last him forty-eight hours in the jungle. All a bit *Boy's Own* for an MI6 intelligence officer, he had to admit, but he hadn't forgotten the old military saying:

'Prior Planning and Preparation Prevents Piss Poor Performance.' Otherwise known as P7.

'It's all there, sir?' asked Coles.

'It's all there,' replied Luke, hefting the rucksack onto his shoulders, testing the weight. 'Thanks, mate. This lot'll do nicely. Now I'd better go and find that lawyer, make sure he hasn't fallen down the loo.'

Staff Sergeant Coles watched him walk out of the door, carrying the heavy rucksack as if it was filled with feathers. In the short time they had spent together he had got the distinct impression that wherever Luke was heading, it smelt of trouble.

Chapter 8

DR GANG KUK Mun felt sick. He knew exactly what he was about to witness. And he knew that he could betray not the slightest hint of emotion. Any glimmer of sympathy for the victims would bring about his own death sentence or, worse, see him trade places with the family being led into the chamber below. Shackled, cowed, terrified and emaciated after months of near-starvation rations, the man, his wife and their two children were being taken into the hermetically sealed laboratory beneath him, condemned as traitors and enemies of the Democratic People's Republic of Korea, better known as North Korea. The hermit state had a well-documented history of conducting human experiments on its own people. As the last truly practising Communist regime on the planet, the ruling Supreme People's Assembly had a deeply entrenched paranoia. Someone close to the top had reportedly been executed before an assembled audience out in the field, obliterated at short range with an anti-aircraft gun. Dissidents, doctors, smugglers and party apparatchiks who had fallen from grace could be found among the half-starved prison population crammed into the gulag of remote labour camps. The luckier ones emerged as broken men and women, looking twice the age they had been when they'd gone in. Many died there, unnoticed and unannounced. But some, mostly the political dissidents, those suspected of directly threatening the regime and the Dear Leader, were selected for a special fate.

Gang Kuk Mun, or Comrade Dr Mun, as his fellow scientists called him, was a loyal citizen, or so he had always thought. He had studied hard, joined the Workers' Party at seventeen and, after excelling at chemistry, had secured a junior position in Pyongyang's prestigious Faculty for Scientific Research and Development. Chemical reactions intrigued him and he was good at his job. As he rose up through the ranks of the faculty he was proud that his skills were of service to the glorious People's Republic. When he was chosen to work in the secretive 'Defensive Toxicology Division' his family glowed with pride. None of them, not even Mun, had any idea what he would one day be required to do.

They sat bolt upright in their chairs, leaning forward to get a clear view. There were twelve in all, eight officers in full dress uniform, their faces inscrutable beneath their huge, sweeping, Soviet-era hats, and four scientists in white coats. Their chairs were bolted to the floor in a circle, arranged around a circular pit, like spectators at a miniature gladiatorial arena. A double pane of hardened glass separated them from the pit and each man had a gas mask beside him, just in case. Down in the pit the two armed guards saluted, awaiting the order. The most senior officer present, a *Sangjang*, a colonel general with three stars on his epaulettes, nodded solemnly. The guards marched out and a steel door hissed shut behind them.

The family looked up in fear at the men who stared down at them as they huddled together. The parents knew what was coming – other prisoners had talked about it in the camp – and fell to their knees, wailing and sobbing, begging forgiveness, swearing undying loyalty to the Dear Leader and to the Party. A lowly Party official, the man's crime had been to make a joke about the Dear Leader in the workers' canteen one day. It was reported, of course, and he had 'confessed his crime', but before the day was out he was on his way to the labour camp. His wife of twelve years still did not know what they had done wrong.

For a few seconds nothing happened, their pleas being mouthed silently on the other side of the thick glass. And then, from a vent high up on the wall, came a pale yellow vapour, heavier than the air. Coiling and twisting like a living creature, it spread along the walls and sank slowly to the floor, where it unfolded like a carpet. The officers and scientists leaned further forward still, some making notes. When the gas reached those in the pit, their bodies were racked with spasms. A derivative of phosgene, a choking agent dating back to the trenches of the First World War, this was Agent MX, the latest addition to the arsenal of massed batteries of artillery units ranged along the border with South Korea, all aimed at its capital, Seoul. The People's Assembly had been adamant: it must be tested extensively on live human subjects.

Dr Mun tried hard to remain impassive as the 'experiment' drew to its inevitable and grisly conclusion. He fiddled with his pen and pretended to write notes as the condemned family writhed and vomited on the other side of the glass, the parents trying in vain to save their two children even as their own lives ebbed away. When their twitching ceased, he joined in the chorus of obligatory applause and stood beaming as the colonel general came up to congratulate him and the other white coats. Then he made a dash for the toilets.

Mun barely had time to check there was no one else in the room before he threw up his lunch of rice balls in the stained lavatory bowl and yanked the ancient flush. He turned the rusting tap and splashed his face with water. He would probably be decorated for this but right now he wished he had never been born. When he raised his face from the sink a man was staring back at him. The insignia on his epaulettes marked him out as a *taejwa,* a senior colonel in the Korean People's Army. Two thin red stripes and four silver stars. A powerful, influential man. 'Comrade Colonel!' exclaimed Dr Mun, pulling himself up to attention. 'An honour!' He stood stock still, wondering if he had washed away the evidence of his disgust. But the officer who faced him looked far from stern. In fact, he seemed equally sickened. The colonel moved slowly to the sink and turned the tap full on. They spoke in low whispers, their exchange masked by the spluttering of the running water.

By the time they went their separate ways Mun felt his heart would burst with the enormity of what they had just discussed. Yes, he could deliver what the Comrade Colonel was asking for. He had the authority – no one would question it – and access to the material, but surely this was treason of the highest order. Should he report the colonel? Was this a trap, a test of his loyalty? What the colonel had asked him to do was almost unbelievable. And yet . . . And yet he could not go on working for this vile regime. If he could play some small part in its downfall he could live with his conscience.

Dr Mun wasted no time. The next morning, at eleven o'clock precisely, he broke off from his work in the lab to go for his customary glass of watery ginseng tea, slipped into a side office and gave an order over the phone. Fifteen hundred grams of highly radioactive caesium chloride were to be diverted from the adjacent waste unit to the Pang Sang Un People's Defence Unit on the outskirts of Pyongyang. There the colonel would take charge of it. Dr Mun knew what this material could do to those exposed to it. Even in news-starved North Korea, word had reached the scientific community of the infamous Goiânia incident in 1987. He had read of how the curious townspeople in the Brazilian city had found an abandoned container glowing blue at an old hospital and decided to prise it open. Four had died from radiation poisoning. Many others had survived with burns, nausea and a lifetime's likelihood of developing cancer. Whatever the colonel had in mind, Mun knew it was destined to hurt people he loathed, the Politburo, whom he considered to be barely human.

In paranoid totalitarian regimes, it is often said the further a person rises up the greasy pole of power, the more they need to watch their backs if they want to survive. In Ceauşescu's Romania of the 1980s, children were encouraged to report their parents if they suspected them of 'anti-state views'. In pre-invasion Iraq, it was often said that President Saddam Hussein had the uncanny knack of being able to tell if a member of his regime was plotting against him, even before that person had decided to make his move. And so it was in North Korea.

They came for Dr Mun that same day, right at the end of his shift, dragging him from the lab, still in his white coat, even as he loudly proclaimed his innocence. His fate had been sealed the moment the colonel had picked up the phone that afternoon to the feared State Security Department. Now Mun was destined to disappear into the gulag, where there was every possibility he would end up on the wrong side of the reinforced glass in that dreadful human laboratory. Yet even now, in his darkest hour, he remained professional. As they bundled him into the Black Crow, the van used to transport political prisoners, he begged them to tell him just one thing. Had the radioactive caesium been safely secured? 'Please,' he sobbed. 'You don't know what this stuff can do. The people must be protected.'

A blow to the back of his head from the butt of a pistol nearly knocked him unconscious. 'No talking!' they screamed. But the arresting officer could not resist a final verbal blow. 'Do not fear, Comrade Mun. Your colonel has been a loyal citizen. All seven hundred and fifty grams have been secured. They will be used as evidence against you at your trial.'

'Wait! Only seven hundred and fifty grams?'

'Silence!' Another crack of the pistol butt and for Dr Mun it all went dark.

Chapter 9

AT FIRST LIGHT they filed out to the flight line, Luke, the lawyer and their Colombian police pilot – black leather flying jacket, reflecting shades and hair slicked back, smooth and shiny, across his scalp. Luke took an instant dislike to him.

'Pacific swallows,' remarked Friend, who was dawdling on the tarmac to admire the birds that swooped and dived in the early-morning sun, catching the midges that hovered above the grass. 'Reminds me of home.'

'We've only been gone a day, John.'

'I know, I know. Just saying.'

One by one, they clambered aboard and strapped themselves in for the three-hour hop from the capital to the Pacific coast. It all started so well, the pilot brimming with confidence, flashing a winning smile beneath his aviator shades. Squashing his tall frame into the Cessna Caravan eight-seater, Luke discovered that the police plane was so small he could touch both sides of the fuselage with his fingertips. The top of his head brushed the cabin roof. There was a brief and noisy commotion in the back as the ground crew struggled to find space for Friend's suitcase. Then they were off, swerving once to avoid a pool of rainwater then taking off west into the wind, lifting clear of the runway with the sprawling, tin-roofed *barrios* of Bogotá spreading out beneath them.

Twenty minutes later it felt like a rough ride at Alton Towers Amusement Park. The tiny aircraft was pitching and yawing, buffeted by the Andean thunderstorm that swept in over the *cordillera*. Battered by rain, the windscreen had only one wiper working, intermittently. The pilot unbuckled his seatbelt and half rose out of his seat to peer through the gloom outside. He sat down, turned to Luke and grinned, still wearing his redundant sunglasses. In the seat behind, Friend heaved twice into a plastic bag. This, said Luke to himself, is not the way I want to go out.

But then the storm clouds of the high Andes gave way to the hot, humid river valleys of Cauca province. A river twisted below, brown and sluggish. And then the jungle was before them, spreading far to the south, leaching across the border into Ecuador. The badlands, thought Luke, as the pilot levelled up to land. Nariño province, the most dangerous of all Colombia's thirty-two *departamentos*, the place with the biggest per capita murder rate in the country, and they were heading for its epicentre, Tumaco port. The natural trouble-seeker in him said, Bring it on, I'm ready. But another, more measured, voice told him to watch his back, get the job done and extract himself in one piece. He had Elise to think of, and Friend to keep out of harm's way.

Their arrival in Tumaco was anything but discreet. They touched down with a bounce, briefly taking to the air again, then landed and rolled to a stop. Luke peered out of the small Perspex window and saw a reception committee lined up and waiting for them, a squad of police commandos in full combat gear, their faces tiger-striped in green and black camouflage paint. He recognized them as the Jungla, Colombia's elite counter-narcotics Special Forces, set up by Britain's SAS in 1989, later trained and mentored by America's Green Berets. Luke remembered being told by someone on an earlier visit: 'It's pronounced *hoongla*.' They had a certain macho reputation, fast-roping down from Blackhawk helicopters into heavily defended jungle labs ringed with Claymore mines and booby traps. But they were not cowboys: they had taken their share of life-changing injuries. A corporal with a prosthetic leg had laughed off his injury and once told Luke: 'You know the only thing we Jungla are scared of? It's *el coralillo*. The coral snake. We have no anti-venom. All our stocks are used up.'

Luke dropped his rucksack on to the tarmac, jumped down from the doorway of the Cessna then strode up to greet the troop commander, who welcomed him to Tumaco.

Out on the edge of the airstrip, not far away, a garbage collector put down his broom and spoke into his mobile phone. There was a pause at the other end. Salsa music played softly in the background, then came a grunt of thanks and the line went dead. He went back to his broom as the convoy of police jeeps swept past him in a cloud of dust.

Far away, up in the cool air of the hills, a message was whispered into the ear of a man they called El Pobrecito. It was an ironic sobriquet, meaning 'poor little thing', a nickname he had earned when he had wept tears of joy after beating his first victim to a pulp with a baseball bat. '*Han llegado*,' they told him. 'They have arrived.'

Chapter 10

'I HATE TO be a bore,' said Friend to Luke, 'but what makes you so certain that this is the right hotel?'

It was mid-morning in Tumaco and their convoy of police vehicles had rolled and jolted its way from the airstrip into town. Their escort had already dismounted and was now urging the two Englishmen to get off the street and inside the generously named Hotel Paradiso.

'Because,' replied Luke, helping the lawyer with his luggage yet again, 'it was mentioned in the latest report from Bogotá station. This is where Benton spent his last day alive.'

Once inside, Luke asked for the room, number 16, that Benton had slept in. He wanted to get right under his skin, to sense his movements and get a feel for what he had been on to. Luke wasn't squeamish: washing his face in a dead man's sink didn't bother him. In his first year at university he had been told he was inheriting his bedsit from a boy who had hanged himself there the previous term. Luke looked up now into the cracked and blotchy mirror and briefly considered the reflection that met him. There were faint creases around his eyes from all those months of squinting into an Afghan sun. Like most of his mates, he had always been more interested in what he was looking out at than in how he appeared to other people, although Elise was definitely working on him in that department. Elise. Just the thought of her brought a smile to his face.

He sat down on the bed, which sagged alarmingly in the middle. 'You fat bastard,' his muckers would have shouted, if he had been in barracks, probably followed by 'Who ate all the pies?' Stuck in that distant hotel room, he suddenly missed the Marines and the banter. Instead, he had John Friend, the Service lawyer, and now the man was knocking insistently on the door.

'I don't suppose you have an adaptor by any chance?' asked Friend, poking his head into the room. 'And what about the water? Do you think we can drink it?'

Luke reached into a side pocket of his rucksack and handed him his own adaptor. 'This is your first time in South America, isn't it?'

'I should say so. Actually it's my first time out of Europe. Well, unless you count Tenerife.' He left, closing the door behind him.

Luke checked his watch. It was time to get started on the investigation. His overriding priority was to find Fuentes, the locally recruited agent who had been working with Benton. Or, rather, for Benton. Fuentes had been the last man to see him alive, apart from Benton's executioners. But if I were Fuentes, reflected Luke, I would have gone very deep underground by now. In fact, I would probably have disappeared altogether. The coroner's office had not reported any more bodies in the last twenty-four hours so he had to assume Fuentes was either still on the run or had been caught by the cartel. So where was he? Perhaps he would get some answers out of the local police chief.

Vauxhall Cross had given him the name before he left, a Major Humberto Elerzon.

The major waved Luke and the lawyer to the chairs in front of his desk and sat down with a flourish. There was supposed to be an interpreter, since Friend spoke no Spanish, but someone was still looking for her, so the lawyer sat drumming his fingers on his briefcase, understanding not one word.

'I think we share the same purpose,' began Luke, diplomatically, in fluent Spanish. 'We all want to get this cleared up as quickly as possible so we can leave you in peace. I'm sure you have lots to get on with.' Major Elerzon nodded and frowned, as if weighed down by the heavy burden of responsibility that came with his job and his title. Luke had seen that look on a policeman's face before and he usually found it to be a façade. The last time he had seen it was in Afghanistan, about five minutes before his patrol had discovered a ten-year-old village boy kept chained and cowering in the police chief's back room. Still, mustn't pre-judge Major Elerzon, he thought. 'Perhaps,' he continued, 'we could start with you telling me what is *not* in the coroner's report.'

'Excuse me?'

'I've read the report,' replied Luke. 'We both have. So we know that Señor Benton suffered several stab wounds from a sharp object – let's assume it was a knife. They caused severe internal bleeding. And he was injected with something before he died. But who do you think did it, and why? Come on, Major, you've worked so many cases down here you must be an expert by now. I'd like to know your gut instincts on this case. What's your professional hunch?'

The major held up his hand as if patting an invisible object. 'Slow down, my friend,' he said. '*Paciencia*. Let us get to know each other a little. That is how we do things over here. This is your first time in my country, yes?'

'I grew up here,' said Luke.

'I see. Well, I can reveal to you that the men who killed your comrade . . .' Major Elerzon placed the palms of his hands together as if in prayer. Luke noticed that his nails were bitten to the quick '. . . the men who did this will most likely be from one of the two cartels down here, Los Rostrojos or Los Chicos.'

Brilliant. I knew that before I left London, thought Luke.

'But, to be certain, my men are working on getting the answers now.'

'Can I ask how?' said Luke.

'Of course. We have nearly forty suspects in custody and some of my best investigators can be . . . how shall I put it? . . . very persuasive.' The police chief's stern features broke into a lopsided grin.

Shit, thought Luke. Abort, abort! It was as if a massive alarm bell was going off inside his head. This would be information acquired through torture and he threw a glance at Friend, knowing the lawyer would have had a stroke if he'd understood what was being said. MI6 and MI5 had got themselves into enough of a legal tangle from their work with local partners in places like Pakistan and Libya. If he wasn't careful on this case, Luke could see himself ending up in the High Court, answering questions from behind a screen. Maybe it wasn't such a bad idea to have legal counsel along for the ride. He looked again at Friend, who was busy making notes. 'Are you following any of this?' he asked.

'Not a word, I'm afraid. You'll have to give me the gist when you're done.'

'We are done,' said Luke. He turned back to the police chief. 'Thank you, Major, for your time. I'll be in touch. Oh. I nearly forgot, I have something for you. A souvenir from Scotland.' He reached into his bag and handed over a bottle of Johnnie Walker.

Elerzon's face lit up, his hands almost caressing the bottle. He opened a drawer in his desk, dropped the bottle into it and took out another. *'Aguardiente,'* he announced proudly, handing Luke what looked very much like a bottle of TCP antiseptic. 'This is Antioqueño, our most popular brand. Please, it is yours to keep.'

Luke knew all about *aguardiente*: 29 per cent proof, it guaranteed the mother of all hangovers. He handed the bottle to Friend. 'Here,' he said. 'You can declare that to Vauxhall in your report!'

'I hope,' continued Major Elerzon, 'that we can provide some entertainment for you here in this town. Perhaps we all drink together. Tonight, if you're free. I know a good place.'

A glance at Friend, wilting quietly in the heat, the jetlag clearly getting the better of him, told Luke he would be on his own for this one. He forced a smile. 'Sure, but my friend here needs to rest. It will just be me.'

'Excellent! I pick you up from your hotel at eight.'

Luke, too, was craving sleep, but back at his hotel he had a visitor. The SIS deputy station chief for Colombia was waiting for him in the lobby. Simon Clements was an unnaturally thin man, and curiously pale for someone living in South America. He and Luke went to sit beside the hotel's deserted pool on white plastic chairs, with no one to overhear them beneath a sunless sky of unbroken cloud.

'Look, you probably know all this from the reports he was sending back to VX,' began the deputy station chief, 'so I'm not sure I can tell you anything massively new. Jerry Benton was overseeing our work with the Colombian joint units, running agents into the cartels and helping to set up the SIGINT telephone intercepts. Oh, and relaying tip-offs in real time on the bulk coke shipments heading for our ports.'

Luke nodded thoughtfully, doing his best to hide a cavernous yawn. He knew all this and, by God, he was tired. 'Anything from Fort Meade? From the Americans?'

'Ah, yes, there is, actually,' said Clements. He reached down to a flat canvas bag at his feet, the sort of thing one might see at an English county book fair, and took out a slim file of printouts marked with the official classification 'Strap 2 Secret'. At the request of Vauxhall Cross, America's giant NSA listening station in Maryland had been on the case since day one, tracking emails, phone calls, text messages and geolocations of everyone sending them. 'There's a fair bit of detail in there,' said Clements. 'Hope it helps.'

'Thanks. And in a nutshell?'

'Well, you'll have to read it yourself,' replied Clements, rather testily, 'but "in a nutshell", as you put it, there's not a lot to go on. Jerry was never much of a one for digital comms – I suppose you could say he was a bit old school. We've got his last call in from this very hotel before he set out, but after that, nothing. There's a bit of chatter from the cartels over the next day or two but, frankly, it's spread all over Colombia.'

'So what about the agent?' persisted Luke. 'What do you have on Fuentes?'

'Only what's on file, I'm afraid. Geraldo Fuentes. Born here in Tumaco, recruited into a criminal *banda* when he was just sixteen. Later arrested for armed robbery, charged, banged up. Jerry went to see him in jail, got to know him, turned him and got him out early. He's worked for us ever since. He's trusted, polygraphed, cleared to level three. He and Jerry were working pretty closely by the end, but I'm afraid I've been too busy up in Cartagena to get involved. You know how it is.'

'I can imagine. Any idea where I might find him?'

'Ha!' Clements snorted. 'You'll be lucky. Fuentes, I fear, has gone to ground. We sent someone round to his family as soon as we heard. You know, see if we could offer any help, get them to a safe place and all that. No joy. Place was deserted. Neighbours say they packed up and left in a hurry. And something quite disturbing too.'

'Go on,' urged Luke.

'Well. Our man said a dead dog was lying on the porch with its stomach slit open and its guts spilling out. I imagine it was some sort of warning.'

You don't say. Luke stifled another yawn.

Clements consulted his watch and got up to leave. 'I've got to catch the next flight back up to Bogotá. Ambassador's been at the Foreign Ministry all day and he wants to confer tonight. I don't mind telling you there's still a hell of a stink about what Jerry was up to. Our Colombian friends are peeved and I can't say I blame them. Let's just be thankful the UK press haven't got hold of it.'

Chapter 11

HEAVY BROCADE CURTAINS, dark velvet cushions, and grandiose faux-colonial arches. This was the décor with which Nelson García liked to surround himself. Of course, nobody called him that – in fact, very few people even knew his real name, or that the well-guarded Spanish-style villa up in the hills of Antioquia, where he liked to spend as much of the year as he dared, was his. When you are running a multi-billion-dollar cocaine empire spanning three continents, with a lot of enemies and a price on your head, you tend to sleep around. Both literally and metaphorically. Two days here, three days there, sometimes in the back-street *barrio* where he had grown up, poor and violent, at others on a luxury yacht moored fifteen kilometres off Cartagena, or in a palm-thatch cabin deep in Amazonas province, where the jungle merged with the great rainforests of Brazil.

Like so many men at the top of their game in the *narcotraficante* world, García had grown up with nothing and now he had everything. With an acquired taste for the finer things in life, it was to this house in the hills, close to the pretty Spanish colonial town of Ituango, that he liked to return most often. Known simply as La Casa, it was built in the classic hacienda style, with whitewashed walls, wrought-iron balconies and handmade roof tiles. It had its own kitchen garden, and for 365 days a year its fridges were kept stocked. Every night, without fail, the crisp bedlinen was turned down by maids in old-fashioned black-and-white uniforms trimmed with lace. Yet weeks and months might go by without a visit from the man the drug world had nicknamed El Pobrecito. Usually the first anyone would know of his arrival was the mounting clatter of rotor blades as he helicoptered down from the skies to a nearby field. Or a convoy snaking up the road from the village in a procession of black GMC Suburbans, gun-toting goons leaning out of the windows, yelling and waving at people to get out of the way.

As Luke was sitting with Clements on the coast, Nelson García was very much in residence at his hillside hacienda. In fact, he was holding court with his most trusted people at the head of a long, highly polished table. The blinds were closed, the heat of the day shut out, and in the lamp-lit gloom of the interior the air was thick with the smoke from countless packets of Pielrojas, loose-packed black cigarettes, not good for the lungs. Every one of the men around that table – there were no women in the cartel's top tier – pulled the strings of international operations that stretched right around the world, into the tattooed gangs of California's Folsom State Prison and San Quentin, into the digital address books of dock workers from Antwerp to the Port Authority of New Jersey, to Customs and coastguard officials from Nassau to Macau.

Today García's instructions were clear: Fuentes, the

informant, was now a dead man walking. It had taken less than two minutes for Benton to give up his name once the cartel had got to work on him in that jungle clearing. Benton was no hero: he had told them everything they had asked, but it still hadn't saved him. So now Fuentes was to be hunted down, along with his family. An example should be made of them, said García, and no time was to be wasted in finding them. But their deaths should be . . . how should he put it? . . . recreational.

García looked around the room, waiting for suggestions, his great bull-like head swivelling from one man to the next. He was looking for ideas, something original that would serve as a warning. Do whatever it takes, he told them, whatever it costs. He didn't care if they had to be traced to LA, Miami or London: the account had to be settled. That was just the way the clan did business.

But now El Pobrecito had more pressing business to discuss. He needed to know: had the project been compromised? That dumbfuck Englishman, that *espión*, who had blundered into his people's jungle rendezvous down in Tumaco, what had he learned?

As always, the words he wanted to hear came from Alfonso Suárez, the head of security, soothing him like a balm. '*El inglés* knew nothing of importance,' he said. Heads turned towards the grim-faced Colombian-American, whose suave good looks had earned him the nickname El Guapo, 'the handsome one'. His track record for getting information out of people was well known within the cartel, and in his younger days his methods had not always involved violence: it was remarkable how much some people's wives and daughters were prepared to reveal between the sheets.

But now his jet-black hair was starting to grey at the temples and he had no time to play games. Suárez would issue an order, on behalf of his boss, and others far further down the food chain would carry it out. He rarely spoke, and when he did it was mostly to whisper something darkly into the ear of his boss, who liked it that way: it kept everyone on their toes.

'We questioned him. Extensively,' said Suárez. They all knew what that meant. 'He gave us some names, including that piece of *mierda,* Fuentes.' He paused to spit theatrically on the marble floor. A maid dashed forward, like a ball-girl on Wimbledon Centre Court, mopped up the spot and retreated to the shadows.

'We have, however, taken some precautions,' continued Suárez. 'We will be putting the word out that the target is . . . Manchester. Only you in this room know the true destination for our gift. So relax, my friends, the project has not been compromised. Everything is still on track.'

El Pobrecito grunted. Now he had another concern. 'There is this other man, this one you say looks like *un soldado,* the Englishman who just landed in Tumaco. Follow him, watch him closely, and if you think he knows anything, deal with him.' He gave a brief, joyless chuckle. His mouth was smiling but his eyes were serious and everyone at the table knew better than to laugh.

'Of course, Patrón,' replied his head of security. 'We already have a team on the case.'

Chapter 12

WHAT, WONDERED LUKE, do you wear for a night on the town in Colombia with a dodgy provincial police chief? Not that he had brought an extensive wardrobe, what with all the survival kit he was hefting around in his rucksack. Tonight it would have to be the chinos, Timberlands and a dark blue polo shirt, nothing flash.

The major was waiting for him in the lobby, in a dazzling tropical sunset of a Hawaiian shirt tucked into contour-hugging white slacks and two-tone loafers. A gold medallion nestling in the man's chest hair completed the picture.

'Major Elerzon!' he greeted him. 'You're dressed for *fiesta*!'

'Please, we are friends now. You can call me Humberto. And you – my God – you are the perfect English gentleman. The ladies will love you tonight!'

'Nice to know,' said Luke, 'but I'm already well spoken for.'

'Ah, we all have someone special back home,' said Elerzon, trying not to think of his embittered battle-axe of a wife up in Bogotá. 'But tonight we forget the world and our troubles, you and me, yes? *Vámonos!* Let's go!'

La Casa Miraflores was everything Luke had expected, and worse. The major's police driver deposited them in the driveway of the 'club' and kept watch as they walked up to the entrance. Moths danced around the bare light-bulb that dangled above the doorway while the purple neon sign that announced the club's name in garish italics fizzed and sputtered with the intermittent power supply. A vast Afro-Colombian doorman was patting people down for weapons, but as soon as he saw the major and his guest he waved them through. 'Don't worry, he works for us,' remarked the major.

It took Luke a moment or two to adjust to the semi-darkness and the rhythmic salsa beat that throbbed through the floorboards beneath his feet. Already his eyes stung with cigarette smoke – he was unused to it: it had been nearly ten years since the UK public smoking ban had come into effect. The major was exchanging jokes with the coat-check girl as Luke took in a trio of bored women in Lycra gyrating slowly on a stage. A man in a stained white shirt and limp bow tie steered them to a table. 'The VIP spot,' he announced. 'Only the best for our esteemed police chief and his honoured guest.'

Luke stifled another yawn. He had managed to pack in a forty-five-minute power nap but his body clock was still all over the place. He had to stay focused, catch the major off his guard and get some insight into what was going on down here, into who killed Benton and what he had been following that was so important he was prepared to risk his life for it. The evening might turn out to be a total waste of time, but he would give it his best shot.

'So, Major, how is the investigation proceeding? Any leads yet?'

'Many, many leads! But first we celebrate!' The irony of celebrating anything in a case that had seen one of his colleagues tortured to death did not escape Luke. But before he could answer, the major was clicking his fingers and summoning a stout, middle-aged woman. She bent over his shoulder as he spoke into her ear above the music, then disappeared through a door. Luke did not like the way the table was set up: he was sitting with his back to a doorway. He was about to stand up and move his chair when the woman returned, leading two girls to their table. The major pushed back his chair, motioned them to sit down and ordered a bottle of sparkling wine from Argentina. '*Vida orgánica!*' he demanded. 'From Mendoza. Your best, if you please.'

Just play along, Luke told himself. Get him loosened up and talking. He was convinced that the major knew a lot more than he was saying. And then, soft as a butterfly, a hand landed on his inner thigh.

It was the older of the two girls and she was smiling meaningfully at him, a slight smear of misplaced lipstick at the corner of her mouth. Luke removed her hand. 'I'm married,' he told her.

'But you have no wedding ring,' she replied.

'*Ladrones*,' explained Luke, with a weary smile. 'Robbers.'

'*Ah, sí, ladrones.*' She nodded in sympathy and moved herself to a respectful distance. They would laugh about this one day, he and Elise, though perhaps it wasn't the smartest idea to tell her the sort of thing he got up to when he was away on an operation.

Across the table, Major Elerzon was clearly in his element, proposing toast after toast, one hand clasped round his glass, the other caressing the girl beside him. She was practically in his lap. When the girls excused themselves to go to the bathroom, he gave Luke a playful slap on his knee. 'Good times, no? Señor Luke?'

'The best,' he lied. He could see that the major was already well on the way to getting drunk. His shirt had somehow magically undone itself by a couple of buttons, and beads of sweat on his chest reflected the flashing neon lights of the dance floor. For a second Luke wondered if this would be him in ten years' time, lost in a loveless world, paying for his own pointless entertainment. Thank God he had Elise.

But he needed to make his move if he was going to get anything out of this character. 'I meant to ask . . .'

'Anything!' The major threw an arm round Luke's shoulders. 'Anything for my English *compadre*!'

'Major, is there anything you would like to tell me about this investigation, any clue, any evidence, just anything that is not in the report?'

'Ah, tan serio! Can you not relax for one night, my friend? Very well . . . there is one thing.' The major was about to continue when the two girls hove back into view, fresh lipstick in place, and he broke off abruptly. Oh, for Christ's sake, thought Luke. He held up his hand, stopping them in their tracks some distance away.

'You were saying, Major?'

'Ah, yes. I have something for you. It is probably nothing but maybe it can help you.' With his thumb and forefinger, the police chief extracted a small black notebook from the breast pocket of his Hawaiian shirt and handed it to Luke. 'It was found,' continued the major, 'on the body of your *compadre* from the embassy. We, er, forgot to give it to the investigators from Bogotá.'

Luke turned the notebook over in his hand. It was damp and the corners of the pages were splayed and frayed. On the back cover there was a brown smear that might have been mud, blood or possibly something more unpleasant. He sniffed it and recoiled. Excrement. What sort of person, he wondered, carries a shit-stained notebook in their breast pocket?

He opened it. The first page was blank, just a dead mosquito squashed flat against the paper. He flicked through the next few pages and found notes and coordinates in Spanish. Benton's handwriting? For a moment he felt almost reverential, handling a relic from a dead man's life. One day, maybe, they would let his widow have it but that might well be thirty years away.

'Is useful?' asked the major.

Luke sensed that the man was eager for him to put away the notebook and get on with some serious drinking but he nodded and turned over. And there it was, staring up at him on a whole page of its own. A single word inscribed in neat Oriental characters he didn't recognize. Was it Japanese? Korean? Chinese? Luke couldn't tell but the analysts back home would have it pinned down in an instant. It confirmed there was an international connection. That must have been what Benton was on to.

And yet it didn't make sense. If this had been found on Benton's body, why hadn't the cartel removed it? Perhaps their people had been careless that night, over-confident even, after beating the crap out of the poor man. And why was the major giving him the notebook? Luke's naturally analytical brain was turning over the possibilities even as he flicked through the remaining pages. Was the major looking for money, a reward perhaps? Or a favour in return? In which case, what was it likely to be? There was something about the man he definitely didn't trust. And what if this was a red herring, deliberately planted on Benton's body to throw investigators off the scent? Well, that would be for a reports officer in London to decide. Right now, though, in the sweaty, sleazy Colombian nightclub, his instinct told him he had something valuable in his hand. Luke slipped the notebook into the pocket of his chinos. 'You did a good thing, Major, I really appreciate this,' he told him. 'Now we should have a toast.'

'*No es nada, no es nada*. It's nothing, really.'

As far as Luke was concerned, the evening's objective had been accomplished and he was counting the minutes before he could leave. First thing in the morning he would photograph every page and send it to VX for analysis. Now he felt a tingling sensation on the outside of his thigh. He turned to his left in irritation, expecting to see Smeared Lipstick coming round for another pass – but it was his mobile phone, quietly vibrating in his pocket.

'Elise!' He could barely hear her. And what time must it be in London? Four thirty in the morning. This was not good.

'Babes,' she said, 'I can't sleep.'

'Hang on, let me find somewhere quieter.' Luke stood up, mobile clamped to his ear, and brushed past the major as he headed for the door.

'Where are you?' said Elise. 'Oh, sorry, I'm not supposed to ask, am I? Well, it sounds like quite a party you're having in there. What's her name?'

'Very funny. You should see this place – it's a crap-hole.'

'Anyhow,' she continued, 'seeing as you're not going to be back in time for the exhibition opening, Hugo's offered to help and maybe take me to dinner afterwards.'

The words were delivered breezily, off the cuff, yet they stung Luke. 'Hugo Squires? That smoothie from Goldman Sachs? I thought you said you couldn't stand him.'

'Oh, he's not so bad – and you should see his place in the country.'

'What? Elise – hello? Hello?' The connection was lost.

They rode away together in the police car, Major Elerzon in the back, wedged happily between the girls from the club. The police chief had 'bought them out' for the night, but Luke sat up front, next to the driver. He was trying hard not to think about the polished investment banker eight thousand kilometres away trying to move in on his girlfriend while he was stuck here, serving Queen and country. Could he blame him? Probably not. Elise was a temptation for any man. Still, maybe they would have a 'conversation' when he got back, him and Hugo Squires. Nothing hard-core, just to get a few things straight. Like, Piss off and leave her alone or I'll break your neck.

'Thanks, just drop me here at the hotel,' he said to the driver. He twisted round to say goodbye to the major but the man was fully occupied. It would take

Luke some time to shake off the image of a girl's head bobbing up and down on the lap of Tumaco's chief of police.

'Que te diviertas! Enjoy yourself,' said Luke, although the words seemed superfluous given that Major Elerzon had his head tipped back and his eyes closed. He shut the car door and went into the hotel past the security guard, patting his pocket to check he still had the notebook. He paused outside the lawyer's room and listened. The faint sound of snoring told him all was well.

Outside his own door, Luke knelt down and shone the torch on his smartphone at the crack between the edge of the door and its frame. Good. The hair he had stuck across the gap before he went out was still in place. It was never 100 per cent proof that no one had been in, but it gave him some reassurance.

Inside his room, he locked the door, then went to the cabinet beneath the bathroom sink. He reached in and felt along the inside roof of the cabinet until he found what he was looking for. With one swift tug, the Sig Sauer came free from where he had taped it to the wooden surface. He popped out the magazine, counted the rounds, reinserted the magazine, cocked the weapon and flipped the safety catch. He went through his rucksack, piece by piece, checking nothing had been removed, then tucked the pistol under his pillow, took off his clothes and fell asleep.

Chapter 13

LUKE WAS RUNNING, pushing his body to the limit, and he ached everywhere. The green webbing straps cut into his shoulders, the SA80 rifle cradled in his hands felt absurdly heavy for such a small piece of kit, and his sopping-wet combat trousers chafed his thighs with every stride. Now he was balanced on a slippery plank ten metres above the ground, taking a running jump and punching his way through rope-mesh netting, then crawling along a single horizontal rope, one leg dangling, the other cocked at an angle and kicking him along, as they'd been shown. Someone was shouting at him, someone unpleasant who wouldn't shut up, someone big and ugly in a tight white singlet with a pair of crossed red clubs and a crown on his chest. A PTI, a physical training instructor. His nemesis. Oh, God, he was back at Lympstone, at the Commando Training Centre on the Devon coast, going through the Tarzan course and the commando tests. Now he was hauling himself up a rope on the Wall of Pain, every muscle screaming. Someone was standing at the top, silhouetted, hands on hips. Another PTI—

Luke woke up. And realized someone was standing at the end of his bed.

There are moments when everything before you suddenly slows down. The cricket ball that hurtles inexorably towards the greenhouse, the drinks tray that slips from the waitress's grasp and takes an eternity to crash to the tiled restaurant floor, the oncoming car that skids and swerves but still hits you. This, for Luke, was one of those moments. How on earth, he wondered, did this person get into my room when I locked it?

'Sssh.' She was whispering to him. '*Relájate.*'

Luke tensed, now wide awake and very far from relaxed. 'Who the hell are you? How did you get in here?' he said in Spanish, reaching for the bedside light. He clicked the switch but it didn't work.

'I saw you in the club tonight,' she replied softly. 'You are . . . *tan guapo* . . . so cute. My friend on Reception let me in. Don't you like me?' She smiled, and even in the dim light that spilled in from the corridor he could see she had perfect white teeth. She was a far cry from the poor souls back in that fleapit of a club and he definitely couldn't recall seeing her there. She was far too pretty to be working in the Casa Miraflores, her oval face framed by a mane of silky black hair.

Luke smelt a rat.

'I'm Carla,' she breathed – and, just like that, she was shedding her blouse, reaching behind her back and unclipping her bra, her breasts tumbling free as she moved towards him like a sinuous, predatory cat. '*Ah, qué bueno, estás desnude,*' she purred, sliding her body up his.

Luke backed himself up against the wall behind the bed, holding out a restraining hand. 'Whoa! This. Is not. Going. To happen.' He spoke emphatically, brooking no argument. And it was then that she gave the game away. Just one glance, a tiny gesture – he could so easily have missed it, but he didn't. Just a minuscule tilt of her chin to one side, and he caught it. She was looking at the door. It gave him the two seconds he needed to prepare.

There were three of them, thick-set and brutish, their muscles bulging through their shiny synthetic gangster shirts as they crashed through the unlocked door from the corridor into his room. The girl had already rolled neatly to one side and off the bed, clearing the way for the first man to lunge towards him. A flat face with a boxer's nose loomed towards Luke as he felt a giant hand scrabbling for his throat, trying to close around his windpipe. There was an overpowering smell of sweat and garlic. And something else he couldn't place. But Luke's senses were on fire. This was what he had trained for. Those two seconds had given him time to reach beneath his pillow and now he slammed the butt of the pistol down on the first man's head. He slumped, pressing Luke down with his bulk. And now the second man was on him, trying to pin back his arms, and behind him the third was preparing some kind of cloth. So he was being kidnapped.

Fuck you, he thought, you're not having me.

In a confined space, like that no-star hotel room, an unsilenced pistol makes a lot of noise. In Luke's firm grip the weapon bucked and roared in a deafening explosion of sound and light. Squeezing off two rounds in under a second came as second nature to him. Time and again he had taken his troop through rehearsals with live ammo in the Killing House back at Poole. Double-tapping, they called it in the trade.

Now, with the flash of each shot, he caught a split-second frame of a man's face, his final moment on earth. Handguns are notoriously inaccurate over distance but at such close range it was hard to miss. Luke heaved the slumped body of the first man off him, rolled off the bed and stood braced, feet slightly apart, both hands on the weapon, poised to fire again, his breath coming in shallow, controlled gasps. Nothing moved, except the girl in the corner, who was shivering with fear. 'Please!' she begged. 'I had no choice.'

'Turn on that light at the wall,' he ordered.

She moved awkwardly at a crouch towards the switch, holding her crumpled blouse against her breasts. Voices sounded in the corridor, and in the harsh, white light that suddenly flooded the room Luke was all too aware of his own appearance. Stark naked, splashed in blood and holding a smoking pistol. Lumps of a pink, blancmange-like substance were splattered across his torso. Human brain. There were two very dead bodies in his room, one unconscious gangster and a half-naked girl. This could take some explaining.

People were jostling in the doorway now, letting out screams of panic as soon as they caught sight of the carnage inside room 16. Someone had gone to fetch the manager. And the incongruous figure of an English lawyer in striped flannel pyjamas was pushing through the crowd.

'Dear God, man, what have you *done*?' exclaimed Friend, clamping a hand over his mouth in horror.

'I know how this looks,' said Luke, putting down the pistol and wrapping a bath towel around his waist. 'But let me take care of it. Just keep an eye on the girl in the corner, will you?' He unzipped a money belt inside his rucksack and drew out a wad of US dollar bills, sought out the hotel manager and pressed them into his hand. Immediately the manager began to disperse the throng, assuring them that the police were on their way.

When they had all gone, Luke sat Friend on the bed. The lawyer was trembling and having difficulty breathing, as if he himself had just had to shoot his way out of a violent kidnapping. Adrenalin was still pumping through Luke's veins but he addressed the lawyer as calmly as he could. 'Look, John,' he began, 'I'm sorry, but that's just how it goes down sometimes. It was them or me. This is a bloody dangerous part of the world. You knew that, right? I'm just glad it was my door they came through and not yours.'

Friend said nothing. He was staring at the floor, shaking his head from side to side.

'John?' Luke gripped his shoulders.

Friend looked up suddenly, eyes furious. 'No!' he shouted. 'It won't do! I won't have it. We can't have you shooting your way around this country, like it's the Wild West. It's against all the rules!'

Chapter 14

'I'M VERY DISAPPOINTED in you, young man.' Sid Khan's voice was so quiet Luke had to press the phone to his ear to make out what he was saying. 'We send you down to South America to help clear things up and what do you give us? Three damned stiffs, Luke Carlton.'

'Two, to be exact. One's still alive. I just gave him a bit of concussion.'

'Let me remind you,' continued the head of CT, 'that this a Tier One Priority, and what are you doing? You end up knobbing some Colombian bird on the Service's time, then turn the place into a free-fire zone, like it's Laser Quest with live ammunition.'

'Look, if I can just—'

'I haven't finished yet,' said Khan. He hadn't raised his voice once: he didn't need to – the message was coming across loud and clear. 'I want a full report on this, sent to me by the usual means, and I want it by the end of today, London time. So you'd better get going. And, Carlton?'

'Yes?' Luke was trying hard to keep the exasperation out of his voice. It was three in the morning in Colombia, five hours behind London, and he had only just finished moving into another hotel room while the night shift began the grisly job of sanitizing his old room. Friend had put himself to bed with a sleeping pill and a chair wedged at forty-five degrees against his door handle.

At least Major Elerzon had played his part. Within minutes of Luke calling him, a squad of uniformed cops had turned up, carted away the bodies and put an armed guard outside the hotel, another outside Luke's room. One of the dead men was quickly identified as a known assassin for the cartels, while the sole survivor and the girl were being questioned.

'I don't mind telling you, Luke,' continued Sid Khan, 'there are people here at VX who think you're a loose cannon, that we should have left you where you were, in Special Forces. I've just spent the last twenty minutes explaining why we should keep you on. This isn't some cowboy outfit where we go jumping out of planes and whack the first people we bump into. We're an accountable arm of government, answerable to the Foreign Secretary. Please tell me you get that?'

Luke stared blankly at the white chipboard door of the bedroom cupboard opposite his bed. 'I get it.'

Not since basic training half a lifetime ago could Luke remember receiving such a bollocking from a superior. He'd really thought he'd left all that behind him. He was being blamed unfairly for what had taken place in his hotel room, but he allowed himself no self-pity. Take it on the chin, write up the report, move on and start getting some results.

First thing in the morning, Luke and the lawyer moved across town, under heavy escort, to the safety of the Jungla Police Commando Barracks. The security people at VX wanted no more chances taken.

Friend had been visibly relieved, patting his briefcase on the short ride over as if comforting a distressed pet. But Luke, now effectively confined to barracks and in bad odour with his masters, felt like a caged beast. Billeted in the officers' quarters two doors down from Friend, he looked out of the window as a squad of shaven-headed recruits jogged past, hoarse voices belting out the corps song in unison, their bodies oozing testosterone.

At a knock on the door, Luke reached instinctively for the Sig. This might have been a police barracks but he was still in South America. It turned out to be Friend, looking rather sheepish. He pulled up a chair. 'I think I owe you a bit of an apology. I mean, are you all right?'

Luke laughed. He was tempted to say that the time to have asked that was last night, but he shrugged it off. Friend had had a baptism of fire and nobody forgets the first time they see a dead body. Already the poor man looked about five years older than he had when they'd left Heathrow. 'No problem, John. They didn't get me, did they?'

'Yes, but you . . . they . . . Well, I suppose you're used to this kind of thing. But I don't mind telling you it scared the hell out of me. How did they know where we were staying?'

Luke smiled. Here was a first-class Oxbridge brain, a man who could dissect reams of legal documents in minutes, probably on three times his salary, yet in a place like this he had absolutely no situational awareness. None. 'Think about it, John. We must be just about the only two *gringos* in town and we stick out a mile. The cartels have got dickers everywhere – they'll have clocked us coming in.'

'I'm sorry. "Dickers"?'

'Scouts. Lookouts. The ten-year-old kid on the street corner, you think he's selling chewing gum but his real job is informing for the crims, that kind of thing.' Even as Luke was speaking a thought occurred to him. Could Major Elerzon have had something to do with the set-up in his hotel room? Surely the police chief had had his hands full with those two ladies of negotiable virtue. Still . . . He tried hard to dismiss the idea but it wouldn't quite go away. He had worked with some fine Colombians in his time, people like Jorge whom he trusted completely. But Major Elerzon was not in that bracket. Luke tended to trust his instincts and he had a bad feeling in the pit of his stomach.

Friend was gazing at him, waiting for him to say something more. When he didn't, the lawyer lowered his head to peer at Luke over the top of his glasses. 'Well, I'd best get the paperwork sorted on those two characters you, er, disposed of last night. I expect Sid Khan has been asking for answers already.'

'You could say that.'

'Let me handle him so you can get on with your work. Just keep me in the loop, if you don't mind.'

'To be honest, I could use your help right now. Can you spare half an hour to go through something? I need your legal, analytical brain.'

'Well, I suppose the other stuff can wait, so—'

'Good.' Luke pulled out the thin classified file of single-sided A4 documents that Angela had put together for him in a rush on the day he had left for Colombia. 'I don't know how much of this you've had a chance to read,' he continued, 'but it contains all the relevant CX reports that Benton filed in the six months before he was killed.'

'CX reports?'

'The raw intelligence he was supplying back to Vauxhall Cross? Before it gets assessed and written up into something ministers can read?'

'Oh, yes, I remember now.'

'Come on, John. I need you firing on all cylinders here.'

'Righto.'

Luke spread the documents on the table between them. One of the legs was shorter than the other three and it wobbled as he touched it. For some unknown reason, Friend seemed more interested in fixing the table leg than in studying the documents.

'Take a look,' said Luke, steering him back to them. 'Because something does not add up. Agent Fuentes – sorry, Synapse, as he's referred to here – was our sole source inside the cartel, right?'

'Right.'

'And everything he was supplying to Benton came from here, from Tumaco, down in the far south-west of Colombia?'

'Yes, I suppose so,' said Friend, lifting his glasses clear of his nose and replacing them in exactly the same spot. 'But I'm not sure where you're going with this.'

'Someone else is in the picture. Someone in another part of this country was feeding material to Benton at the same time. Someone inserted in deep cover, way upstream in this cartel, someone I haven't been told about. John, what the hell is going on here?'

If Luke had looked hard enough at Friend in that moment he might have caught it: the pulsing vein in his temple. Friend certainly looked uncomfortable, but then he always did.

'Well,' said the lawyer, 'I'm sure we've both been given the same brief. Look, I hear what you say and I think you should take it up with Khan. But I really must get on now and tie up the paperwork on these two fatalities. There'll be a coroner's inquest, you know, and the Service will want your name kept out of it.' He stood up, avoiding Luke's gaze, and let himself out of the room.

Luke watched him leave. *He knows something I don't.* He didn't like that. But now he needed to turn his attention to Benton's notebook. Had it really been less than twelve hours since Major Elerzon had handed it to him in the club? It felt like months.

Luke couldn't help himself, he sniffed the cover again and recoiled. It still smelt of crap, and now he was down to his last packet of anti-bacterial wet-wipes. He took out his smartphone and painstakingly photographed every page that had been written on. As he did so, a memory came floating back: his uncle, who had worked at MI6 in the seventies and eighties, showing him his old Service camera, a beautiful leather-bound Agfa Silette with a Carl Zeiss lens, 'Made in West Germany' stamped on the side – a throwback to when the country was divided in two by the Iron Curtain. His uncle, long retired, had shown him how to photograph documents in double-quick time, clicking the shutter and shuffling the papers with all the swiftness of a casino croupier. This was good old-fashioned spy work, he had told him, stealing secrets in a hurry before someone comes through the door and catches you red-handed.

But Luke was alone, in the sparsely furnished officers' quarters on a secure base with the police commandos, and he took his time getting it right.

First he transferred the images in his phone to the Service laptop, formatted them for transmission, then attached the 'Squirter', the encryption device that would send the data in a burst transmission up into space, then bounce it off a satellite back down to earth to be collected and decrypted at Vauxhall Cross.

It took quite some time and when he had finished he sat back and opened a packet of dried plantains, left behind by the previous occupant. It was more for something to do than anything else, while he worked out his next move. In fact, Luke decided, as he popped the last one into his mouth, he didn't like plantain. Just then his secure phone beeped and shuddered. Incoming text from VX. He half expected another rocket from Khan, but it was from Angela: *Nice work on the notebook L. Translation completed. It's Korean. That isolated word was Hungnam. It's a port. In North Korea.*

Chapter 15

BETWEEN THE EAST Pyongyang Market and the giant triple statue of the Workers' Party Monument lies the district known as Munsin-Dong. Amid the uniform white tower blocks and the smaller green-roofed office buildings of the North Korean capital sits a discreet organization called simply Bureau 121. Unheard of until recently, the unit has achieved a certain notoriety in foreign intelligence circles. It is widely believed to be the nerve centre of North Korea's cyber-hacking industry, a nationwide enterprise employing at least six thousand people and absorbing more than 10 per cent of the country's military budget.

It was not the job of Bureau 121 to record what happened to the disgraced scientist Comrade Dr Mun and his family. Those details were written down, with clinical precision, by another government department. The confessions, the trial, the sentencing and the transport to the labour camp, all recorded and logged in the annals of North Korea's disappeared. But in the week following his arrest the morning shift at Bureau 121 noticed something unusual: there had been a spike in online communications between an IP address, an internet user in South America and another inside their country. The team on duty traced it to the Pang Sang Un People's Defence Unit on the outskirts of Pyongyang. This could be serious, a matter of national security. But should they report it or should they back off?

The unit leader, Comrade Goh, was summoned and for several long minutes he stood behind them, leaning over their shoulders and peering through his spectacles at the streams of code and intercepted messages. What puzzled him most was that they were not written in Korean but in English. Why would anyone be communicating in English from inside the People's Defence Unit? This was a hard call to make, careerwise. Get it wrong and he didn't want to think about what might happen to him and his team. Eventually, without saying a word to his colleagues, Comrade Goh straightened, removed his spectacles, went to his glass-sided office and closed the door. They saw him pick up the phone and speak, nodding vigorously.

Thirty minutes later there was a commotion in the corridor, the sound of booted feet running down the linoleum. A dozen men from the State Security Department, the dreaded SSD, burst into Bureau 121 and ordered everyone to stand up, away from their consoles. Nothing was to be touched. A photographer moved among them, walking right up to each analyst, letting his camera flash go off right in their faces, catching their anxious expressions, recording their reactions as he methodically worked his way through everyone in the room. Inside Comrade Goh's office three of the men from the SSD sat him down and fired a stream of questions at him in quick succession.

'Why did you not report this earlier?'

'When did you first discover this?'

'How long have you been monitoring this interaction?'

Goh, an academic by training, was as bewildered as the rest of his team. Surely, he protested, he had done the correct and patriotic thing by calling it in at once. Could he venture to ask what this was all about? Then perhaps his team could assist in the investigation. The men from the SSD turned away from him and conferred among themselves. 'The reason we are here,' announced the lead investigator, 'is that the IP address you told us about belongs to a *taejwa,* a senior colonel.'

'But that is why I called you!' exclaimed Comrade Goh. 'We could see that the online traffic was originating from inside the People's Defence Unit. Did I not do the right thing? If not, I am humbly sorry.'

'You acted as you should,' replied the SSD team leader, 'but now we must begin a thorough investigation. We will need all your team to work with us on this.'

'But I don't understand,' protested Goh. 'Surely you can put these questions to the colonel himself.'

'That is no longer possible.' The three men from the SSD looked at each other. In the paranoid regime, this was a potentially dangerous situation for all of them and they knew it. 'It is not possible,' repeated the investigator, 'because yesterday Colonel Kwon Gangjun deserted his post.'

The cyber team leader's jaw dropped.

'Yes,' continued the investigator, 'this running dog of the capitalist West has defected. We believe he has left the country by ship. He was last observed in Hungnam port.'

Chapter 16

SECURE, CONFINED, FRUSTRATED, Luke was totally unable to sleep. It was one in the morning, and in his bunk at the Francisco Santander police commando base, watching a spider crawl across the ceiling, he was still wired from what had happened the previous night. Shooting his way out of a kidnapping was not something he felt particularly proud of, although all day the Colombian officers had nodded respectfully to him. Even the cleaner had asked to shake his hand. But clearly there was a contract out on him from the cartel so he was going to have to up his personal security a notch.

Yet it wasn't this that was keeping him awake. It was the notebook and, specifically, the North Korean connection. What, in Heaven's name, could link a Colombian drug cartel with that isolated and unpredictable Cold War relic? Nothing good ever comes out of North Korea, he reflected. If they're not test-firing their latest ballistic missile or banned nuclear device they're busy flogging Scud blueprints around the Middle East and harassing exiled dissidents. A Colombian narcotics–North Korean partnership?

The only person alive, Luke realized, who could possibly shed some light on this was Fuentes. He had to find him before the cartel's thugs did. The odds on this happening were not good, but by the morning he had an idea where to start.

As soon as dawn broke, grey and misty, over the camp, Luke was rapping on the door of the base commander's office. He was already up and an orderly let him in. 'Señor Luke!' Commander Rojas beamed. 'Perhaps we should call you "Tirofijo" – Marksman! Two of those *putas* dead and one in custody. Nice going! Maybe I keep you here and make you an instructor! Coffee?'

'Please.'

The commander went to a table where someone had left a jug and some cups, and poured *café tinto* for them both. He was tall for a Colombian, and well built, with alert, darting eyes. Halfway across the room, with a cup in each hand, he stopped and smiled again. 'You're looking at my tracksuit, right? It's the morning run in twenty minutes. I take the men out every day. They expect me to set an example. You should come too.'

'Maybe I will,' said Luke, 'but the reason I'm here is that I have a favour to ask.'

'Tell me.'

'If I wanted to go for a drink tonight . . .' began Luke.

The commander threw his head back and laughed. '*Dios mío!* My God, you British have *cojones*! You want to go out partying again already? After what just happened?'

Luke held up his hand and laughed with him. He could see how that must have sounded. 'Hear me out,' he said, when they had both calmed down.

Commander Rojas sat down at his desk, folded his hands and gave him his full attention.

'If I was Señor Benton,' continued Luke, 'and I wanted to meet someone in a public place near my hotel, somewhere I'm not going to attract a lot of attention, where would I go?'

The commander was nodding before Luke had finished his sentence. He opened a drawer, rummaged around, closed it, then opened the one below it until he found what he was looking for: *Mapa turístico de Tumaco.*

'We had a guy from the US Drug Enforcement Administration here on the base for a month last year,' said Rojas, unfolding the map. 'Man, he wanted to see everything. And I mean everything! OK, so here's your hotel, El Paraíso . . .' The two men leaned over the city street map as the commander traced a route with his finger. 'And I'm guessing your Señor Benton could walk, if he felt like it, to this place here, Las Olas del Mar.'

'The Waves of the Sea?' said Luke.

'Exactly. Very popular at weekends, close by the beach, great margaritas.'

'So if I wanted to check it out this evening could you provide a discreet security escort? You know, you're there but you're not there, if you catch my drift?'

'It will be our pleasure. This is our *especialidad.* We even teach this on a course here to our friends from Honduras and Guatemala.'

Outside the window the grey mist of dawn had turned to a fine drizzle. Luke noticed a solitary figure pacing up and down near the parade ground, holding up an umbrella. 'Chadwick & Partners' read the logo.

'For All Your Legal Solutions.' It was Friend and he seemed to be lost in thought. Luke left Rojas's office and went out to catch up with him. 'Sleep all right, John?'

Friend whirled round, then relaxed. 'Ah,' he said. 'Not really, no. But I'm glad I've bumped into you because I've got something to tell you. I have to fly up to Bogotá this afternoon and sort out the paperwork for the repatriation of Benton's body. I'm afraid that means you're on your own down here. I know you can take care of yourself, but just . . .' He tailed off.

'Just don't go slotting anyone else?'

'Precisely. Look, um, I've been thinking. About that second source inside the cartel that you mentioned.'

'Yes?'

'Well . . .' Friend was shifting uncomfortably now, giving Luke the impression he rather wished he hadn't broached the subject after all '. . . obviously, there's nothing I can tell you but, um, I wouldn't entirely steer you away from it.'

Luke stared hard at him, his earlier suspicions confirmed. *He's been told something. And I haven't. So I'm down here working this thing with one hand tied behind my back.*

'Look,' said Friend. He could see how this was going down with Luke. 'Why not talk to the Cousins?'

'You mean the CIA?'

Friend winced, as if stung by an insect, and glanced round to see if anyone was within earshot. They weren't. 'Yes,' he continued. 'I take it they've given you a number for the liaison officer on this one? Good. Well, I'd give him a call and hook up if I were you.' And with that, Friend and his umbrella were gone.

*

Anyone strolling past the Olas del Mar bar that evening might have noticed several short but well-built men sitting drinking on bar stools. If they had taken a really close look they might have noticed that for all the swigs they took from their beer bottles they never seemed to finish them. Luke's escorts from the Jungla were very much alert and on duty. He arrived a few minutes after them, having been dropped off nearby, pulled up a bar stool, gave them a cursory nod, as a stranger would, and ordered himself a beer. He was dressed in pretty much the only clothes he had brought with him: beige chinos, dark-blue polo shirt and a pair of grey, springy shoes. 'Approach boots', they were called, nothing too military about them but they allowed you to walk for hours and tread softly when you needed to.

Tonight, mid-week, the bar was practically deserted, open on all sides to the damp breeze and the sound of the Pacific surf crashing ashore just down the beach. A young girl in a sleeveless dress was behind the bar, bending over to get Luke's beer from the icebox. For a moment he was reminded of Elise, though there was probably ten years' difference between the two women. What would she be doing now? Tucked up in bed, hopefully.

When the girl brought his beer, which was cocooned in a Styrofoam jacket to keep it cold, he asked, 'Do you get many tourists from Europe here?'

She laughed. 'None! You are the first for a long time. Why?'

'Well, my friend from England was here in Tumaco a few days ago. Staying at the hotel just down there. He's a bit older than me. He's, er, missing and I'm trying to find his friend, a *Colombiano*. You didn't see them here together, by any chance?'

The girl put a hand on her hip and bit her lower lip in thought. 'When?' she asked.

'Five nights ago. About the same time in the evening as now.'

She shook her head and gave him an apologetic look. 'Sorry, I was off then. Can I get you some *tapas* with your beer?'

'In a while,' replied Luke, and pulled out his phone. He should probably check in with Friend.

Two girls walked in, arm in arm and giggling, brushing unnecessarily close to Luke and making eye contact with him as they sashayed to the other end of the bar. They certainly had the attention of his Jungla escorts, he noticed. They wore tight, fluorescent crop-tops, spray-on jeans and rather too much make-up. The girl behind the bar turned her back on them, and when they ordered some green fizzy drink with ice she took her time serving them. Evidently she did not approve. The girls smiled at Luke from across the bar and a thought flashed through his head: would Benton have known them? Would he have . . . 'When in Rome' and all that? Surely not. He got up and walked over to them.

'*Hola, chicas.*' That sounded pretty tacky. He'd better get straight to the point. 'Has either of you met another Englishman here, a man a bit older than me?'

They gave him a coy look. 'It's no problem,' said the older one, thrusting out her chin. 'You can bring him too. Which hotel you in? The Paraíso?'

Luke sighed. He was not easily embarrassed but his cheeks were reddening. He sensed the bar girl staring at him, her disapproval burning into the back of his neck. 'No. I meant have you seen any other *inglés* here, in this bar, last week?'

Their smiles evaporated. This man was a time-waster. They turned away, bored of him now. Luke exchanged a glance with his close protection team and gave a barely perceptible shake of his head. It was time to move on.

It was as Luke was paying for his beer that a boy came in, a wooden tray suspended round his neck on frayed straps bearing lottery tickets and sticks of chewing gum. *'Loto! Millones de pesos!'* he called. He made straight for Luke, tugging at his elbow and holding out a wad of printed lottery tickets. Immediately there was a hiss from one of the well-built men at a nearby table, telling him to leave the tourist in peace.

Luke had never bought a lottery ticket in his life and he was not about to start now. But the lad was so insistent that he took out some pesos to give him and was about to send him away when he noticed something that made the words die on his lips. It was the pen poking out of the top pocket of the boy's shirt. It was nothing special, just a cheap plastic giveaway, but the words printed on it were plainly visible: Scarborough North Cliff Golf Club.

Chapter 17

LUKE PULLED UP a chair for the lottery-ticket boy and made him sit down, his heart racing. 'Let me buy you a Coke, a Merinda, a Sprite? Whatever you want.' He knew exactly how this must look to everyone else in the bar but his explanations could come later. 'Where did you get that pen?' he asked the boy. 'Who gave it to you?'

'No lo sé. Por qué? I don't know,' said the boy, shrugging his shoulders. 'Why? What's it to you?' His eyes darted around the bar, looking for a way out.

This was the most tangible lead Luke had had and he could not afford to blow it. He reached into his pocket and pulled out a single fifty-dollar bill. The boy's eyes widened. 'Listen, *chico,* you see this money?' Luke told him. 'Well, it's all yours if you can take me to the man who gave you that pen, the one in your pocket. Can you do that?'

He could see the boy hesitating, sensing trouble. Smart kid, he thought. You don't get to survive on the streets of Colombia without an antenna for danger. But the boy's eyes kept flicking back to the banknote and eventually he nodded. Without another word he took Luke's arm and led him away. As they left, Luke looked at his escort and inclined his head towards the exit. They would be following at a discreet distance.

As soon as they were outside, the boy quickened his pace. People talked in these parts and Luke didn't blame the kid for not wanting to be seen with a *gringo*. Word might get back to the cartel and that would not be good for either of them. They passed a solitary streetlamp that lit up the fine mist of rain that had begun to fall, then turned down a muddy, unpaved road. The night felt close and, far out to sea, jagged forks of purple lightning split the sky. Luke walked quickly, just behind the boy, who sidestepped neatly around the puddles, still holding his tray against his chest. Luke still had good night vision, a product of all his years in Special Forces, but this kid was almost supernatural – he seemed to know every inch of the road. Was he being led into an ambush? Luke was all too aware of the possibility, given the failed kidnap attempt. But he could feel the comforting bulk of the Sig Sauer pistol tucked into his waistband beneath his polo shirt, and a glance over his shoulder confirmed that his Jungla escort were shadowing them some distance back, one on either side of the road.

When the shot rang out from in front of them Luke dropped immediately to the ground, flattening himself against the rain-soaked mud of the track, the Sig already in his hand. '*Bájate!*' he shouted to the boy. 'Get down!' But the boy just stood there, laughing. '*No es nada*,' he said. 'It's nothing.' Something was coming down the road towards them at speed now – Luke readied the weapon in his hand. And then he relaxed. A stray dog, half running, half limping, tore past them into the night. Luke stood up, his clothes soaked in mud. They pressed on.

At a fork in the road the boy steered them to the left and the track soon narrowed to a footpath. They were right on the edge of town now, leaving the lights of Tumaco behind, and Luke could hear the unwelcome whine of the first mosquitoes beginning to seek them out. His escort, he noticed, had closed the gap between them. They came to the outline of a large shed, pitch black against the night sky, and the boy pointed to a flight of steps that led down at the side to a basement. Luke wished he had his NVGs with him, but instead he took out a pencil torch with a red filter, standard military practice to avoid using a white light that can be seen for miles.

'*Y entonces?*' he asked the boy, pointing to the steps. 'So what now?'

The boy went first, picking his way down. Luke could feel underfoot they were wet with slime, and in the shadows something scuttled away, abandoning a chicken carcass. Luke grimaced: the air reeked. At the bottom of the steps they came to a door, black with grime and mould. The boy knocked.

'*Oye!*' he called. 'It's Julio. I have someone with me.' Now he turned to Luke, holding out his hand for the promised fifty dollars.

'Whoa,' said Luke. 'Who's behind that door?'

'You ask me about your friend, the Englishman,' said the boy, defensively. 'He is a kind man. He give me a present. So,' he pointed to the door, 'this is his friend. Sometimes I bring him food.'

Together they pushed open the door to the basement and Luke's torch probed the room with a dim beam of red light. There was a rustling in the corner, then silence. As the torch played over the detritus in the room it lit up broken chicken baskets, discarded plastic buckets and crumpled newspapers, and there was an overpowering smell of excrement. A foot was poking out from beneath the rubbish. Luke moved towards it, squatted and nudged it with the muzzle of the Sig. It recoiled, and its owner leaped into view, then huddled against the wall. His red-rimmed eyes were bright with terror, his hands pressed together, imploring. He had found Agent Fuentes.

Chapter 18

THREE HOURS LATER Fuentes had showered, shaved and put on a green military-issue tracksuit. Now he was nursing a glass of Fanta Orange and was ready for his debrief.

A radio call back to the Jungla base that night had summoned a nondescript pickup truck to extract him and Luke from the warehouse cellar, while the boy with the lottery tickets was dropped off on the edge of town. The Jungla police commandos were taking no chances and they made Fuentes lie down behind the front seats with a blanket over him. He was a marked man.

Luke was pacing up and down outside the debriefing room, running through all the questions he needed answers to. Do not cock this up, he told himself. He took a deep breath and pushed open the door. Fuentes barely looked up when he walked in. He had, Luke noted, the thousand-yard stare, which was hardly surprising, given what he must have seen and heard. His hair was black, short and curly, there were worry lines across his forehead and his face had deep, open pores. To Luke, he looked about forty-five but was probably ten years younger. The strain of being an agent, an informant, inside one of the most dangerous cartels in Latin America would be taking its toll.

'OK,' began Luke. 'Let's start at the beginning. How long were you working with Señor Benton?'

Fuentes looked up sharply, his mouth half open. 'I thought you said you worked with him?' he said. 'You are from British intelligence, no?'

'Yes, I am,' Luke reassured him. 'And I have most of his reports here.' He gestured to the thin file in his hand. 'But I still need to hear it in your own words. What, exactly, was your position within the cartel? How far did they trust you? What were they planning?'

Fuentes answered slowly at first, his comments interspersed with long pauses, but Luke didn't hurry him. This man was a classic candidate for PTSD – post-traumatic stress disorder – and he would certainly need counselling. But now, his words were coming faster, like a dam bursting on a mountain stream, coursing through the narrative of what had happened that dreadful night when Benton had been caught and killed. Fuentes recalled the beach-bar rendezvous with Benton, the night-vision goggles, the camera, the ambush, the screams. Luke watched Fuentes and made notes as he recounted all this, reliving every detail. When the agent had finished, Luke got up, walked round to the fridge by the window and took out two more Fantas, one for each of them. He sat down again, handed one to Fuentes, then held his own can against his forehead, savouring the cool, moist metal surface against his hot skin. Fuentes watched him, bemused, then broke into a laugh and did the same with his. It was the first time Luke had seen him relax.

'So,' Luke continued, 'my Service needs to know – and this is why they've sent me all the way down here – what you and Benton were chasing that night that made you take such a big risk. You went into the jungle with no back-up and there's nothing in Benton's last report that gives any hint of that. What . . .' Luke searched for the right Spanish phrase '. . . what were you on to?'

Fuentes took a long swig of his drink. 'Señor Jerry – excuse me, Señor Benton – he was my friend. He was like family to me. Even my wife, she cooked for him in my house. I trusted him and he trusted me. We took every decision together.'

'So what made you take this one?' Luke regretted his abrupt tone. This was meant to be a debrief, not an interrogation.

'Just one day before I was in the Café San Andres, here in Tumaco. You know it?'

Luke shook his head.

'I am there with my wife when this guy comes in. He's a big shot in the cartel, like an enforcer. Nobody likes him. And he beckons me over. I'm like, "Hey, I'm with my wife, you know?" But he just gives me that look and I know what that means. You don't argue with this guy. So he sits me down next to him and looks me in the eye and says it right out. "Geraldo," he says, "I think we have an informer in our ranks."'

'Jesus,' whispered Luke.

'*Hombre*, you have no idea!' Fuentes was smiling now as he remembered the encounter. 'I tell you, man, I was shitting my pants.'

'But he obviously didn't think it was you?'

'No, *gracias a Dios*. They caught one of the drivers, got him through his cell phone. Turns out he was moonlighting for another cartel. Anyway, this big shot tells me they've got visitors coming in from somewhere in Asia. China, maybe, somewhere like that. Really important visitors, he says, with a lot of money involved. Then he tells me there's a meeting at the Tree House the next evening.'

'The Tree House?'

'It's what they call the cabin out on the edge of the jungle. It's miles from anywhere. The cartel uses it when it wants total privacy.'

'So hang on,' said Luke. 'Why's he telling you all this? Was it a test?'

'That's what I'm thinking too,' said Fuentes, 'but then he tells me I have a role to play. He wants me take care of these visitors during the day, house them somewhere safe, show them round but keep it discreet.'

'How soon could you alert Señor Benton?'

'It wasn't easy. There was so little time. I had to use the emergency frequency.' Fuentes suddenly placed his hands flat on the table and stood up. 'Hey, I need the toilet. It's all that Fanta!'

'Of course.'

Alone in the room, Luke went over what he had just heard. Asian visitors, a jungle rendezvous and the notebook recovered from Benton's body with that single word, 'Hungnam', the name of a North Korean port. What was all this stacking up to? He should probably get word out to the Colombians to pick up the Asian men but they would be long gone, slipped out of the country by sea to avoid detection.

'Tell me about those visitors,' he asked Fuentes, when he came back into the room.

'*Ay* . . . Well, they didn't talk much, not to me anyway. They brought an interpreter with them but his Spanish was terrible. They looked kind of military but were dressed in very dull clothes, almost like factory overalls.'

Luke was having trouble picturing them but he needed to understand what had happened next that night in the jungle. 'How did you know where to go to shadow that meeting they held at the Tree House?'

'Tracking beacon. Magnetic, GPS. Señor Benton showed me how to use them after he recruited me. There was an opportunity and I took it. When I handed over the visitors to the others I placed it under one of their pickup trucks.'

Luke nodded, impressed, then leaned forward, his arms on the flimsy table, which creaked under the pressure. 'Do you still have the receiver?'

Fuentes gave a short, bitter laugh. 'Are you serious? I fled for my life from that *infierno.* I knew what they were doing to him – I could hear it.' He shivered at the memory, still uncomfortably fresh. 'I left that place with nothing but my life.'

His words hung in the room. Then the silence was broken by the revving of a lorry outside. Luke leaned back in his chair and tapped his fingers on the table, thinking. 'You should know,' he said finally, 'that my Service is incredibly grateful for the work you've done here. You'll be looked after now, I can promise you. And I'm sorry about Benton. He was a brave man and he's going to be missed by a lot of people back home, believe me. But we owe it to him, don't we, to get to the bottom of this?'

Once more Fuentes looked hunted. *He probably thinks I'm going to ask him to risk his life again.* 'It's all right,' said Luke. 'I'm not going to ask you to do anything more for us. But I do need to know what's in your head. Let's suppose that this deal, whatever it was, has gone down between the cartel and the Asian men you looked after. Which way is it going?'

'I don't follow you?'

'I mean who's buying what? Is the cartel exporting their product into Asia? Or is there something they want from the Asians?'

'I see.' Fuentes lowered his head, ran thick fingers through his curly hair and scratched the back of his head. He suddenly looked very tired. Luke knew he should probably let the man get some rest but if he had a personal motto it was *carpe diem* – seize the day. He had to assume the cartel would stop at nothing to find Fuentes and finish him off. He also knew that, on a medium-sized military base like this, there was a fair chance the cartel had dickers on the inside reporting back. He had to get Fuentes out of there first thing in the morning and preferably on a plane out of the country. This might be his one and only chance to question him.

When Fuentes spoke he looked Luke straight in the eye and enunciated his words very carefully. '*Cigarros mojados*,' he said.

'Wet cigars?'

'Yes. It's what the cartel call their miniature submarines. I think you call them mini-subs. They launch them out of the swamps up the coast from here, near Buenaventura. Normally they're taking the coke shipments up to Mexico or wherever but this month I've heard them talking about something else, some kind of special delivery.'

'From the cartel to Asia?'

'No,' replied Fuentes. 'The other way round. They are bringing something in, I think, from across the Pacific.'

Luke's mind was racing. What could the Colombian cartel possibly want from North Korea – if it was North Korea? They already had all the weapons they could buy, didn't they? 'Did you tell this to Benton?'

'Of course,' said Fuentes. 'First chance I got. That's why he was so preoccupied with this thing. Didn't he put it in his report?'

Luke shook his head. Benton must have had his own reasons for keeping it to himself but, for the life of him, Luke couldn't figure them out. 'But there must be more to it than that, or why would Benton have risked his life?'

It was well past midnight now and Fuentes was yawning. Luke wasn't feeling too fresh either, but he had to press on. At last, he felt he was making real progress.

'There has been talk,' said Fuentes, 'of *la venganza*. Of revenge. The cartel really hate you Brits, especially your Service. You – we – have done a lot of damage to their operations recently.'

Luke sat bolt upright, very much awake and listening. 'Go on,' he said.

Fuentes tilted his head to one side. 'It's only whispers,' he said, 'they don't tell me everything, but it seems they want to punish your country for all the arrests and confiscations, the millions you have cost them. I think they are buying in some kind of unusual weapon. They say it is to teach the *ingleses* a lesson. And they say it will travel by sea. This, my friend, is what Señor Benton was working on, and this is what he died for.'

Chapter 19

LUKE SAT ALONE on a hard wooden chair, facing a room full of senior officers. They made no attempt to hide their contempt: it was written all over their faces.

'Your plan sucks,' said one. 'You haven't thought this through, have you?'

'You don't have much of a tactical brain, do you?' said another. 'Have you decided to ignore all the information we gave you?'

Luke was exhausted. He had been on the run for a week, hadn't slept for nearly seventy-two hours and his last meal had been a half-cooked rabbit. He had had diarrhoea for two straight days now.

'Please enlighten us, Carlton,' said a senior officer in the front row, leaning forward and fixing him with an icy stare, 'because I for one just don't get it. How the hell are you going to extract yourself and your team without a helicopter?'

'If I could just explain—'

They cut him off with more questions.

'Your men are out of rations. They're tired, they're pissed off, they've lost all confidence in you. Basically, Carlton, you're a complete failure.'

Officer Week. Part of Special Forces Selection. The worst week of your life, they had warned him, and he wouldn't dispute it. For the third time, Luke took them through his plan, but now there was a persistent whining, getting louder by the second. Soon it was drowning his voice, filling his head with an urgent, rhythmic clatter. Blackhawk helicopter. He recognized the sound of the rotor blades.

His eyes popped open. Not quite five a.m. and it had been another dream, another flashback. He was not in Wales. He was on a Colombian police commando base, his room annoyingly close to the helicopter landing pad. And he was bathed in sweat, his heart racing. Awake now, the enormity of what he had learned from Fuentes came back to him in a rush. The agent had had no more details to offer, but already Luke sensed he was standing on a precipice, looking down at something very big and very sinister. The investigation had taken a whole new turn and now he had to pace himself. The obvious thing to do was to call VX: that was what they would expect of him. But he wanted more answers first, something more concrete to give them than a second-hand rumour overheard by an agent.

He got up, splashed some water over his face and stood by the window. He could hear the Blackhawk powering down on the landing pad, the yelping of the camp dogs beginning to subside. He stood there at the window, gazing out at the grey pre-dawn half-light and chewing the inside of his cheek. He knew exactly what he had to do. Friend, the Service lawyer, might not like it, and neither probably would Vauxhall Cross, but Luke had made up his mind. He needed to take the fight to the enemy.

Chapter 20

THE PRISONER WAS slumped on a metal chair that scraped on the floor each time he moved. His hands were cuffed behind his back, his head was bandaged and a barrel-chested guard kept watch on him from the door. The prisoner's pudgy, bovine face bore a look of concentrated defiance and his eyes narrowed as he watched Luke and the police chief walk into the room. '*Malparidos!*' he muttered, under his breath. Bastards. He spat quietly on the floor.

He was the man Luke had knocked unconscious with the butt of his Sig Sauer in his hotel room a few days ago. A phone call to Major Elerzon had secured him access to the prisoner, and now he had questions for him. He pulled up the only other chair in the room and put his face about ten centimetres from the prisoner's, invading his personal space.

'Listen, *caraculo*, I'm going to make this really easy for you to understand.' Luke spoke in Colombian street slang, addressing the man as 'arse-face'. 'You're going to tell me what I want to know or I swear you'll never leave prison.'

'Never,' echoed Major Elerzon, from just behind Luke. Part of the deal for access was that he should be present at the interrogation.

'I shot dead both your *compañeros* in that hotel room, remember? You only lived because I knocked you unconscious. Your life in prison will be shit if you don't cooperate. So, you need to make some choices fast. Because this opportunity is not going to come around twice.'

The man's eyes flicked momentarily towards the guard by the door, then towards Major Elerzon. Luke understood immediately what that meant. There were things that could be said, at some personal risk, but not with policemen in the room. Luke stood up, went to the guard by the door and bent to speak quietly into his ear, simultaneously pressing a twenty-dollar bill into his hand. The guard left.

'Major.' He turned to the police chief.

But the major was ahead of him. 'You need privacy. I understand.' He too left the room. Probably going to listen in from next door, Luke reckoned. That didn't bother him, he just needed to get the thug talking.

So now it was just himself and the prisoner.

'So here's how it is,' Luke began. 'After the trial you'll likely be sent to La Modelo prison. Twelve years for armed assault and attempted kidnapping. I hear the overcrowding there is worse than ever. But who knows? With a bit of input from us they'll send you to La Tramacúa instead. You can spend the next twelve years picking out the lumps of shit your fellow inmates put in your food.'

The prisoner said nothing, just stared at him blankly. Luke found it impossible to know what he was thinking or if he was even getting through to him, but he continued. 'You're probably thinking your cartel connections will see you through, that you'll get some kind of special treatment. But you know what? At La Tramacúa it doesn't work like that. The guards there really don't like you people, but they do like their tear gas and pepper spray. In fact, they love firing it into an enclosed cell. Then there are the daily beatings with table legs. Big lad like you can probably take it for the first few months. But the bad food and dysentery will get to you – it gets to everyone there eventually. It's all the maggots in the food and mould in the water bottles. You'll lose your will to resist after a while. And that's when you'll start bending over to be the duty bitch for the *patrón* on your wing. Sound good?'

The thug sat there, silent and passive. He just gave the faintest tilt upwards of his chin. Luke took this to mean, Go on, what are you proposing?

'Let's start with a simple question. Who sent you to kill me?'

The man looked up in surprise. Slowly his face creased into a grin and finally a great rasping laugh that betrayed a lifetime of smoking cheap unfiltered cigarettes. 'You don't know? It was El Pobrecito, of course. My God, it's common knowledge! You people really know fuck all!'

The man was every bit as stupid as he looked. In his eagerness to insult Luke he had given away a vital clue. El Pobrecito, the Poor Little Thing. Luke recognized the nickname: he had seen it in Benton's earlier reports. But now the dots were starting to connect. If the man had ordered a hit on him, he had something to hide. Had he also given the order for Benton to be killed? It was certainly starting to look like it. Yet something was troubling him. If it was such common knowledge that El Pobrecito was behind the attempt to kidnap Luke, why hadn't Major Elerzon shared it with him? He must have informants on the inside here. Luke would take it up tactfully with the police major.

'So where is El Pobrecito now?' said Luke. 'Where's his base, his centre of operations?'

The thug said nothing. Luke could almost see the cogs in his mind turning, the realization slowly dawning on him that he had probably let slip something extremely dangerous. For this failed assassin, prison had just got a whole lot more dangerous. Finally he spoke, in the coarse language of the *barrio*, but not the words Luke wanted to hear.

'You think you know this country? You think a few words in your stupid Cachaca slang will get you through?' The prisoner shook his head, his eyes narrow slits of hate. 'You are a fool, English. You should leave Colombia today. Get your police friends to drive you to the airport. The same one we watched you arrive at. Because the next time we send people to find you, you will not be so lucky.'

'Right,' said Luke, calmly. 'Except you're the one in prison now. I hope you enjoy your next twelve years in La Tramacúa.'

Chapter 21

THE DOOR CLANGED shut behind him and Luke walked down the green-painted prison corridor behind Major Elerzon and the guard. Had they been listening in on his 'conversation' with the thug? He didn't really care: the prisoner had given away so little. But now, at least, he had a name to put in his report. Dark arms were reaching out of barred cells trying to touch him as he went past, the unhappy inmates of Tumaco's overcrowded penal system. The stench was overpowering and Luke quickened his pace until they left the prisoner wing and reached the guardhouse. Now was perhaps a good time to tackle Major Elerzon about El Pobrecito. But first he had some urgent business.

Luke sat himself in a corner of the guardhouse, away from the policemen, who paid him little attention. On his personal mobile he sent an email to Commander Jorge Enríquez at the Colombian Embassy in London, asking for anything he had on El Pobrecito, his known locations, his organization and his TTPs – his tactics, techniques and procedures. Next, on his secure phone, he took a deep breath and sent the briefest of messages to Sid Khan back at Vauxhall Cross:

Progressing here. Benton closing in on transnational deal. N. Korea? Possible weapon headed from Colombia to UK by sea. Target is UK. Much to discuss. Talk in 2 hours.

He knew this would set the hares racing and that his phone was about to start glowing red hot with frantic calls. So he turned it off. He still needed more answers and now it was time to turn to the Americans for help.

Luke's police escort was waiting for him just outside the main gates of the prison. *'A la base militar, Señor?'* asked his driver, already putting the vehicle into gear and revving up.

'No. The Hotel Paraíso.' Not exactly his first choice for a rendezvous with the CIA but their local station chief had apparently classified it as 'secure'. This, to Luke, was unbelievable irony. But the CIA station was adamant. He was to meet his contact out by the pool, where he had met Clements, from MI6, on his first day down there.

Luke walked through Reception and was relieved to see a different manager on duty. Only the cleaner recognized him from his earlier eventful stay and she crossed herself before hurrying away down a corridor, throwing anxious glances behind her in case Luke was pursuing her. He wasn't. He made his way out to the pool area. He was fifteen minutes early, a habit he had acquired long ago in the forces, preferring to check out a place for entrances, exits, hiding places and ambush points. He wondered how the hotel made any money as, again, it was practically deserted, just a couple of old Colombian men playing draughts in the corner and ignoring him.

Luke pulled up a white plastic chair, sat on it with

his back to a wall and contemplated the lime-green water of the swimming pool, which reflected the lowering sky. The minutes ticked by and nobody came. Luke glanced at his watch and frowned. It had gone eleven forty, ten minutes past the agreed time. It was unlike the Yanks to be late. He'd give it five more minutes, then head back to the base. Bloody CIA. And now one of the old men was lurching towards him. Luke groaned inwardly. He really didn't feel like striking up a conversation with a stranger right now.

'Easy, kiddo,' said the 'old man', in perfect English. 'I'm not asking you to join in our game.'

Luke nearly fell off his chair. He should have spotted this one coming.

'Sergio Ramirez,' said the man, holding out his hand in greeting. 'Station chief for Tumaco.' He was clearly enjoying Luke's reaction. 'Guess you were expecting some clean-cut Ivy League type?'

Luke grinned. 'I guess I was,' he said non-committally. All he really cared about was whether the man could help him.

'I'm Colombian-American, in case you're wondering,' continued Ramirez. For a spy, he certainly had a lot to say. 'That's right. Raised in the *barrio*, emigrated with my dad, got my degree from UCLA, then joined the Agency. And now, all these years later, for my penance, they've sent me to this shit-hole.' He threw a tanned arm around Luke's shoulders. 'Welcome to Tumaco, my friend. May your stay be short and profitable.'

'Thanks,' said Luke. 'I've had a ball so far.'

'So I hear.' Ramirez pulled up a chair and sat down heavily. They were a generation apart, him and Luke, and while they had both done the hard yards in their own ways, their physique was very different. While Luke was lean and fit, he reckoned it had been some years since Ramirez had darkened the doors of a gym. Now he was pulling out a packet of cigarettes, Marlboro Lights, the smokers' equivalent of a Diet Coke. He lit one, then waved the packet in Luke's direction. 'Thought not,' he said. 'So, buddy, how can I help?'

'El Pobrecito,' replied Luke, cutting straight to the chase. 'I was hoping you could give me what you've got on him.'

'You mean García, right? Nelson García?' Ramirez looked at Luke for a moment, then squinted towards the shack beside the pool. An attendant in a white baseball cap with a whistle round his neck was arranging fresh towels in a stack, waiting for customers. 'Well, he's one nasty SOB. Does a lot of bad things to bad people to stay at the top of his game. He runs a fair bit of the trade that leaves this part of the country, mostly by sea. You Brits have been hurting his business plenty, though, and I guess we've been doing our share too.'

Luke looked at the CIA man as he spoke, pausing between sentences to drag on his cigarette. From the way he was talking it didn't sound to Luke as if Benton had shared with anyone his fears about the cartel buying in a weapon. Which was odd, given the Five Eyes mutual intelligence-sharing agreement between the UK, the US, Canada, Australia and New Zealand. Maybe Benton had been keeping his cards close to his chest until he could be sure of what was really going on.

'So where would I find him?' said Luke.

'Whoa there, fella! Let's take this down a notch. You asked for this meeting at short notice and I'm more than happy to oblige. Jerry Benton was a good friend of mine. But see here . . .' the American took a deep breath as if trying to explain something very simple to someone very stupid, 'there are things in play right now that you may not be aware of, things that . . . Well, let's just say there are things you might not want to go upsetting.'

Luke looked at him questioningly. Was there more? No, Ramirez had finished. So was this patronizing spiel all the help he could expect from the CIA, Britain's closest intelligence partner in the world? 'Let me get this straight,' he said evenly. 'You guys know where to find him but you'd rather not share it just yet?'

Ramirez chuckled. 'Something like that,' he replied. 'We can give you NSA phone intercepts and testimonies from some of his people we've caught over the years. Just, you know, don't go stirring up the hornets' nest. Like I said, there's a lot of things in play here.'

The conversation was not going the way Luke had hoped, or expected. It was time to come out with the question that had been bothering him. 'Can I ask if you guys have someone on the inside? Someone on El Pobrecito's team?'

'Phone intercepts and witness testimonies,' replied Ramirez, getting up to go. 'I'll have them brought round to your base by this evening. Pleasure meeting you, Carlton.'

Chapter 22

SEVENTEEN MISSED CALLS. No surprises there, Luke had known his last message to Vauxhall Cross would set the cat among the pigeons.

'What the hell do you mean, "Possible weapon headed from Colombia to UK by sea"?' shouted Khan, as soon as Luke called him back. 'What weapon? And do you have any idea how many people have been trying to get hold of you in the past hour? I had to share this with the Chief and tell him you'd switched your phone off. How do you think that makes us both look?'

Luke didn't care how it looked, to Sid Khan or to anyone else. He just wished he had a bit more hard intelligence to offer up. And now, just when he was getting going, he felt the window was about to close.

'I want you back in London by the weekend,' announced Khan. 'We're sending a full team out to take over.' He sounded calmer now, his naturally analytical brain resuming control after his brief emotional outburst.

'With respect,' said Luke, 'I'm just starting to get somewhere. I need more time. Wouldn't it make more sense for me at least to work with them down here, this new team?'

'Decision's already been taken,' said Khan. 'You're being recalled. Plenty for you to do here when you get back. That's all there is to it.'

Luke knew it was pointless to try to enlist help from Angela, or even John Friend in Bogotá. Even if they agreed with him, which they probably wouldn't, they would end up deferring to Khan. And, besides, office politics were not his thing. He was back on the Jungla police commando base, sitting on his sagging bed with the mosquito net flipped up and the ceiling fan turning in the midday heat. It was quiet, everyone at lunch in the canteen. His phone buzzed with an incoming email. Elise? It had been a while since he'd heard from her. No, it was from Jorge.

Hola, Lucas! That's what Jorge always called him. *Got some intel attached here on your player García. He moves around a lot but looks like he's at Ituango right now. Happy to assist if you need.*

Bingo. Out of the darkness of despair, a shining ray of light. Luke couldn't have wished for better news. He opened the attachment and scrolled down. It was all there: profiles of García, his top team, their modus operandi, the estimated strength of their security units, even a detailed description of their weapon systems. There were photos of Ituango too, taken from the air on slow flypasts by the Colombian police air wing. They showed a villa surrounded by a wall, fortified but not impregnable. A plan began to form in Luke's head. What did he have to lose? He was facing a forced recall to London with the job left undone and him no closer to learning what the 'weapon' was or where it was heading. What was the worst they could do to him at VX? Fire him for ignoring orders? He'd had worse days in Helmand Province.

It was 1400: time to catch Commander Rojas as he came back from lunch.

'Comandante,' he said, as the Colombian officer trotted up the metal steps to his office. 'Can we talk?'

'Of course. In fact I was expecting you to come by.'

'How's that?' said Luke.

'I just took a call.' Commander Rojas, that smile playing once again around the corners of his mouth, his eyes sparkling, almost mischievously. 'A call from London. From a certain Jorge Enríquez? At our embassy there. It seems I'm to give you every cooperation and it's to remain classified. Sounds like you have some useful friends, Señor Carlton!'

This time the Jungla commander didn't trouble to ask if Luke wanted coffee. He went straight to the side and poured some for them both. It was going to be a long session.

'Nelson García,' Luke began, as they took their first sips of the rich, dark liquid from tiny white china cups. 'The guy who calls himself El Pobrecito.'

'That piece of shit,' barked the commander. 'His people killed three of my men last month in an ambush. I've got another in the infirmary who will never see his legs again. We have some scores to settle.'

'Good. I think I can help you. He's up at Ituango right now, in northern Antioquia province, just up from Medellín.'

'I know where it is,' said the commander. 'Nice place, if it wasn't for García. Hills, churches, farms . . . airstrips.'

'I think we agree the world would be a better place with him out of the game. But he knows some things we need to find out fast. We need him alive.'

The commander was staring at Luke now, his eyebrows half raised. Luke could tell this was an officer who cared about his men, that he was not about to put them in harm's way without a decent plan.

'What I propose,' said Luke, 'is that I work up a plan with twelve of your operatives. We'll need to go over aerials, floor plans, routes in and out – and we'll need airlift by helo, medevac and an extraction plan. I'll come back to you shortly with our CONOPS, our concept of operations. If you approve it, we'll go for a start time of twenty hundred hours tomorrow.'

Commander Rojas got up and walked to the window, his hands clasped behind his back. A woman in a blue tunic was sweeping methodically at the side of the road, going through the motions rather than having any effect on the leaf litter that had gathered in piles along the gutter. 'You don't ask for much, do you?' he said finally.

But Luke caught the twinkle in his eye. He knew enough about him already to understand that he lived for exactly this kind of operation.

'*Bueno*,' said the commander, after only the briefest of pauses. 'You can have Captain Martínez and his squad. They have considerable experience in this area.'

Luke held out his hand in thanks, but instead of shaking it, Commander Rojas gripped it and did not let go. 'Just one other thing,' he said. 'I take it your office has approved this mission?'

Luke was surprised by how easily a lie could spill from his lips when needed. He didn't hesitate, even looked the commander in the eye as he said it. '*Por supuesto*. Of course.'

*

At that exact moment, in another corner of Colombia, an unremarkable light aircraft was taxiing down the runway at a small military airfield. On board, a woman and her four children were experiencing their first ever flight. Frightened beyond their wits, they clung to each other as the aircraft lifted clear of the tarmac. They had nothing but the clothes they wore, and the youngest boy had already wet his trousers. But there was a silver lining. The family of Geraldo Fuentes was safe, flown out of South America to Miami, into the waiting arms of the FBI, and a new life under a new name. The family of Agent Synapse had been safely extracted.

Chapter 23

MUD BROWN, ALWAYS mud brown. Did the Thames ever look any other colour? Elise watched the eddies and whirls drift past the window of the river bus. She loved sitting in her usual seat, takeaway latte in her hand. Such a great way to commute, she told her friends, just a hop across the river from Battersea, then a short tube ride up to Piccadilly Circus and she could be at her desk in the Stratford Gallery within forty minutes. More for something to do than for any other reason, she fished out her phone and scrolled through the news headlines and the online papers. Since she had started going out with Luke, she had been taking a keen interest in global affairs. In turn, he had been doing his best to learn a bit about the art world. So far, she was making rather more progress than he was.

As the boat slowed to dock at Embankment she was about to put away her phone when she clamped her hand to her mouth, muffling a cry of dismay. From the tiny screen in her hand the headline stared out at her and Elise's world went cold.

MI6 SPY MURDERED IN COLOMBIA –
a *Guardian* exclusive by Steve Drayne in Bogotá

He had never told her that was where he was heading, but Elise was not stupid. She knew Luke had had a childhood in Colombia and she knew he had been back more than once. Although he never spelled it out she got the impression it was his time in the SBS that had taken him there. And now, of course, he was on contract to SIS. That much he had confided in her, nothing more.

It's Luke, oh, God, I know it is. She called his number at once but it went straight to voicemail. Suddenly she felt profoundly and inexplicably guilty about how she had spent the previous weekend. Hugo Squires's house party in the country had been rather more fun than she had expected. The invitation had been for them both, of course, but as Luke was away she had gone on her own, driving down to Dorset with her favourite MP3 playlist plugged into the car stereo.

Hugo had been the perfect host, lavishing just enough attention on her. There had been croquet on the lawn with the other guests, a tour round the walled herb garden, drinks on the veranda, then a glittering candlelit dinner beside a roaring log fire. It had not escaped her notice that everyone was in a couple, apart from her and Hugo. At one a.m. he had politely escorted her to the door of her room, and there they had kissed, drunkenly, his hands around her hips, gently pulling her close to him. He was certainly keen. Elise had let it go no further, eventually breaking off and placing an elegant finger on Hugo's parted lips, then firmly closing her door, but she felt incredibly guilty. And now this. She read on.

In an exclusive report we can reveal that a serving British intelligence officer has been found murdered on a top-secret mission in a South American jungle.

Name him, just name him. The other commuters were pushing past her now, queuing to get off at Embankment.

In order to protect his family we have been asked not to reveal his name, but it is understood he was a father of two and originally from Scarborough in North Yorkshire –

Elise closed her eyes and breathed out. Scarborough. So not Luke then. She hardly needed to read any more.

Less than a kilometre from Elise, in the sandstone-and-green palace of Vauxhall Cross, a crisis meeting was under way. In the boardroom the directors had gathered, with Sid Khan seated at the head of a long table of anxious faces. 'Two items on the menu today,' he began. 'First, the so-called "weapon" that our man Carlton has alerted us to, down in Colombia.' Everyone in the room noted that today Khan had swapped his customary pink- and plum-coloured polo shirts for a sombre suit and tie. 'We need to know what it is, where it is, where it's heading and what we're doing about it.'

Khan held up a copy of the *Guardian*. 'Second, my friends, there's this.' They had all seen the headlines in that morning's paper, but the words 'MI6 Spy Murdered in Colombia' still had a chilling effect.

'The news is out, we can't change that,' said Khan,

looking around the group. 'So this, clearly, is about damage limitation. Do we know how it leaked out?'

'We do,' said a voice behind him, causing Khan to swivel awkwardly in his chair. It was Vikram Sharma, the head of Corporate Communications, his bald head gleaming in the tungsten spotlights embedded in the ceiling. 'Sorry I'm late – just off the phone to the Foreign Secretary's office. C wants an agreed party line on this one.' Sharma reported directly to the Chief of MI6, sitting in an outer office and responsible for handling the press and media. News of Benton's murder had got out on his watch and now it was his job to pick up the pieces.

'It seems the local Colombian media got hold of it first,' said Sharma, pulling back a chair and sitting down. 'It appeared in yesterday's edition of *La Prensa.* Someone down at the police station in Tumaco blabbed to the press – I'm afraid it was bound to happen eventually – and the *Guardian* had a stringer in Bogotá with good government contacts. He managed to get the whole story. Well, at least the stuff about Jerry Benton's body being found in the jungle. But we've moved quickly and the DA notice people in Whitehall have asked editors to exercise caution.'

'Exercise caution?' said Khan. 'What does that mean, exactly?'

'It means an email's gone round to all the mainstream media reminding them of their responsibility not to publish the names or photographs of any intelligence officers, past or present.'

There was a loud grunt from the far end of the table. It came from a thick-set man in a pin-striped suit, his hair grey at the temples, his fingertips yellow with nicotine.

'Gary? You have a question?' said Khan, addressing the head of Security Section, MI6's own internal security cadre that looked after everything from online digital footprints to safe routes into a war zone. Gary had been in the business most of his life.

'Well, come on,' said Gary, 'who are we kidding here? This is the twenty-first century. Do we really think they're going to abide by those rules? If they want to publish, they can get a US subsidiary to do it. It's happened before. Remember Edward Snowden?'

'Well, it hasn't happened this time,' said Sharma, rather testily. 'Jerry's name has been kept out of it. We've got a close eye on what pops up online.'

'OK,' said Khan, calling the meeting to order. 'So here's where we are now. The media will obviously get the narco connection – it's a bit of a no-brainer, given where it is on the map. But there's no reason to suppose they'll dig any deeper than that, is there? FCO are putting together a press release as we speak. With any luck, that will draw a line under it and they can move on. Plenty of other news for them to get their teeth into and Colombia's a long way off. There's the new SARS outbreak, the Baghdad bombings and now that backbench bloke sexting pictures of himself to an undercover reporter.'

'Sorry, am I missing something here?' asked Greg Sanderson, head of Latin America. 'If the media know about Jerry's murder that's pretty big news. Surely it's only a matter of time before they send people down to Tumaco to start poking around. The next thing we hear they've run into our guy down there, Carson or whatever he's called, and this whole op is blown wide open.'

'It's Carlton, Luke Carlton,' Khan corrected him. 'And he's being recalled.'

'Is he?' said another voice at the table. The head of HR. He put down his pen and took off his glasses. 'I don't think I was told about that. When's he back? Because with what happened in that hotel room a few nights ago we may need to arrange some counselling when he gets here.'

'He's flying home this weekend,' replied Khan. 'I've asked John Friend from Legal to escort him onto the plane in Bogotá. We can't have him rattling around South America racking up dead bodies. And his comms are appalling. He switched off his phone for two hours after he messaged us about the weapon.'

'But he did produce that notebook,' pointed out another figure at the table. It was Craig Dalziel, head of Agent Handling. 'And he's tracked down Jerry's principal agent, Synapse. I think we should give him some credit.'

'I take it,' said Sanderson, 'that he's now in contact with Tradewind. I don't mean to sound disrespectful to Jerry Benton, but it's obviously important Carlton's able to pick up where Jerry left off. Wouldn't everyone agree?'

Khan and Dalziel exchanged meaningful glances and there was a brief, awkward silence, before Khan replied: 'No. To answer your question, Carlton does not know about Tradewind.'

'Hold on a minute!' exclaimed Sanderson. 'You mean we sent him out there without telling him? Any good reason? Aren't we effectively making him fight this battle with one arm tied behind his back?'

'Absolutely not,' retorted Khan. 'We took a decision—'

'You mean *you* took a decision.'

'No. Craig and I took a combined decision based on

the grounds of operational security. Tradewind is in deep cover, and when the time is right we'll let Carlton know. But right now,' continued Khan, 'he's safely on the police commando base. Under orders not to move off it without referring back to me. I don't think we'll be having any more shoot-ups like last week's shenanigans.'

Chapter 24

LUKE LOOKED DOWN at his thumb and winced. Blood blister. That was careless. He was loading so much ammunition into so many magazines that he had accidentally jammed his thumb between a cartridge and the metal lip of the M4 clip. One of the Jungla police commandos had noticed his missing middle finger and offered to help him load his rounds.

'Thanks, but I can manage just fine,' Luke had said, with a grin, which was when he'd messed up his thumb. No more mistakes from now on, he told himself. He and Captain Martínez had worked hard on the plan, anticipating the questions that Commander Rojas would ask, putting in last-minute bids for extra resources and firepower, all granted.

Now they were on final prep for the mission to take down El Pobrecito, and Luke felt a familiar knot of tension deep in his abdomen. He was about to go seriously off-piste. The Colombians might have approved this mission but Vauxhall Cross had not. Technically, this would put him in breach of duty to the Service – and quite possibly put the Service in breach of its duty to its political masters in Whitehall. This was already a sensitive mission that had needed sign-off from several people on both sides of the river. Now he was about to take it to a whole different level. Yet Luke had an unerring sense that what he was doing was right, given the opportunity he now had.

He smiled to think of the look on Friend's face if the lawyer could have seen him now – in body armour, with two personal weapons strapped to his sides, his face streaked with green-and-black camouflage paint. Friend had checked up on him by phone a short while back and Luke had been somewhat economical with the truth. 'I'm using my last two days in-country to follow up a possible lead in Antioquia with the Jungla,' Luke had told him. 'Can't promise mobile reception will be that great up there but I'll do my best to ring in.'

Luke knew full well he had only to switch on his mobile and the NSA would have his location triangulated and pinpointed on a map. He would not be switching it on and he had no intention of 'checking in'. He was going out on a limb. This mission had to work because if it didn't he would be looking for another job, another career.

The Colombians had been gratifyingly enthusiastic about his plan. They had had the rehearsals: the 'actions-on-contact', the back-up plans, the comms checks and the last-ditch mission-aborts. The HUMINT reports provided by the Colombians on the ground had confirmed that García was 'in residence' at the fortified farm, though no one could ever tell for how long.

He glanced around the briefing room, where men in full combat gear, like himself, were quietly going over their kit, checking and rechecking the M4 carbines slung across their chests, spare magazines taped on. Faces he had been getting to know were almost unrecognizable beneath tiger-stripe paint. Radio call-signs were being run through, ration boxes broken open and distributed. From outside came the familiar whine of the helicopter rotors starting up. The sound took Luke back to another time, another war, on a different continent: the Blackhawks preparing to carry him and his team into the dangerous badlands of Afghanistan. Here we go again, he thought.

'Listo, Señor Carlton? You ready?' It was Captain Martínez, technically the mission commander, though it was agreed Luke would be driving it. At twenty-nine, Emilio Martínez had a deep mahogany tan from a life spent almost entirely outdoors. A curved scar ran halfway down his cheek towards a thick moustache, and Luke noted that his gravelly voice seemed to carry instant authority with his men.

'I'm good to go,' he replied.

'Vámonos. Let's go.' They filed out to the helipad, Luke the lone Englishman among twelve of Colombia's most highly trained police special forces, each weighed down with equipment, rations and the sheer enormity of what they were about to undertake. It was 2000 hours and starting to rain again.

Chapter 25

CRAMPED, IRRITABLE AND thirsty, the two submariners could agree on only one thing. This would definitely be their last voyage in one of these metal coffins. At three metres below the surface of the Pacific Ocean, conversation in the tiny craft had all but dried up. Four days of chugging along at minimal depth, breathing bottled oxygen and diesel fumes, eating freeze-dried food, then urinating and defecating into plastic bags, had left them craving fresh air and sunlight. Undetected from the air, from the surface, or even from up in space, their six-metre miniature submarine had inched its way northwards up Colombia's Pacific coast from the swamps just south of Buenaventura. The vessel's confined cabin had few creature comforts, just two hard aluminium bucket seats, a periscope, a basic navigation panel and an empty cargo compartment. It had been left up to the pilots, in the final days before they had slipped their moorings in the muddy jungle berth, to source a pair of makeshift cushions, fashioned from jungle hemp by the local indigenous Indians. The cushions had now started to unravel and rot, leaving their backsides sore and aching. But the money was good. Oh, yes. Fifty thousand dollars each in cash and a bonus when they reached their destination.

Their instructions were simple: steer the vessel to a point exactly 7.50 degrees north and 79.14 degrees west, then rendezvous with the mother ship. Out in the maritime no man's land of the eastern Pacific, this would be well outside the territorial waters of either Colombia or Panama and far from the prying eyes of their nosy government coastguards.

But the mini-sub was making painfully slow progress, battling a swell that held it back to just eight knots while the pilots fought constant nausea. One had thrown up three times, the vomit slopping around the metal floor at their feet before drying into an acrid, foul-smelling crust. It had turned the unpleasant into the intolerable and now the space between them crackled with silent tension.

On the fifth day at sea, the submariners brought the vessel slowly up to the surface on a steamy equatorial morning. They unwound the airtight hatch to the deck, pushed open the lid and took in great lungfuls of fresh air. In the grey light of dawn they scanned the waters around them. Nothing. As the temperature rose the horizon began to wobble in the haze, the sea blending almost indistinguishably into sky.

'*Oye! Mira!* Look!' shouted one, pointing at a distant silhouette. 'Quick, fetch the helix.' Together they stood on the crudely welded iron deck and signalled the approaching ship. Nothing. '*Mierda*. Maybe it's the wrong ship.'

'Or maybe you've brought us to the wrong place,' muttered his co-pilot.

But then came an answering signal, flashing clear and bright across the narrowing gap between them.

The ship's silhouette matched the image on the print-out they had been handed before leaving Colombia, wrapped in waterproof cellophane. It certainly resembled the hulking rust-bucket of the 9,000-ton bulk cargo ship they were expecting. Lit by the slanting rays of the rising sun, it was close enough now for them to make out the chestnut-brown streaks that poured down its side from a socket where the anchor was secured. The superstructure had been painted white, an unfortunate choice for so filthy a ship, but down towards the waterline the hull was a dingy grey. A man in overalls and a white hard hat peered over the side at them, then disappeared. On the side of the ship, outlined in peeling grey letters, they read '*Maria Esposito*. Manila.' They had made the rendezvous.

Chapter 26

FOR CLOSE TO three hours they flew north-eastwards through the night, their camouflaged faces lit dimly by the eerie green light of the Blackhawks' cockpit instrument panel. Only the door gunners moved, constantly shifting left and right as they scanned the vegetation below with their helmet-mounted night-vision goggles. Their gloved hands were clenched around the grip handles of the chain guns mounted in the helicopters' open doorways, ready to spit out a stream of bullets if they took fire from the ground. Nariño, Valle del Cauca and Chocó provinces slipped past beneath them as the helicopters powered on unseen, bolstered by external fuel tanks.

So much for putting this shit behind him, thought Luke, but it certainly beats a day in the office. He shuddered briefly to think what Elise would say if she could see what he was up to. What would she be doing right now? It would be about four in the morning in London and he liked to think of her in their bed, her perfect face turned to one side on the pillow, with maybe a dab of lavender oil to help her sleep. Tonight was that exhibition opening she'd worked so hard for, and where was he? Helicoptering into a hostile landing zone in South America. He felt a twinge of remorse at not being with her – he knew how much the show mattered to her. But, if he was honest with himself, he often felt like a fifth wheel at those things. People were always coming up and asking him questions about the artist that he couldn't answer. This was the world he knew and he was glad to be back in it.

A sudden jab in the ribs from Martínez brought him back to the moment. It was time to 'switch on', as the military were so fond of saying. They had crossed into Antioquia province and were circling for the landing, the pitch of the rotors changing as the pilots steadied their craft for the touch-down, the blades slicing through the rain they could see through the window, now falling in sheets. Luke spared a brief thought for the reconnaissance team, who would have gone in at last light to stake out the landing site, a disused field close to the forest, now calling in the Blackhawks on a prearranged frequency. They must be soaked. He glanced one last time around the interior of the helicopter – the canvas seats, the silvery metal floor, the boldly marked fire-fighting equipment – then scanned the men's faces. He searched for any signs of fear but he could see only determination beneath the helmets and face paint. Only one man, the medic, crossed himself.

The loadmaster was on his feet now, his harness attached by wire to the Blackhawk's ceiling. Next thing the door was fully open and in rushed the noise, the rain, the roar of the rotors and the wind whipped up by the downdraught. It was like opening a door to a miniature tempest. Luke was second out of the helicopter, putting his feet on the wheels then jumping out in almost pitch darkness, trusting that the pilot had judged it right and had them at the hover no more than a couple of metres above the ground. He landed, rolled clear and hugged the sodden vegetation, protecting his head from the small branches and leaves that whipped around him in the downdraught. In one continuous stream the Jungla commandos followed, throwing themselves out of the open door, then fanning out to form a defensive perimeter, a protective circle around the Blackhawk, while the second aircraft remained above them, door gunners at the ready. In less than a minute the team were all on the ground and then the Blackhawks were gone, lifting clear and tilting to one side as they clattered off into the night.

In the curious quiet left behind by the departing helicopters, Luke tuned into the sounds around him: the distant bark of a village dog, the soft whoop of an owl, the insistent electronic whine of cicadas as they clung to trees in the nearby forest. The sounds of his Colombian childhood.

They had put down in farmland, just over fifteen kilometres short of the objective, far enough away to avoid detection by García's perimeter guards, near enough to be able to patrol in on foot. Before they set off, Luke and Martínez huddled beneath a rain-lashed poncho with the recon team, going over the route on the map.

'Cuidado aquí,' said one, pointing to a stream. 'Be careful here. One of the farmers says he's seen García's people planting mines along the banks.' Luke and Martínez took careful note: they had both seen what an anti-personnel mine can do to a man's leg.

Shortly before midnight the team moved off down a path, treading almost noiselessly, spaced ten metres apart, Martínez behind the front man on point, Luke following him. The ground rose and fell, and at times the foliage closed in tight around them, but mostly it was easy going. It was hill country, much of it cleared for grazing, very different from the dense lowland tropical jungle that blanketed so much of southern Colombia. The air was cooler and there was a welcome absence of mosquitoes. The team gave the stream a wide berth and skirted an abandoned farmhouse before entering the forest that overlooked the hacienda of Nelson García, the man they called El Pobrecito.

They had not gone fifty metres into the trees when the commando on point held up his hand and they all sank slowly to one knee. Word was passed down the line in hisses: '*Cuerda de trampa*. Tripwire. Right across the path.' They all knew what that meant. It would most likely be connected to a Claymore, a curved shield packed with plastic explosive that would blast around seven hundred steel ball bearings at everyone in its path. Set one of those off, and the entire patrol would be hit.

Luke conferred briefly with Martínez and it was decided they would take no chances and retrace their footsteps, adding a necessary hour to the journey. In the dark of pre-dawn, under cover of the rain, they stopped and took up position on a forested hillside. Through a small gap in the trees, the lights of some outbuildings and what looked like a farm down below were just visible. Luke tilted down the night-vision goggles on his helmet and snapped the magnification to the maximum. It took a while for the images to settle down and come into focus but there it was, unmistakably, García's fortified farm. He checked the layout against the laminated plan in his hand and nodded to Martínez. They would go firm there for the next twenty-four hours, burrowing into the side of the hill, observing, noting routines, numbers of guards, their weapons and changeover times. Only when Luke and the Colombian commandos had a thorough sense of the drug lord's security precautions would they make their move.

They settled quickly into a routine. Two men on 'stag', on lookout, while two crawled forward with high-powered binoculars or night-vision goggles. Four hours on, four hours off. They lit no fires, left no litter, and made almost no sound that could be heard above the constant chorus of tree frogs and cicadas.

'Sometimes after a mission,' confided Martínez to Luke, 'I can't get that damned noise out of my head.' Slowly, he unwrapped a strawberry-flavoured boiled sweet, popped it into his mouth and pushed the crumpled wrapper deep inside his breast pocket. 'I know what you mean,' concurred Luke, who had stripped down his weapon, oiled it and was now reassembling it in a short respite from the rain.

García's *finca*, his farm, was well fortified. You didn't need specialist equipment to see that. It was laid out atop a gently sloping hill, a wall surrounding it. There appeared to be some small hovels clustered around it, rather like those found outside a medieval castle, and Luke was pretty sure he had identified dog kennels, which they would need to take into consideration. After observing for a full twenty-four-hour cycle he and Martínez had done their own counts and come up with the same figure: twenty-six guards, no more than twelve on duty at a time. Three on the front gate, the others spaced at intervals around the perimeter. They all carried Israeli-made Galil assault rifles,

Luke noted, and there was a 'technical', a pickup truck with a mounted machine-gun – it looked like a Russian PKM – hidden just behind the guardhouse on the gate. A paved road led from there down the hill, through a wood and towards a distant village. They could not detect any pedestrian traffic, but twice they watched a convoy of two vehicles leave the compound and return, García in the rear, his bodyguards in front.

To Luke it felt strange, and almost wrong, not to be reporting in all these details, feeding them up the chain of command to appear in some intelligence officer's situational briefing on 'Enemy Forces'. But, of course, he couldn't do that now. He looked at his watch. In around twelve hours he was supposed to be meeting John Friend at the check-in desk at Bogotá airport for the 23.05 Avianca flight to London. That was not looking too likely. But Luke had made a contingency plan. If he was still on this mission at 1000 hours then the Jungla commander on the base would call Friend, assure him all was fine and buy Luke some more time.

On the evening of the second day Martínez and Luke conferred once more, this time beneath Luke's basha, the thin stretched camouflage-pattern tarpaulin that was keeping most of the rain off them. They spoke quietly, despite the rain.

'So we know García travels in a convoy of two cars,' began Luke, brushing a trickle of rain off his cheek. Just beyond the basha the fronds of a fern were trembling with the onslaught of rain, and rivulets of mud streamed past them down the hill. It was impossible to stay dry in this, and Martínez had expressed concern that it was only a matter of time before one of the team was sneezing. It was time to firm up their final plan for the snatch.

'The chassis on their vehicles are so low to the ground we've got to assume they're armour-plated,' continued Luke, 'and you've got the kit to deal with that. His close protection team travels in front, we've established that, and both the drivers will have done defensive driving courses. My guess is they're Colombian ex-military.'

'It happens.' Martínez shrugged. 'You should see my pay cheques, *amigo.* My wife complains every month!' Luke laughed with him. In the short time he had worked with the officer he had grown to like and respect him. Dead professional on the things that mattered, yet he didn't sweat the small stuff. A man after Luke's own heart.

'So, the way I see it,' continued Luke, sketching out a diagram of the fortified farm and the road that led from it, 'there's only one place his convoy has to slow down and that's here.' He jabbed a finger at a bend in the road just before it crossed a stream. 'We're going to need to set the main charge right there, beneath the lead vehicle. We'll have to get our own Claymores pre-positioned and the M60 machine-gun to try to punch through the armour plating. That should take care of Vehicle One.'

Martínez was nodding. A veteran of several such operations, he was under no illusion as to the risks. 'You know that by this stage in the plan those sons of bitches are going to come swarming out of the farm like ants?'

'Yes, they will,' agreed Luke, 'so we need two of your guys set up with the M60 where they've got a free field of fire, right across the front wall of the farm. This is not going to be pretty.'

'And you?' Martínez raised an eyebrow. 'Because, I

tell you, my bosses will hang me out to dry, Señor Carlton, if you get hit. I have orders to keep you safe!'

'We can argue about that when it's over,' replied Luke. 'I'll take care of myself. You just concentrate on the prize: García. He'll be boxed in by then and he'll want to go down fighting – you may have to use the Taser.'

'Timings?' asked Martínez.

'H hour will be oh five hundred local. We need all your team in place by then, ready for García's oh six thirty convoy out. That's if they follow their routine.'

'And if they don't?'

'We wait. If it's two cars we execute the plan. If it's three we abort and come back the next day. We'll need that extraction by Blackhawk thirty minutes after we launch – and make sure they've got a medic onboard.'

'Claro,' Martínez grunted. He was about to get up when he gave Luke a light slap on the back. 'I like your plan,' he said simply.

Now Luke gripped his arm. 'Martínez? Don't forget the plasticuffs and sandbag. We're taking this bastard alive.'

Chapter 27

AN HOUR AFTER dawn a cloak of mist still hung about the gullies and ravines of Ituango. For a few brief minutes the sun broke through, bouncing off the tin-roofed livestock pens and lighting up the white-washed walls of houses down in the valley. At least, reflected Luke, it had stopped raining for the first time in two days. They had been in position now for more than an hour, Martínez and the rest of the snatch team, with Luke a short distance from them, where he could control the action and issue orders.

The adrenalin that had coursed through their veins as they crept down from their hillside hideout in the forest to the ambush site by the bend in the road had given way to something else. Not quite boredom but certainly frustration. Nothing was stirring at the farm, and the only sound was the murmur and burble of the stream that flowed nearby. Perhaps, after all, today was not the day.

But the Jungla commandos remained poised and alert, their index fingers extended flush with the trigger guards on their US-supplied M4 assault rifles, waiting for the order to engage. For some reason that Luke could never quite figure out, his body had its own way of dealing with a long wait. The scarred knuckle of his middle finger would start to ache in the place where the Taliban bullet had taken it clean off a couple of years back. He rubbed it now, straining his eyes and ears for any movement from the farm three hundred metres up the road.

'Señor Carlton!' One of the Jungla police commandos crouched beside him and gripped his arm to alert him but Luke had already seen it. The farm's reinforced gate had swung open. First one, then another car nosed out of the compound and drove towards their concealed position. A pair of customized black 4x4s, low to the ground, almost certainly armour-plated, probably bullet-proof glass. The gangster's choice. They seemed to be in no hurry, which puzzled Luke but he spoke calmly into his mouthpiece, reminding every member of the team through their headset not to jump the gun. '*Espera,*' he told them. 'Wait.' Timing was everything: he needed the convoy to pass the exact spot before he gave the command. Two hundred metres . . . one hundred metres . . . The gap between them was closing and still the vehicles were not speeding up. Fifty metres . . . and . . . 'Execute!' shouted Luke into his head-mike. He braced himself instinctively for the hot blast of a remotely detonated explosion followed by the ear-splitting cacophony of automatic gunfire when his team would open up on the lead vehicle.

Nothing happened.

In a sickening moment, Luke knew immediately that this was no accident. It wasn't just that the device buried in the road had failed to detonate: it was the fact that no one was firing. And now both vehicles had stopped in front of them. '*Disparar!* Shoot!' he ordered into the head-mike, but the response was silence. His team had vanished. As if watching a film in slow motion Luke saw the doors of the second car swing open and two men step out.

They were in no hurry at all. Nelson García was a big man, his chest made bulkier by the Kevlar body armour he wore beneath his tailored hunting jacket. Now he was looking straight in Luke's direction, as if he knew where he was hiding. His voice boomed across the few metres between them.

'You can stand up now, Señor Carlton,' he called. 'Your stupid games are over.'

Luke's training kicked in. Fight or flight? His finger was on the trigger and he had less than a second to decide. And in that moment, he knew the decision had been taken out of his hands. From out of the undergrowth around him gunmen appeared, scruffy, unshaven, heavily armed, training their weapons on him. García's men. It was a hopeless situation and he knew it. He might be lucky and take a couple with a quick burst but then it would be over: they would cut him down in seconds. Luke placed his weapons on the ground and raised his arms. Who had betrayed them? Surely not Martínez. He felt sick.

The second man from García's vehicle stepped forward and stood beside the drug lord, smoothing the creases in his police uniform.

'What the fuck . . .' Luke was almost lost for words.

It was Major Elerzon, the chief of police in Tumaco.

Chapter 28

COLD AND BORING. That was how Luke remembered his teens. Almost five years on from the accident that had killed his parents, his life had not turned out as he had hoped. Still blaming himself for what had happened that day in Colombia, he was growing up fast on his uncle's farm in Northumberland. By his fourteenth birthday he knew a lot about sheep. He could help deliver lambs in the freezing dawn of an April morning on the moors and could tell from a hundred yards off if one of the flock was infected with parasitic flukes. Older than his cousins by several years, he had been given the one-day-all-this-will-be-yours speech and had worked hard to show his gratitude. He knew that, after what had happened to his parents in South America, he was lucky to have a family to take him in and treat him like a son of their own. There had been nothing on the windswept patch of northern English farmland he couldn't do.

But what Luke really liked to do, when he had finished his jobs around the farm, was to hang a rucksack on his back and set out through the heather to a place called Otterburn. It was a military training area, its sixty thousand acres of wild, rain-lashed hills and fenced-off forestry blocks home to one of the largest live firing ranges in Britain. When the bullets were zipping across the valleys, and tiny, distant figures moved slowly across the landscape, fourteen-year-old Luke Carlton was not put off by the red danger flags or the stern 'Keep Out' signs. He would jump over the stone wall to hide where he could watch without being seen, making his own judgements about where was safe and where was not. It was a game he played, lying low, concealing himself deep in the heather, then bringing out a notebook and binoculars and noting down everything he could see. On certain days, he would watch them firing the MLRS, the great batteries of multiple launch rocket systems that could deluge an area the size of a football pitch with high explosives in just a few seconds. But mostly he envied the men on foot, sprinting and ducking among the rough terrain, rifles cradled in their hands, shouting commands, taking cover, crawling, their faces streaked with paint and mud.

At seventeen he had made up his mind and broken the news to his uncle and aunt. He was never going to take over their farm because he had chosen a different path: he was going to join the Royal Marines and become a commando. And that was the path that had led him to this moment. Face down in a wet Colombian field, bound and gagged, his hands cuffed behind his back while some bearded and bandoliered thug held down his neck with a boot and every nerve in his body told him he was in deep, deep trouble. To think that he could have lived frugally but happily as a Northumberland landowner, playing the part of a country gent, probably with a brood of children by now . . .

Out of the corner of his eye Luke could see two things approaching. The first was a column of ants, surging through the wet grass that grew along the riverbank. As they grew closer he could just make out their dark red heads and black abdomens. South American fire ants. Nasty. He remembered some painful bites from them as a child, and having to be taken by his mother to the pharmacy on the corner of their street for some ointment. But the ants were the least of his problems. Now he could see a pair of patent-leather cowboy boots with angled Cuban heels coming into his line of sight and stopping centimetres from his face. 'You screwed up, didn't you, inglés?' said a voice above the boots. 'This is Colombia, my friend. You should have taken more care.' García's voice carried all the menace of his trade.

He squatted down, bringing his broad, flat face close to Luke's and shoving a fistful of crisp hundred-dollar bills under his nose. '*Plata, Señor Carlton*. Money. You have to know who to trust in this country and who can be bought. And your Major Elerzon here . . .' García tilted his head towards the renegade police chief, standing there in his uniform '. . . he likes the *plata* too much. So he works for us. He is a rich man now.' He broke unexpectedly into laughter. 'You'd be surprised who we have on our payroll. D'you know my people even watched your helicopters take off from Tumaco two days ago? Hmm? We watched you land here in Ituango. You thought you were watching us, but we were watching you, *amigo*.' García sighed theatrically, and straightened. 'Sadly, these lessons come too late for you. And now it is time for *la fiesta*.'

The man they called El Pobrecito spoke rapidly to his bodyguards. Strong arms reached down and hauled Luke upright, his joints crying out in pain. A man behind him grabbed his hair to hold his head in place. Luke's mind was racing now, running through his ever-dwindling courses of action. His wrists were tied behind his back but his legs were free. If this was execution time, he wasn't going down without a fight. Probably end up with the same result but he was damned if he was going to submit like a lamb to the slaughter. He readied himself to back-kick the man behind him, hard enough to break one of his shins. He would then sprint for the edge of the forest a hundred metres away, 'hard-targeting' by zigzagging to avoid the inevitable fusillade of bullets that would follow him. Not the greatest odds of success, he had to admit, but it was better than the alternative. He steadied his breathing.

He was on the point of making his move when the scene around him suddenly changed. One by one, the members of his team started to appear, bound, gagged and stumbling towards him, tripping as they went, pushed on by García's gunmen with the muzzles of their rifles. The captured commandos' faces were already purpling with fresh bruises. This was his patrol, his team, betrayed by a corrupt police chief and whoever García had on the payroll on the inside. How had they been disarmed and captured without a fight? And then he knew. Two of the team stood off to one side. They still had their weapons and were exchanging jokes with García's bodyguards. The mission had been compromised on the inside from the first moment.

Luke felt physically sick. He wasn't scared of death. God knows he had looked it straight in the eyes enough times in Afghanistan. But this had been his plan, his initiative, and now it was about to consign these good men to their deaths. They would nearly all have families, a young wife nursing a child in some distant village, unaware that she was minutes away from widowhood. And then there was Elise. He could picture it now: the quiet knock on the door from the Service welfare officer, the invitation to sit down and prepare herself for bad news, a cup of tea perhaps, such cold comfort for the hammer blow of bereavement, and then the limp offer of counselling at some future date. Nice one, Carlton. You brought this on yourself.

García's men were making the prisoners kneel now, forcing them to the ground and standing behind them as they looked expectantly at their boss, awaiting his orders. Luke could barely recognize them as the same highly motivated police commandos he had got to know over the last few days. Stripped of their weapons, their body armour, their helmets and their dignity, they were pale reflections of the fighting men he had known. Perhaps this was how he, Luke, looked to them.

García was standing not far from them, his hands on his hips, his paunch protruding over his belt, only partially hidden by the flaps of his unbuttoned hunting jacket. Luke watched in horror as, slowly and deliberately, García's men trained the muzzles of their rifles on the backs of their captives' heads from a few centimetres away. García gave a brief, curt nod, then turned away, as if bored and quite uninterested in what was to follow.

The shots rang out, not quite in unison, and even though Luke was braced for it, he still caught his breath, his heart racing. He was being forced to witness an extrajudicial execution by firing squad, a synchronized mass murder carried out by worthless *narcotraficantes,* criminal lowlifes in the pay of a ruthless drug lord. When it was over, there was just a line of bodies slumped on the wet grass. For a few seconds nobody moved. But it was not over. The narcos still had one more prisoner and they brought him over now. They had kept their tenth victim, Captain Martínez, until last. They took their time, making him wait for the bullet he knew was coming. Luke looked across at him and saw a man devoid of fear, his scarred, tanned face defiant, his jaw held high. When the narcos tried to push him to his knees he was having none of it and remained standing. Luke caught his eye and, incredibly, Martínez winked. Massive respect there. He was giving them nothing. Then the metal butt of a Galil rifle slammed into Martínez's ribs and he buckled, letting out a muffled groan through the gag around his mouth. But still he remained on his feet. A frown passed over García's face and he called out to his men, '*Terminarlo!* Finish it.'

Luke closed his eyes, flinching at the roar of the single gunshot that rang out just metres away, echoing across the valley. Then there was just the sound of the babbling stream. Luke could not bring himself to look at Martínez's corpse. He stiffened himself for what was to come – surely he was next. He should make his move before it was too late. But now García was almost in front of him, a fat Melia Cohiba cigar clamped between his fleshy lips.

'Such a waste,' scolded García, his face contorted in a hideous parody of pity for the people he had just had murdered. 'Such brave young men. And they all had to die because of you, Inglés. You feel good about that? Because you had the chance to leave, did you not? We gave you warnings, so many warnings. But, no, you had to be a *burro*, a stubborn mule, and outstay your welcome.'

Luke's eyes held his. He hoped García could see the contempt in them but he doubted it would bother him. What was the death of one more agent to this man? Probably nothing, given his long, bloodstained track record.

'Shall I give you an easy end, like them?' said García. He waved a fleshy hand towards the line of dead police commandos. 'Something nice and quick, huh? A hero's death, you'd probably call it.' He exhaled, the acrid smoke of his cigar briefly coiling around the air between them. 'No, I think not. Because, you see, you British have been getting in the way of my business. Spoiling it. In return, we are sending you *un regalito,* a little present. Your people will learn about it soon enough. And what about you, you must be asking? What does the future hold for Señor Carlton? Hmm?'

García came another step towards him, placing his great flat face so close to Luke's he could have kissed him. Suddenly he reached up with his hand and grabbed Luke's jaw. 'Look at me, inglés,' he whispered, his breath a toxic blend of stale cigar and cooked garlic. 'Because I am the instrument of your death. Soon now, very soon, you will be calling out my name and begging me to finish you.' He turned abruptly and shouted, 'Marquez! Take Señor Carlton to Buenaventura and check him into the Chop House.'

A man approached with a strip of black cloth and moved to wrap it around Luke's head in a blindfold. In the second before it went on the last thing Luke glimpsed was Major Elerzon, lounging against a 4x4, one hand in his pocket, the other holding a cigarette. He was looking straight at Luke, shaking his head and laughing.

Chapter 29

ELISE TOOK A sip of her chilled Marlborough Sauvignon Blanc, picked up her napkin and dabbed discreetly at the corner of her mouth. 'This,' she said slowly, 'has got to be the most amazing crab I've ever tasted. I'm loving the sauce. How did you know about this place? I never even knew it existed!'

Hugo Squires gave her a knowing look. 'One of the best-kept secrets in Chelsea,' he replied. He had chosen tonight's venue with care. Absolutely not a date, he had reassured her, yet the 'friends' who were supposed to join them had mysteriously never materialized. A quiet word with the maître d' when they arrived and Elise was handing over her coat, and the table for four had been neatly switched for a cosy corner setting for two. Candles were lit with a click and a flourish, and the menus arrived in padded crimson leather binders. A sommelier had appeared from nowhere to enquire discreetly: 'Would Mademoiselle care to choose from the wine list?' She had opted, as she usually did, for a New Zealand white.

Hugo had worked out his strategy in advance. As long as Elise was with Luke he knew he didn't stand a chance, but he was falling for her, and he knew he had one weapon in his armoury that Luke lacked. He was dependable, always there when she wanted a chaperone, because Luke was on his travels somewhere he couldn't even tell her.

Tonight, as they tucked into their main course of Dover sole on the bone with a shared dish of spinach on the side, Hugo knew what would be playing in the back of her mind. Were they going to broach the subject of that kiss, the one they had had at his house party in Dorset? He wondered, not without some trepidation, if she had mentioned it to Luke.

'So . . .' he began, twirling his wine glass to tease out the bouquet and looking meaningfully at Elise as he did so. 'How's Luke's trip going? I expect he's been keeping in touch.'

Elise blushed. Hugo wondered why. 'Oh, you know,' she replied, non-committal. 'He's pretty tied up with work right now. He calls me whenever he can.'

'That must be hard for you,' said Hugo, his thick black eyebrows arched in sympathy, and gave her hand a friendly, comforting squeeze. 'He's quite the globetrotter, isn't he? So where is he now? Timbuktu? Vladivostok?'

'Overseas somewhere,' replied Elise, her eyes wandering elsewhere in the room. It was a clear signal that she would say no more about Luke's whereabouts, so Hugo swiftly changed topics.

'Any plans for skiing this year?' he asked. It was a loaded question. 'As a matter of fact,' he went on, 'a bunch of us from Goldman's are taking a chalet in Verbier first week of February. Always room for one more if you're interested. There's no pressure!' He mimicked a line from an old *Blackadder* TV episode and laughed at his own joke as Elise smiled politely.

'That's sweet of you,' she replied, 'but Luke and I were thinking of going Nordic skiing in Sweden this winter.'

'Seriously? That sounds a bit hard-core. Where's the fun in that?'

They talked on about skiing, the merits of off-piste versus prepared slopes, chalets versus apartments, and whether it was worth trekking all the way out to the Rockies to catch the fine dry powder the US resorts seemed to have in abundance.

It was during the warm, fuzzy stage of the evening, when they were cradling glasses of golden dessert wine, that Elise's mobile rang in her handbag. She flinched and apologized at once. This was not the sort of place where ringtones were welcomed, and hers was a particularly striking BeeGees song. She scrabbled to locate her phone, got up and hurried out of the restaurant to disapproving stares. Outside, in the chill evening air of autumn she saw that the number calling was Luke's and her heart leaped with excitement.

'Babes!' she cried. 'Come home immediately! I miss you!'

But instead of Luke's voice she heard something else, a high-pitched whine that sounded like . . . Like what? An electric drill?

'Luke?' she said, anxiety creeping into her voice. 'Come on, don't play games. Where are you? When are you coming home?'

It was then that she heard a scream. A human scream, one of sheer animal agony.

'Luke!' she cried, clamping her hand to her mouth. But the voice that answered was not his. It was nasal and coarse, and sounded as if it came from far away. *'Buenas noches, Señorita Elise,'* said someone, and laughed. In the background someone groaned and gasped. Luke? The line went dead.

Chapter 30

HUGO DROVE HER home. Elise sat beside him in the passenger seat, as stiff as a corpse, staring rigidly ahead, focusing on the traffic, her make-up smudged with tears, her hands clenching and unclenching, fingernails digging into her palms. Their candlelit dinner had screeched to a halt after that phone call, Hugo's romantic plans replaced by something else, something tender and protective. He hated to see her like that but he felt helpless. Whatever kind of fix Luke had got himself into did not sound like something he could resolve. He was an investment banker, not an international security consultant. But the least he could do was to take care of Elise.

'Look, I'm really sorry about all this,' she said, snapping out of her trance as they pulled up outside her flat. 'It was good of you, Hugo, to take me out tonight. I just . . . I had no idea it was going to end like this.'

'Don't even think of apologizing. I'm going to get you through this. Now let's get you inside and sorted while you figure out who you need to call.' His eyebrows raised in genuine concern as he steered her up the steps and in through the communal ground-floor doors to the building. They rode up in the lift to the fourth floor in silence. He had never seen her so shaken. Hugo wanted so badly to hug her, to envelop her in his arms and tell her that everything would be all right, but something told him that probably wouldn't be the case.

'Where are your mugs?' he asked, once she had let them into the flat and he was rooting around in the kitchen.

'Top cupboard,' she replied, her voice flat and listless. She excused herself, went into the sitting room and to the desk Luke used, in the corner by the window. She remembered him showing her a plastic card, like a credit card, with a government logo printed on the back. It had a phone number on it, he had told her. She was only to use it in a genuine emergency. She rummaged around in the drawers until she found it and dialled the number printed on the front.

Hugo came in and set down a steaming mug of camomile tea. 'Hope you don't mind,' he said, 'but I've added a tot of whisky. I reckon you need it.'

Elise flashed him a smile. 'Thanks,' she said, and nearly called him 'babes'. Then she held up her hand. Someone was answering the phone.

Forty-five minutes later the door buzzer rang and she moved to get up, but Hugo put his hand gently on hers. 'Let me get this,' he insisted. He opened the door to a rather plain-looking woman in a raincoat. She was carrying an umbrella.

'Can I help you?' Hugo enquired politely.

'I'm Denise Wilcox, Joint Family Liaison Team. I've been sent over from, er, Vauxhall. Is this the residence of Miss Mayhew?'

'It certainly is,' replied Hugo, opening the door wide and stepping aside to let her in. 'She's just through there on the sofa.'

Denise Wilcox went into the sitting room and sat down next to Elise, turning her back to Hugo. She was kind, she was sympathetic, and she had absolutely no information about Luke. But there was a procedure to follow when anyone from the Service was kidnapped and she was going through the motions of it now.

'I've been asked to come here,' she began, 'by your boyfriend's employers. You do know who they are?' Denise Wilcox looked meaningfully at Elise as she asked. Elise nodded.

'I do have to check,' continued her visitor. 'It was you who alerted them this evening?' She reached for a notebook and glanced quickly through the details she had been given.

'Yes,' replied Elise, impatient now. Something about the woman didn't inspire her with confidence.

'So, Eleanor—'

'Elise.'

'So, Elise,' she checked her notes again, 'you did the right thing. Now, you'll appreciate there was a good deal of concern after you made that call.' She looked up at Hugo, who was standing in the doorway, not sure what to do with himself. 'Is this gentleman your next of kin?' she asked.

'Hugo? No, he's a friend. He's been very kind tonight.'

'I see.' Wilcox smiled up at him. 'It's probably all right for him to go now. I'll be staying here tonight and we have a few things to discuss, in private, as it were.'

'Oh, right. Yes, of course.' Elise's voice was distant and mechanical, as if all of this was happening to someone else. She was still finding it hard to get Luke's scream out of her head. Hugo took his cue and came over to give her a peck on the cheek, then saw himself out, closing the door gently behind him.

'OK,' continued Denise Wilcox when he had gone. 'We'll have to keep your mobile on the whole time, I'm afraid, in case they call again. If and when they do, we need you to get them to call the landline here in the flat. That makes it easier for us to track and record what's being said.'

'But what if I'm at work?' asked Elise.

'I don't think you'll be going anywhere until this is resolved. You'll have to let your employers know in the morning. Say it's a family emergency, nothing more. We don't want this getting out. What matters now is that we get Luke back unharmed. That's the outcome we're all working for.'

Elise studied her. 'Can I ask you something?' she said.

'Please. I'm here to help.'

'Have you worked on a lot of kidnap cases? I hope you don't mind my asking, it's just this is pretty unsettling for me and . . .' Her voice trailed away.

'Well, we cover them in training, of course,' replied Wilcox, 'but no, I suppose you're my first. I'm currently on secondment to Vauxhall Cross. I actually work for the other lot, down in Cheltenham. GCHQ. Mostly I'm dealing with traffic accidents and breathalysers.'

Elise nodded. A thought occurred to her. 'But you know where Luke is, right? I mean you know which country and you've got some idea where that call came from?'

Wilcox hesitated, unsure of just how much she should say. 'I believe the people who need to be aware of that do know, yes,' she replied.

'Can you at least tell me which country he's in?'

'I'm sorry, but I'm not authorized to tell you that.'

Elise was tempted to say that there was not a lot of point to her visit if she had so little to tell her. But she was tired now, so very tired, so she helped the woman make up a bed on the sofa, then went to her room. On Wilcox's suggestion she swallowed a sleeping tablet and eventually drifted off.

She slept fitfully, passing from one dream to another. In the one she remembered when she woke up the next morning they were Nordic skiing, she and Luke, striding through forests of Norwegian firs on thin, pointed skis that cut parallel grooves in crisp snow. The low Scandinavian sun cast long shadows and she laughed as she tried to push him over. In her dream, Luke was by her side and Elise, asleep in her bed, was happy.

Chapter 31

ELISE HAD NO idea of the train of events triggered by her single phone call to that emergency number at Vauxhall Cross. All through the night and into the morning there was a frenzy of coded electronic activity criss-crossing the Atlantic, between VX and SIS's Bogotá station. Frantic requests for help went to Washington, to the CIA at Langley, Virginia, and to the headquarters of America's giant eavesdropping organization, the NSA, at Fort Meade in Maryland. SIS had lost their second man in South America in less than two weeks, and now they were in a race against time to find him, while he was still alive.

Sid Khan had been in Ronnie Scott's jazz club when he had got the call. Working late, day after day, it was unlike him to give himself a night off, but this was special: it was his brother's birthday, and they had come to Soho to listen to some authentic Cuban jazz. Stepping outside to take the call on his mobile from the night duty officer, the words in his ear sent a chill down his spine. 'Carlton's been taken. The narcos have got him.'

Within thirty minutes Khan was back at his desk at Vauxhall Cross and, despite the late hour, the Chief was demanding answers. Who authorized Carlton's mission? Why wasn't John Friend with him? And, most pressingly, what were they doing to get him out? Khan rubbed his palms over his face. To lose one intelligence officer on active duty in Colombia was unfortunate. But to lose a second? And then there was the unknown device, the weapon to which Luke had alerted them. He was supposed to be giving a proper handover briefing to the relief team Khan had sent out to Colombia. Instead Luke had become the problem. Khan kicked himself for not reeling him in sooner. Well, now it was too late and the Service's whole South American operation looked like it was starting to unravel.

Shortly before midnight Khan sat down with Craig Dalziel, head of Agent Handling. They were in Khan's office, each with a mug of Tetley's tea beside them. Distracted by the business at hand, neither had bothered to remove the teabag. Khan handed him a single-page memo from Clements, now acting head of the station in Bogotá. 'This just came in,' he said. 'It doesn't look good.'

Dalziel started reading then looked up sharply at Khan. 'Jesus Christ!' he said. 'It was a massacre! They killed everyone there. All those policemen dead.'

'Everyone except, it seems, our man Carlton,' replied Khan. 'They'll be keeping him somewhere they think we won't find him. And they'll be torturing him – we know that from the phone call his girlfriend got. They'll be doing it first for information, and then for fun.'

'Christ!' repeated Dalziel, under his breath.

'NSA are doing a surge operation on all comms in the area where he was taken,' continued Khan, 'but it's coming up blank so far. The narcos aren't stupid – they cleared out pretty fast after the executions. Nobody left in that farmhouse but kitchen staff and cleaners. The Colombian military have been through on a sweep and found nothing but bloodstains and spent cartridge cases.'

'Any word from Tradewind?' asked Dalziel.

'I was going to ask you the same thing,' replied Khan, picking up his tea and blowing on it to cool it.

'Nothing.' Dalziel had just noticed the teabag floating in his mug and was looking for somewhere to dump it. 'At least, not yet. The transmissions are infrequent, as you know. There's no knowing when the next chance will come up.'

'Well, can we fire off a request anyway?' said Khan. 'See if the agent has any clue where Carlton's been taken? If García's people are holding him there must be gossip, surely.'

'We can but try,' said Dalziel, getting to his feet. He still hadn't found anywhere to put his teabag and Khan obviously hadn't noticed so he left the mug on his desk. 'Let's stay closely in touch,' he said, and left.

There was a sofa in Khan's office and he went over to it now, plumped up a couple of cushions, lay down, stretched out his legs and closed his eyes. Two hours later the phone on his desk purred and he rolled off the sofa to answer it. It was the night duty officer again, with more bad news, this time putting through a call from the substantial SIS station in Washington DC. It seemed the NSA had managed to triangulate the approximate origin of the call Elise had taken in the restaurant barely five hours ago. The NSA analysts had pinned it down to a town called Buenaventura on Colombia's Pacific coast. The SIS man in Washington added, rather unhelpfully, that

Buenaventura was considered to be the most lawless and dangerous city in the whole country, if not the whole of South America.

Khan remembered that name from Luke's briefing to the board on the morning after Benton's body had been discovered. He went over to his computer and pulled up the most recent security advisory on it. 'Parts of this port city,' it read, 'are no-go zones even for Colombian security forces. UK government staff advised to avoid at all times. Entry into Buenaventura only to be undertaken in extremis and with reinforced security envelope.'

From the river outside his window he heard a long, mournful blast on a horn. A barge passing by. Right now, Khan wished he was on it.

Chapter 32

THE MAN STOOD over Luke and leered into his face. 'Do you know why they call this the Chop House?' he asked. Luke looked up through his unswollen eye and saw one of García's men swaying, swigging from a beer bottle. Behind him, packing cases, lots of them, were stacked on top of each other in untidy piles. They appeared to be in some kind of warehouse.

'No?' continued the man with the beer.

Luke knew the answer but said nothing. He was trying not to think about it, but the screams he had heard from beyond the packing cases had left little to his imagination. The pain in his own left foot was still excruciating from where they had taken the drill to him. The last thing he remembered, after they had smuggled him into the place and strapped him down, was a man holding a mobile phone up to his face. It was his. Then the drill was biting into his flesh, churning through skin and sinew, spraying everyone with blood. He had blacked out then and he still didn't know who had been at the other end of the phone. He just prayed it wasn't Elise.

'So, let me give you a clue as to why they call it the Chop House,' said Beer Bottle. He wasn't going to let this one go. Luke strained his head to look round at a circle of men, all narco thugs, standing there watching, with their Uzis, their MAC-10s and their stolen M4 assault rifles. They wore filthy ragged surf shorts mostly, and stained white singlets, the tropical coastal heat coating their dark, muscled skin in a constant, glistening sheen of sweat. He was struck by how young they seemed, and how desperate. Some had wild, staring eyes, tinged with pink. How many were hooked on some toxic drug?

Luke could see Beer Bottle ambling slowly to a corner of the room, then selecting something. From where Luke lay, strapped tightly to a hospital gurney, he couldn't make out what the man was doing but he had an inkling. And for the first time he felt real fear.

The man returned with a sickly smile, displaying prematurely yellowed teeth. He must have discarded his bottle somewhere in the corner, because now he was using both hands to carry something else. 'So,' he said, presenting his burden to Luke as if it were a gift. 'Here is one we made earlier.' He winked at the men standing around watching and then, with a slight heave of his wiry frame, he tossed something wet and heavy onto Luke's chest.

They say that the adult human eye can focus clearly on an object as close as eleven centimetres away but that the distance grows longer with age. Luke had good eyesight, even with one eye swollen shut from the beating, and he had no difficulty in making out what had been dumped on top of him. It was a human arm, severed high above the elbow, the skin thick with black hair, the blood still only half congealed, the jagged white bone sticking out from where it should have joined a man's shoulder. The lifeless hand was reaching out towards his face, as if the broken fingernails were scrabbling for purchase on his chest. He struggled to suppress the urge to vomit. Who the arm had belonged to, he had no idea, probably some nameless gangster on the losing side of a narco turf war. This was Buenaventura's calling card: its 'chop houses' were the rat-infested sheds down by the waterside where rival gangs lopped limbs off their living victims, before killing them.

'Oye, inglés!' Beer Bottle had wandered off but now he was back, hovering over Luke. 'Would you like to see more?' he asked. The men were loving this, giggling like children and giving him whoops of encouragement. Beer Bottle threw something else on top of Luke, something so long and heavy it knocked the wind out of his lungs, leaving him gasping for air. It was a leg, black and scarred and missing a foot. The victim had suffered two amputations on the same leg. Luke said nothing, but Beer Bottle had not finished. Back and forth he went to the corner of the warehouse until a small pyramid of limbs was piled up on Luke's chest. Unable to move, he was starting to find it hard to breathe. And now the flies were descending in earnest, following the scent of death, oblivious to whether they settled on a severed limb or Luke's lips and eyes. His ears filled with their constant droning as they crawled about and tried to get inside his nostrils.

He fought to stay calm. You are truly in the shit here, he told himself, but you've got to start working on a plan, any plan, to get out of this place.

Beer Bottle had recovered his drink and was taking another swig but he still had lots to say. 'What do you think it feels like,' he said, 'to have your arms and legs cut off, one by one? Huh? You see, I don't know because I still have all of mine!' He did a little drunken dance and waved both arms in the air. 'And today,' he said, frowning and concentrating on getting his words out, 'you still have all of yours . . . but tomorrow . . .' His face lit up in a grin as he turned to the men with the submachine-guns for approval. 'Tomorrow you are going to find out. Maybe we make it nice and slow. Take our time. Do you want to see what we will use? You do? Here . . .' He bent down and picked something up from the floor. It was a vicious-looking machete, the blade stained brown with dried blood, a small chunk of decaying flesh stuck to its surface and a thin leather strap dangling from the handle. 'Why don't we let you have a good look at it?' he said. 'Let you sleep with it, really get to know it, because tomorrow, my friend, you will know each other very well. This baby . . .' he tossed the machete onto the severed limbs piled up on Luke's chest '. . . this baby is going to be the instrument of your death. You should learn to love it.'

Chapter 33

NO ONE TOOK much notice when one more rusting cargo ship joined the flotilla of vessels lining up to enter the Panama Canal from the south. It was just past eight in the morning and the air above the port of Balboa was thick with flocks of marauding frigate-birds, wheeling and diving, searching for any scraps of food tossed overboard. Each year fourteen thousand vessels made the day-long crossing from the Pacific Ocean to the Caribbean and on to the Atlantic beyond, saving themselves a 12,800-kilometre detour round the storm-tossed waters of Cape Horn. The *Maria Esposito* had submitted her notification of arrival with the Panama Canal Authority two days earlier, using the EDCS electronic collection system. Registered in Manila, and with her last stated port of embarkation listed as Batangas in the Philippines, her details attracted little attention when they flashed up on the computer in the harbourmaster's office. Her arrival was logged and the ship's captain informed that prior to transit an inspection would take place in two days' time. The *Maria Esposito* was instructed to drop anchor and wait.

On the bridge, Captain Hector Jiménez passed a damp flannel over his forehead, wiping away the beads of sweat that had formed in the muggy heat of the morning. The air-conditioning on the bridge had stopped working a week ago. Two days' delay . . . *Mierda*. He had never had to wait that long before and he had not taken this into account. He needed to let them know back home. But at least it gave his crew time to make the final checks, to make sure everything onboard appeared completely 'normal'. The *Maria Esposito* was certainly no beauty, with her stained hull, her filthy superstructure and her ageing cranes, which looked as if they might topple over the moment they were put to use. Her manifest declared she was carrying agricultural equipment destined for the port of Antwerp. Quite what use the good farmers of Flanders would make of antiquated North Korean-manufactured tractors and ploughs was a question that might well be asked when she reached her destination. But in Panama there was a rule book for crossing the Canal and the *Maria Esposito* was treated no differently from any of the other ships that made the transit.

First to board her was the inspector from the Admeasurers' Office in Balboa. A rotund man with a moustache and wispy comb-over, he bustled about the bridge in his short-sleeved shirt and epaulettes, demanding to see certified records of the ship's weights and measurements. He talked Captain Jiménez through the lockage arrangements for the coming transit, reminding him there were three locks in total to negotiate between the two oceans, then arranged for his subordinates to come aboard for the below-decks inspection.

It seemed to go badly. As the first inspector climbed down the metal ladder into the hold, he found it impossible to grip the last few rungs, almost as if someone had left them smeared with grease. In his panic he let go and fell the final two metres onto the steel floor, landing with a thump and a howl of pain. No bones were broken but it was enough to put off his companions. After peering down and holding a brief discussion they went to inspect the deck while the man got back to his feet, nursing his bruised ankle and muttering under his breath. He hobbled around the cargo hold, peering at the steel-grey farm equipment and patting the piles of stacked boxes. He could hardly wait to finish. Perhaps, if he had had more time and inclination, and a bit more curiosity, he might have noticed the signs of recent welding on the bulkheads, or the application of fresh paint on a vessel that was otherwise in a shabby state. But he didn't.

By midday, with the sun beating down directly overhead from a white, colourless sky, the *Maria Esposito* riding calmly at anchor, Captain Jiménez was shaking hands with the departing inspection team, the all-important Admeasurement Clearance form clasped in his hand. He instructed payment of the transit fees to be made to a nominated bank in Balboa. Within the hour confirmation came back and the *Maria Esposito* was placed on the transit list. Given the powerful new arc lights installed at the locks and along part of the transit route, Jiménez was hoping they would send him clearance to proceed that afternoon. But rules were rules, and they stated that a south-to-north transit across the isthmus must start first thing in the morning. It meant a further delay. Alone in his cabin that night, Jiménez chewed his fingernails in nervous distraction. They had got through the inspection, but a three-day delay? It would not go down well with his bosses.

In the morning he was up, dressed and had breakfasted by the time the Canal Authority pilots came alongside and onto the bridge. They had done this journey so many times, and with ships much larger than the *Maria Esposito*, that their relaxed manner was infectious. Captain Jiménez found himself starting to unwind in their company – they were fellow mariners, after all. Just eight hours after they had boarded, the haulage hausers were disconnected and the ship passed through Lake Gatún under its own steam and then through the last of the Canal. When they entered Limón Bay, the pilots waved farewell and lowered themselves over the side into the waiting harbour launch that would take them to shore at Cristóbal and a nice cold beer.

Captain Jiménez waited until they were well clear of the Colón Breakwater and out into the moonlit waters of the Caribbean before he instructed his radio operator to transmit a single-word message to those he knew would be listening: '*Benicio*.' It would mean nothing to almost anyone who heard it, but it meant a great deal to a tight group of men waiting for news in Colombia.

Chapter 34

LUKE WAS RUNNING out of ways to hold the pain at bay. The straps that bound his limbs to the gurney were digging into his upper arms and threatening to cut off the blood supply. He could feel them going numb. His chest ached with the oppressive weight of all the severed limbs that Beer Bottle had piled on top of him, and his throat was parched, but worst of all was his foot. Every few seconds it sent lancing through his body a fiery pulse of pain so intense it threatened to block out everything else. He tried to focus on a distant corner of the shed, but whatever he looked at kept looming in and out of focus, coming towards him and then retreating. He recognized the signs and knew there was a serious risk he could black out here.

Would he ever walk again? He wouldn't know until he put his weight on his foot but, right now, the more pressing question was whether he would still be alive in twenty-four hours. He had lost all track of time – they had taken his watch within the first few minutes of capture up in the hills at Ituango. But he could see it was late from the crack in the roof rafters that let in a faint, intermittent ray of moonlight, and guessed it must be some time after midnight. The flies, at least, had gone to sleep.

After dumping all those severed limbs on him, Beer Bottle had eventually got bored and wandered outside some hours ago, but the half-dozen men with machine-guns had stayed on for a while, drinking and amusing themselves by walking up to Luke, making chopping noises then pretending to scream. They're like children, thought Luke, but children with automatic weapons.

Eventually, they, too, had grown bored. One had come over to check the straps that held him in place and then spat casually into his face. He had nodded to the others and they had all left together, their weapons dangling menacingly by their sides. So now Luke was alone in the warehouse, tied to a gurney and half buried beneath decomposing body parts. This was surely about as bad as it could get. Dawn could not be more than a few hours away and when the narco thugs woke up he could look forward to an excruciating death. What a bloody waste of a life, all that education and training, just to end up dying a squalid death in a Colombian waterside shed, murdered by men he didn't know and who probably wouldn't outlive him by much more than a year, if they were lucky. It was that bastard police chief, Major Elerzon, he had to thank for this, for betraying his operation and selling him out, not just him but so many of his countrymen. But Luke knew there was no point going over dead ground: he needed to focus one hundred per cent now on an escape plan.

And that was when he saw it. Out of his one unbattered eye, peering through the gloom of the darkened warehouse, he spotted the machete. In his half-drunken stupor, Beer Bottle had left it out of Luke's reach amid the pile of severed limbs that covered his body. But now it was tantalizingly close to his right hand, dislodged by the thug who had checked his bindings. Luke shifted a fraction, which was all that the straps would allow him, and extended his arm as far down his body as he could. His fingertips clawed towards the handle of the machete, fighting their way up the damp expanse of dead flesh. No. It was still beyond his reach. He tried again, straining every muscle in his aching body, and this time his fingertips made contact with something. The leather strap that hung from the handle. His fingers closed tight around it. If he could only pull it to him, then get a purchase on the handle . . .

He heard the door to the warehouse open and he froze. It was Beer Bottle, still swaying, still drunk. The man tottered over to the gurney and stood next to Luke's face. In the semi-darkness Luke could see him fumbling with something: he was unbuttoning the fly on his shorts and taking out his penis. The next instant a hot jet of urine hit Luke's face, spraying him up and down, stinging his one open eye with the acrid tang of ammonia. Beer Bottle was laughing, rocking back on his heels as he relieved himself all over his prisoner, then he did up his flies, croaked, '*Dulces sueños*, sweet dreams,' and lurched out of the door.

Luke waited a full minute, ignoring the stench of the urine that was dripping off him. He had kept his hands perfectly still throughout, not daring to lose his grip on the machete strap. But now he was alone again he got to work, fast. He extended the fingers of his right hand so that they gathered in the slack on the strap, pulling the handle closer, then felt the crude wooden shaft and his hand closed around it. Now he needed to shake some of the limbs off him, but softly, without bringing any of the thugs running into the room. It wasn't easy. They had tied him so tightly to the gurney he had almost no room for manoeuvre. But by clenching and unclenching his muscles he was able to shift his position ever so slightly. Luke set up a rocking motion, tilting his supine body from left to right and back again until at last something fell off the pile on his chest. A severed leg. He kept going until, one by one, he had shaken off around half of the dozen or so limbs Beer Bottle had placed on him. Breathing more easily, he filled his chest with a whole lungful of air, then wished he hadn't. The smell was rotten, fetid.

As a small boy, Luke remembered, he had been double-jointed: he used to show off to the other boys in his class how he could bend his hands right back at the wrists so that the tips of his fingers were touching the back of his arms. He didn't have quite the same flexibility now but, still, it was about to serve him well. Gripping the machete with his right hand and using his wrist as a pivot, he was able to sweep the blade back and forth so that it knocked the remaining limbs to the floor. But now came the hard part: cutting through the coarse ship's ropes they had used to bind him. Lying flat on his back, with only his hand able to move, he had almost no purchase, no means to bring his weight and power to bear on slicing through the two-centimetre-thick coil. He decided to start with the one closest to the blade binding his legs. He flicked the machete down onto the rope and immediately it bounced off, nearly causing him to drop it. He was about to try again when a beam of light burst into the room and there was the sound of salsa from beyond the door. Again he froze, knowing that this time they were bound to spot what he was up to. This could be the showdown. But no one came in. The door banged shut and he was alone. Luke resolved to work even faster – he might have only minutes to save himself.

He swung the machete blade once more down onto the rope, the muscles in his arm straining with exertion, a vein around his biceps pulsing, and this time it connected. The blade was razor sharp and when he began a sawing motion, moving it back and forth just a few centimetres at a time, the rope began to split in two, then parted with a gratifying pop. It was as if a coil that had bound his whole body was suddenly released. At last, for the first time in hours he could move his legs, but as the blood came back to them, so did the pain. Luke fought through it, pushing it to the back of his mind as he turned the blade to point up his body, towards his chin, and sawed at the rope that bound his chest and arms. Twice he nearly dropped the machete, his hand slipping constantly with the wetness of his own sweat mixed with Beer Bottle's urine. Because of the odd angle this was far harder and it took him nearly ten minutes, but then came the second, blissful release as the rope that had bound his chest and arms sprang apart. It was as if a voice in his head was screaming at him, 'Go! Go! Go!'

But it wasn't as easy as that. Luke had lost count of how many hours he had been tied to that gurney. Then there had been the beating and, of course, the drill to his foot. He was in no shape to leap up and out of the door. Slowly at first, like an old man with arthritis, he raised himself into a sitting position and rubbed his joints as he felt the circulation returning. He swung his legs over the side and looked down at his injured foot.

He could just make out a dark circle of congealed blood around the point where the drill had gone in, right at the top of the arch. He knew the last thing his body wanted was for him to put any weight on that foot, but he also knew he had no choice. At any moment that warehouse door would swing open and then it would all be over.

Luke took a deep breath, steadied himself with a hand on the gurney and put his full weight on both feet. Immediately, red-hot pain shot up his leg from the drilled foot and seemed to sear right into his brain. Jesus H. Christ! That hurt! Luke fell back onto the gurney, gasping. Then he tried again. This time he clenched his teeth and fought through it. He had to keep going or he would die, like so many others, right there in that godforsaken shed, in a corner of Colombia that no one in their right mind would ever choose to visit.

He picked up the machete and hobbled around the room, looking for an exit. There had to be another way out of the place other than the door with García's men on the other side. His punctured foot was oozing fresh blood and he looked around for his shoes, craving the cushioning that his approach boots would give him, but the narcos had taken them away long ago, probably drawn lots for who would get to wear them. He continued his search, peering through the gloom of the warehouse interior, where the only light came faintly from a lamp outside. He dragged himself to the inside wall of the shed and worked his way along it, gasping with each step. His foot was on fire. His eyes settled on something and he reached out to touch it. It was another door and he tried it now. Locked. Well, of course it was. He was stuffed.

So, what now? He could wait behind the other door and take on the first narco who came through, maybe grab his weapon if he was lucky. But Luke knew the odds were stacked against him. There were at least ten of them, all armed, and while they might well be off their heads on drink or drugs by now, he was in no fit state to put up a fight. No, he had to find another way out.

A sound from the other side of the shed made him stand perfectly still, straining his ears to listen. It was the sound of someone unbuckling their belt and dropping their trousers to the floor, the sound of someone using an outside lavatory. Luke shuffled as silently as possible across the darkened floor of the shed, almost tripping over what he took to be a severed hand, until he drew level with the sound on the other side of the wall. Whoever was in there was making heavy weather of their business, groaning and grunting. But Luke wasn't listening: he had found what he was looking for. There was a door, leading from the interior of the warehouse to the outside lavatory. He readied the machete in his right hand and put his left on the door handle, turning it slowly and quietly.

Beneath the single bulb that dangled from the ceiling the man sat hunched on the toilet with his back to Luke. He was heavily built and looked older than the young thugs who had taunted him earlier with Beer Bottle. But he was still a narco, still one of García's men – Luke could see that with just one glance at the MAC-10 machine pistol that lay on the floor beside his crumpled trousers. As Luke moved towards him a floorboard creaked and the man started to turn his head.

'*Quién está ahí?*' he called. 'Who's there?'

Luke moved with lightning speed, his reflexes taking over. In one single movement he covered the remaining distance between them and drove the pointed tip of the machete deep into the back of the man's neck, severing his spinal cord and his upper vertebrae. There was remarkably little sound. He died instantly, but Luke had to move round quickly to catch the body before it fell to the floor with a crash. Gently, he laid the dead man on his side, then snatched up the MAC-10. A gangster's favourite, the 9mm version had a thirty-two-round magazine, fully loaded, and a folding stock. Luke checked that the safety was off and squatted down in a firing position, ready for anyone coming through the outer door to investigate. Inwardly, his spirits soared. He was tooled up now: the odds had suddenly changed in his favour and he was back in the game with a fighting chance.

Chapter 35

HE GAVE IT thirty seconds, no more. When no one came, Luke made his move. Holding the MAC-10 out in front of him, he eased open the outer door of the lavatory and adjusted his senses to the night outside. A hot, rank breeze blowing off the muddy shore, a distant dog barking, the light and shadow cast by a lamp placed just around the corner of the warehouse. Luke was still in shadow but now he could see his situation all too clearly. The warehouse was built on stilts over the water. He hadn't noticed that before because of the blindfold he'd had on when they had brought him here. He was standing on a wooden walkway made up of crooked, uneven planks – a nail protruded from one just beyond his bare feet. He could hear some people talking in low voices, not far away, round the other side of the warehouse: García's men, with guns, he had to assume. The problem was, the wooden walkway led directly past them, bringing him out into the pool of light given off by the single lamp hanging from the wall. The urge to take them on was overwhelming. He had a full magazine on his weapon, the advantage of surprise and, yes, if he was honest with himself, he wanted payback for the hell they had put him through. A hell that was as nothing compared to what they had in store for him when morning came.

But the burst of automatic fire he would let rip – and that was assuming the MAC-10 didn't misfire – would rouse the whole neighbourhood in a second. He could see there were other sheds and shanty huts nearby, doubtless housing more of García's men. They would be swarming over to him like rats, hunting him down the moment his ammunition ran out. No, there had to be another way, a subtler way. What would he do, Luke asked himself, if he was still in the SBS? And almost as he posed the question, the answer presented itself. It was obvious when he looked down. He eased himself into a sitting position, dangling his legs over the side of the walkway, relishing the small relief it gave his tortured foot.

He had left the machete in the lavatory, preferring his chances with the machine pistol, but the gun had no strap and he had no means of fastening it to himself when he made his next move. He had hoped to lower himself into the oily black water as quietly as possible by dropping fully extended from the edge of the walkway, holding on with his hands until the last moment. But it was that or the MAC-10, he couldn't have both, and he wasn't leaving it behind. Would it work after it had been dunked under water? He honestly didn't know.

Maybe he should have stuck with the machete – at least it had a carrying strap round the handle. But he wasn't going back in there now. Adrenalin was coursing through him, pushing back the throbbing from his foot. Luke held the weapon in one hand and used the other to lever his backside off the walkway. Then he jumped.

In the stillness of the tropical night he hit the water with an almighty splash. For a brief, blissful moment he was submerged under water, cocooned in a different world, but the impact had been far louder than he had hoped and he knew that the second he surfaced all hell would break loose. So he didn't.

Under water, he made an instant decision to ditch the machine pistol: he couldn't swim with it so he let it drop to the bottom of the harbour as he struck out away from the shore. The water was filthy. He could taste the fuel of boat engines, but that was the least of his worries. Beams of light were probing the water around him and as his lungs screamed for air he knew he had to surface. He was a good ten metres from the warehouse when a cry went up as the torch-beams found him. A crackle of shots followed. Bullets zipped past him in the darkened water of the bay, sending up small plumes of spray.

Luke dived vertically downwards to escape the gunfire. It wasn't easy on a full gulp of air: his lungs were acting like a lifebelt, preventing him from descending, so he exhaled in bubbles. He had about thirty seconds left before he would have to surface again. When he came up for air a second time he thought he might, just, have got away with it. The torches were playing on a patch of water some distance behind him, and García's men were firing blindly at the wrong place. Perhaps he could make it out to the open sea and take his chances there. But then he heard a sound that made his heart sink: an outboard engine. Once they started criss-crossing the bay in a speedboat with lights it was only a matter of time before they found him. Even his powerful swimmer's lungs couldn't keep him submerged for the minutes he would need to stay hidden. So he took a difficult decision, a totally counter-intuitive one. He turned and swam back towards the shore.

He had no intention of giving himself up, so he aimed for a patch of mud he could see beneath another building on stilts, the darkest place he could find. As the narcos' speedboat swept the waters of the bay in front of him with its lights, Luke did what he did best. He vanished. He positioned himself at the point where the tidal seawater lapped against the stinking black mud of the shore and proceeded to smear it all over his face, arms and feet. He still had his trousers on so he coated them too. Soon he was almost indistinguishable from the mud that surrounded him. Only his eyes would have given him away to anyone who came close, shining with a desperate intensity as he fought to survive.

But Luke was not alone. His arrival had disturbed the rats, dozens of them. They swam around him in confusion, setting his teeth on edge with their manic, high-pitched squeaking. The less he moved, the bolder they became, scuttling towards him on the mud and bumping into his legs below the waterline. He slapped the water, just enough to send them retreating, but soon they were back, ever more fearless. How long before they started to take a few chunks out of him? He couldn't stay there.

The narcos' speedboat was some distance off now, scanning another empty expanse of the bay, and Luke reckoned he could make it undetected to a small fishing boat he could see riding at anchor, about two hundred metres away. He was about to launch himself back into the water when he became aware of footsteps on a wooden walkway directly overhead.

Through the cracks in the planks he could see a man silhouetted against a nearby light, pacing slowly up and down, holding what looked like a shotgun. Another of García's men searching for him? Almost certainly. He would have to put up with the rats.

After ten minutes the man coughed, hawked up some phlegm, spat it into the water below, then wandered off. Luke scanned the darkened bay for any sign of the speedboat but it was gone. He smiled to himself. All those armed narcos and they had lost their prisoner. García was not going to be happy. Someone would be punished and, with any luck, it would be Beer Bottle. But Luke was not out of trouble yet. Silently, he detached himself from the muddy shore and struck out into the bay, pushing his way through discarded oil cans and plastic bags. He was aiming for the fishing boat and taking care to disturb the surface of the water as little as possible. Polluted as it was, it acted like a balm to his injured foot, but now an unwelcome thought occurred to him. It was probably still bleeding. Sharks, he knew, could detect a molecule of blood in 25 million molecules of water and he was guessing there would be hammerheads and bull sharks in the eastern Pacific. If there were any in the vicinity they could probably close in on him in under two minutes. Still, even a shark was preferable to the horrors of García's Chop House. He intensified his efforts, slicing through the water at a fast crawl, making for the safety of the fishing boat.

Gasping for breath, shoulder muscles burning, Luke slowed his pace as he approached the small craft. What would he do if someone was asleep on board? He was unarmed now, in no condition for hand-to-hand combat. He circled the boat, guessing it to be about seven metres in length. It had a covered wheelhouse upfront. With his head bobbing just above the surface, he ran his eyes along a line of white, hand-painted lettering on its side. It spelled *La Macarena*. And it was then he noticed two things. His swollen eye had re-opened. And if he could read the lettering, dawn could not be far off. He was running out of time.

He made his way round to the stern and gripped the rungs of a metal ladder that hung down into the water. With an immense effort he hauled himself out of the sea and nearly howled as he put his injured foot on the lowest rung. He climbed slowly up, keeping his profile low as he rolled his body over the side and down into the well of the boat. It was empty. There was nothing in it but a crumpled tarpaulin that someone had neglected to put away. All his body wanted to do, all it yearned for, was to curl up in that tarpaulin, go to sleep – what, and wake up back in the Chop House? His body might have been close to exhaustion but Luke's mind was still firing on all cylinders.

As the sky to the east over Buenaventura took on the pinkish tinge of dawn he crawled to the side, reached for the anchor chain and pulled. Nothing happened. He gave it another tug but it was stuck fast. His heart sank. He just didn't think he had it left in him to dive down and free the anchor. He sat on the tarpaulin and held his head in his hands. This was not despair: he was absolutely knackered and wondered how much longer he could keep going. He went back to the side and gave another pull on the anchor chain and there it was, coming free in his hands, like the sword Excalibur. He hauled up the chain and put away the anchor. Almost immediately he faced another problem. The tide was coming in fast and the boat was already drifting towards the shore. At this rate he would be bumping up against the side of the Chop House in no time.

He made a quick assessment of his options. Start the outboard and make a break for it? Too risky. It was a feeble fifty horsepower and looked as if it had seen better days. The narcos would overtake him in seconds. Put the anchor back down, stay hidden under the tarpaulin and wait till dusk, in the hope no one came aboard to find him? Not smart. There were no other boats within a hundred metres, so they were bound to come looking here once they had finished searching the shore. There was nothing else for it: he was going to have to muster his final reserves and do this the hard way. Still staying down, Luke lowered himself over the stern and back into the sea. He clenched his fingers around the rusty metal rungs of the ladder, extended his arms and kicked out like a frog. At first it had no effect, but he kicked out again with all his strength and gradually the momentum began to build and the boat was moving. After several more kicks he glanced over his shoulder at the shore. Yes! It was marginally further away. He kept going, heading diagonally out to sea and northwards, keeping the murderous shanties of Buenaventura on his right, straining to put as much distance as he could between himself and the men who lurked there. He tried not to think of the sharks.

Luke's arms and legs were numb with tiredness, his hands wrinkled and sore where they gripped the rusty rungs, but it was as if he was on auto-pilot now, kicking out rhythmically and robotically. This was more gruelling than anything he had faced in Special Forces Selection but he had to keep going. The alternative was unthinkable. He picked a distant rocky promontory on the shore far to the north as his marker and focused his efforts on pushing past it. Now a distant memory floated back, a half-buried moment from his childhood. The butterfly. The promontory was like the butterfly he had followed all those years ago as a boy lost in the jungle, the day his parents had died. Well, he'd survived then and he was bloody well going to survive now too.

By the time he drew level with the rocky outcrop the sun was bearing down on him out of a thin haze of white cloud, scorching his shoulders through his tattered shirt. He could feel his forehead and nose blistering, imagining them glowing bright red with sunburn. In his desperation to get away he hadn't stopped to search the boat for water and now he was tormented by thirst. He stopped kicking and pulled himself back onto the deck, then surveyed where he was. On either side of the outcrop thick, lush vegetation tumbled down a steep slope to a deserted beach of uninviting black sand. He was alone, adrift on this stretch of coast, and he could feel the current sweeping him northwards.

He went into the covered wheelhouse, grateful for some shelter from the sun, and rummaged around in a bucket until his fingers closed around a warm can of Coca-Cola. He wiped it on his sleeve, pulled back the ring-pull and drank it in one go. His teeth were gritty with sugar so he continued his search for water. Slopping around in the bilge beneath the wheel he found a half-empty plastic litre bottle. He unscrewed the top, sniffed and recoiled. It smelt faintly of fuel.

But a further search revealed that it was the only water onboard. It would have to do.

Now he needed to find the key to start the engine. The empty silver socket in the dashboard was staring back at him, taunting him. If he couldn't get the engine started he would make slow progress along the coast and this was still narco territory. Luke got down on his hands and knees, trailing his fingertips through the bilge water on the floor in case someone had dropped the key there. Nothing. Whoever owned the boat had taken the key with them when they had gone ashore. For a moment he felt a pang of guilt, knowing he had just robbed some Colombian fisherman of his livelihood. But this was survival and he'd had no choice.

The soft, rhythmic lapping of the waves against the hull, the torpor induced by the noon heat and the gentle rocking motion as the current bore him northward were all starting to have an effect. Luke could resist it no longer. He dragged the tarpaulin into the wheelhouse, made himself a bed amid its creases and folds, then sank into the deep sleep of exhaustion.

The kick that woke him seemed to come from nowhere. One moment he was fast asleep, the next he was staring up at a man with a machine-gun. '*Levántate!*' he ordered. 'Get up!' Dazed, dehydrated and slightly delirious, Luke did not react at first, so the man jabbed the muzzle of his weapon into his chest. '*Levántate!*' he repeated, louder this time and more urgent. Luke struggled to stand up but his legs felt like lead ballast and suddenly everything was spinning – the man, the boat, the sun, the sky – and he fell helplessly into oblivion.

Chapter 36

'GO HOME.' IT was more than a suggestion. Craig Dalziel had come into Sid Khan's office at seven a.m. to find him slouched forward on his desk, his head in his hands, his eyes red-rimmed, testimony to an almost sleepless night. The news that Luke Carlton had been kidnapped, most likely by the same cartel that the Service was working to dismantle, then taken to one of the most violent towns in Colombia, had left him drained. This was his mission, his alone: he had sent Luke there and now the buck stopped with him. There was no place in Vauxhall Cross today for his usual cheerful bonhomie: people would expect him to pull out every stop to save Luke. But there was a limit to how effectively someone could operate on almost no sleep and Khan had reached his.

'I'm going, I'm going,' he replied, making a half-hearted attempt to tidy away the papers on his desk. 'But before I head home, something's bothering me here.'

Dalziel let out a snort. 'That's putting it mildly! This whole thing has turned to a bag of shite. I won't even tell you how many agents we've had to pull out of that country since we lost Benton.'

'I know, I know,' said Khan, holding up a hand defensively. 'What I meant was, something doesn't make sense here.'

'Which is?'

'That phone call the narcos made to Carlton's girlfriend, Elise. Putting him on the line while they beat the crap out of him. I mean, why take the risk? Now we know they've got him, and they must know we'll stop at nothing to get him back.'

Dalziel sucked in his cheeks and pursed his lips. It was an odd habit but it gave him time to compose what he was going to say. 'Look, Sid, we've both come up against some highly unpleasant people in this business. In Agent Handling it still comes down, as it always has, to persuading some very brave people to do very dangerous things on our behalf, right?'

'Sure, but where are you going with this?'

'All the reports I've read from Bogotá station suggest that these narcos are about the worst you can imagine. They're sadists. They kill people slowly for fun. You said it yourself, they'll be torturing our man for information, then do it just for kicks. Twisting the knife into his girlfriend is part of the same deal. It's what they do.'

For several seconds the two men stood there without speaking, consumed by their own dark thoughts. Then Dalziel spoke briskly. 'Right. You need to go home and get some sleep. Ask someone to sort you a car – you're in no fit state to drive. I'll call you if we get a breakthrough.'

'Cheers, Craig. Appreciate it. Where's C today? Is he up to speed on all this?'

'He's in Brussels at NIS, the NATO Intelligence

Summit, remember? Mullens is with him and taking calls if you need to get hold of him.'

The Chief of MI6 was listening through headphones to interminable speeches from various Baltic intelligence chiefs about Russian covert activity along their borders. It was late in the afternoon, soon after they had all come back from the tea break, when Mullens, his PA, tapped him on the arm and motioned for him to follow him out of the conference chamber.

'C, it's Clements,' Mullens said, as soon as they were in the corridor. 'Our acting head of station in Bogotá. Says it's urgent.' He handed his phone to the Chief.

'Any news?'

'They've found Carlton,' said the voice down the line. 'He's alive.'

The Chief leaned against the corridor wall and breathed a sigh of relief. With his free hand he massaged his temples. 'Go on,' he said.

'The Colombian coastguard found him drifting just south of the Panamanian border. Seems he hijacked some local's fishing boat to get away from the narcos. He's been knocked about a bit, needs a thorough medical, but he's in one piece. They're flying him up here to Bogotá now for the debrief, and then we'll get him on the first plane home.'

'Thank Christ for that,' said the Chief. 'Is that chap from Legal still with you?'

'John Friend? Yes.'

'Tell him he's to stick to Carlton like glue the moment he reaches Bogotá. He's not to let him out of his sight, d'you hear? And I want a word with him when he gets back.'

Chapter 37

MOTORCYCLE OUTRIDERS. NICE touch, thought Luke. The Colombian security people were taking no chances. In a convoy of four they swept down the leafy avenue of gum trees and into the courtyard of the *finca*, the discreet farmhouse north of Bogotá that served as MI6's Colombia station. Several people offered to help him out of the car but he waved them away.

'I'm fine, honestly.' But they all saw him wince as he put his weight on his right foot. One of the Colombian intelligence men from ANIC whispered something to a policeman. He hurried away, returning moments later with a large hospital wheelchair.

'Para usted, Señor Carlton. Por favor . . .'

'Seriously?' said Luke, looking from the wheelchair to the circle of pitying faces. Could he really not make it from the car to the front door by himself? He made an effort to straighten up. He could do this. 'No, thanks,' he told them. 'I'll manage.'

He hobbled slowly to the door of the main office, trying not to show the pain he was in from the wound in his foot. Then he stopped and grinned. 'John!'

There in the doorway stood the lawyer. Luke hadn't thought he would be happy to see him but today, after all he had been through, he was. Now John Friend crossed the courtyard to greet him. There was a dab of blood on his collar, Luke noticed, where he had probably nicked himself shaving. 'Come on, you old bastard,' he said. 'Give me a hug.' The two men embraced awkwardly, Luke finding he was doing all the back-patting. The Colombians looked on approvingly.

'My word, you've been through the mill,' said Friend, stepping back to take a good look at his colleague. And Luke was quite a sight: there was a livid purple bruise beneath his eye where they had hit him hard soon after his capture. His face was scorched with sunburn from the boat, his hair matted and unwashed, he had a few days' growth of beard and he smelt appalling.

'Let's get you cleaned up,' Friend said. 'The doc will need to check you over and there's a heap of stuff Khan wants me to go through with you but that can wait. D'you fancy a fry-up? Carmen here can do you some bacon and eggs. I believe we've even got some baked beans in the kitchen.'

'Right now, I can think of nothing better on earth. Lead me to it!'

Chapter 38

'YOU'RE PUTTING ME on the spot here,' said Sid Khan. 'Look, no one's more relieved than I am that he's alive, but I just can't do what you're suggesting. Not today, not now.'

Angela stood in the doorway of his office on the fourth floor at Vauxhall Cross, one hand on her hip, and regarded him coolly. The head of Counter-terrorism was wearing a suit and tie again today, she noticed. Must be a reason for that. 'I'm just saying it would be a good idea if you met him off his flight, that's all,' she said. 'After all he's been through. I mean, it was you who sent him. And Luke was progressing well on my team. He'd had some successes already and his probation was nearly up. I think he'll make a first-class case officer in time – that's if we haven't put him off by now. As his line manager, I'm obviously going to the airport, and we're taking his other half along, plus the family liaison officer. The Met can keep any press away.'

Khan fidgeted with his pen. He seemed to be only half listening. 'We're going to have to agree to disagree on a few things here, Angela. As I say, no one in this building is more relieved than I am to see Carlton come back in one piece. I don't have to tell you that.'

And yet you just have, twice, she thought. 'But he went completely off the grid for several days. He took it on himself to set off on an unsanctioned operation that ended up with ten Colombian policemen killed—'

'He was betrayed, though, wasn't he?' she interrupted. 'As I understand it, the local police chief the Colombians assigned him to work with turned out to be playing for the other side. That's hardly Luke's fault!'

'That's by the by,' said Khan. 'He'll have to face an internal inquiry when he's well enough to come in. Meanwhile . . .' Sid Khan pushed back his chair from his desk, rose heavily to his feet and buttoned up his jacket '. . . we still have a potentially serious CT situation building here and I've been asked to chair a COBRA meeting in Whitehall in less than an hour.' That would explain the suit, thought Angela. She had never seen him like that before, all self-important and formal. It was not like the Khan she knew at all.

Then, as if he had read her mind, Khan relaxed a little and let his shoulders slump. 'I'm sorry,' he told her. 'I don't mean to come over all official – it's not my style, as you know. But I'm under a lot of pressure here and I feel like I haven't slept in weeks. That last report Carlton sent after debriefing our agent, Synapse, has set a lot of hares racing, I can tell you.'

'You'll have to remind me which report that was,' said Angela. 'I've been rather focused on whether or not he'd survive getting kidnapped.'

'The transcript's right here,' replied Khan, picking up a thin file from his desk and passing it to her. 'Have a look on page two. Carlton transcribed the exact words the agent told him. We've marked it up in bold.'

Angela opened the file and read:

It seems they want to punish your country for all the arrests and confiscations, the millions you have cost them. [I think] they are buying in some kind of unusual weapon. They say it is to teach [you British] a lesson. And they say it will travel by sea. This is what Señor Benton was working on, and this is what he died for.

TRANSCRIPT OF AGENT SYNAPSE
DEBRIEF, TUMACO, COLOMBIA

The colour had drained from Angela's face. 'I hadn't seen this,' she said.

'Well, you have now,' Khan replied. 'I'd best be getting to COBRA.'

Chapter 39

AT THREE IN the afternoon, as Luke's flight descended on its final approach to Heathrow, Sid Khan sat at the head of a rectangular table in a windowless wood-panelled room. He was not alone. Of the twenty-two seats around the table, nearly all were occupied today, many by people he knew, with whom he had had dealings in the twenty months since he had taken up the reins as director of Counter-terrorism at MI6. As the room settled down to business, Khan nodded as he recognized them. There was Andrew Crowthorn, his opposite number at MI5, the domestic Security Service; next to him was a senior policeman, Andy Grimshaw, who ran SO15, the Met's Counter-terrorism Command; then some suit from the Home Office, whose name he could never remember. He spotted Maria Stanikowski, the CIA representative from the US Embassy, dressed in a dark suit and crisp white shirt, and they exchanged rather exaggerated bows. Khan liked her: she always spoke her mind and got straight to the point. There were also a few military types he didn't know, so he glanced quickly at his list, the crib sheet of attendees printed up and handed to him by the Cabinet Office just minutes earlier. Royal Navy . . . more Royal Navy . . . Special Forces . . . He read down the list, pausing to look at 'the exotics', as he thought of them, the science brains from the Atomic Weapons Establishment at Aldermaston in Berkshire, then the Defence Science and Technology people from Porton Down in Wiltshire.

They were in a basement beneath the pavements of Whitehall and Khan was about to preside over a session of COBRA, the acronym coined by the media for Cabinet Office Briefing Rooms, where a committee meets whenever the government is facing a national emergency. Ebola, hostage situations in Nairobi and Algeria, and a host of other threats to Britain's security had all triggered COBRA meetings in their time. But this was different. Those had been known threats that had triggered a clear, calibrated response. Here they were dealing with something unquantifiable, so a whole range of frightening scenarios had to be planned for.

'Right.' Khan stood up. 'Thank you for being here promptly. Before we start, can I just check we've got the live feed from Bogotá station?'

'Coming online now,' replied one of the tech operators, from just behind Khan's chair.

At the other end of the table a large TV screen took up the whole of the wall, divided up into eight separate images. Some were blank, some were maps, but in the top left-hand corner a man's face flickered into view. It was Clements, acting head of MI6's Bogotá station since Benton's death. His pale, pinched face was rather too close to the camera and he was wearing a pair of horn-rimmed spectacles that gave him an owlish, professorial air.

'Good,' said Khan. 'Now, I'm going to be brutally honest and tell you exactly what we know and what we don't.' Every head in the room was turned towards him.

'We have a high level of confidence that an organized criminal network in South America is trying to smuggle an unconventional weapon into this country by sea.' It did not escape anyone's notice that he avoided using the toxic term 'WMD'. It had taken ten years and two chiefs for MI6 to move on from the fiasco of those shaky intelligence assessments about Saddam Hussein's mythical weapons of mass destruction.

'We have some handle,' continued Khan, 'on who is behind this and why they are doing it. It's one of the Colombian drug cartels. But . . .' he looked around the table '. . . we do not, as yet, know what this weapon is, where they are planning to bring it ashore or what the intended target is.'

'Bloody brilliant,' sneered Andy Grimshaw, under his breath.

'If I could ask you all to look at the screen,' he went on, 'I'm going to get our man in Bogotá to update us on what we know about this particular cartel.'

Clements's face suddenly filled the entire wall. One or two people round the table flinched as his bookish features jumped out towards them. His lips were moving but no sound was coming out.

'Tech?' called Khan.

'Sorry, sir. We seem to be having a problem with the audio but we're working on it.'

Clements was in full flow now, apparently speaking with passion, but not a word could be heard in London. Khan motioned to the techie at the console and at the click of a button Clements's face was demoted back to its place at the top left of the screen.

'OK, moving on,' said Khan. 'As you would expect, my Service has been working closely with Counter-proliferation at the FCO and we're pooling our efforts with Aldermaston and Porton Down. We've also made discreet enquiries with the UN's International Atomic Energy Agency. Our assessment is that the cartel does not possess a thermonuclear device.'

Several pairs of shoulders around the table visibly relaxed.

'But that still leaves the chemical, biological, radiological and explosives strands of the whole CBRNE piece,' continued Khan. 'Until we know what we're dealing with, my Service has briefed the Prime Minister that we need to prepare for every eventuality. Our American friends,' he gestured towards the woman from the CIA, 'have been very helpful with extra satellite coverage over the Atlantic, while both Cheltenham and Fort Meade are hoovering up anything they can catch in the cybersphere. But so far there's not a great deal to go on. These people in Colombia appear to have gone to some lengths not to leave a digital trail.'

Khan rested his hands on the surface of the polished table. 'Now, I mentioned at the start that we think this weapon is coming in by sea. That's from a single, trusted source, but we have to be open to the possibility they could change their plans at short notice. Right now this makes it a maritime problem. So I'm going to ask . . .' Khan stopped to look down at his list of attendees '. . . I'm going to ask Rear Admiral Paul Maddox from the Royal Navy to give us his assessment. Over to you, Admiral.' Khan sat down heavily, took out a handkerchief and wiped his forehead as the naval officer walked briskly to the far end of the briefing room and stood by the screen.

A tall man with jet-black hair, Maddox was in uniform, his two-star rank displayed by the thick gold braid around his cuffs and a further thin one with a curl insignia. He picked up the remote control, and a map of the Atlantic filled the screen. He turned to address the room.

'Right, ladies and gents. This will take about ten minutes of your time so bear with me. I'm going to cover routes, means of delivery and counter-measures.' Maddox took what looked like a black fountain pen from his jacket pocket and flicked a switch, directing a thin green laser beam at the map. 'Colombia is down here on the bottom left of the screen. There are three container sea ports that could act as a point of departure, here, here and here.' He pointed the laser pen at the cities of Barranquilla, Santa Marta and Buenaventura. 'Anything leaving from the Pacific coast would have to transit the Panama Canal, which takes several days longer and incurs additional searches, so we think that's less likely.'

'Excuse my interrupting,' said a voice from the other end of the room. It was Maria Stanikowski. Maddox did not look like the sort of person used to being cut off in mid-flow but he let her speak. 'Please,' he said, 'go ahead.'

'How do we know they're transporting it by container?' she asked. 'The DEA have all those terminals under surveillance. Wouldn't they think of something a little more subtle?'

If Maddox was irritated by her interruption, he took care not to show it. 'You are absolutely correct,' he replied. 'I was coming to that. There are smaller vessels leaving a number of other ports every day, not all of them capable of making the Atlantic crossing. And then there are the mini-subs – the miniature submarines the drug cartels use to ferry their product up the coast to Mexico and the Caribbean. They're an integral part of their smuggling operations and they can launch from pretty much anywhere along the coast that's hidden by undergrowth. But let's be clear here. These are basic jerry-built sardine cans. They don't have the range or the stability to cross the Atlantic.'

'Which means?' It was the CIA woman once again.

'Which means,' continued Maddox patiently, 'that we are most likely searching for a small to medium-sized cargo vessel coming in from the south-west. Its destination need not necessarily be a UK port. It could be Antwerp, Rotterdam, Le Havre. We have to keep an open mind here. But the bottom line is, we must assume that whatever device is onboard that vessel, it's on its way to us right at this moment.' He let that sink in.

Khan cleared his throat. 'Thanks for that, Admiral. If you would be so good as to tell us what measures we can have in place to intercept it?'

'Absolutely,' said Maddox, putting down the laser pen and walking back to the table. 'In an ideal world we would set up a naval screen on the hundred-fathom line just west of the English Channel to stop and search every vessel coming into our waters. But that's just not practical. There are tens of thousands of ships making the Atlantic crossing every year, hundreds at any one time. Even if we had the means to do it, the effect on trade would be catastrophic. So this has to be intelligence-led. We'll go with everything the agencies can give us.' He looked pointedly at Khan. 'We're after deadweight, cargo, port of origin, anything that narrows it down.'

'Sorry to butt in, but can I just get something straight?' This time it was a senior Army officer, Major General 'Chip' Cutler, the director of Special Forces. Unlike Maddox, he was in civilian dress, wearing a well-cut suit and silk tie from Jermyn Street. 'If the vessel is IDed at sea, we're going for a maritime interdiction, right?'

Maddox was already nodding, but Khan answered the question. 'As you know, General, that would be a decision for the PM or the Secretary of State to make on the day. But that would be the most likely scenario, yes.'

'Sounds like Groundhog Day, then,' said Cutler drily.

'Excuse me?' said Khan.

'Groundhog Day. History repeating itself. Remember the MV *Nisha* back in 2001?'

There were a few murmurs of recognition from the older people around the table, but Khan was silent. In 2001, as an applied mathematician at GCHQ in Cheltenham, he had been so knee-deep in codes and algorithms that he must have missed that moment.

'The MV *Nisha*,' explained the director of Special Forces, 'was a freighter coming from Mauritius and heading for these shores. There was an intelligence tip-off that she might be carrying terrorist material hidden inside her cargo. So there was an interdiction at sea, off the Sussex coast, I believe. SF teams assaulted from RIBs – rigid inflatable boats – and fast-roped down from helicopters. They found nothing.

But all the protocols are in place to do it again if we need to.'

'I have a question.' This time it was Andy Grimshaw. Khan noticed to his surprise that he appeared to be chewing gum. 'We want to stop this thing out at sea before it gets here, right? How many planes have we got to do the search sweeps off the coast?'

Khan narrowed his eyes a fraction. He could not be sure if Grimshaw was being mischievous or genuinely curious. Either way, there was a short, embarrassed silence before Rear Admiral Maddox, still standing, gave an abrupt answer. 'None. The UK scrapped its maritime patrol aircraft, the *Nimrod*, some years ago.'

'Genius,' muttered the policeman.

'There are other options,' replied Maddox sternly. 'There are helicopters out of the naval air station at Culdrose in Cornwall with horizon-scanning radar, as well as sonar, and they can fly eight-hour sorties at a time. Weather permitting, of course. And we have ScanEagle drones that can fly off one of our frigates in the Channel.'

'So when does all this get started?' asked a woman from Number 10. To Khan, who was far from being the oldest person in the room, she looked impossibly young. Her auburn hair was scraped back into a ponytail, a pink blouse showing beneath a tweed jacket of muted green. 'And when do we tell the public?' she added.

'The answer to your first question,' replied Maddox, 'is that it's already begun. The first Sea Kings took off on patrol from Cornwall this morning.'

'And I can address your other question,' said Khan, standing up and reasserting his role as chairman.

'We're not telling the public anything,' he said. 'At least, not yet. The last thing we want is some tabloid-generated panic when we don't even know what we're dealing with. Once we've got a better grip on the situation we can consider putting out an official line through the Cabinet Office. But until then, can I remind everyone present that what we have just discussed is classified Strap Two-level secret. Absolutely nothing you have heard today is to leave this room.'

Chapter 40

'IT'S CALLED BELLE de Provence,' whispered Elise. 'It's lavender oil from the South of France.' Luke, his upper body propped on pillows, his legs extended along the bed, found himself caught between pleasure and pain. After all he had been through in Colombia, Elise's touch was soothing as her hands worked gently on his legs, massaging the scented oil into his muscular calves, her eyes never leaving his. But when she turned her attention to his injured foot he winced with pain. It was still too raw to touch. There was a vivid purple mark, like a bullseye, on the upper arch of his right foot where García's thugs had taken the electric drill to him. He had given them the passcode to his mobile phone pretty quickly after that, especially when they had threatened to start on his hands.

Now he was going to put all that behind him. Since landing back at Heathrow he had been pumped full of antibiotics and a thorough two-hour medical had found no lasting physical damage. After an initial debrief the Service had told him to take as much time off as he needed to recuperate from his ordeal so he and Elise were enjoying something akin to an unofficial honeymoon. Both naked on the bed, their bodies still steaming from a hot bubble bath, they had lost all track of time.

For Elise, the days since Luke had returned had been uninterrupted bliss. She wanted never to let him out of her sight again. True, at times he seemed a little withdrawn, a little preoccupied, as if something was weighing heavily on his mind, but she put it down to his ordeal and didn't press him. He could tell her everything in his own time and that was fine by her. Now she leaned over his legs, caressing them with her hair as it fell loose, and began working her way up them, planting kisses higher and higher. Suddenly his whole body tensed and she stopped, fearful she might have touched some damaged nerve. But it was something else: his work mobile was buzzing. Elise's eyes said, 'Please, not now, just ignore it,' but Luke reached over and grabbed it from the bedside table, looked at the number and sucked in his cheeks. Covering the phone with his hand, he whispered, 'Sorry, got to take this,' and kissed her softly on the lips before rolling off the bed and carrying the phone into the next room. He was no longer hobbling.

'Luke?' said the voice at the other end. 'It's Angela.' And there it was, *bang*, just like that: the 'honeymoon' was over. Luke perched himself on the arm of the sofa in the sitting room, recognizing the subdued office voices he could hear in the background. 'Look, I'm sorry to ring you,' continued his boss, 'I know you're officially on medical leave, but I thought you'd want to know—'

'Know what?' snapped Luke, suddenly impatient for news. 'Don't keep me in suspense! Please tell me you've found the weapon.' Serene as his reunion with

Elise had been, he hadn't been able to get the thought of the unknown device out of his head. While Elise had slept peacefully beside him, he had lain awake at three in the morning, racking his brain for what it might be and how they could track it down before it was too late.

'No,' replied Angela. 'Let's not get ahead of ourselves. We think it's still at large somewhere out in the Atlantic, but things are moving very fast on many levels. Washington are redirecting a lot of their assets over the Channel approaches. Fleet HQ at Northwood are deploying a destroyer to the Scilly Isles, HMS *Dauntless*, I think. They've sent one of our nuclear subs to patrol off the entrance to the Bristol Channel. And . . .'

'And?' Luke dug his fingernails into the soft material of the sofa as he waited for Angela to reveal why she was phoning.

'You'll not be surprised to hear that your old mob from Poole are deploying,' she said. 'They're sending the Maritime Counter-terrorism Squadron. They're setting up a forward base in Cornwall, ready to move the moment we can identify the incoming vessel. Some place called Culdrose. I expect you know it? They're giving them a corner of the base cordoned off from everyone else. They've got Merlins and Sea Kings down there. Director Special Forces has tasked the SBS to take down the ship and secure the weapon as soon as we have a lead. It's crunch time, Luke.'

'And you're telling me this because?'

'Well, you are still on the payroll and—'

'Angela, I want in, you know I do. My foot is fine now.' It was a lie and she probably knew it. Even as he spoke he felt a faint throb emanating from it, but it was nothing he couldn't handle. 'I'm good to go,' he told her. 'I'm seeing this one through.'

'I thought that might be the case. But are you absolutely certain you're up to it? You've just been through much worse than most of our agents ever risk if they get caught.'

Luke hesitated. He was wondering how Elise would take it. Not well, he suspected.

'I'm in,' he said.

'Good. Because I've already gone ahead and nominated you as Service liaison on the Poole team. I had a bit of pushback from HR. They want you to spend all next week sitting in a country house in Buckinghamshire going through some "situational re-evaluation programme", but I've batted that away. You need to be ready in an hour. They'll pick you up from Battersea heliport and fly you down to Culdrose by Chinook. Best pack for a few days. This could take a while.'

Luke walked back into the bedroom, his bare feet noiseless on the thick carpet. Elise was sitting up in bed, a towel around her shoulders, staring silently at the bookcase. She had heard most of his side of the conversation and now there was nothing more to be said. The moment between them had passed.

Chapter 41

LIFE FOR CECILIA Cruz had not turned out the way she'd planned. Her husband had brought her from Colombia to London after the birth of their first child and she still crossed herself each time she thought of him, God rest his soul. A merchant sailor from Barranquilla, he had showered her with presents. She'd never asked where he got the money to pay for them and he'd never offered to tell her. Cecilia had, at first, found it hard to adapt to life in Britain, with its dull grey winters that sometimes seemed identical to its summers. She missed the colour, the heat, the vibrant passion of her Caribbean village just west of Cartagena. Somehow, she had ended up trading *fiesta*, friends and family for a tiny one-bedroom basement flat in Ealing. When her husband's drinking and his tempers became so bad that his employers, the shipping agents, fired him, the hard truth had dawned on her. From now on she would have to be the breadwinner. Cecilia found herself a job as a cleaner, working double shifts and doing her best to raise her boy. When the cirrhosis eventually got the better of her husband she buried him just before her fortieth birthday.

It was in the week after the funeral that there was a ring at the doorbell.

'I am a friend of your late husband,' said the man in the corridor outside. 'Well, more of a business contact from the old days, you could say. May I come in?' Cecilia looked him up and down with suspicion. Nobody came to their flat, except to try to sell her something or pester her for overdue rent. But this man was different. His shoes were polished, his tie was shiny, his hair slicked back in the way the *muchachos* used to wear it back home. What did she have to lose?

'I understand,' said the man, sitting at the kitchen table and resting his hands on his lap, 'that you are in the cleaning business, no?'

'I am a cleaner, yes.'

'These must be difficult times for you, with your husband gone and . . .' He looked down at the cracked lino where her son was playing with a cheap toy. There was a ragged hole in the elbow of his sweater. 'So I have a proposition for you,' he said brightly. 'Because we Colombianos must do all we can to help each other, yes? There is a job starting on Monday at an establishment just west of here. It pays good money.'

'How much?' she demanded.

'Let me ask how much you take home now, Señora?'

'Nine pounds fifty an hour. And I pay my taxes.'

'How does twenty-five pounds an hour sound? Cash in hand.'

Cecilia's eyes narrowed. Was this a trick? A cruel joke? For a moment an absurd thought flashed through her mind, but she dismissed it at once. She was much too old now for anyone to want to put her on the game. There had to be a catch, so what was it?

'Twenty-five pounds an hour is a lot,' she replied.

'What do you want from me?' She was no fool: she knew from bitter experience that if something seems too good to be true it usually is.

'Only your cleaning skills, Señora. We hear you are a perfectionist!' He flashed her a crooked smile. She did not believe him for a second, but twenty-five pounds an hour? She could hardly afford to say no. Perhaps it was best not to ask too many questions.

'*Bueno.* The job is at Northwood, a place just outside London. You will be part of a contract team that cleans the premises. It is some sort of government headquarters. They call it PJHQ for short, but that is not important. Now, I have arranged a day of extra training for you tomorrow and—'

'I don't need training,' she interrupted. 'I am a good cleaner.' Really, this was an insult.

'Ah, but you do,' insisted the man. 'This is special training. Tell me, Señora, do you own a laptop?'

Cecilia shook her head. They had computers at her son's school, but she had never owned one, never needed one. What use would she have for it?

'No? I thought not,' he said slowly, with that sickly smile. 'But that is no problem, no problem at all. We will give you one and teach you everything you need to know. And enjoy it! After all, it's free!' This left her more confused than ever. What did she need a laptop computer for if she was to clean some government office? This made no sense. But the man was standing up now, buttoning his jacket with an air of finality and handing her a piece of paper with an address on it.

'If you would be so good, Señora, to present yourself at this address tomorrow morning at nine, they will take care of everything. And here, in this envelope, is a little something to help with expenses. Maybe treat yourself to a cab on the first day.'

In the silence left by his departure Cecilia Cruz wondered what she was letting herself in for. She felt as if she were being herded onto a bus going somewhere she didn't want to go. She might not own a laptop but she wasn't stupid. It was obvious something distinctly fishy was going on. The envelope lay open on the kitchen table, with crisp twenty-pound notes spilling out. This was rather more than a cab fare.

She moved to the gas cooker, all scratched and stained with rust, and put the kettle on to boil. Then she sat down with a sigh. Her options were not good, that was clear. She was on her own now, although in truth she had been on her own for quite some time. What chance did she have of finding another husband? And these people, these 'business associates' of her late husband, they were offering her a lifeline. Cecilia Cruz poured herself a cup of milky English Breakfast tea and glanced at her son, Emilio, still playing with the same toy on the cracked lino. Yes, she decided, she would accept the offer. She would take it with both hands and she would play their games, if only for the sake of beloved Emilio.

Chapter 42

NUMBER 94 ASHBURNHAM Gardens was not at all what she was expecting. Cecilia Cruz had had little difficulty in making her way to the address she had been given in Westbourne Grove but somehow she had imagined something more down to earth, more like the basement flat she and Emilio shared. Now she stood on the front porch, clutching the crumpled piece of paper she had been given, looking up at an elegant white façade with black wrought-iron balconies and tidy windowboxes. She squinted at the list of names beside the door buzzers. Standish. Duckworth. Trenton-Smith. This was a fancy neighbourhood, no question, but which button should she press? As her finger hovered uncertainly, the front door opened and a woman stepped out to greet her. She was tall, expensively dressed in a silk blouse, jacket and pencil skirt, and she exuded an air of confidence that Cecilia could only envy. One thing struck her immediately: this woman smelt of money.

'Señora Cruz? *Bienvenida!* I am Ana María. Please, come in. Here, let me take your coat.' She addressed her in Spanish. 'What can I get you to drink?' Cecilia wasn't used to this – the people she cleaned for barely acknowledged her presence. But she soon got over her surprise because there was something warm and welcoming about the elegant woman with the long, lustrous hair and beautifully manicured nails now leading her into the living room. Her lispy Castilian accent revealed her to be Spanish rather than South American, and she moved around her apartment so gracefully.

'I understand,' the woman said gently, motioning her to sit down on a soft sofa, 'that you are new to computers.' Cecilia didn't answer at first: she was too busy studying the bookcase set into the wall beside her. It held all the books she had ever wanted to read: *One Hundred Years of Solitude, Love in the Time of Cholera* and *Chronicle of a Death Foretold*, all by the Colombian writer Gabriel García Márquez.

'Señora Cruz?' the woman prompted her, coaxing her out of her reverie.

'Perdón,' Cecilia apologized, turning back towards her and giving the lady her full attention.

'Don't worry,' said Ana María. 'We have all day and will not be disturbed. By the time you leave here you will know everything you need to know.'

Everything I need to know for what?

Together they worked through the morning, with Ana María patiently explaining and encouraging, at times holding her own hand over the cleaner's to move the mouse and the cursor on the screen. By midday Cecilia Cruz had sent her first email and by lunchtime she was ecstatic: with Ana María's help she had found her old village on the Caribbean coast on Google Earth. Laughing, she zoomed in and out of the page, watching the pixels forming and re-forming, the landmarks of her childhood swimming up into focus.

At lunchtime they broke off for tortillas, freshly made and warm from the oven. Cecilia was enjoying herself now and they talked over the clatter of plates and cutlery, comparing childhoods, hers in a poor *barrio* in Colombia, Ana María's in a leafy suburb of Madrid. Of course, Cecilia was itching to ask how she knew someone as shifty as that slick *muchacho* who had set up their day – they seemed like creatures from two different planets – but she thought better of it.

Lunch over, Ana María poured them each a cup of *café tinto* and led her into another room. On the table was another, larger computer, and beside it a printer. 'This one is a desktop,' she said lightly, 'but of course you know that. You must have cleaned around them so many times.' She stepped a few paces back from Cecilia and looked her up and down, as if admiring a work of art.

'I am pleased to tell you, Cecilia – may I call you Cecilia? – you have made such good progress this morning that we can now move on to the next stage. This is your advanced lesson. You are fast becoming an expert!' Cecilia watched her lovely features crease into a smile, showing perfect teeth. She felt a sudden burst of pride: she had discovered a talent she'd never known she had. Now, maybe, she could escape her life of poverty. Her earlier misgivings were forgotten.

Ana María picked up a small black rectangular object, about the size of her little finger, and held it out for her. 'You will recognize this, I expect? It is a USB stick, a memory stick, no?' Cecilia nodded uncertainly. It was true that she had seen them a few times in the offices she cleaned, sticking out of computer drives under the desks where someone had left one, but she had never given them much thought.

'*Sí, claro*,' she replied, 'but I have never thought to ask what they are for.'

'Ah, you need not concern yourself with that,' said Ana María, in that soothing tone. 'Instead, I am going to show you how to attach it to the printer. Like this. Here, you try.' Cecilia picked up the USB stick and slotted it into the socket. '*Bien hecho!* Well done!' exclaimed her coach. 'You see? Didn't I tell you you would soon be a natural with technology? Now, I want you to pick up that object there, the other one, that's right. It's called a three-into-one connector. I want you to fit that one into the printer, go on – yes, that's perfect – and then I want you to fit the USB stick into that. Can you do that for me? *Mira!* You did it! Please practise taking them out and putting them back in while I go next door for a moment.'

When Ana María came back into the room she was carrying a sheaf of papers, which she now spread out on the table. Cecilia could see they were diagrams.

'Now,' she said, her voice dropping lower, suddenly more serious. 'This is a layout of the office you will be cleaning tomorrow night.' Tomorrow night? Cecilia's brow furrowed briefly; the man had not mentioned anything about working a night shift. Could she leave Emilio alone in the flat while she worked? This was a worry and she was only half listening as Ana María continued.

'The office will be on the third floor of this building here.' She laid a finger, the nail varnished, on a schematic layout of Permanent Joint Headquarters. 'It is at Northwood, the government place. Please, Cecilia, I need your full attention. The door is marked here, the windows are here . . . and over in this corner is the desk of someone very important to us. To me. You understand?'

Cecilia nodded, saying nothing. Here it came. The catch. Well, it was not as if she hadn't been expecting it.

'I want you, Cecilia, to take these two objects we have here and attach them to the printer in the corner. Exactly like you have been doing here today. *No es nada complicado.* Nothing complicated. But this is the important bit. Nobody, and I mean nobody, must see you do this, you understand? You are to wait until you are alone in that room and there is no one coming. And then I want you to place the waste bin in front of it, so it hides it. You follow me?' Cecilia followed her. She just didn't like the direction this was going in.

'And that's all I have to do?' she asked in a guarded tone. The warm glow she had felt all day had evaporated.

'Not quite,' said Ana María. 'You will be working night shifts for your first week – everyone has to when they start. On the second night you are to remove both devices from the printer and hide them somewhere personal.' Ana María glanced down meaningfully at the Colombian woman's ample bosom. 'I'm sure you will think of a hiding place. When the night shift is over and you leave Northwood in the morning you are to turn right out of the gate and walk down the hill through the woods towards the station. At the first layby on the right a man will be waiting for you in a car – you know him. He has come to your home. You will give him the two devices and he will give you a lift to the station. You will tell no one about any of this.'

Cecilia stepped back a pace from the table and looked at the woman she had thought was becoming her friend. A hard edge had crept into Ana María's voice and she, Cecilia, was deeply uneasy about what she was being asked to do. Of course, she knew that her late husband had been mixed up in all sorts of business but that was his concern, not hers. Her record was squeaky clean. And this smelt like trouble. 'I'm not sure,' she said. 'Can I think it over?'

'No,' said Ana María flatly. 'There is no time.'

'I think maybe I have made a mistake in coming here today,' said Cecilia, gathering up her coat and preparing to leave. 'Can we just forget this? I will tell no one, you have my word.'

Ana María stepped to one side, neatly blocking her exit. She was nearly a head and shoulders taller than Cecilia and now she looked down at her, staring hard at the Colombian cleaner's face. Gone were the soft, coaxing tones of this morning as Ana María said, 'Of course, you can refuse, but I wouldn't advise it.' She pronounced each syllable carefully. As she did so she pulled out a photograph from inside her jacket. 'I believe this is your son, Emilio?'

Cecilia staggered backwards, both her hands going to her mouth to stifle a cry. 'Where did you get that?' she demanded. 'Leave my boy out of this. What could you want with him?'

Ana María gripped Cecilia firmly by the shoulders and held her gaze. 'I want there to be no misunderstanding between us. If you refuse this small task, I promise you will never see your son again. Is that clear enough?'

Chapter 43

THE CHINOOK IS a giant twin-rotored beast of a helicopter, a metallic pterodactyl of the skies. At thirty metres long and able to carry up to forty fully laden troops, it has been the workhorse of Western military operations since as far back as the Vietnam War. Naturally, Luke had spent more of his life in them than he cared to think, strapped into a canvas bucket seat, his helmet strap chafing his jaw, exchanging glances with fellow Marines as they helicoptered into some sandblasted battlespace in Iraq or Afghanistan. Today, though, was an airborne cab ride to the West Country, and he felt a familiar wave of exhilaration as he ducked his head to meet the blast of downdraught from the rotors and strode quickly up the rear ramp, a day sack of essentials slung over his shoulder. He was alive, he was back in play, and he was heading for the action.

Curiously, the throbbing pain in his foot, such an unwelcome feature of the last few days, had subsided, pushed into second place by the adrenalin that flowed through his veins. He felt a pang of guilt at the lengths to which Elise had gone to speed his recovery. In return he had abandoned her again, slipping out of the door just forty minutes after that phone call from Angela. Still, it was not as if he was going back to South America, he had reassured her, just a quick trip to Cornwall, should be back in a few days. Hopefully.

The loadmaster gave Luke the thumbs-up, indicated where he should sit with a vertical slicing motion of the hand, and spoke into his helmet-mike. The ramp went up and seconds later they were lifting clear of Battersea heliport, dropping the nose, angling the tail and powering westwards along the Thames, rising quickly over the traffic jams on Putney Bridge and heading for the checkpoint on the map that RAF helicopter pilots call Hotel Two. At three hundred metres above the M3, the pilot spoke briefly into his headset to welcome Luke aboard, and in no time at all they were over the south coast, heading out to sea, then west for Falmouth and the nearby Royal Naval Air Station at Culdrose.

They landed into the wind a short distance from a giant green hangar. As the pilot powered down, Luke caught sight of a short, broad-chested man in a camouflage smock striding forward to greet him.

Once the ramp had gone down he disembarked. 'Buster!'

'Hey, Carlton. Heard they were sending you.'

The two men shook hands, old comrades-in-arms from operational tours with the Royal Marines in Kajaki and Sangin, two of the most dangerous places to serve in Afghanistan. A fearsome operator in the field, Buster Loames had always had a certain reputation. Once, after losing a bet in a Plymouth pub on a Saturday night, he had shed his clothes and run butt-naked up Union Street before the police could catch him. It had nearly cost him his commission. Well, those antics were in the past now, thought Luke, as he noticed the woven crown on Buster's combat smock. 'Can't believe they've actually given you a squadron to command,' he said, as they walked away from the Chinook towards the hangar. 'Major Loames . . . It just doesn't sound right. What's the Corps coming to?'

'Easy there, Carlton, or I'll have your bedding moved into the latrines.'

Luke gave him a back-handed punch to the solar plexus. It was rock hard.

Banter over, the two men fell silent as they walked into the hangar, recent memories of Afghanistan coming fleetingly back to them. Inside, several dozen men with large chests and unruly hair were perched on the edge of green camp beds, cleaning their Diemaco assault rifles, checking the laser sights and muzzle-suppressors. An SBS assault troop preparing for an op.

A chill passed down Luke's spine as he experienced a flashback. This had been almost the exact scene in another country just over two weeks ago, at a Jungla barracks. Ten good men had died on that op, Luke the only one to walk out alive. All that training, all that experience, gone in a blaze of bullets. The thought of it haunted him.

'Care for a wet, boss?' A corporal was standing in front of him, holding out a Styrofoam cup of steaming grey liquid. Military tea. Luke knew it would taste like dishwater but he took it anyway and thanked the man.

'We're still getting set up here, as you can see,' remarked Major Loames. 'The troop only got here this morning and we're having a few problems with the comms, but we should be good to go from tomorrow. We're currently minus one of the Fleet divers – he's on his way down from Arbroath – but otherwise we're operational.' He motioned for Luke to follow him over to a corner of the hangar, where several men were discussing a laminated map, balanced on an easel. It showed the Cornish coast and the south-western approaches to the English Channel, with the locations of various vessels and distances between them marked in purple chinagraph pencil.

'Let me introduce you to our ops officer,' said Loames, turning to a well-built figure with a squashed boxer's nose. 'Luke, this is Captain Chris Shaw. Chris, this is the bloke from London I was telling you would be joining us as liaison. He's from the dark side now, but he used to be one of us, so be nice to him. Gents, I'll leave you to it.' And Loames was gone, off to chase down a hundred and one things on his mental checklist.

The ops officer held out a giant hand to Luke, then dismissed the men he had been talking to. 'I'll see you later, guys . . . So,' he said, turning to Luke with a lopsided smile, 'good to be back?'

'Yeah, it is.'

Shaw peered closer at Luke's face, with its faint traces of purple bruising beneath the eye, the healing cuts and fast-fading South American tan. 'I won't ask where you've just been,' said Shaw, 'but it looks like you got knocked about a fair bit.'

Luke shrugged. 'You could say that.'

'Right, let's talk shop,' said Shaw, sweeping a hand over the map beside them. 'You know we're lining up for an interdiction at sea. The lads are on thirty minutes' notice to move. Question is, which vessel is our target? That's where we're hoping your people at Vauxhall Cross can enlighten us so we can get the job done and all go home. J2 intel says it's coming from the Caribbean, and Fleet reckon it's a small- to medium-sized freighter. Which means we've got every port from Merseyside all the way round the south coast and up to the Humber on standby.'

'What if it's heading for Scotland?'

'Good question, well put,' replied Shaw. 'Fleet HQ, in their wisdom, don't seem to think that's a possibility. We're focusing on a south-westerly approach. Task Force HQ have offered us a mix of helos on call – Merlins, Sea Kings and CH47s. I've put together a package that can deliver enough of our operators onto the deck to take it down and secure the cargo the moment we get the word.' Shaw dropped his voice a shade lower, even though there was enough activity going on inside the hangar to mask whatever he was going to say. 'Speaking of that, um, the boss and I would really appreciate it if you were able to give us an early heads-up on timings. Strictly on the down-low, you know.'

Luke smiled. He'd have been asking exactly the same thing if he were in Shaw's position. 'I'll see what I can do,' he replied.

Shaw looked up at the roof of the hangar as a low drumming started above them. Rain. 'That's another thing. NCI say the forecast is truly crap.'

'NCI?' All these acronyms.

'National Coastguard Initiative. It's the volunteers down at Lizard Point. They've got their own radar and their reports tend to be spot on. They're currently giving us a sea state of four to five. If it's still up that high when we get the off, it's too much for a boarding at sea – the waves will smash the lads to pieces.'

'I remember,' said Luke.

'Of course you do, sorry.' Shaw grinned. 'Whatever it is that's steaming in here across the Atlantic, it's going to have some seasick matelots onboard by now. Anyway, it'll be helos all the way for us on this one. I'm putting eight operators into each of two Sea Kings and the rest on a Chinook. That will include the medics, signallers, bomb disposal and a liaison bod from Police National Counter-terrorism. And yourself. I take it your people want you in on this one? Oh, and if you see any blokes walking on in space suits, that's the HAZMAT guys. Task Group Headquarters are taking no chances with this thing.'

'Any idea how long you're going to be standing by for, if we don't get the word in the next day or so?'

'How long's a piece of string?' said Shaw. 'It'll be a case of hurry-up-and-wait, won't it?'

For the first time since leaving London, Luke felt the pain in his foot returning. It was always the waiting before an op that got to him.

Chapter 44

AS THE CORNISH weather closed in around the Royal Naval Air Station at Culdrose and Luke went off to sort out his accommodation, his nemesis was standing before a full-size copy of his favourite painting, thousands of kilometres away on the other side of the world. Nelson García admired the work of Francisco Goya. He liked his dark, sinister colours and particularly the picture of the god Saturn devouring his son. But that wasn't his favourite. The prize went to Goya's early-nineteenth-century depiction of Spanish patriots being executed by a Napoleonic firing squad. It was a deeply unsettling picture to look at, which was exactly why García had ordered several copies to be hung in his various safe houses around Colombia. The anguished young faces of the Spanish patriots stared out, pleading for their lives as the muskets were levelled at their chests. For García, its message was explicit: there was to be no mercy for anyone who betrayed him.

'So,' he began, turning away from the Goya on the wall to address Vicente Morales, the cartel's head of information technology, 'you asked to see me in person?'

A maid, dressed in the old-fashioned Spanish style,

poured them cups of *café tinto*, bowed deferentially and backed out of the room, closing the door behind her with a soft click. It was just the three of them now, García, security chief Suárez and Morales. They sat in deep leather chairs draped with crimson embroidered shawls.

Morales met his boss's cold, cruel eyes and tried not to imagine what it would be like to disappoint this man. He shuddered to contemplate what had happened to the idiots in Buenaventura who had let the British spy escape from under their noses. A lifetime's fascination with computer coding, a half-completed degree at an obscure US university, then a fruitful career in the criminal underworld had led him to the cartel's top table. Morales cleared his throat.

'A zero-day bug, Patrón,' he said quietly, letting the words fall on uncomprehending ears.

'A what?'

'A zero-day bug. It is a computer virus that can reveal all your secrets. You count down from the first day it starts to work and everything from that moment on is compromised.'

García's thick, dark eyebrows knitted together in a frown and his face formed into an angry snarl. 'You come here today,' he shouted, 'to tell me you have let this bug into our systems?'

'No! Absolutely not, Patrón. It is the other way round! We have succeeded in planting it into our enemies' systems.'

It was as if the sun had come out from behind a cloud. The cartel boss's face melted into a leer of satisfaction. 'Go on.'

'You are familiar,' said Morales, 'with a USB stick?

A memory stick? Some people prefer to call it a flash drive.'.

Suárez had been watching the exchange in silence but now he chose to speak. 'The *patrón* has many responsibilities. He cannot be expected to get involved in petty details. Please, hurry up and get to the point.'

Morales proceeded to pick his words carefully, as if tiptoeing through a minefield, anxious to explain without appearing to patronize his boss. That would be unwise. '*Bueno* . . . We have succeeded in getting our own USB stick into the headquarters of Britain's military operations. Using this, we have introduced a zero-day bug. Think of it . . .' Morales hesitated, hunting for the appropriate simile '. . . think of it like opening a door, yes? Now that it has let us in, we can see many things.'

El Pobrecito raised those heavy eyebrows, impressed. 'And how was this possible?'

'We have a woman on the payroll, a cleaner. Her company has the contract to clean the offices at night, at a base called Northwood. It is from there that they direct all their naval operations around the world.'

'*Y entonces?* And then?'

'Our people in London showed her how to insert one into their printer. It intercepts all the messages coming from the naval people's computers. She put it in one night, the next day they come in to work, they boot up their machines and, *iya está*! All the information flows into this little device. That night she is back. She takes it out and passes it to our people. *Un trabajo bien hecho!* A job well done, I hope you would agree, Patrón?'

García shifted his weight in his leather chair, his belly flopping from one side to the other, straining against the confines of his white silk shirt. He stroked the side of his jaw, considering the IT man. Suárez stared at him too, saying nothing.

'I see,' said García at last. 'And what did you learn that can be of use to us?'

Morales reached down to retrieve the attaché case he had brought with him. He took out a thin manila envelope and passed it to his boss. 'In there, Patrón, are printouts of the latest positions of all Britain's naval vessels in the Atlantic and the English Channel. We can see exactly where they are and where they are heading.'

García flipped through the dossier and passed it to Suárez. The world of IT might largely have passed him by – he was essentially a street thug who had bullied and butchered his way to the top with a combination of animal cunning and extreme violence – but he knew the questions that mattered.

'This is all very impressive, Vicente.' The IT man relaxed visibly at these words. To be addressed by your first name by El Pobrecito was an honour afforded to only a very few. 'But is this information not already out of date?' asked García. 'Because I see a date stamp on it from yesterday. What use is this to us?'

'Ah, but that is exactly why I asked to see you, Patrón. We have a problem. We have studied the Royal Navy's movements and we think they may have identified the *Maria Esposito*. Some of their ships have altered course towards her. They are getting close to where she is heading. Dangerously close.'

García held up his hand and inclined his head towards Suárez, raising a single eyebrow. His chief of security shrugged. 'We had anticipated this,' he said quietly, 'and we have allowed for it. With your permission, Patrón, we will have to launch early.'

García was already rising to his feet. 'Do it,' he said. As he walked out of the room, passing between the two men, he patted Morales affectionately on the shoulder. *'Un trabajo bien hecho,'* he murmured, with a smile. 'A job well done.'

Chapter 45

IN HIS CRAMPED cabin on the *Maria Esposito,* Captain Hector Jiménez turned the signal over in this hand and frowned. This was undeniably bad news. So near to their destination and now this. He threw an anxious glance towards the porthole. Just as he'd thought: still lashing rain and heavy seas. Typical. A smooth passage nearly all the way across the Atlantic only to run into this storm at the last minute. But the signal from Colombia was unequivocal. It was short and to the point: 'Your position identified. Interception imminent.'

Mierda, he thought. When you're running a suspect cargo into another country it was always a fine judgement whether or not to switch off the ship's automatic identification system, which shows up its name, port of origin and disposition. Keep it on, hide in plain sight, act the innocent and hope that nobody spots what you're up to. Switch it off and you're anonymous, but you're not invisible and, of course, it shows you have something to hide. The North Koreans, he remembered, had switched off their AIS on that run from Cuba to Panama in 2013 and they'd still got pinged by the Americans with a load of useless old Soviet-era aircraft parts, hidden beneath sacks of sugar. In the view of Captain Jiménez, it was usually safest not to know what you were carrying. He was aware that somewhere down in the false hold of his ship, inside the mini-sub they had taken in off the Panamanian coast, there was probably something highly illicit. He just preferred not to know what it was.

'Señor Capitán.' The radio operator was still standing in the doorway, waiting for orders.

Captain Jiménez sighed. 'Send up the two pilots and tell the crew to prepare to launch.'

'*En serio?* They want us to launch in this weather?'

The captain was silent, thinking. This was a hell of a gamble. If they tried to launch the mini-sub now, in these heavy seas, it could easily end in disaster. They could lose the sub, and the precious cargo he was being paid so handsomely to deliver intact. Besides, in these conditions, he could not be 100 per cent certain if the covert hatch in the hull would function properly without letting in half the Atlantic. Maybe he should alter course, give the Navy the slip and wait for calmer seas before delivering their cargo. On the other hand, was he prepared to risk having a load of commandos swarming all over his ship and spending the next ten years in a British prison? It was a tough call.

'Cancel that,' he told the signals operator. 'I need more time to think about it.'

A little over fifty kilometres away, Luke was in the sauna, his body slick with sweat, his shoulder muscles aching: he had pushed himself through twenty lengths of the twenty-five-metre indoor pool. Two days he had been stuck on this naval air station, cooling his heels, waiting for the mission. He was bored with watching the operators from his former unit clean and re-clean their weapons, jog circuits round the base perimeter with thirty-kilo packs on their backs, lift weights in the gym or join in the daily boxercise weight-management classes. He had to hand it to RNAS Culdrose, there were worse places to be stuck. HMS *Seahawk*, as it also called itself, seemed to have every facility going and Luke had decided he might as well use it for a continuation of his rehab after Colombia. Twice a day he had been checking in with VX for updates, offering advice where he could, passing on the occasional snippet of info to Buster Loames so he could fine-tune his plans for taking down the ship when the call came. But time had hung heavy and they were all getting restless.

And that was when he'd got the call. It came in just before 1900 hours on his third day in Cornwall. Luke apologized to the other two people in the sauna and took it outside the door, feeling the sweat dry rapidly on his torso.

It was Sid Khan, and he sounded dead tired. 'I'm giving you the heads-up, Carlton. Just thought you ought to know.' His tone was matter-of-fact, not unfriendly, but Luke detected a definite coolness in his voice. They had yet to meet face-to-face since the bloodbath in South America. There was clearly some unfinished business still to go over, but now was not the time. Khan cut straight to the point.

'You're on,' he said. 'TGHQ will be alerting the assault commander about now. We've identified the inbound vessel. It's the MV *Maria Esposito*.' He spoke the words slowly, almost phonetically. 'Last port of call was Colón, Panama. She's got her AIS beacon switched off, the only ship for miles around to do that, a bit of a giveaway. Don't know what nasties she's got aboard her yet, but you're about to find out.' Before Luke had time to cover the phone there was a loud whoop from behind him, followed by a double splash, as two off-duty seamen dived into the pool a few metres away, their voices echoing around the indoor hall.

'What was that? Where are you?' demanded Khan.

'Still on the base,' he replied. That much was true. 'The lads are getting some final training in.'

'I see.' Khan sounded unconvinced. 'So, listen. We're throwing everything in the toolbox at this, so let's bloody well hope it's the right ship.' It was the first time Luke had ever heard him swear. 'Bogotá station has come up with some background on the ship's captain. You should be getting it shortly. He's a known player, a career cartel guy. You're going to need to get him alone in a room, lay out his options and make him spill the beans. Use your powers of persuasion – within the law, obviously. Time is against us, because once the Met and the CPS get their hands on him it could take weeks, months, and we haven't got that luxury. The PM is following this one personally. You're my eyes and ears down there, Luke, and no heroics this time. Let the SBS do the sharp stuff. It's what they're paid to do.'

Luke ended the call, snatched up his towel and was moving rapidly towards the changing rooms when a young marine caught up with him. 'Sorry to disturb you, Mr Carlton, sir,' said the lad, 'but the boss asked me to come and find you urgent, like. There's a briefing in the main hangar at nineteen thirty hours. Says you need to be there.'

Luke glanced down at his wrist. It was not his own

watch that stared back up at him – García's henchmen still had that. This was a borrowed standard military G10 Pulsar stainless-steel job on a nylon strap. It told the time, nothing more. And he could see he had precisely sixteen minutes to get dry, get dressed, and get himself over to the briefing. He was used to that.

There was an almost palpable sense of expectation in the hangar as Luke joined the forty or so men gathered under its roof. After two days of squalling winds a metal sheet up there had worked itself loose and was now rattling and banging like a demented carpenter. 'Somebody fix that fuckin' roof,' murmured the man next to Luke. 'It's doin' my head in.'

The men fell silent as Major Loames strode in, accompanied by Chris Shaw, who towered over him. Loames was not vain – other men might have stood on an upturned crate to make up for their lack of height. Instead he jacked up his voice several notches and boomed out what he had to say. 'Right, gents, I've just taken a call from TGHQ.'

Word had already got round. Everyone in that hangar knew the mission was on.

'We've had a suspect sighting fifty kilometres out, just south of the Scilly Isles, so this is an emergency response. We're going for a takedown at sea. The J2 int cell have sent us images of the vessel and also of Bravo One, the main player. That's the skipper, Hector Jiménez. The helo pilots are being given the coordinates now. H hour is fifteen minutes from now. I say again, H hour is in one five minutes. Take-off is at twenty hundred hours. Guys, we've trained for this a hundred times. You're going to have to think dynamically on your feet. Make it a good one. See you on the ship.'

Chapter 46

FOUR HUNDRED KILOMETRES east of Culdrose, Elise was alone in her flat, which, she reminded herself, she was supposed to be sharing with Luke. She was back from her first night out with friends since she had taken that terrifying call in the restaurant, and the evening had not gone well – at least, not for her. Three of her girlfriends had coaxed her out, saying it would be good for her to get away from the confines of the flat and forget about everything that had happened, just for an evening.

They had met up in an overpriced bar in Clapham, and were served frilly cocktails with pink umbrellas and swizzle sticks by a Polish waitress wearing a Mexican sombrero. The place had an air of enforced jollity.

'So come on, Lise,' one had said. 'How's your man, these days? We don't hear much about him.' Jess never needed more than one drink to speak her mind.

Elise had looked down into her cocktail glass, rather too quickly, then up again brightly. 'Oh, you know . . .'

'No,' persisted Jess. 'I don't know! Is it on or off?' Another friend, Hannah, nudged her gently in the ribs, but she wouldn't let it go. 'Sorry, just putting it out there. I mean, one minute he's back and you're all loved up with your phone switched off and we don't hear a word from you, the next he's buggered off again. I thought you said he'd left the Army.'

'The Marines,' Elise corrected her. 'Luke was in the Royal Marines. He wouldn't like anyone to think he was in the Army. He's very particular about that.'

'Yeah, whatever. But are *you* getting any action?'

'Jess!' scolded Hannah. 'Can we drop this?'

'No,' said Elise, 'you're right to ask. The truth is, I sometimes feel like I'm on a roller coaster. When he's here it's like the best feeling in the world and I don't want to be with anyone else. But then, yes, I suppose you're right, he's off again on his travels. And I don't want to pin him down, I really don't – he'd hate that. Besides, he's got a lot on his plate and the last thing he needs is a snippy girlfriend.'

Becca gave Elise's hand a supportive squeeze. 'Honestly, Lise, I don't think anyone could call you snippy. Seriously, though, what exactly does Luke do for a living?'

'He works for the FCO,' replied Elise, perhaps a little too quickly.

'A diplomat?' said Becca. 'My uncle's a diplomat – I think he's an ambassador somewhere. Maybe you'll end up living in some grand embassy.'

Elise shot her a withering look. 'Becs, can you really see me handing out canapés and making small-talk with the Belgian ambassador's wife?'

'Hmm. Maybe not.'

'So,' Jess started again, 'back to what I was saying. There's this guy at work, he's new, doesn't know anyone in London. He's quite hot. But I'm spoken for, *as* we all know. So I was thinking maybe I could introduce you both. You know, something to take your mind off things when Luke's not here?'

'Who? Me?' Elise looked shocked.

'Well, yes, you. I wasn't talking to the wall!'

'Jess! What the fuck? I'm with Luke, remember? End of.'

Elise had got up abruptly and gone off to find the Ladies. She hadn't needed the loo, she hadn't needed to freshen her make-up, she had needed something else: a text, a voicemail, anything, from Luke. Now more than ever. She had keyed her six-digit passcode into her phone – it was the date Luke had first walked into her gallery – then waited for the little red message circle to pop up. Nothing. She had checked her emails. Nothing. Then WhatsApp. Nothing. Luke had gone cold on her yet again.

And now, the evening having drawn to its own desultory close, she sat on the sofa in their silent, empty flat, contemplating the blank, black screen of the switched-off TV. Maybe her friends had a point after all.

Chapter 47

ON A BEARING of 235 degrees they flew south-west. Skimming low over the tossing waves, the helicopters were heading right into the teeth of the storm, the assault teams up ahead in the two Sea Kings, the follow-on force close behind in a Chinook. Standing off six kilometres from the target, a Lynx helicopter from 815 Squadron was in position to vector the assault force in, sending back live feeds to Task Group HQ in Poole, Dorset, and to Regent's Park barracks in London. Sid Khan was watching from Poole too, sitting wedged into a chair with a set of headphones clamped over his ears, staring at a flickering monitor, while an SBS captain took him through what was going on out at sea. In these conditions it was questionable how much use the blurred and rain-splashed images were to anyone. The latest signal from Fleet said the *Maria Esposito* had altered course. In these heavy seas she was making slow progress towards the coast of Cornwall. Her AIS beacon was still switched off and she was barely doing eight knots.

Strapped into his seat in the Chinook, Luke had forgotten how deafening the noise could be inside those things. Buffeted by the storm, the aircraft's frame lurched and jolted. They were flying at less than three hundred metres above the surface of the sea and already he was aware of the cold and damp seeping into his bones. As well as his Kevlar flak jacket, he was wearing a Gore-Tex waterproof, cargo trousers, mountain boots and a borrowed helmet with night-vision goggles, appropriate kit for an op like this where he would be putting down on the deck in the second wave. The armourer at Culdrose had issued him with a replacement Sig Sauer pistol, and Luke preferred not to wonder which low-life Colombian gangster now had his sweaty paws on the other.

His headset crackled into life and he recognized Buster Loames's voice. 'Gold One Alpha. Listen in, gents. The wind's too strong to put down on the bridge wings so we'll be going for alternate RDPs aft on the main deck. Call-sign Gold One Alpha goes in first, then Gold Two, then Three. Out.'

RDPs? Luke racked his brains to recall what this stood for, then remembered: rope down points. The means by which the commandos would drop onto the ship.

'Contact target,' said the pilot in the lead Sea King. 'Five hundred metres. Eleven o'clock.'

Luke craned his neck, trying to peer through the round Perspex porthole of the Chinook. But it was pitch dark out there and the glass was splattered with rain. Instinctively he reached up and felt for the night-vision goggles on his helmet, pulling them into position over his eyes. If anything, he could make out even less of what was outside the window. Maybe he was just sitting on the wrong side to see the ship. He pushed the goggles back up. They could wait till he was off the helicopter and on the deck. In the pit of his stomach Luke felt a knot of tension. It had been there ever since he'd taken Khan's call in the sauna. He knew a hell of a lot was riding on this mission – for him, for the Service, for the unknown future victims of whatever device the narcos were propelling towards Britain. Whatever it was, it needed to be stopped in its tracks, right here, right now, before it came ashore.

Down on the *Maria Esposito* it was the second mate who spotted the approaching silhouettes, all blacked out, no lights. He had been smoking a cigarette on one of the bridge wings, the steel viewing platforms that stuck out from the ship's superstructure at either side of the bridge. He dropped the remains of his cigarette underfoot, ground it out with his heel and raced back inside the bridge. '*Capitán! Cuidado!* They're coming!'

Hector Jiménez had been expecting this and took it in his stride. 'Be calm,' he told the man, 'and precise. What, exactly, is coming?'

'Helicopters! Many of them!' They could hear them now, even above the roar of the storm, the rising throb of massed rotor blades slicing through the wind and rain. The second mate's words triggered a minor panic on the bridge. Men started dashing about, unsure of what to do. In the confusion someone switched on the ship's arc lights, illuminating the deck, while someone else broke open the emergency cabinet and took out the flare pistol. It was a young deckhand, and he rushed out impetuously onto the bridge wings, about to fire a flare straight at the first approaching aircraft, a Sea King helicopter lining up to hover over the deck, when a blow to his jaw knocked him over.

'*Careverga!*' shouted Jiménez, leaning over the

deckhand with a clenched fist. 'You dickhead! Are you mad? They will kill us all! Give me that thing!' He grabbed the pistol and flung it overboard.

Through the reinforced glass of the bridge window the crew could see them clearly now, dropping like spiders on silken threads down onto the deck. First came the teams in the Sea Kings, fast-roping down with incredible speed even as the ropes swayed in the wind and the ship heaved in the swell. In less than two minutes the assault teams were aboard and moving in two parallel lines up both sides of the ship towards the bridge and the living quarters. Behind them the Chinook's dedicated Special Forces pilot struggled to keep his craft in a steady hold with its ramp down, just high enough above the deck for the follow-up team to jump off without breaking their legs. This was extremely close to being suicidally dangerous, but he managed it.

Luke, one of the last few to disembark, landed with a thump, banging his knee on a metal pipe that ran across the deck. It occurred to him that this was the second time in a few weeks he had launched himself out of a helicopter on a live op. Maybe this one would turn out better than the last.

Up on the bridge Hector Jiménez braced himself for the inevitable, but it was still a shock when it came. The heavy metal door to the bridge came crashing open so fast it nearly came off its hinges. Within seconds the room was swarming with heavily armed, black-clad men in black helmets. Their night-vision goggles were clamped on their faces, lending them an almost extra-terrestrial appearance. They were pointing their weapons at him and his crew.

'Al Suelo!' shouted the leader. 'Down on the floor! Now!' He motioned with the muzzle of his assault rifle towards the floor of the bridge so there could be no mistaking his meaning. Jiménez dropped first to his knees, then lay flat while his crew followed his example. One by one, the SBS team handcuffed them.

'Gold Two. Bridge secure.' The leader spoke into his helmet-mike. 'Five Bravos detained.' Then he motioned for one of his team to come over. The man he signalled to was smaller and slighter than most of the other operatives. He wore body armour, a helmet that was slightly too big for him, and carried no weapon. He looked as if he might be sick at any moment. This was the 'terp', the Spanish language interpreter. 'Tell the captain,' said the leader, 'that I need him to address the crew. He is to tell them to cooperate and they won't be harmed.' One of the operatives spotted the bridge-mike attached to a curled phone cord and passed it to Jiménez. Face down on the floor, his hands tied behind his back, it was obvious he was in no position to address anyone, so two men hauled him up and put him into a sitting position against the bulkhead. 'There you go,' said the team leader, gesturing to the microphone. 'Make the call.'

Jiménez, seemingly meek as a lamb, did as he was told, ordering his crew to offer no resistance. This was no time to be stubborn. He needed to keep his cool. Then he reckoned he could come through this unscathed. They were just soldiers, after all, doing their job, and he doubted they would know what to look for. And if they did? Well, so what? It would be too late now anyway.

Jiménez looked up as the bulkhead door swung

open, letting in a tall man with a pistol strapped to his thigh. He spoke briefly to the leader, who pointed straight at him. It was then he noticed the man was missing the middle finger on one hand. The next thing he knew, two large men were lifting him to his feet and dragging him backwards into the radio operator's room behind the bridge. They sat him down at the small table and left. The tall man walked in and shut the door behind him. What was he? Jiménez wondered. A detective? A lawyer? Maybe he could get him to take the cuffs off his wrists. They were already starting to chafe.

The tall man sat in the only other chair in the room and took out a slim laptop from the day sack he was carrying on his back. He still hadn't said a word. He placed it on the table between them, opened it, then typed something in. He swivelled the computer round so Jiménez could see it. He was half expecting it to be some sort of confession they were about to ask him to sign but, no, it was a photograph of a man's face.

'*Lo reconoces?*' said the man, addressing him at last. 'Do you recognize him?'

Jiménez did – instantly. It was Nelson García. He pretended to lean closer, frowning as he studied the image. Then he shook his head sadly. 'I don't know this man,' he told him. 'Why, who is he?'

'I think you do, Capitán Jiménez.'

'No, I swear, he is a stranger to me.'

The tall man sighed, almost theatrically. He had taken off his helmet and body armour, placing them on the floor beside him. Jiménez was surprised that a *gringo* with blond hair could speak such good Spanish. Now the man was typing something else into the laptop and once again he turned it round to face him.

Capitán Jiménez went very still. He said nothing.

The other man broke the silence. 'Let me be clear,' he said, fixing Jiménez with an unflinching gaze. 'That man there is on the Colombian government's Wanted List. He is a known *narcotraficante.* And there's no dispute about who is beside him, with his arm round his shoulders. It's you.'

The room seemed to heave violently as the *Maria Esposito* hit a particularly big wave and the laptop nearly slid off the table. Jiménez, whose hands were still cuffed behind his back, had to brace himself with both legs to stop himself falling off his chair. The ship lurched in the opposite direction and then steadied itself. The door opened. An operative poked his head in. 'Just to let you know, we're taking her into Falmouth with everyone onboard,' he said, and shut the door.

Jiménez was thankful for the interruption: he needed time to think. These gringos were clearly smarter than he had taken them for. Where the hell had they got that photo from? He didn't even remember when or where it had been taken.

The man had started speaking again. 'So where do we go from here, Jiménez?' he was saying. 'Because, you see, we can have you arrested, right here and now, on suspicion of links to international organized crime. We can hand you over to the Colombian Embassy, who will have you on a plane to Bogotá by tomorrow. You think I'm bluffing?'

Jiménez stared blankly back at him, giving nothing away. Inside his head, he was seriously worried. This man was building up to making some kind of impossible demand from him, he could feel it, and now they had that photograph, his options were not looking good.

'Let me tell you,' continued the tall man with the missing finger, 'my people in Bogotá have done their research. You're looking at a long stretch in one of your country's worst prisons. By the time you get out, your bank accounts will have been frozen, your family will have fallen into poverty, your wife will have left you for someone who can take care of her, and your children will have grown up forgetting what you look like. You'll be an old man and they won't even know you. Sound good?'

It was quite a speech, and the tall man sat back in his chair, arms folded, considering him. Jiménez felt like spitting in his face and was half tempted to do so. Instead he stared at the table in silence. He was waiting to hear the alternative and, sure enough, here it came.

'So here's what I can offer you,' said the blond man. 'My Service – my organization – can make all of that go away. No need for arrests or charges. La Modelo has quite enough prisoners already. But, in return, you have to help me.'

Jiménez looked up into the man's eyes and saw ruthlessness. They were ice cold, like the snow on the windswept summit of Pico Simón Bolívar back home.

The man leaned forward and spoke into his face. 'Señor Jiménez . . . Capitán Jiménez . . . You need to tell me what this ship has hidden on it. What is it you're carrying that's so secret it made you switch off your AIS beacon? We need to know where to find it and you need to tell us now.'

Hector Jiménez held Luke's gaze, his face now set hard in an attitude of defiance. His mind was made up. If he betrayed the cartel he would end up a hunted man all his life. It wouldn't matter where he fetched up, Miami, Madrid, San José, they would find him eventually. Take the rap now and he and his family would be well looked after. Even in prison they would take care of them. The cartel looked after its own, everyone knew that. And if they found the right judge, well, he might even be out in a year.

'I have nothing to say to you,' said Jiménez, and stuck out his jaw.

Chapter 48

'NOTHING, BOSS. SHE'S clean. We've searched her top to bottom.' A grim-faced Major Loames was up on the bridge speaking into the high-frequency radio. Raising his voice above the noise of the pitching, rolling Atlantic outside, his call had gone through to Task Group Headquarters at the SBS base in Poole, Dorset. He was speaking directly to the commanding officer.

'As far as we can see,' added Loames, 'she's carrying nothing but tractor parts and empty beer cans. The HAZMAT guys have been all over her with the Geiger counters and the readings are normal. We're taking her into port for a closer look. We'll need to get the Fleet divers to check out her hull. That bit we couldn't do in this sea state.'

In the ops room at Poole, the SBS commanding officer swore, turned to his regimental sergeant major and shook his head. Now it was his turn to have a difficult conversation, this time with Permanent Joint Headquarters at Northwood. There, in a windowless room, they put him on speakerphone as they stood around the table waiting for the word. It was a heavyweight audience gathered there that night: the director of Special Forces, a Royal Navy captain from Fleet Intelligence and Britain's Joint

Force commander, a four-star general whose command included all Special Forces and Joint Operations. This was not the news anyone was hoping to hear. Level by level, it worked its way up the chain of command, prompting sighs of disappointment and tired heads resting on hands, until finally a secure cell phone was handed to the Prime Minister at Chequers. His response was far from charitable. They had drawn a blank. This maritime counter-terrorism operation had failed.

Onboard the MV *Maria Esposito* Loames turned to Luke with an expression as black as thunder. 'Looks like Fleet fed us dodgy intel. Or was it your spooks? Doesn't really matter now, does it? We're stuck with this rust bucket all the way to Falmouth.' Capitán Jiménez had been placed under guard in a room down below while the second mate, released from his handcuffs but still closely watched, was now steering the vessel to port. There, a crew from the harbour-master's office would come out to meet them and take over the helm.

Luke felt about as low as he possibly could. He was deflated, weary and angry, all at the same time. And his foot was throbbing. It wasn't just the massive let-down of an intercept that had turned up nothing. That he could live with. No, it was the growing possibility that this whole Colombian venture, right from the first awkward boardroom meeting in Vauxhall Cross, might be about to culminate in failure. Failure for him, failure for the Service, and potentially a nightmare for Britain, if the device, the weapon, whatever it was, ever went off. And what about Elise? All these days away, unable to tell her what he was doing, where he was going, her worrying if he was safe. Which he clearly wasn't. And yet, for some reason he could not figure out, he was holding off calling her. Perhaps it was because he preferred to have no distractions while he was on this job. And that reminded him: he'd better have a conversation with Khan, get it over with.

He sat in the ship's radio room, being patched through to Sid Khan's secure mobile. He braced himself to hear a gloomy run-through of damage-limitation measures coupled with some fairly dire predictions. Instead, he heard Khan's voice, animated, combative and strangely upbeat.

'Here's the thing, Luke,' he began, almost as if he were taking him into his confidence. 'We just don't accept the result. That ship is carrying something: our analysis team is absolutely positive on that score. They've backtracked her routing across the Atlantic and, frankly, its erratic and evasive. Oh, and NSA picked up a signal she put out soon after she came through the Panama Canal.'

'What did it say?' asked Luke.

'It was a single word, and that's unusual in itself – doesn't exactly fit the pattern of normal commercial maritime comms. It was "Benicio". Any thoughts on that?'

It was just a name, nothing more, and Luke could think only of the actor, Benicio del Toro, which didn't really help. 'Sorry. Doesn't ring any bells.'

'Anyway, moving on,' said Khan. 'What did you get out of the skipper? How did he react to that photo of him with García?'

'It seemed to take the wind out of his sails. That was impressive research.'

Khan gave a quiet chuckle. 'Research?' he repeated. 'More like Photoshopping!'

Nice one! There had never been a photo of García with the ship's captain.

'Whatever,' said Luke. 'He's holding out, obviously decided where his loyalties lie. How long can we keep him when we get to Falmouth?'

'Forty-eight hours,' said Khan. 'Then he'll be handed over to his embassy. But the Navy divers will have been all over the ship by then. So, with any luck, Captain Jiménez might change his tune.'

A Colombian drug cartel miniature submarine is not built for rough seas. Unable to dive to any great depth, fundamentally unstable in the water, it is intended for calm equatorial waters, like mangrove inlets and balmy tropical reefs. Certainly not the English Channel in a Force 5 wind, gusting to Force 7. Buffeted and battered by the Cornish waves, the two submariners were battling to keep the craft on course. They were a very long way from home and partially disoriented by the past few weeks at sea, cooped up aboard the MV *Maria Esposito* as the ship ploughed eastwards across the Atlantic, followed by that last-minute emergency exit from the hull. That was surely not the way it was supposed to be. They hadn't trained for it and it was a miracle, they agreed, that nothing had gone wrong with the launch.

'Ay! Mamá!' wailed the pilot in front as another giant wave rolled over them, causing him to hit his head on the welded steel bulkhead. 'How much further in this shit can?' he called, to the man seated behind him. They were just below the waves, close enough to the surface to feel the effects of the storm

yet unable to see anything with the naked eye. In the bare, barren interior of the mini-sub the navigator sat behind him, his knees squashed practically up to his chin, struggling to keep a grip on his charts as the sub rolled and dipped in the surf.

'Just keep going on the same heading,' he replied, rather unconvincingly.

'You don't know, do you?' retorted the pilot. '*Imbécil.* If you get us lost in this, I swear I will kill you.' The weeks of enforced idleness aboard the *Maria Esposito,* as she made her way from Panama to the English Channel, had done nothing to improve their relationship. There were only so many games of Parqués, the Colombian board game – the navigator had brought it with him – that two people could play before they felt like killing each other.

But right now, as they made their tortuous way through the dark and turbulent seas off the south coast of Cornwall towards the designated landing site, both submariners were thinking the same thing. *This is madness and it is quite possible that we may not make it.* Since the rendezvous off the coast of Panama they had done precious little maintenance on the mini-sub, largely because it had been hidden in the false hold at the bottom of the *Maria Esposito.* But they were paying for it now, as rivulets of sea water streamed alarmingly down the walls of the interior. The bilge pump had packed up.

They had argued against the decision to launch in this weather, both men telling Capitán Jiménez it was insane to put to sea in a jerry-built mini-sub in a gale. But he had shown them the signal and the terse order from the cartel, then practically pushed them off his ship into the Atlantic. What the two men didn't know was that he had had good reason to follow orders. Within twenty minutes of the launch from the *Maria Esposito* he'd had the SBS fast-roping down onto the deck. When they had put those handcuffs on him and the tall Englishman had led him off to the radio room to offer that absurd deal, Jiménez had known what none of those *cabrones* knew: a miniature submarine containing something extremely dangerous was less than five kilometres away, heading for the darkened Cornish coast, and they had missed it by minutes.

Chapter 49

'ONE MORE FOR the road, Jack?' The barmaid leaned across and tapped old Jack Hammill's arm. He seemed to have gone to sleep where he sat.

'Dreckley,' he replied, using the Cornish equivalent of 'Soon, but not just yet'.

'Wozza madder withee?' she continued. 'You used to be the life and soul, you did. Now look at yers.'

'I'm getting old, that's what,' said the retired policeman, and shuffled off to answer the call of nature. Occupied. 'Bugger that,' he muttered, pushed open the door of the Halzephron Inn and tottered out into the night. The wind came barrelling in off the Atlantic waves below and caught him full in the face. For a moment he stood there, rocking gently, then walked on down the hill to find a bush.

'That's odd,' he muttered to himself, as he fumbled with his zip in the dark. He could swear lights were flashing dimly down on Gunwalloe Cove. Who would want to be out on Porthleven Sands on this kind of a night? Probably some young surfers, stoned out of their minds, he reckoned, camping in the storm for a dare. Stupid bloody grockles. Might check up on them in the morning. Jack had hung up his uniform years ago but in his heart he had never stopped being a copper.

For the five men working in the dark in the bleak, windswept cove, it was lucky that nobody other than Jack Hammill noticed them. When he toddled back into the bar, a few tell-tale dark splashes showing on his trousers, nobody paid him too much attention. Even if he had got within earshot of the men, Jack would not have understood a word they were saying, because they were talking in low, hoarse whispers, speaking the language of the red-brick Colombian *barrios.* The cartel's men were working against the clock to bring something ashore in secret. They knew that everything, even the lives of their families in Colombia, depended on their getting the job done and disappearing before anyone saw them.

Chapter 50

FROM THE NARROW shingle beach of Gunwalloe Cove, an unpaved road just wide enough to let a vehicle pass leads up the hill between wind-blasted bushes and dry-stone walls. The van made its way, in the darkness before dawn, up onto the flat, rolling heath, past the gorse and along winding lanes slick with rain. The man in the driving seat gripped the wheel, his knuckles white, staring dead ahead as his lights illuminated the uneven road. Beside him sat a man with a gleaming gold tooth, his clothes cleaner than those of the others in the vehicle. Only his boots bore the marks of the beach where he had stood for over an hour giving orders, cajoling, cursing and, eventually, congratulating, once the cargo was finally hoisted into the vehicle.

It was just before the junction with the A3083 that they saw the Military Police patrol vehicle. It was parked discreetly beside the road, close to the rusting barbed-wire coils that ringed the Royal Naval Air Station at Culdrose. It was already too late to avoid it.

'*Cuidado!* Watch out!' shouted Gold Tooth, as the driver, unsure of what to do, swerved to one side, then braked hard. Immediately the patrol car's flashing lights went on.

'Pull over,' hissed Gold Tooth. 'I'll speak, not you.'

The RMP Land Rover drew up behind them. A man in uniform got out and walked up to the window on the driver's side. His red armband bore the thick black letters 'MP', he wore a pistol at his side and in his hand was a heavy standard-issue right-angled torch. He shone it straight at the face of the driver, then peered beyond him into the interior of the van. Several sleepy figures looked back at him, shielding their eyes from the intense beam of white light.

'Pescadores,' the driver explained to the policeman. 'Fishermen. We are fishermen.'

'Could I see some identification please?'

The driver turned to his passenger, the man with the gold tooth, who passed over two valid British driving licences. The policeman turned the pink laminated cards over in his hand, checking the ID photos against the two men in the front of the van.

'So what might you be up to at this time of night?' he asked. 'Could one of you step out of the vehicle and open the rear doors.' It wasn't a question.

Gold Tooth smiled obligingly, unbuckled his seatbelt, got down from the van and walked round to the back. After a brief fumble with some keys he unlocked the rear doors, pulled them open and stood back to let the policeman shine his torch where he wanted. Neatly stacked, all the way from floor to roof, were plastic crates of fish packed in ice. The policeman tugged at one, pulling it out just far enough to see the silvery forms that glittered and sparkled in his torchbeam. All seemed to be in order. His radio crackled into life and he moved away to take the call as Gold Tooth stood patiently by the open doors of the van.

'You'd best be on your way,' said the policeman,

when he returned. 'Don't fall asleep at the wheel now, will you?'

Gold Tooth returned to his seat in the van. As they resumed their journey, turning left towards Helston, past the clumps of Scots pines and the home of 771 Search & Rescue Wing, where Prince William had served, the two men in the front exchanged a nervous glance and said nothing. That, they both knew, had been way too close for comfort.

From Helston they drove on in silence. After that heart-stopping encounter at Culdrose the men in the van would be extra careful from now on, driving with the saintly obedience of a nun. They crawled through deserted 20 m.p.h. zones and negotiated empty, darkened roundabouts. Their instructions were simple and they followed them to the letter. Proceed north to Truro, then take the A30 up to Bodmin and on up onto the moor. At Bolventor they were to turn off the dual carriageway, drive under the bridge and proceed to a grey stone inn. The gates to the car park would be locked overnight so they were to carry on to the next layby. When the gates opened at seven a.m. they were to drive to the car park on the left, and head for the furthest corner by the bush that looked like a Christmas tree.

The Jamaica Inn is famous, steeped in the history of contraband changing hands in the dead of night, of deals done on the adjacent moor beneath jagged tors where the mist can hide many things. And as the Colombians drove into the car park, the fog swirled around them, lying low in the troughs and hollows that swept down from Brown Willy, the crag that towers over Bodmin Moor. Visibility was a few metres at most. But through the gloom, the headlights of a parked truck flashed once. It was enough. Five men spilled out of the van, stretching their limbs and stamping their feet in the cold and damp.

'Ay, qué frío!' they complained. *'Esto es insoportable.'* Some began to compare the weather unfavourably to the home country and the balmy Caribbean heat of Cartagena. But for Gold Tooth, overseeing what was about to take place, the foul weather was exactly what he had hoped for. So late in the season, so early in the morning and on such a miserable day, there should be nobody around to observe them.

Beneath the fir tree in the corner of the car park the two teams made contact, shook hands and embraced. It was a fleeting moment of companionship and human friendship in an otherwise grim endeavour. One by one, the crates of iced fish were removed from the van to reveal the precious cargo: a heavy lead-lined box. Its carrying handles were still in place. It had not been opened since it had left the port of Hungnam in the People's Democratic Republic of Korea, discreetly stowed on the *Maria Esposito*.

It took six of the men twenty minutes to manhandle the box from the van into the small trailer that would be towed behind the truck. The exchange had been made. The first van would be delivered to a recycling depot just outside Bristol and crushed to the size of a suitcase. By the time the gift shop at the Jamaica Inn opened for business, the truck, its trailer and its contents would have vanished into the fog, hurrying north across the moor towards the M5, Bristol and London.

Chapter 51

AS THE TRUCK drove, unnoticed, towards the capital, Elise Mayhew was sitting in a Chelsea pub, racked by doubts. Her relationship with Luke was not in a good place. When she thought about it, which she had a lot recently, things had not been right between them ever since he had taken off for South America. Now the clichés came crowding in. It's just a blip, she told herself. Every couple has them. Put it in perspective. Your relationship is stronger than this. 'You two are so good together,' her friends told her, as she confided her doubts to them. 'We'd hate to see you split up.' A big part of her was secretly proud of what Luke did for a living. All he had told her was who he worked for, not what he did or how he did it. She had become adept at covering for him in conversations, telling people he worked for the Foreign Office or 'some boring part of Whitehall'. She quite enjoyed doing that: it made her feel they were a team. But now, with Luke constantly away, and the glaring absence of any calls from him . . .

'Four days,' she told Hugo, as they sat at a table hewn of rustic wood in a Chelsea gastropub. It was the sort of place where the simple single-sheet lunch menu belied the exorbitant prices. Elise glanced at it in dismay. Ballotine of guinea fowl: £28? Assiette de jambon en croute: £23.50? She was glad he was paying.

'Four days,' she repeated, holding up four elegant fingers. 'That's all I've had with Luke this month.' She knew that Hugo, as an interested party, was probably not the right person to confide in, but she was starting to think of him as a dependable elder brother – a generous one too.

He reached out and topped up her glass of crisp white Gavi. He was a good listener too. 'Where is he now?' he asked gently.

Elise pursed her lips. 'I have absolutely no idea. He seems to have gone completely off the grid again.' She didn't know why she was so angry. It was unlike her and already she could feel a pang of guilt at her disloyalty. Luke was the man she loved. She just wished he was more there for her. It was all very well dating a good-looking superman but not if he was going to turn into the Invisible Man every few days. She took another sip of her wine as Hugo changed the subject, but her mind was made up. Something in her relationship with Luke, she resolved, had to change.

If Angela could have heard that conversation she might have insisted Luke take some urgent domestic leave. God knows he had earned it. But at that moment she was standing in a pew at St Laurence's Church in Scarborough, attending a memorial service for someone who had once been quite special to her. Jeremy Benton, long-serving intelligence officer, fluent Spanish speaker, murdered in the line of duty in Colombia. Even now, in the serene Yorkshire church, with its ancient yew trees and its neatly laid out cemetery, she still couldn't take in the fact that he had been killed.

She looked down at her hymn sheet and silently mouthed the words to 'Abide With Me', then sat down for the eulogy. An old schoolfriend had gone up to the pulpit and was starting to tell the congregation about Benton's early prowess on the cricket pitch. There would be no mention from anyone, of course, of his past affair with Angela, the brief in-house fling before he was married. It had fizzled out soon after, when he had got his next posting, and they had gone on to pursue their own separate lives.

The words from the pulpit washed over her. Right now her concerns were for Luke and the ongoing operation. Sid Khan was running it but she was Luke's immediate boss and felt a strong duty of care towards him. As his line manager she was in two minds whether or not to insist that now was the time to take him off the case. No one, not even a superfit operator like Luke, could keep going at that pace indefinitely, and they had ridden him hard ever since the crisis emerged. Maybe HR had been right: maybe she should have sent him off for that re-evaluation course and spared him the ordeal of a night-time maritime interdiction in the English Channel. But set against that was the harsh reality of the situation they were now in, trying to intercept the still unidentified device.

Only the day before Angela had attended a deeply worrying event: a briefing for the directors at VX by the Counter-proliferation team. WMD were right up there with international terrorism as a top priority for SIS. There were people in that building whose entire working lives were dedicated to stopping terrorists and rogue states acquiring WMD. In the case of North Korea, with its plutonium warheads and its fledgling hydrogen bombs, it was already too late. And now they faced the threat they had always feared most, that of a WMD getting into the hands of a non-state organization, a group with no obvious return address to threaten with retaliation. Against this backdrop, she had no choice when it came to Luke. There was no one else in the Service with quite the same skill set as him. Until they could locate and defuse the weapon there would be no let-up for any of them. Angela knew exactly what Benton would have said – she could almost hear him now, whispering it to her in this old Yorkshire chapel: *Keep your eyes on the prize, girl, and keep going.*

Chapter 52

NELSON GARCÍA WAS in a genial mood. Dressed in nothing but a pair of black silk shorts, a thick fuzz of hair covering his back from the nape of his neck to the cleft of his buttocks, the man they called El Pobrecito lay face down on the bed. Protruding from the back of both of his knees was a pair of ultra-slim needles, so thin that anyone walking in would easily have missed them. The girl leaned over him and, with great care and precision, placed two more acupuncture needles right behind his kneecaps. 'Meridians,' she said softly. 'What I am doing here is all about your meridians. You have fourteen meridian lines inside your body. The Chinese call this one *wei-zhong*. It means "urinary bladder meridian".'

He grunted, his face resting sideways on the pillow. How did this girl from the village know so much about what went on inside his body? It surely wasn't natural. Well, it didn't matter as long as she could fix his problem. As far as his people were concerned, even his closest confidants, like Suárez, she had come to fix an intestinal issue. Three sessions every week, cash in hand, and he was generous because she was the only one he could share his secret with. No one else must know. It would be disastrous for his reputation in the cartel, a big man like him, running a multi-billion-dollar global operation, a man who could choose at the click of his fingers if someone lived or died, and whether it was a swift or slow and painful end. No, it would not do for them to know that in the last few months El Pobrecito had become impotent.

'Stay still,' she commanded. 'I'm going to place more needles close to your spine.' The drug-lord did as he was told, a great slab of meat beached on the bed, putty in her hands. 'This one,' she continued, 'is called *shensu*. It reaches the two meridians that run either side of your spine. Like a railway track.' He laughed, and she placed a warning hand on his shoulder blade. 'Don't move,' she scolded him. 'This is delicate work and I have no wish to hurt you.' No one in the cartel could speak to El Pobrecito like that, and Valentina had only been around a few weeks but already he was growing fond of her, in an almost paternal, protective way. The girl from the village, with her nimble fingers, her soft touch and her surprising knowledge of Chinese medicine, was like an island of innocence amid the sea of violence in which he swam. She was careful never to ask him about his business and he respected that. Perhaps she reminded him a little of his sister when they were growing up together in the *barrio*, before she'd married that idiot from Cali and moved away to have his babies.

Twenty minutes later Valentina plucked the needles out, one by one, and laid them carefully in the box with the clasp. '*Hemos terminado*,' she announced. 'We're all done.'

García let out a contented sigh and rolled onto his side, propping his head up with his fist and considering her carefully as she tidied away her things. 'Really, *chica*, you are *una artista* with your hands,' he told her. 'You are becoming almost a part of *la familia* here. Listen, I have a proposition for you.' He looked down at his free hand, examining his fingernails. Valentina had slowed her movements to listen to what he was about to say. 'Why don't you move in here with us? You can have a room of your own, with a balcony. Would you like that? No more trudging back and forth from the village? No more patting down at the gate from my . . . over-enthusiastic guards?' García was giving her his most charming smile as he said this but the undertone was clear. This was not an offer, it was an order, and it would not be wise to turn him down.

Valentina tilted her head ever so slightly before she answered. 'You know I have to get back now,' she replied. 'My *papi* will be expecting me. He gets worried if I am late. But . . .' she gave him a coy smile in return '. . . if the kind *señor* is serious, then that would be a most generous offer. I will fetch my things from home tomorrow.'

He was about to tell her they would send a car for her, but someone was approaching on the other side of the door. It was Suárez – he recognized his footfall even before he knocked. After years of working together, you get to know someone's traits.

'*Entra*,' he called. 'Come in.'

The heavy wooden door swung open, and his security chief came over and spoke quietly to him as Valentina put away the last of her things, folding towels and wiping down surfaces. 'I have the information you asked for, Patrón,' he said. He paused, staring meaningfully at the girl. It was in his nature to be suspicious, and the *chica* who had found her way into his boss's inner sanctum – well, in his view she was still on trial.

'Her?' García caught his gaze and waved a hand dismissively at Valentina. 'You don't need to worry about my little Valentinita. You can speak freely.'

Still, Suárez lowered his voice as he continued. 'You asked about the girlfriend of that Englishman, Carlton, who got away.'

García chuckled as he remembered something. 'You mean,' he said, 'the one we told them to call while he was our guest in the Chop House?'

'That one.' Suárez passed him a photograph, printed out on an A5 sheet of laminated paper. 'This is her. She works in an art gallery in London. Ana María has the address. She is arranging everything now.'

García held the photo at arm's length. He did not have his glasses to hand and his eyesight was not what it used to be. He let out a soft whistle, then tutted. 'What a shame,' he said sadly. 'So young and so pretty.'

Chapter 53

IN A COLD and draughty aircraft hangar at RNAS Culdrose, Luke sat sprawled on a folding metal chair, his long legs stretched out in front of him. After the tension of the night-time intercept of the MV *Maria Esposito* at sea, shepherding her into Falmouth harbour had been something of an anti-climax. They had handed her over to the Royal Navy for a fuller inspection in the early morning and now he was back on the base, his kit packed, waiting for the transport that would take him up to Truro and the fast train back to London. A bit more low-key than the ride down in the Chinook. Already that seemed like a lifetime ago. He had phoned Elise that morning, breaking the silence between them, and they had agreed to go for an early Italian once he'd got into Paddington. Luke could tell from her tone there were things she was holding back, for now. Hardly surprising, really, given that he hadn't exactly been there for her.

The sound of a Land Rover pulling up outside the hangar had him springing up and reaching for his pack. The passenger door swung open and a naval rating half ran towards him.

'Easy,' said Luke, 'No rush. My train's not till eleven twenty-five.'

'Don't think you'll be catching it, sir. Something's come up. You're wanted in the ops room. I'm to take you there right away.'

They were waiting for him: the base commander, a senior policeman from Falmouth and two young men who looked barely out of their teens. Luke took in the scene, noting the serious expressions on the officers' faces and the lads' bewildered look. His first thought was that they were trespassers and he wondered why they were involving him. But then he saw what they were wearing: black neoprene dry suits, the sort worn by scuba divers in cold Atlantic waters.

'These two,' explained the commander, 'are from the Porthmorgan Diving Club on the other side of the Lizard. I'll let them tell you in their own words what they've just discovered.'

They both started speaking at the same time, then fell silent. One laughed nervously.

'Take your time, guys, no rush,' said Luke.

The taller of the two, his face tanned and wind-burned, his long blond hair knotted into Rastafarian dreads, spoke up, his well-enunciated syllables hinting at a private education.'Yes, well, we set off this morning just before seven for a drift dive off Porthleven.'

'We being?' asked Luke.

'Oh, right – me and Josh here, and four others from the dive club. We'd been waiting days for the wind to drop so this was our first dive in a while. Got to be careful this time of year. Those rip tides can be totally gnarly.'

A grunt from the senior policeman, his way of saying, 'Just get on with it.'

'It took us a couple of hours in the inflatable to get round the Lizard before we moored up off Gunwalloe. It's *literally* just two kilometres from here.'

Luke stole a glance at his watch – he was going to miss his train at this rate.

'We'd heard there's still part of an old trawler down there,' continued the young diver. 'It's twenty-five metres down, part of a wreck from the big storm of 'eighty-seven. Well, we found something, just not what we were expecting.'

'And?'

'And we found – you tell it,' he said, turning to Josh.

'We found a submarine,' said the other abruptly. It was his first and only contribution to the conversation so far and it certainly got Luke's attention.

'A submarine?' repeated Luke. 'You mean, like a Second World War job?' He turned towards the base commander. This was something for the local history society, surely, not for someone sent by MI6 to work on a national crisis.

'No!' Dreadlocks corrected him. 'Not as big as that. More like a submarine in miniature. You know, a bit like those craft in *The Cockleshell Heroes*, except this wasn't a kayak, it was definitely a submarine.'

Luke's pulse was racing. There were only two groups he knew of who used mini-subs: the Russians, off the Baltic coast, and the Colombian narcos. 'Did it look new or old?' he asked. 'How long d'you reckon it had been there?'

'Definitely new,' interjected Josh.

'And you know that because?' said the base commander.

'There were no barnacles. Anything we find down there is usually covered in them after just a few weeks.

I could show you photos of things growing down there you wouldn't believe.'

'So,' said the senior policeman, 'the craft they found has been in the shallows for a day or two at most. Somebody's abandoned it.'

Luke exchanged glances with the base commander. As the senior officer at Culdrose, he would have been well aware of last night's abortive maritime interception of the *Maria Esposito*. He would also know this was a Tier One national priority. The discovery of a mini-sub so close to where she was sailing was now a potential game-changer. 'Does Major Loames know about this?'

'He's getting the Fleet divers on to it right now. They should be deploying on-site as we speak. Then they'll go for a recovery and bring the hull into Falmouth. Fleet Intelligence are sending a couple of experts down from HMS *Collingwood* in Hampshire.'

Luke's mind was busy fitting the pieces into place. An abandoned mini-sub. Only there a day or two. Uncovered just hours after the *Maria Esposito* raid. No wonder that ship's captain was so bloody sure of himself. He must have known he was clean. They would have launched already.

Luke's earlier despondency and fatigue were gone, the news had hit him like a double shot of espresso, waking him up.

Dreadlocks and Josh were still standing there, unsure what do with themselves but vaguely aware that they had probably done something right.

'Any chance of a coffee?' asked Josh, but the older men in the room weren't listening.

Luke addressed the base commander again. 'There's someone else you need – we need – on this.'

'Who's that?' The commander was a seasoned Navy man on his final posting. He had known a fair few dramas on his watch, but now he wore the wary look of someone whose patch was about to be invaded by a lot of people from London.

'Commander Jorge Enríquez,' replied Luke. 'He's the naval attaché at the Colombian Embassy in London. Knows all about mini-subs, which boats can carry what cargo. He can even match them to the cartels. We're going to want him ASAP in Falmouth the moment they bring this thing in. I wouldn't mind getting him to give the ship the once-over too. Trust me, he's the real deal.'

The base commander hesitated. Evidently he wanted to play it by the book.

'Well, that'll have to be cleared with the FCO and the MoD. It might take some time.'

'It really shouldn't,' said Luke. 'I'll get it cleared right now.' He moved away to make a phone call.

'So, um . . .' he heard Josh say as he went towards the door '. . . do we, like, get any kind of reward?'

Luke hurried down the corridor and into a side room, where he called Khan, who was already on his way back from Poole to Vauxhall Cross.

'Yellow,' came the response. It sounded as if Khan was travelling at speed in the back of a car.

Yellow?

'What?' said Luke.

'I said, yeah, hello,' replied Khan. 'Go ahead. Who is this?'

'Luke Carlton. There's been a development. And it's a pretty major one.'

Chapter 54

THE EVENING SHIFTS were often busy in A&E. In the five years she had been working at Plymouth General Hospital, Nurse Jovelyn Flores couldn't remember a week without some drunk stumbling in, bloodied and bruised, his knuckles broken or his face cut. She had seen a lot worse in her native Philippines. She shuddered to think of the knife wounds she had dressed in her time at the Golden Gate General Hospital in Batangas. Plymouth was tame by comparison. Of course, there were always the teenagers, dumped half-conscious in the doorway by their mates who roared away in cars with souped-up engines. She had seen some bad cases, boys barely out of school overdosing on chemical pills sold in cellophane wrappers, probably by some unscrupulous dealer in a thumping nightclub.

Tonight was set to be no different. As the triage nurse, Jovelyn sat in her booth behind a glass window, neat and organized, wearing her regulation blue uniform with white trim, making those all-important decisions on who got to see the doctor and when. The words 'Take a seat, please. We'll call you when it's your turn' tripped off her tongue like a mantra – she practically mouthed them in her sleep. Looking up from her computer she surveyed the waiting room. At least three of the faces she recognized, serial brawlers. They would not be top of her list tonight.

Then something caught her attention. A man had just come through the sliding doors, stumbling, confused. She was about to mark him down as another drunk when she caught her breath. His face and hands were covered with red blotches, like blisters or welts. Burns? She couldn't tell, but it was obvious that he needed immediate attention. He stood swaying, just inside the doorway, as others in the waiting room noticed him and recoiled.

Nurse Flores buzzed the intercom to the receptionist. 'Can you take his personals then send him straight to me?' But the man didn't even make it across the floor to Reception. He collapsed where he was, his body seemingly turning to jelly before her eyes. There were gasps of horror from the waiting patients. She raced over to where he lay and saw that his lips were perforated with unsightly ulcers. They were moving – he was trying to say something – but no words came out. She bent over to hear better but he was seized by a series of convulsions. Then he was violently sick on the pale green floor, with flecks of tell-tale crimson in his vomit. He was very ill indeed.

Other patients nearby had abandoned their seats and were standing with their backs against the far wall, keeping as far away as possible. A young boy, sitting with his mother, started to film the scene on his mobile phone. 'Wicked,' he kept saying, until she took it off him and put it in her handbag. Nurse Flores told Reception to summon a cleaner, and after a few minutes, a man in overalls emerged with a mop and an angry frown.

Oblivious to the pool of vomit at her feet, the nurse examined the red welts on the man's skin. On his wrist she found a blue mark, like a bruise. She looked more closely and saw that it wasn't a bruise but a tattoo of an anchor. And then she noticed something else: a clump of his hair had fallen out and lay matted and sodden in the vomit. He had lost almost half the hair off his scalp, but not evenly. It was falling out even as she watched.

Something was very wrong. 'Get the house doctor in here now!' she called. The man twitched at her feet and vomited again, feebly this time. Then he lay perfectly still.

Chapter 55

IN THE A&E waiting room at Plymouth General there was a ripple of excitement. Cuts, bruises, sprains and fractures were all temporarily forgotten – everyone was more interested in the man who lay silent on the floor. While she waited for the doctor to arrive, Nurse Flores stood over him, like a bird defending her brood, scolding anyone who tried to sneak a picture on their mobile phone. He was in a dreadful state. In addition to the vomit that had pooled around his head, he had soiled himself and the stench filled the room. People were clamping their sleeves over their noses, a child wailed, and several patients got up and left.

The duty matron was the first to arrive on the scene. A tough but kind-hearted woman in her late forties, Rhona Braddock had seen it all, or so she thought. As a clinical professional, she did not flinch when the smell hit her nostrils. Symptoms, treatments, cures, this was her world. She leaned down, touched the man's forehead with her gloved hand and nodded. 'He's running a fever. Must be at least forty degrees. Get him into isolation and page Dr Patel,' she said. 'I want a clinical nurse specialist on this one. See who's in tonight.'

Nurse Flores spoke to her as quietly as she could.

With so many people listening in, she didn't want to start a panic. 'Is it . . . Ebola?'

The matron shook her head vigorously, then motioned the nurse to follow her out into a side room. She spoke in low tones, almost conspiratorially: 'Without the burns,' she told her, 'I'd have said Ebola was near the top of the list. He's haemorrhaging badly and he has a high fever. Classic symptoms.' She peeled off the purple latex gloves and dropped them into a bin, then pressed hard on the disinfectant dispenser on the wall and rubbed the gel into her hands. 'But this is something else. It'll be for the doctor to make the call, but I can tell you one thing. We've never had anything like this before at Plymouth General. It's one for Public Health England. We'll need to inform the authorities.'

After that, things happened very quickly. The senior medical staff at Plymouth included a number of military medics on secondment and at 10.30 p.m., as the two women returned to the collapsed patient on the floor, the sliding doors hissed open and a team swept in, led by a surgeon commander. He took one look at the scene and issued a terse order. 'Clear the waiting room. Move everyone away from this man and keep a three-metre cordon from him. Do it now.'

In the early hours of the morning a convoy of vehicles drew up outside, escorted by police outriders. It was just as well that the public didn't see what followed, which could have been a scene from a Hollywood disaster movie. Four figures, dressed from head to toe in white bio-hazard protection suits, entered the now-evacuated waiting room, breathing loudly through their respirators. Methodically and efficiently, they passed red-and-black contamination monitors over the prone man as he lay breathing weakly, starting at his head and working their way down to his feet. They paused to check the digital readings, then passed the devices over him once more. One spoke briefly into a radio-mike attached to the inside of his helmet.

'It's positive, five hundred and fifty millisiverts. He's contaminated.' His voice was rising. 'We're going to need to file a JSP392 straight away.'

A small group of hospital staff huddled in the car park, oblivious to the autumn chill as they watched the proceedings. The surgeon commander was with them and when he heard the reading he swore quietly. Nurse Flores had noted the worry on his face and she moved close to him. 'What are they doing? Who are these people?' she asked. She was scared for the first time since she could remember.

'They're from the Defence Radiological Protection Service. They've come down from Alverstocke near Gosport – drove through the night as soon as we alerted them. Um . . .' he looked Nurse Flores up and down as if noticing her for the first time '. . . I'm afraid you're going to have to get checked over as well, you and the duty matron. We need to follow procedure here.'

'Checking for what?' But Nurse Flores already knew the answer.

'Radioactive contamination. Our man here has received a potentially lethal dose of radiation poisoning. If I was a betting man, I would say his odds were not great.'

'Oh, my Lord.' Jovelyn Flores' hands flew up to her face. Then she made the sign of the cross.

Chapter 56

LATER THAT MORNING, shortly before ten a.m., anyone walking along Whitehall might have noticed a number of figures converging on the entrance to the Cabinet Office. They would have seen them trot briskly up the three wide stone steps, push through the blue-framed glass doors, stencilled with the government's coat of arms, and turn sharp right.

They gathered in a windowless conference room, an unusually large group this time, their numbers swollen by several technical experts rushed up to London. A COBRA crisis meeting had been convened at extremely short notice, chaired by the Home Secretary. Sid Khan sat beside him.

'I'd like to thank you all for getting here so promptly,' the Home Secretary began. Youthful and energetic in his movements, his jet-black hair glistening with a hint of product, Alan Reynolds had been in the job just two months. After a bruising row with the Police Federation about overtime pay in his first two weeks, he was still getting to grips with the unwieldy leviathan that is the Home Office. 'As most of you know by now,' he continued, 'the Prime Minister has asked me to chair this session because of the developments overnight in the West Country.' He removed his spectacles, with their thin, scarlet frames, and folded them away in his top pocket. 'A man has shown up at a hospital in Plymouth with symptoms of acute radiation poisoning.' He let those words sink in. Ten years had passed since the Russian dissident Alexander Litvinenko had died a slow and painful death in a London hospital from the same complaint.

'We are still awaiting all the facts, but we are obviously taking this extremely seriously. It is absolutely imperative that we identify the source of that radiation, isolate it and secure it. The man in question is unconscious. I understand he's very sick indeed and we can't be sure that he'll survive. Detectives from the Met's SO15 are waiting to interview him – if he wakes up.'

Reynolds stopped and glanced down at the bare table, as if a sheet of notes lay there. 'We need to move as fast as possible on this one, so the PM and I wanted you all to be fully briefed. To that end,' he nodded at two men sitting halfway down the long table, 'I have asked two of our Defence Radiological experts to come in today. Professor Lynton Macaulay and Dr Frederick Böhse. Over to you, gentlemen.'

The two scientists got to their feet but seemed unsure of where they should stand, so Reynolds gestured them to the far end of the table. Macaulay spoke first, buttoning up his suit jacket before he began. A senior figure at Britain's Atomic Weapons Establishment at Aldermaston, he had a soft, soothing Scottish burr, which to those present seemed strangely at odds with the unpleasantness of the topic.

'You will all have heard, no doubt, of the Brazil cobalt case back in 1987, yes?' he began. There were some nods around the table but others looked blank.

'And the one in Mexico in 2013?' Even fewer nods this time. 'And I wonder how many of you in this room have heard of the Polish cobalt-60 theft in 2015?'

Reynolds interrupted: 'Let's assume we're not familiar with any of these, Professor. Please go on.'

Macaulay's expression suggested he found it hard to comprehend that anyone could not know about them. 'In early March 2015 twenty-two canisters, each containing pellets of radioactive cobalt-60, were stolen from a warehouse in a Polish town called Poznań. Cobalt-60, along with strontium-90 and caesium-137, is a radioactive isotope that, left unshielded, emits harmful gamma rays.' There were worried looks of recognition around the table. Everyone had heard of gamma rays. 'They can cause horrendous burns but they also pass right through human skin to attack the body's cell walls. Put bluntly, you start to decay rapidly from the inside.'

'Like Litvinenko?' interrupted a young man from the Foreign and Commonwealth Office's Counter-proliferation Department.

'Not quite,' answered Macaulay. 'Litvinenko died from alpha-emitting particles that he had ingested from drinking poisoned tea. It had been laced with polonium-210. Unlike gamma rays, alpha rays are very weak. They can't penetrate our outer membranes, but once ingested they cause enormous damage. It took us quite a while to figure out what was wrong with him. It was his urine that gave it away in the end, positively brimming with radioactivity. By then it was too late and even the best care possible at University College Hospital couldn't save him. When the poor man died he had so much radioactivity in his body they had to bury him in a lead-lined coffin.'

The Home Secretary interrupted again: 'Sorry to have to move you along, Professor, but time is pressing.'

'Of course,' said Macaulay. 'So, Poland. It was several days before the Polish authorities reported the theft to the UN's nuclear watchdog, the International Atomic Energy Agency, the body that tries to keep tabs on all this stuff around the world. As long as the radioactive material is shielded with enough lead lining it can't harm you. We call it a "pig container". Please don't ask me how it got that name.'

Several people exchanged glances.

'Sorry, could you elaborate there?' That was Laura Deane, deputy director of MI5, who had spent much of her career running agents inside extremist groups.

Macaulay took a moment to locate who had asked the question. 'A pig container,' he replied, peering straight at her, 'is basically a thick metal cylinder, like a really heavy Thermos, with handles. It has a hollow centre where the radioactive source is inserted. If anyone is stupid enough to go unscrewing the top of the pig and removing the source they're likely to get a lethal dose of radiation in under five minutes.'

'Just so we're clear,' said the Home Secretary, 'is that what you believe has happened here? In Plymouth?'

Macaulay held up his hand authoritatively. He was definitely enjoying bringing his pet subject to this Whitehall audience. 'That,' he said, 'is not a judgement for me to make. I'm going to let my colleague answer your question. I expect many of you have come across Dr Böhse's work?' he asked. 'No? Well, Dr Frederick Böhse is the senior consultant at the Defence Radiological Protection Service, part of the government's defence science labs. He was the author of the Omon Report last year. So, Doctor . . .'

The man who stood beside Macaulay at the far end of the table could not have looked more different from everyone else in the room. In contrast to the sombre business suits and uniforms arrayed around the table, Böhse wore a green tweed jacket with a loud yellow check and a flamboyant bow tie.

'That's a brave choice,' murmured a man from the MoD to the policeman beside him.

From the front, Böhse appeared to be quite bald, but the moment he turned his head they could see that what hair he had left was tied into a neat little ponytail. Dr Frederick Böhse was no Whitehall clone.

'And so,' he began, as if finishing off an earlier sentence, 'the reason we are all here today is that we believe that the man who presented himself to the hospital in Plymouth last night has received a potentially fatal dose of radiation from an unknown source that is emitting gamma rays.' He spoke with just the faintest trace of a German accent, but it did not go unnoticed. 'It is the job of my agency to find that source and secure it. We cannot do this alone, naturally, so this will be a combined effort.'

Reynolds prompted him: 'Thank you, Doctor. And the RDD? Could you summarize what you told me on the phone?'

'Ah, yes. An RDD.' The scientist's eyes shone with fervour as he scanned the faces in the room. 'It stands for Radiological Dispersal Device. Short of an atomic bomb going off, an RDD is perhaps our worst nightmare. Some people call it a dirty bomb. Essentially, this device combines radioactive material with high explosive to scatter it over a wide area. In a city like London, it would make a whole district uninhabitable.'

'Could you be more precise, Doctor?' asked Reynolds. 'What sort of timescale are we talking here?'

'My department has done projections,' replied Böhse, 'and we estimate that if terrorists got their hands on enough material for a small- to medium-sized RDD and detonated it in, say, the centre of Birmingham, the entire business district would have to be evacuated.'

'For how long?' asked a woman from Public Health England.

'It depends on the clean-up operation,' answered Böhse, 'but we are talking weeks. Whole city blocks could potentially be contaminated.'

'Jesus . . .' she breathed. 'So how did we suddenly get from a sick man walking into A and E in Plymouth to talking about a dirty bomb going off in Birmingham?'

Reynolds cleared his throat and addressed the room: 'It's time we shared something with you so that we're all on the same page. Some of you,' he nodded towards the MI5 deputy director, 'already know what you're about to hear. But I think everyone needs to hear what Syed Khan of SIS has to say. Sid?'

When he stood up to address the room Khan chose his words carefully, weighing them up as he spoke. 'As most of you are aware, we are already facing a national security threat in the form of an unknown weapon being sent, by sea we believe, to this country's shores. My service has been working flat out on this for weeks now. We've just had a significant development.' Even those in the room who knew what he was about to say were giving him their full attention.

'And that was the discovery, just off the Cornish coast, of a miniature submarine. Intelligence is, as we all know, an imperfect science. We rarely get our hands on every piece of the jigsaw. Instead, we try to make the connections between the pieces we do have.'

Khan stopped as the door opened and a civil servant came in and whispered something in the Home Secretary's ear. Reynolds nodded, the man left and Khan resumed.

'So we now have three pieces of the jigsaw.' He held up three fingers for emphasis. 'There's the suspect ship, the MV *Maria Esposito,* which our Special Forces raided unsuccessfully two nights ago. We're still holding her and her crew in Falmouth while the Navy goes over her with a fine-toothed comb. Then there's the mini-sub that's been found very close to where the ship was intercepted. A coincidence? We don't think so. And now we have a man showing up in A&E with acute radiation sickness.'

Khan looked down at the Home Secretary, who nodded just once. Khan took a short breath, then delivered his *coup de grâce.* 'As of this morning,' he told the room, 'it is our belief, with a high degree of certainty, that in the last forty-eight hours an RDD – a dirty bomb – has been brought ashore in this country.'

Reynolds stood up once more as Khan sat down. 'So let me be clear on our priorities before I close this meeting. I want every possible resource deployed to locate this device, neutralize it and arrest the people involved. I want every precaution taken to protect the places we think they might try to set it off. In the meantime, we have no choice but to follow the recommendation of JTAC, the Joint Terrorism Analysis

Centre. I am raising the national terrorism threat level to Critical.' Most of the people in the room had expected that, but some hadn't and one man dropped his spectacle case on the table, causing it to spring shut with a loud snap. 'Sorry,' he mumbled.

'In case anyone needs reminding what Critical means,' said the Home Secretary, 'it means an attack is expected imminently.'

As they filed out, grim-faced, it occurred to many of those attending the COBRA session that this was the moment things had changed. A line had been crossed.

Chapter 57

THE CORNISH TOWN of Falmouth, with its picturesque harbour and cobbled streets, is not a mainstream naval base like Portsmouth. But it is home to something just as vital to Britain's defence industry. With one of the largest deep-water harbours in the world, Falmouth has the biggest ship-repair complex in the country. Sheltered from the Atlantic by the promontory of Pendennis Head, Falmouth docks are a confusing maze of engineering and electrical workshops, cranes, gantries and vast sheds. With three large docks and the capacity to take in vessels of up to 100,000 tons, the Port Authority had had little difficulty in accommodating an 8,000-ton freighter registered in Manila, even at short notice. The MV *Maria Esposito* was moored, under Royal Navy guard, at Dock No. 2. Floating beside her, hidden beneath a frayed grey tarpaulin and likewise under guard, lay a patchily dark-green vessel just six metres long. The salvaged mini-sub had been brought in to join her.

Luke had wasted no time in calling Commander Jorge Enríquez at the Colombian Embassy: he needed his expertise. The young naval attaché had cleared his engagements for the next day, and by the morning after the mini-sub's discovery he was on the 09.25 Flybe scheduled flight from London Gatwick to

Newquay. As Dr Böhse was briefing the COBRA crisis meeting in Whitehall, Luke was meeting Enríquez in the arrivals hall.

'*Madre de Dios!*' exclaimed Enríquez. 'You've been through it, my friend. I heard what those bastards did to you.' He gave Luke a bear hug then held him at arm's length to look him up and down. 'Seems you lost weight too. I guess those narcos didn't feed you too well!' Luke shrugged, picked up Enríquez's overnight bag and walked him to the waiting Land Rover. He had only the slightest of limps now, and the pain in his foot had almost disappeared.

By eleven fifteen they were on the A30, driving south to Falmouth. At the entrance to the dockyard Luke produced his government ID and signed in his guest. They proceeded past the gatehouse, keeping to the designated 5 m.p.h. speed limit, and parked on the quayside next to where the mini-sub lay tethered beneath its tarpaulin. A pair of armed naval ratings in camouflage stood guard in front of it. Once again, Luke flashed his ID card on its coloured lanyard and the sailors moved aside a barrier to let them pass.

'That's a bit pointless,' remarked Luke, when they were out of earshot.

'What is?' said Enríquez.

'Those sailors on the barrier. Both carrying weapons with no magazines in. Not much use if we were terrorists.'

They stopped just short of the edge of the quay. There, wallowing in the water, lay the salvaged mini-sub, its crude iron hull stained, pitted and streaked with rust. Someone appeared to have given it a coat of dark-green paint some time ago, but most of that had worn off to reveal the scarred metal beneath. At the stern, a pair of tiny propellers was just visible above the waterline between two hydro-vane flaps that protruded on either side, giving it the means to dive or ascend in the water. On top of the hull, slightly aft of centre, there was a round access hatch with its lid open. Luke and Enríquez descended the metal ladder embedded in the wall of the quay then jumped onto the mini-sub's hull, steadying themselves on its smooth, curved surface with their hands.

'So, what d'you think?' asked Luke, as he straightened. 'How does this thing compare with the sort of craft you've been catching in Colombia?'

'I'll tell you one thing,' replied Jorge. 'If this boat belongs to anyone other than a cartel then it's a damned good copy. We've been busting vessels like this all up and down the Pacific coast for at least seven years.'

'Which begs the question,' continued Luke, as he approached the access hatch, 'what the hell is one of your country's mini-subs doing all the way over here? Shall we?' He pointed to the hatch, hauled himself over the lip and started to let himself down the inside of the funnel, rung by rung. Almost immediately, he stopped and came back up. 'No,' said Luke. 'I've got a better idea. You go. You'll know what to look for.'

Enríquez moved past him and paused to extract his wallet from his pocket. 'Look after this, will you? It's a tight squeeze down there.'

Commander Jorge Enríquez was big for a Colombian, a well-fed descendant of a long line of Spanish *conquistadores*, and a whole head taller than some of the indigenous Indians in his country. It took him a few seconds to squeeze his broad shoulders through the hatch and into the gloomy interior.

Just as he had expected, it was intolerably cramped. He guessed that whoever had piloted the craft had been chosen as much for their small stature as for their navigational skills. He reached down and took out a small pencil torch that he had brought with him from London with exactly this in mind.

'You OK down there?' called Luke.

'Yeah, no problem.' He began to scan the interior. Back home, he had crawled into vessels like this to find them stacked high with cellophane-wrapped parcels of pure cocaine, but this one was empty. There was a basic steering-wheel console at the front and a couple of crude metal seats. For whoever had piloted the craft, he noted, there had been absolutely no view, nothing to look at, just a bare metal bulkhead. It was enough to drive a man crazy. Enríquez could see that whatever navigational equipment there had been had vanished.

Jorge Enríquez was about to call it a day when his torch caught something in its beam. He arched his body closer to get a better look. There, on the wall of the coffin-like cabin, someone had used a sharp implement to carve their name. Except it was not a name. It was a phrase, a gang totem, a marking of the turf. Enríquez froze. He recognized it at once. It brought back memories of mutilated bodies dumped in back streets, hostage videos of grown men crying for their mothers as they went to their deaths. It was just two words: Los Inocentes. To Enríquez, that meant everything. It meant that someone, or something, very bad had been in the submarine.

'Luke?' he called, a brittle edge to his voice that even he didn't recognize. He knew in that moment that Colombia's murderous drugs war had crossed the Atlantic. The narcos had brought their war to Britain.

Chapter 58

IN THE STRATFORD gallery that afternoon, everyone noticed the difference. Elise, only recently back from her extended leave, was unusually happy, even radiant. For days she had appeared drawn and stressed, something clearly playing on her mind, but now she tripped into the gallery from her lunch break with a smile.

'Someone's in a good mood today,' said Samantha on Reception. 'Care to share?'

'It's Luke,' she replied, putting her bag on the desk, brushing her hair back then retying it. 'He's coming back tonight!'

If Elise had known the true circumstances of Luke's return to London that day, it might have tempered her good mood. The inscription found inside the mini-sub at Falmouth dockyard had triggered a flurry of frantic phone calls to London. The Colombian naval attaché had rung his ambassador, and Luke was on the phone to Vauxhall Cross, speaking to his boss. Los Inocentes, he told Angela, was another name for García's cartel, the very people he had gone after in Colombia. Angela, in turn, told him about the man who had collapsed the previous evening in Plymouth

A&E with acute radiation sickness. Khan had yet to return from the COBRA crisis meeting but, one by one, the pieces of the jigsaw were slotting into place. At least now they had some idea of what they were up against: a radioactive dirty bomb, smuggled into Britain. A task force was being set up, she told him, inside Thames House, the headquarters of MI5, to coordinate the hunt for the radioactive material and the people behind it. Luke was to represent SIS and he was to report there first thing the next morning.

Luke chose to share none of this with Elise when he rang her on her lunch break. Instead he tried hard to keep the tension out of his voice. He wanted more than anything to put a soft cocoon around her, an invisible blanket that shielded her from all the unpleasantness he had to deal with in his job. It was bad enough that he had come back into their Battersea flat nursing a weeping hole drilled into his foot by psychopathic criminals. He certainly didn't want her having nightmares about the full horrors of a dirty bomb.

Elise retrieved her bag from Samantha's desk in the gallery. 'Any messages while I was out?' she asked.

'No – but I almost forgot. There's a lady here to see you. Wants to take a look at those new watercolours. She's in the Quiet Space.'

Elise walked through to the inner room. As an art dealer, she had acquired the knack of knowing if someone was serious or not about buying. Of course, these days you couldn't always tell for certain where the money was. More than once she had nearly made the mistake of ignoring some unshaven young man in a T-shirt and trainers, only to find he was a dotcom millionaire with a black Amex Centurion credit card or something similar. But this lady definitely had money, Elise concluded. Mulberry oxblood handbag, pearl earrings and matching necklace, a tailored jacket that looked like Armani and killer heels – were they Christian Louboutin? Probably.

'Hello! How can I help you?' Elise greeted her with a warm smile and a practised familiarity, intended to make customers feel at ease.

The woman was still studying the softly lit paintings on the wall as Elise held out her hand. 'Elise Mayhew, head of International Sales.' It was a pretentious title, really, given that there were only three of them on the sales side, but it sounded suitably grand.

The woman turned to face her and removed her glasses, which had ultra-modern thin steel rims. She seemed to be studying her, which Elise now found a little disconcerting.

'Ah, yes, thank you,' said the woman. A faint trace of an accent, and a slight lisp, Elise noticed. 'I am looking for works by the Portuguese artist, Agostinho Bacalao. You have him here?'

'Agostinho Bacalao?' Elise's forehead furrowed into a frown. 'I don't think I know him. Is he in the catalogue? Let me go and check.'

But the woman was already moving towards the door. 'Is all right,' she said. 'I have to go now. Maybe I come back later.'

How odd, thought Elise, as she walked her to the door. 'Do you have a card, maybe? Then we can let you know if we come across any of his work? Oh, and I didn't catch your name.'

'It's Ana María,' said the woman, and closed the door softly behind her.

Chapter 59

THE NEXT MORNING the taxi dropped Luke in the forecourt of Millbank Tower on the north bank of the river and he covered the final hundred metres on foot. Thames House is an imposing sight, a stolid Grade II-listed building that sits like a grumpy uncle, guarding the western approaches to Whitehall, a fitting place for the headquarters of MI5. As he walked up the wide, sweeping steps, he knew immediately he had made the wrong call on dress. He was wearing a suit, and almost everyone else here was in casual clothes.

What with the Colombia trip, the MV *Maria Esposito* debacle and, yesterday, the mini-sub, it felt like an age since he had set foot inside an office. It was not a prospect that filled him with joy. But, physically, he felt on top of the world. His injuries from Buenaventura had almost healed and last night had been brilliant: a tentative reunion with Elise that had culminated in their cancelling their dinner reservation and staying in bed for nearly ten hours. He smiled. This morning he ached in places he had almost forgotten about.

At the top of the steps he fished out his Intelligence Service ID on its coloured lanyard, pressed the pass to the electronic reader and keyed in the code that Angela had told him to memorize. For a split second he caught sight of his reflection. He hardly recognized himself in a suit. The cylindrical Perspex door slid open and he stepped forward onto a round black mat. The door closed behind him with a click. He felt as if he was on the set of a sci-fi film, walking into a teleporter to be beamed onto some alien planet. In front of him another Perspex door opened. On either side of him, men and women, mostly young, some in jeans and trainers, were streaming into work. How many of them knew about what García and his narcos had sent to these shores? How many of them were still chasing the jihadists, the Russian spies, the Chinese cyber hackers and the 'Real IRA' diehards that accounted for MI5's daily workload? And how many would now be redirected to this latest, most terrifying priority? He would soon find out.

From the lobby, a corridor extended to both left and right, and he could see several widescreen LCD televisions on the wall, showing a silent rolling stream of Sky and BBC twenty-four-hour news.

A woman was coming forward to greet him. She was short and neat, dressed in a dark blue jacket and skirt and no-nonsense black shoes. Perhaps his suit had not been a mistake after all.

'Luke Carlton?' she checked.

'Yes, that's me.'

'Hi, good morning. I'm Sangita Lal, from Task Force Support. Welcome to Thames House. I'll take you through to meet the team.' She led him through a set of swing doors, then into the lift, up to the second floor and along another corridor. Somehow, possibly because this building was so much older than MI6's

1990s headquarters at Vauxhall Cross, Thames House felt more institutional, with its cream-painted corridors and massive walls. It reminded Luke of any one of a dozen Defence Ministry sites he had had the displeasure to walk into. Invariably he couldn't wait to get out.

'Here we are,' said Sangita. They had stopped outside an unmarked door. 'You're going to need an extra security code to get in here,' she told him, indicating the swipe reader on the wall. 'It's printed on the card I'm going to give you now. Can I ask you to memorize it? We prefer it that way.'

'Sure.' Luke took the card, glanced at the numbers on it, then handed it back to her.

'Coffee and tea are just down the hall there,' she added. 'Do you want to give that code a try? We'll go in and meet the team.' Love it, Luke thought. I'm being tested like I was at school. After all he had been through, there was something strangely comforting about this. Sangita, he suspected, would probably not have been told about his ordeal in the Chop House.

Luke swiped his ID card through the reader and keyed in the code. After a series of beeps a tiny light flashed green and the door clicked open to reveal a room crammed with desks and a window that looked out onto a blank wall. The first thought that came into his head: This looks exactly like a classroom. No view, not much natural light, just walls of pale, fluorescent-lit, lavatorial green. The desks were arranged in a U round the room, all facing towards the principal workstation at the apex. Around fifteen people were at work, most of them staring intently at computer screens; at each desk there were printed title cards with roles like 'Team Leader A', 'Investigative Desk Officer', 'Support Worker' and so on.

'Let's get you introduced, then I'll leave you to it,' said Sangita, leading him to the man at the head of the room. 'This is Damian Groves, the group leader on this investigation,' she said. 'Damian, this is Luke Carlton. From across the river.'

To Luke, the man bore an uncanny resemblance to the actor who played Harry Pearce, the spymaster in the TV series *Spooks*. A red lanyard hung around his neck with 'National Security Council' printed on it. 'Thanks for joining us,' he said. 'Welcome to the Crisis Cell. In fact, welcome to the Security Service. We're still just setting up in this room, as you can see. I've come across from G Branch myself, our agent-handling division – sorry, I expect you knew that.' Luke shrugged. He hadn't known it. 'We've allocated you a workspace over there by the printer. I'll get someone to give you the log-ins for the secure network. That way you'll be able to talk directly to VX from your laptop.' He turned to Sangita. 'Before I forget, Sangita, can you tell Cheltenham we'll book the line from here for the video conference call at three?' He turned back to Luke. 'Sorry about that. Got rather a lot going on today. I'll let you get settled in. I'm addressing everyone in ten minutes, so best not to take any comfort breaks just yet.'

Luke thanked him, then walked beside Sangita as she gave him a whistle-stop tour round the task force. 'Basically,' she told him, 'we've pulled together a lot of different disciplines from a number of different agencies and we're all crammed into this one room.' She pointed out various people at various desks but almost no one looked up. 'So you've got Covert

Surveillance over there, that's my service. Next to them is Agent Handling, also MI5. Over there is GCHQ, Public Health England, the Metropolitan Police, and next to them you've got the National Crime Agency.'

'And those four?' asked Luke. He indicated a group sitting slightly apart, almost like a cell within a cell. They appeared to have an enclave all of their own at one end of the room, and he could just make out some graphic charts flickering on their screens.

'They're the scientists, the defence radiological experts from DRPS,' she replied, lowering her voice for no apparent reason. 'They're absolutely key to all this. OK, it looks like Damian's about to start so I'll head off. I'm on extension triple-five-zero if you get stuck for anything. Best of luck.' She flashed Luke the briefest of smiles, then let herself out.

Damian Groves was standing and looking at his watch. 'Could I have everyone's attention, please?' he said, as he waited for phone calls to end and the room to settle down. 'Before we begin to zero in on our intelligence targets,' he continued, 'we need to have a clear understanding of what we're dealing with here. I want each and every one of you to be fully conversant with the nature of the threat we're facing.'

The threat. How many others in this room, wondered Luke, had come as painfully close as he had to its sharp end? As a young marine, and later as an SBS operative, he had always held a certain disdain for deskbound analysts. But his months with SIS were whittling away that prejudice. Quietly spoken men and women he had dismissed as backroom pen-pushers were turning out to have rather interesting field records, running agents in the dark recesses of Moscow back streets, the souks of Dubai and across the porous Turkish–Syrian border. Luke leaned forward and gave Groves his full attention.

'So to that end, I want to introduce you to a subject-matter expert.' He gestured towards the woman standing next to him. She was dressed in a black jacket and scarlet shirt with a wide, open collar and she had one of those frosty, brittle hairstyles that left not a single hair out of place. Luke put her at around fifty. 'This is Dr Sheila Morton,' continued Groves. 'She's from the DCU. That's the Divisional CBRNE Unit based here in London. Anything chemical, biological, radiological or nuclear that's liable to go off inside the M25 is their call.'

It occurred to Luke that it might be a bit presumptuous to narrow the target down to Greater London when they still didn't have a fix on it, but day one on the task force was probably not the best time to interrupt.

'Good morning, everyone,' began Dr Morton. 'I've been asked to give you a basic scientific briefing on what we think we're dealing with here. RDDs.' She looked round the room, searching for recognition. 'There are essentially two types of radiological dispersal device – those that go bang and those that just quietly emit dangerous isotopes. Both can kill you if you get close enough and both are, potentially, a national security threat.' She moved out from behind the desk and began to pace slowly up and down. 'Now, we don't yet know,' she said, 'which type of RDD the players are planning to detonate or where they're hoping to hide it, but as of yesterday afternoon we've got every single radiological detection device out and deployed around the country.' She stopped pacing and thrust both her hands deep into her jacket pockets.

'Washington,' said Dr Morton, 'is understandably concerned. They're sending over a team of nuclear physicists from the National Laboratory at Argonne, Illinois. If that man walked into A and E in Plymouth with acute radiation sickness, that means the material is not properly shielded. Which means that, wherever it is now, it should be detectable. We're starting with Plymouth and working outwards from there. We'll be using detectors in every major city up and down mainland Britain.'

'Not Belfast, then?' interjected an MI5 intelligence officer at the front. His voice carried a soft Ulster burr.

'No. Our assessment is that if the players have gone to the trouble of bringing this thing ashore in Cornwall, then dumping the mini-sub that carried it in, they're not going to bother shipping it off by sea a second time.'

'Fair enough,' said the Ulsterman, and scribbled a note on his pad.

'So, let's assume for now,' continued Dr Morton, 'that this is a classic RDD. That's going to be a combination of high explosive with a radioactive isotope. The blast itself won't kill any more people than a normal bomb would, but it will do two other things. It will aerosolize the isotopes into the atmosphere, exposing anyone within range to radiation.' *Aerosolize?* This expression was new to almost everyone and several people were jotting it down.

'Gamma rays go through human tissue, so anyone who comes into contact with it will be affected,' she added. 'The closer you are, the higher the dose, and the more chance you have of being poisoned, possibly fatally.'

'And the second thing?' The Ulsterman at the front again.

'The second thing is panic.' She was perched on the edge of the desk now, facing the room and swinging her legs. 'When radioactive dust settles on surfaces after an explosion we call it "groundshine". Depending on which isotope is used, it can take years to decay. It's called a half-life – some of you might remember that from GCSE science.' There were knowing nods from her trio of colleagues in the DRPS cell. 'In some cases you're looking at a half-life of thirty years. Imagine what that can do to the centre of a city like London. It could make several boroughs uninhabitable for a generation.'

Her briefing had plunged the room into a mire of introspective gloom. Truck bombs, IEDs, suicide bombers, marauding machine-gun attacks and kidnappings were the staple fare of the terrorist plots that MI5 had been working to prevent. Known threats of a known magnitude. But this was a whole new order of terror. A young woman from Public Health England raised her hand with a question.

'Yes?'

'I understand that there are ways of mitigating the effects of radioactive contamination. I mean, it can be cleaned up, can't it?'

'Yes . . . it can,' Dr Morton answered with some hesitation. 'But I wouldn't want to give you the impression that that's all in a day's work. It's intensely laborious and eye-wateringly expensive. Believe me, I've seen the projections. It would still take months to pronounce the centre of a city the size of, say, Leeds free from that sort of contamination.'

Dr Morton tilted her head to one side and appeared to reconsider the question. 'But you're right. New treatments are being developed the whole time. There's some great work being done by the US nuclear research people over at Argonne. Spray-on and peel-off polymer gels that soak up the isotopes, that kind of thing. But let's not beat around the bush. An RDD going off in Britain would still be the worst terrorist attack this country has seen since . . . well, ever. The economic impact alone would be catastrophic.'

Another young woman had her hand up, her long, silky black hair cascading halfway down her back. When she spoke, Luke detected a very slight trace of a Chinese accent. 'You mentioned earlier,' she said, 'that an exploding RDD wouldn't kill any more people than an ordinary bomb. Is that right?'

Dr Morton stiffened, misunderstanding the question. 'Excuse me, are you questioning my analysis?'

Groves got to his feet, ready to defuse the situation, but the woman was ahead of him. 'Not at all,' she replied hastily. 'I just wanted to make sure I'd heard you right.'

'Oh. I see. Sorry.' Dr Morton's shoulders relaxed. 'Yes, that's right. At least in the initial blast. Give or take one or two extra casualties, that's our projection. It's the after-effect and the ensuing panic that would raise this thing to another level.'

'Dr Morton, I have a question.' It was the Ulsterman again. 'I'm still not completely clear why this RDD threat is such a big deal. What exactly does this stuff do to you?'

She got up and walked over to where he sat. 'D'you

ever watch films?' she said, facing him square on. 'Go to the cinema? Watch Netflix at home?'

'Yes, of course. Why?'

'Ever seen a Harrison Ford film called *K-19: The Widowmaker*?' She turned to address the entire task force. 'Because I recommend that when you go home tonight you should all order it up and watch it. Just fast-forward to the bit where the Russian sailors enter the crippled submarine's nuclear reactor core to try to repair it. Because that is about the most graphic depiction of acute radiation sickness you'll ever see on telly. Skin peeling off, raw welts and blisters, vomiting, men collapsing as their legs give out from under them. And it's a true story, by the way. Everyone who went within a few metres of that radioactive core died soon afterwards. That, ladies and gentlemen, is what we're up against.'

Chapter 60

THE TURRET LODGE Guest House in Plymouth was not the sort of place where anyone would want to spend their holiday if they had the choice. Its grimy pebbledash walls and scratched frosted-glass windows had seen better days. Outside, on the pavement, discarded polystyrene fast-food cartons skittered along in the wind. A newspaper, curled and yellow with age, had made a home for itself wedged between the wall and a rusting lamp post. The Turret Lodge was cheap: it offered rooms for £29 a night. No breakfast, no Wi-Fi, no questions asked.

When the two men with wind-burned faces and Latin looks had asked to check in without producing ID, the landlady had scowled at them. Meg Tucker was well used to taking in strangers, but there was something about these two she didn't care for. 'Thirty-eight pounds a night,' she grunted. 'Take it or leave it.' They had taken it. All the next day they had kept to their room, ordering pizzas to the front door and watching TV on the small boxy set that sat on top of the cupboard. Meg Tucker reckoned they were up to something and tiptoed onto the landing to listen outside their door. Soap operas: that was all she could hear. Twice she'd had to bang on the door to tell them to turn it down.

The second time, the door had opened a crack and she'd caught a glimpse of the younger man lying on the single bed by the window. He did not look well. She detected a faint smell of vomit mixed with stale pizza. 'Is he all right, your friend?'

'He is OK,' said the other man, gently pressing the door against her furry slippered foot.

'He don't look well to me,' she insisted. 'D'you want me to call a doctor?'

'No. Is fine,' said the older man, and closed the door on her.

It was later that evening, after she'd finished her tea and tidied away her things, when she heard a car draw up outside. Meg Tucker peered out from behind the net curtains of her tiny kitchen window – she always liked to know who was coming and going. It was a radio taxi from Dial-a-Cab: she recognized the illuminated logo on the roof but she didn't recall ordering one for any of her guests. The driver was opening the back door and the two foreign men were getting in. One didn't look at all well – his friend seemed to be holding him up as he walked. She couldn't be sure in this light, but he seemed to have blotches all over his face. She'd have to give that room of theirs a good going over when they left.

Meg Tucker put it out of her mind as she sat down to watch *The Graham Norton Show*. But half an hour later, when she heard the taxi return, she was sure only one pair of feet went up to the room. She padded back onto the landing outside for a listen, but this time there was silence, not even the TV. It was an odd business, no doubt about it, and she thought about calling the police, but what would she tell them? After all, they hadn't done anything wrong and they'd paid up front, in cash. Besides, she needed the money. There was not a lot of demand for rooms at this time of year at the Turret Lodge Guest House.

Chapter 61

LUKE BOUGHT A sandwich from the trolley for lunch and ate it at his desk in Thames House. Avocado and bacon on wholemeal bread. He chewed it methodically as he worked at his laptop, hovering the cursor over an interactive digital map of the UK. As it passed over certain points a box would flash in the top right-hand corner enclosing a brief set of data. These were the CTUs, the Counter-terrorism Units, distributed around the country, showing where MI5 had combined forces with the police, running agents into local communities. 'SECTU,' read the first line in the box as he paused at a village just north of Oxford. Then 'South-east Counter-terrorism Unit,' followed by the name of a detective superintendent, the head of ops and their mobile numbers.

Next, Luke pulled up a page of statistics from the Met's Intelligence Unit detailing every criminal conviction among the 200,000-plus South Americans living in England and Wales, with their registered home addresses and place of arrest. He cross-referenced that with data supplied by Colombia's National Crime Bureau on known criminal gangs smuggled into Britain, mostly by Eurostar, often on forged Mexican passports. He sighed and leaned as far back in his chair as he could, closing his eyes and ruffling his hair. This really wasn't his thing. Sid Khan had asked him to do it, to send a report back to VX that combined what SIS knew about Colombian international criminal gangs with whatever the Met, the NCA and MI5 had on their activities in Britain. Which, as far he could see, wasn't very much.

Luke could certainly see the value in this as a starting point. If they were to have any chance of catching the people holding the weapon, they had to start second-guessing where they would most likely be hiding and with whom they would be in contact. Unless, of course, it was a completely self-contained cell sent in for this sole specific purpose. In which case they were in even deeper trouble. But this was an analyst's job: Luke saw himself as an operator, not a desk jockey.

'Need any help?' It was the girl with the Chinese accent and the long silky hair. She was standing over him, hand out in greeting. 'Jenny Li. I work here at Five, as a case officer.' She had delicate Asiatic features but not fully Chinese. Mixed parentage, he guessed.

Luke catapulted forward in his chair and shot out his hand to shake hers. 'Luke Carlton. I've been sent from across the river.'

'I know.' She smiled. 'I read your biog.' She indicated the space at the desk next to his computer. 'May I?' She sat down without waiting for an answer.

'You read my biog?' repeated Luke. Was she flirting with him? Surely not, today of all days.

'Don't flatter yourself,' she replied crisply. 'I've read everyone's biog in this room. I like to know who I'm working with.'

'And?' Luke was half expecting her to quiz him about his time with the SBS, or what he knew about García and his cartel.

Instead, she replied, 'It looks like you could do with some IT instruction! You know, there's an in-house program for what you're trying to do there. It's called Circuit. I can load it for you, if you like. Save you a lot of time.'

'Wait,' said Luke. 'You've been tracking what I'm pulling together? But you're sitting on the other side of the room.'

'We're all paid our salaries out of the Single Intelligence Agency account, remember? We're all on the same team. Now, d'you want me to load that program?'

Before he had a chance to answer their attention was requested: Groves had an announcement to make. He looked rather shaken.

'I've just taken a call from the surgeon commander at Plymouth General,' he said. 'The patient who presented himself at A and E two days ago with radiation sickness has just died.'

There was an audible intake of breath. This was a further reminder, as if any were needed, of the urgency of their task.

'He had internal bleeding and raging infections,' added Groves. 'He took a cumulative dose of five hundred and fifty rads and his white blood cell count had dropped off the scale. Unfortunately he never regained consciousness so SO15's detectives never got the chance to interview him. That means we're none the wiser on where he received his lethal dose.'

Dr Sheila Morton, who had briefed them first thing that morning, had left some hours ago. In her absence, one of her colleagues from the radiological protection cell posed an all-important question.

'Did the surgeon commander mention what the isotope was that killed him?' The man asking had thick, black-rimmed glasses and, despite flecks of grey in his hair, retained the faint scars of teenage acne on his face and neck.

'Yes, he did,' replied Groves, hunting for a note he had scribbled down. 'You should be getting the details any minute through your own channels from DPRS. But here it is.' He held up a piece of paper to the light so he could read it. 'It's caesium chloride. I'm told it's used in medical laboratories.'

The trio of scientists exchanged knowing glances. 'That's true,' said the man with the glasses. 'It's also soluble in water and can get into all sorts of cracks. It's hard to clear up, even with a polymer gel.'

'So what are we talking about here?' asked Groves. 'Is this isotope a solid, a powder or a liquid? I'm confused.'

'Most likely a powder,' answered one of the scientists. 'Caesium chloride has about the same density as talc, and it's white. Think of it like a large bag of sugar or flour, except it will be held in a shield container.'

'A container that obviously leaks, or has leaked,' added Groves. 'So it should be possible to plot a trail from everywhere that shows up traces of it. Just as the Met did with Litvinenko.'

'Unless,' said Luke, 'that trail is at sea, not on land.' Several faces swivelled round to him. 'Can I ask how long it would take for someone to show up with symptoms of radiation sickness?'

'That depends on how big a dose they got,' answered the man with the glasses. 'It could be hours or days. But if Plymouth are saying their patient got five hundred and fifty rads . . .' he blew through pursed lips '. . . well, that would take effect within twenty-four hours.'

'Right,' said Luke. 'So if – and we don't know this for certain yet – but if the cartel brought this material ashore in that mini-sub, the one down in Falmouth Dock, it's quite possible that was where the contamination took place. Which would make our dead patient a submariner.'

Even as he spoke, a terrible thought struck him. Jorge Enríquez had been crawling around inside that mini-sub only yesterday. He had to alert him immediately, tell him to go and get himself checked out. There would be questions asked, of course, since no one had authorized him to go inside the sub, but that could come later.

Luke excused himself from the meeting and took his phone out into the corridor. He scrolled down his contact list and dialled Jorge's mobile but it went straight to voicemail. He called his friend's work number at the embassy and a woman's voice answered: '*Oficina del Comandante Enríquez. Buenas tardes.*'

'May I speak to Señor Enríquez, please? It's Luke Carlton from the FCO.'

'I'm sorry,' she said. 'Commander Enríquez has gone home, he is not feeling well.'

Chapter 62

NOBODY TOOK MUCH notice when Luke let himself back into the task force ops room. His face wore a look of profound concern but that was hardly surprising, given the circumstances. Britain was facing a catastrophic threat and he was one of the privileged few to be burdened with that knowledge.

Groves was still speaking as Luke returned to his seat, wondering if he should report his fears about the Colombian naval attaché and the mini-sub. But the prospect of seeing his friend carted off and quarantined in an isolation unit when he was probably fine put him off. He would give it one more hour, no more.

'Carlton. Glad you're back,' said Groves. 'We've had another update. I've just been sharing it with the team here. That ship, the one you intercepted off the coast?'

'The *Maria Esposito*?' said Luke.

'That's the one. It turns out there's considerably more to her than we thought.'

More than *you* thought, reflected Luke. We always suspected she was hiding something, just needed more time to search her.

'The Navy divers and search teams have finally been all over her, top to bottom,' said Groves. 'It took them a while to bring in the right equipment but they've come up trumps. It transpires she had a false hold with a concealed hatch. She'd had a lot of work done before the voyage. Enough to hide a six-metre mini-sub beneath all those useless tractor parts from North Korea. They're holding the crew in Falmouth. Devon and Cornwall Constabulary are working on the charges now. So,' Groves raised his voice to include everyone in the room, 'now that we know how they got this stuff over here, we can move forward. This is what needs to happen.'

At that moment Luke's mobile vibrated quietly in the breast pocket of his suit. As discreetly as possible, he lifted it out to see who was calling. It was Jorge Enríquez, the Colombian naval attaché, returning his call.

'Carlton,' said Groves, looking straight at him.

'Yes?' His phone was still vibrating, he had yet to answer it. He really needed to take this call but now was not the time: Groves was about to issue a tasking order.

'I'll need you to coordinate everything we have coming in from every CHIS inside the Colombian international criminal networks, both here and overseas.'

'Sorry to interrupt,' said a scientist. 'But what's a CHIS?'

'Apologies for the jargon,' said Groves. 'It stands for Covert Human Intelligence Source. They're our moles inside whatever group we're trying to penetrate.'

With the attention off him, Luke stole a glance at his mobile. Enríquez had rung off. Keeping his eyes on Groves as far as he could, Luke tapped out a text. *Are u ok? U ill?* He pressed send.

'Conor.' Groves was talking to the Ulsterman now.

'I need G Branch to shake up every CHIS we have with any connections to the South American underworld.'

'I'm going to be straight with you,' the man replied. 'We don't have a lot of traction in that area. We tend to leave it to the NCA and the Colombian Embassy. They've not really been on our radar as a national threat priority. Until now.'

'Understood,' said Groves. 'Cross-check with the NCA if you need to, but keep it discreet.'

Luke's phone was buzzing again. It was Jorge. This was getting really awkward. He excused himself and slipped out into the corridor.

'What's up, buddy?' said Jorge. 'What's with the messages? I'm nursing a hangover here.' He certainly didn't sound like someone dying of radiation poisoning.

'I'm going to cut straight to the point. That minisub you climbed into yesterday? Down in Falmouth?'

'Don't tell me you want me to go back?'

'No. Quite the opposite. It's possible – we're not sure yet – that it's contaminated . . .'

There was a long pause at the other end.

'Jorge? You still there?'

'I'm still here. I'm not happy to hear this, Lucas, but I'm still listening.'

'You need to get yourself checked out for radiation poisoning.' Luke told him to go to University College Hospital in Euston Road. It was the best he could offer right now.

When he walked back into the ops room Groves shot him an irritated look. 'If we could keep your attention in here for just five minutes, Carlton,' he told him. 'There's been another development. It seems every time you step out of this room we get a new piece of the jigsaw.'

'Sorry, sick relative,' Luke lied.

'I've had Plymouth General on the line again. They've just taken in another casualty with suspected radiation sickness. And this one's conscious. They're transferring him up here immediately. He'll be coming in by air ambulance and going straight to the isolation ward at UCH.'

'That's the death ward,' said a man from the Met. 'It's the one they put Litvinenko in.'

Groves ignored the morbid remark and looked at Luke. 'Carlton, you speak fluent Spanish, don't you?'

'Pretty much, yes.'

'Good. Because apparently that's the only language the patient speaks. You'll get first crack at him. Jenny, go with him to the hospital. Oh, and please listen to the medics there. Don't go taking any chances on protection when you interview this patient. I don't want anybody else getting contaminated.'

Chapter 63

ELISE MAYHEW WAS not a worrier. Since paying off her student debts early, with a bit of help from her parents, she had had few financial worries, although the art gallery, it had to be said, did not exactly pay her a generous wage. But she was acutely observant – that was partly what had got her the job in the first place and perhaps why she had spotted Luke at that party. Now something had registered with her that just didn't seem right.

It was halfway through the afternoon when she looked up from the digital archive she was skimming through online.

'Samantha,' she called, to the girl on Reception, 'did that woman from yesterday ever call back? You know, the one who was waiting when I came back from lunch?'

'I don't think so, no.' Samantha had been eating a biscuit and she had to swallow the last of it before she could answer fully. 'Why? I mean, let's face it, most of them don't come back, do they?'

'It's not that,' said Elise, biting her bottom lip distractedly. 'She asked about a Portuguese artist, Agostinho Bacalao. She was very specific about his name.'

'And?'

'He doesn't exist! There's absolutely no record of him in any catalogue. I Googled him too. Nothing. And that surname just means "codfish". You don't think that's odd?'

'Maybe. A bit. If she comes back and you're out I'll make sure I get her card.' With that, she replaced her earphones.

Elise put on her coat, walked outside, lit a cigarette and observed the shoppers of St James's as they scurried along the pavement. Should she mention it to Luke? She knew he was incredibly busy right now and probably wouldn't welcome the call. No, it could wait. Besides, she was holding out for the right moment to broach something rather more delicate with him.

Chapter 64

'FRIJOLES,' HE GROWLED. 'Simple refried beans. *Nada más*, nothing more. So what the fuck is wrong with my chef that he can't cook them the way I like? Hmm?' El Pobrecito was not a happy man that morning. Since the massacre of the police commandos at the fortified farmhouse at Ituango, Nelson García and his entourage had moved their base deeper into the hills to avoid retribution from the state. They had chosen an uninhabited coffee planter's villa as their new headquarters. The place was crawling with ants and García had been grumbling constantly as he pined for the lost comforts of his farmhouse.

'Tranquilo, Patrón,' Valentina purred, as he lay face down on the makeshift acupuncture table. 'You give yourself too much tension. Here . . . I'm going to make it better.' Gradually, like an angry dragon being lulled to sleep, the cartel boss's bad mood subsided and his shoulders slumped. A smile of contentment settled on his coarse, pockmarked features and his eyes closed. For a man with five mobile phones, a multi-billion-dollar drugs empire and a great many enemies, this was perhaps the only time of day when he could completely relax. Outside the window the rain fell in sheets, drenching the untended crimson

helliconia shrubs that crowded up against the wall and soaking the lush foliage that cloaked the hills.

Valentina looked down at the bear of a man beneath her as she removed the needles, one by one, then began to knead and massage his shoulders. His street-fighting days were far behind him but the muscle bulk was still there, built up over long hours in his mother's filthy backyard, endlessly lifting two concrete breeze blocks stuck on the ends of a scaffolding bar. Valentina, too, was stronger than she looked, her slender frame hiding a toughness that few could see from the outside.

Now there was an interruption, a soft but urgent knocking at the door. Nelson García roused himself with a scowl. His time with Valentina was supposed to be sacrosanct, regardless of which safe house she was summoned to. Had he not issued a standing order that he was never to be disturbed at this hour unless it was a matter of great urgency? The door opened and Suárez stepped into the room, the only man permitted to come into his inner sanctum. García sat up and faced him with a mixture of weariness and expectation.

'*Entonces?* So?'

'You need to come down to the signal room, Patrón. There's something you'll want to see.'

The drug lord threw a glance at Valentina. 'Can't it wait?' he said.

'No, it's happening now. You have to see it with your own eyes. Believe me, Patrón, you won't want to miss this.'

El Pobrecito threw on a Hawaiian shirt, wrapped a towel round his waist and followed his security chief towards the door. To his surprise, Valentina asked if she could come too. 'Am I not, as you say, part of *la familia* now?' she said coyly. García laughed and beckoned her to follow, but Suárez stood where he was and shook his head firmly. What he wanted to show his boss was sensitive and he still didn't trust the girl. To him, she would always be *una persona ajena*, an outsider. Valentina looked crestfallen but she returned obediently to her station beside the acupuncture table.

Down the steps the two men went, along a corridor damp with humidity, until they came to the door of a room that served as the nerve centre for the cartel's global operations. The two guards posted outside stood up when they heard them coming, cradling their Galil assault rifles and nodding deferentially to García and Suárez as they swept into the signal room. Suárez was still working on beefing up the physical security measures for the place, but when it came to online digital security, Morales, the cartel's cyber wizard, was way ahead of him. Every phone call made over the internet, every text message, every email, incoming and outgoing, was routed and rerouted through a bewildering chain made up of thousands of different IP addresses dotted around the globe. At each stage it was re-encrypted so that anyone thinking of intercepting, like the NSA at Fort Meade, for example, would have to get very lucky: they would need to know exactly what they were looking for. It was not so much a question of searching for a needle in a haystack, more that the haystack was built of needles and nearly all of those needles would lead to a dead end.

'It started ten minutes ago,' said Suárez. He was standing next to his boss with his arms folded, watching his reaction. 'Can you see now why I wanted you to be here?'

'Incredible,' whispered García. For once, he was almost lost for words.

The thing about being the boss of a super-rich drug cartel is that when an invention comes out, you don't have to wait around for it to hit the mainstream retail market. At the urging of Vicente Morales, the cartel had acquired one of the most advanced models yet of a three-dimensional printer and now here they were, in a coffee planter's discreet villa on a Colombian hill-side, watching it do its stuff. In the centre of the room a shape was taking form before their eyes, rising up from the floor like a phantom. Made of pale yellow resin, it was growing and morphing as if it had a life of its own.

'Dios mío,' breathed García, and crossed himself. He didn't trust it at first, yet still it fascinated him. 'Is this the replica of . . .?'

'Sí, Patrón. They phoned to alert us it would be coming through.'

'My God! This is amazing!' García erupted into a great belly laugh and hugged Suárez. 'I want them to tell me all about it. Get them on the line now. Wait! We should give it a name first.' García's face bore a mis-chievous expression. 'We will call it . . . we will call it La Palomita. The Little Dove.'

Chapter 65

WITH CALLOUSED HANDS García stroked the shape before him. Then he rubbed his thumb and forefinger together, held them to his nose, sniffed and wiped them on his Hawaiian shirt. This creation, he decided, was *un monstruo,* but it was a beautiful monster: it was *his* monster. It reminded him, for just a moment, of the container they had put his little brother's ashes in all those years ago in the *barrio,* after he had swallowed the rat poison someone had placed around the drains. But this replica, this avatar, which had miraculously built itself in quick-setting resin, here in the communications room of his villa, it was a source of pride, not of sadness. It had been Morales' idea, buying a 3D printer so the boss could see for himself the instrument of his own very personal revenge on the British. And Suárez, never far from his boss's side, had approved it.

It had taken more than two years to get to this point, two years of mounting bitterness and frustration, as one shipment after another had been stopped and impounded, all due to the meddling of the British spies and their sons-of-bitches informants at the ports. The idea had come to them in 2014, soon after that terrible, terrible April day in Cartagena. Seven tons!

Those *malparidos*, those bastards, at Customs had seized the lot, all those sealed packages carefully hidden in an innocuous consignment of pineapple pulp bound for Rotterdam. It wasn't all his, of course. A massive shipment like that needed to be shared with other players, like the KIA and the Yamaha cartels. But it had cost his people dearly. Over US$250 million at a conservative estimate. More, when you took into account the revenues that washed back into the network from the sales on the street.

From that moment on, vengeance had been only a matter of time and careful planning. Suárez and those who worked for him had done their research diligently, then trawled through their international contact base until they found the right connections. A meeting was arranged with the North Koreans on neutral ground in Havana. A down payment was made and a 'memorandum of understanding' was agreed as to when the material would arrive and how it would be delivered. But when disaster struck again a year later off Scotland, with three tons being seized at sea by Britain's Border Force and the NCA, García had erupted in fury. That had been the final straw. The project, he had demanded, must be brought forward without delay.

'Get them on the line,' he told Suárez now. 'I want to know how my Palomita will work.'

'I can explain it to you myself, Patrón, if you would like?' As the cartel's security chief, Suárez preferred to avoid unnecessary phone calls whenever he could. He believed he would live longer that way.

'No!' insisted García. 'Call our people in *Inglaterra* right now. Have them explain it to me. I want to hear from the *científicos*, the scientists.'

Minutes later they handed him the phone and the voice crackled through the earpiece from across the Atlantic. García stood there, listening, still in his Hawaiian shirt and with a towel wrapped around his waist. He nodded, impressed and inquisitive at the same time.

'I understand,' he said. 'So three component parts . . . *el explosivo* and the nuclear thing and the shield. So what am I looking at here?' García patted the 3D-printed replica beside him. 'Which bit did you send us, hmm? . . . All of it? . . . I see. And when will my Little Dove be ready?'

Those in the signals room that morning noticed that it was at exactly this moment that his demeanour changed markedly. For the worse.

'What do you mean, *un problema*?'

There was a pause on the line and he could hear urgent whispering.

'Don't talk when I can't hear you!' he shouted at them. 'What problem?'

The voice at the other end sounded hesitant, even afraid. That was natural: García expected people to be scared of him. He liked it that way. But it was not him they were afraid of.

'Señor Patrón . . .' said the voice. 'The device, it is making people sick. The two *submarinistas* who sailed with it, they are not well, not well at all.'

'Then prepare it quickly. Waste no time. Suárez will tell you when it is time.'

He cancelled the call and handed the phone back to his security chief. 'If there are any more problems,' he said, as he left the room, 'I don't wish to hear of them. Just tell me when it is ready.'

Chapter 66

AS GARCÍA SAUNTERED back to his private room in the villa, a midnight-blue BMW eased quietly out of a London side-street and merged into the afternoon traffic on Millbank. It took a right turn at the roundabout, crossed Lambeth Bridge, passed the IMAX cinema, then crossed back over Waterloo Bridge and headed north along Southampton Row and beyond that towards a hospital on Euston Road. In the back sat Luke and Jenny Li, a slew of scientific papers spread on the seat between them. He was unsure why Groves had assigned her to go with him when he really needed a radiation expert from DPRS, not a case officer from MI5.

'How much do you know about CBRNE?' he asked. His tone was neutral enough but it was still a loaded question. Not very much, was his guess. When she didn't answer straight away he added: 'Sorry, that's chemical, biological and—'

'I know what it stands for, Luke. I did a degree in chemical engineering. My thesis was on industry safety protocols.'

'Ah.' So that was why Groves had assigned her to this. They had stopped at the lights beside Holborn tube station, and through the tinted rear windows

Luke looked out at the streams of pedestrians crossing in both directions, blissfully unaware of what he and his team were striving to prevent.

'What about you?' said Jenny.

'Excuse me?' He had zoned out there for a moment.

'I was asking how much you knew about CBRNE?'

'Only what I picked up in the military,' he replied. 'The Cold War was well and truly over by the time I joined up so it wasn't considered too much of a priority.'

'Not a problem,' she replied. 'The Cabinet Office commissioned quite a good paper on this that you might want to read. It's among this lot somewhere.' She rummaged through the papers on the back seat, then handed him a slim pamphlet. 'Here you go.'

'*Strategic National Guidance.*' Luke read the title page out aloud as he took the booklet and started to flip through it.

'You might want to go straight to page forty-four,' she told him. 'It's an appendix on radiological substances. Gives you the basics.' She flashed him a superficial smile and went back to sorting through the documents on her lap. Luke read on.

'Gamma rays are the most energetic of the three types of radiation and can pass through the body. Gamma rays can penetrate most materials and require a substantial thickness of lead or concrete to provide an effective barrier.' How the hell had the two submariners been poisoned? Had the protective shield broken? And what about Jorge Enríquez? Luke was seriously worried about him. And now he was probably going to bump right into him at the hospital. This was getting messy.

'And there's this one.' Jenny handed him the

confidential report on the various stages of Alexander Litvinenko's terminal decline. 'It's all in there,' she told him. 'The urine tests, the hair falling out, the attempts to reverse it with Prussian blue. I think we should brace ourselves to expect something similar with our guy.' She looked up as the car slowed. 'Oh, we're nearly there.'

The MI5 driver let them out in the forecourt of University College Hospital, parking just behind a St John's ambulance. They pushed through the double doors, making room for a woman being wheeled in on a gurney, then approached Reception. A man emerged from behind the desk to meet them. 'Luke Carlton? Jenny Li?' he asked. 'Welcome to UCH. Follow me this way, please.'

Through a set of swing doors and down a spotless corridor, where every few seconds a disembodied voice in the wall above them admonished everyone, in a stern, matronly way, 'Please help us to protect our patients. Gel . . . your . . . hands.' Up in a lift, along another corridor, then they came to an abrupt halt outside a room. Two armed uniformed policemen stood guard at the door.

'They're here to see the patient brought up from Falmouth,' said the receptionist quietly, as if confiding a secret, even though no one else was around.

'Sorry, can't let you in.' It was the older of the two policemen who spoke.

'I think you can,' said Luke, his voice carrying an authoritative hint of his years as a Royal Marines officer. He produced his Security Service pass and Jenny Li did the same. 'Someone should have told you we were coming,' he added.

'No one's told us anything,' replied the policeman,

studying Luke's ID and handing it back like an unwanted flyer. He might as well have shown him a library card for all the good it did. 'We're going to have to ask you to move back now. This is a secure area.'

'Seriously?' said Luke. This was unbelievable.

'Seriously,' replied the policeman, moving closer to Luke now and squaring off opposite him. They were about the same height but the policeman was heavier, his body made bulkier still by his stab vest and utility belt. 'No one goes through unless we get told by Gold Command. Now, please, sir, I'm asking you once more to move along.'

The man who had escorted them from Reception seemed suitably embarrassed. Clearly this was above his paygrade too. 'Can I suggest,' he said to Luke and Jenny, 'that I take you both down to the cafeteria while we sort this out? It shouldn't take long. Really, I'm very sorry.'

Jenny Li had a face like thunder. 'I've taken that man's badge number,' she hissed to Luke, as they walked away. 'He's not heard the last of this.'

Precious time was lost as they sat in the café on the ground floor, drinking weak tea and making small-talk while the receptionist worked the phone, chasing authorization. Luke's mobile vibrated twice with an incoming text message from Jorge Enríquez. He read it and felt like shouting for joy. *Had the scan. All clear.* That was a massive burden lifted off his conscience.

An hour later, when authorization had arrived, all three returned to the isolation room and saw, with some satisfaction, that the policemen had changed shift. They were let in immediately.

The smell hit them as soon as the door closed behind them.

'Sorry about that,' said a voice behind them. 'It's glutaraldehyde. We use it as a broad-spectrum disinfectant. I'm Tomasz Kracjek, the consultant here.' He smiled but kept his hands at his sides. 'We operate in a sterile zone,' he added. His white medical coat was partially open, revealing a crisp Charles Tyrwhitt shirt and designer jeans. His patent brown leather shoes looked strangely out of place in the clinical, aseptic environment. 'Look,' he seemed to be gathering his thoughts, 'I'm afraid our patient is not in a good way. His immune system is heavily suppressed so any infection could finish him off. We're having to take every precaution.'

'Is he well enough to talk to us?' asked Jenny, cutting straight to the point.

'If he wants to. Yes. But I'm afraid you've just missed your chance for now. He's back under sedation – he'll be out for the next few hours. His body needs all the strength it can get to fight this thing. I can call you when he comes round . . . I must say, we were expecting you a bit sooner. He was wide awake just fifteen minutes ago. Was it the traffic then?'

Chapter 67

'CAN'T SAY I'M a fan of this coffee,' observed Jenny Li, then, for the nth time that hour, glanced at her watch. 'This is just so annoying,' she said, jiggling her foot distractedly. 'I can't believe those two on the door blocked us like that. If they had any idea how much this is setting us back! And what if he never comes round? We'll have missed our best chance. Aaargh.'

Luke had been using the enforced waiting time to read up on radiological half-lives and the different properties of caesium chloride. He smiled to himself. This was a very different Jenny Li from the cool, calm and collected individual who had come up to him in his lunchbreak. 'You can't blame the coppers,' he told her. 'They were only doing what they'd been told to do. And, besides, the patient may not know anything useful – or tell us, even if he does.'

'In human intelligence,' Jenny said slowly, 'everything is useful. Every phrase, every offhand remark. Trust me, you let nothing go to waste. So when we get up there, Luke, we'd better make damn sure every second counts.'

Luke was about to reply when the receptionist rushed into the cafeteria. It was the same man who had welcomed them hours ago. 'You're on,' he said.

'He's awake and lucid. Best be quick in case they change their minds upstairs.' Luke and Jenny were on their feet even as he said this, cups abandoned on the table. Back the way they had come, dodging past groups of hospital staff heading home after their day shifts, they half walked, half ran to the isolation room.

Tomasz Kracjek was in the anteroom, looking tired but animated, his Charles Tyrwhitt shirt less pristine now. 'I can let you go in,' he said, 'but you'll have to put on these first.' He pointed to a pile of what looked like white spacesuits. 'They just go over the top of your clothes.'

'Just us in there with him, right?' checked Luke.

'That's the access we've been told to give you,' replied the consultant. 'But we'll be watching from next door. On the monitor. If we think he's getting distressed or needs medical attention, the interview has to stop as soon as I say so. I'm afraid that's the deal.'

They nodded as they struggled into their protective suits.

'One last thing,' said Kracjek. 'I'm sure I don't need to remind you. Just don't touch the patient! OK, in you go.'

Luke wasn't sure what he expected to find when he pushed open the door. A scene from the biological disaster movie *Outbreak* perhaps, with a man only vaguely visible beneath an oxygen tent. But there was no tent, no drama, just a solitary man in a light-green hospital gown, lying slack and listless, an IV drip in his arm, his scalp smooth as a billiard ball, his eyes barely open. They hardly registered a flicker as he and Jenny walked in.

Luke pulled up a chair and sat as close to the patient

as he dared without actually brushing against him. Jenny remained standing in front of the closed door. There was a strange, sickly smell in the room that he couldn't quite place. Urine? Yes, probably. He spotted a bag of golden liquid suspended beneath the man's bed and winced inwardly: he had been in a bed like that not so long ago himself, recovering from his Afghan wounds, at the Queen Elizabeth in Birmingham, drips going in and tubes coming out. But he had made it, and one look at this man told him there wasn't going to be a happy ending here.

There was no time for preamble or introductions. Luke decided to go for broke. *'Tú estás muriendo,'* he told him flatly. 'You're dying.' A flutter of eyelids in response. 'These people here,' Luke continued in Spanish, gesturing to the door behind him and the hospital in general, 'they're doing their best to save you. They're trying to help you, to make you comfortable.' The patient groaned quietly and turned his head to one side, against the pillow. He didn't look very comfortable. His eyes were open now but they were dull and vacant. If they were focused on anything it was the blank expanse of wall next to the window. Luke couldn't even be sure that he was listening so he put his head closer still, close enough to hear the rasping of the dying man's breath.

'What did you do?' Luke whispered. 'What did you bring into this country? You need to tell me. You have nothing to gain by keeping it secret now.'

Slowly the man turned back to face Luke. He seemed to be trying to raise his head and now his lips were moving. Luke strained to catch the words. Even Jenny Li had left the safety of her post to edge closer to listen.

'Es . . . es una bomba.' His head sank back onto the pillow, as if the effort of saying just those four words alone had exhausted him.

'Where?' There was no point in asking complicated questions. For all he knew, this was the man's last hour on earth. 'Where is the bomb hidden?'

Again his lips moved, soundlessly this time. Luke could see he was trying to purse them but they were trembling. 'Ma . . . Mancha . . .' Luke looked at him sharply. La Mancha was Spanish for the English Channel and he knew the device was already ashore. But the patient hadn't finished. His lips were still moving. 'Manchest . . .' he gasped.

Luke looked at Jenny. She had heard it too.

'Manchester?' repeated Luke, making eye contact with him. He needed to make sure he had heard him right.

The sick patient didn't move, didn't say anything in response, but his eyelids blinked twice. Then he closed them and was still.

Chapter 68

THE LIGHTS WERE burning long after dark at Vauxhall Cross that evening. Nothing unusual about that: sometimes they stayed on all night, blazing like a candelabrum across the muddy waters of the Thames.

It was after seven o'clock when Angela Scott knocked on Sid Khan's door. For once, she didn't wait for an answer but marched straight in and confronted him.

'I've been waiting all afternoon for you to be free,' she barked. 'Just what kind of an operation are you running in Colombia?'

There were other directors who might have taken great offence at her tone, but not Sid Khan.

'And good evening to you too, Angela. Please, have a seat.' Khan waved at a chair and put away his glasses. 'Cup of tea?'

'No, thank you.' Angela remained standing, her pale, freckled face slightly flushed. 'I want to know why you allowed one of my team – and you know who I'm talking about, Luke Carlton – to be sent off on an extremely hazardous assignment without giving him the full intel picture.'

'Sorry, I'm not following you.'

'You know exactly what I'm talking about, Sid.' She walked up to his desk, placed her hands flat on its polished surface and leaned towards him. 'I'm talking about Tradewind.'

Khan flinched, but said nothing.

'When were you going to tell him we have another agent in place? An agent who just happens to be absolutely crucial to this whole operation?' Khan studied her but still said nothing. 'Because d'you know what I'm thinking?' said Angela, her face more flushed than ever now. 'I think you've done the dirty on Luke Carlton. If I didn't know you better I'd say you set him up to fail. You may be two ranks my senior but I swear to God there had better be a good reason for this or I'm taking it upstairs.'

'Please, Angela, it's just us in here.' Khan looked rattled now but he gestured once more at the empty chair. 'I'm asking you to sit down.'

Reluctantly, she did so, straightened her charcoal-grey skirt and faced him square on.

'I spoke to Carlton over at Thames House today,' she began. 'I needed to bring him up to speed on that Joint Intelligence Committee meeting we attended.'

'And?'

'He wasn't born yesterday. He's not some spotty school leaver who's watched too many episodes of *Spooks* and happens to have passed the psych analysis and come up clean on developed vetting. He's already served his country with distinction. He's an ex-Special Forces officer, for Christ's sake, with a Conspicuous Gallantry Cross. He pretty much worked it out for himself.'

'How's that?' said Khan. His forehead had started to shine with sweat and she couldn't help noticing that damp patches were appearing at the armpits of his polo shirt.

'How's that?' she repeated sarcastically. 'Try looking at what's been coming in from Bogotá station. Luke's been given access to everything Clements sends us from Colombia but he's noticed some material he didn't recognize. It didn't match anything from Langley or Foreign Liaison with the Colombians either. So he asked me to check it out with Agent Comms. Turns out it came in on a separate, standalone satellite feed. You've been running Tradewind off-the-books without telling him.'

'I hear you.' Khan held up an admonishing hand.

'I haven't finished yet. Ordinarily, I'd say this is none of my business. But given the current threat level – and the fact that Luke was tortured and narrowly escaped being macheted to death – I'd say it's every bloody bit my department's business!'

'Angela. You've been in this organization long enough to know some things are so sensitive that the fewer people with access the better – for everyone. Tradewind is one of those situations. I can't tell you who he – or she – might be. There is an extremely tight circle of people who know about this, all within this Service, and we need to keep it that way.'

She waited for him to say more. So far he had told her nothing.

'Okay,' said Khan, relenting now. 'We do have an undeclared agent down there. That person is in deep cover, really deep cover. Their ability to communicate with us is severely limited but the product we get – when we get it – is pure gold.'

Angela took a deep breath and shook her head.

'Would you mind closing the door?' he said.

'Why? They've all gone home on this floor. That's why I waited until now.'

'Can't be too careful. Remember what happened in Baku? Anyway, I'll level with you, Angela. Tradewind is placed extremely close to the principal we're focusing on. So close that most of this building doesn't even know.'

'And you chose to keep this from Luke? You don't think he deserves to know? Given that he's been down there at the sharp end, not you or me?'

Khan shrugged. 'I'm afraid I've said all I'm going to say on this. You'll just have to manage the situation. I'm sure you'll find a way.' He smiled at her. 'Now, if you don't mind, it's getting late, and I've still got a heap of stuff to get through here.'

'All right.' She got up to leave. 'I'll defer to you on this one. You're the director of CT, not me. If there's a reason to keep Luke in the dark, I can accept that. But, please, just make sure it's a good one.'

Chapter 69

BY THE TIME Luke got home it was nearly midnight. Day one on the Thames House task force and already he felt exhausted. The second he and Jenny Li had left the isolation room at UCH they had paced quickly down the corridor until they found a quiet corner to call in what they had gleaned from the desperately sick patient. They agreed that Jenny would call Groves, while Luke would alert Khan. They stood a few metres apart, their backs to each other, beside a broom cupboard on the second floor.

'It's Manchester,' said Luke. 'At least, that's what he's telling us. And he says it's a bomb. Which we pretty much knew.'

'Go on,' said Khan.

'That's it. That's all there was. Believe me, it wasn't easy getting that out of him.'

'Young man,' replied Khan, 'you need to go straight back in there and try again. We need a lot more than you've just told me. Like, where in Manchester? The town hall? The cathedral? The Etihad Stadium? Come on, we need names, addresses, phone numbers.'

Luke waited for him to finish. 'Sid, I don't think anyone's told you just how far gone the man is. He's at death's door – he can barely speak. He is very, very sick. We can give it another go, if they'll let us back in, but I thought you should know about Manchester straight away.'

'You did the right thing,' said Khan. 'Is he fit enough to be polygraphed?'

'Not in his present state,' Luke replied.

'Do we believe him?'

'Hard to say. I think he knows he's at the end of the road, so what's he got to lose by telling us?'

Khan was silent, digesting this new development. 'Does Groves know about this?' he asked eventually.

'One of his case officers is telling him now.' Luke ended the call and turned to Jenny.

'Let me guess,' she said, and they recited in unison: 'Names, addresses, phone numbers!' It was the only light moment in a very dark day.

After that Jenny had left quickly, heading back to Thames House to work with Groves and others on the Manchester angle. Luke had stayed on at the hospital, waiting for the green light to revisit the patient, but it never came. A different consultant had taken over for the night shift. Every half-hour or so he had come out to see Luke: the patient was alive but unresponsive. At 11 p.m. Luke had called it a day and caught a cab home to Battersea.

Which was where he found Elise, still up, dressed in a black and silver kimono, and holding a glass of wine. She came over to greet him, put a slender arm around his neck, pulled him towards her and gave him a lingering wine-wet kiss. 'Welcome home, babes,' she said softly. 'I've missed you today.'

After the day he had just had, which seemed to Luke to have lasted about thirty-six hours, he had envisaged tiptoeing quietly into bed and crashing straight out. Now he slumped on the sofa, resting his head on the back and closing his eyes. Elise walked round behind him and reached down to loosen his tie, then gently massaged his shoulders. 'I won't ask you how your day was,' she said, 'because I bet you can't tell me. Instead I've booked us a nice surprise.'

'And what might that be?' asked Luke, looking up at her from his position on the sofa. 'A Secret Escapes weekend for two? A visit to Victoria's Secret?'

She gave him a deadpan look, then a fixed smile. 'No, Luke Carlton. I have not been shopping for lingerie. I've got us tickets to see Ellie Goulding at the O2.'

'Great. When?'

'Next Saturday.'

Luke said nothing.

'Oh, come on,' said Elise, 'don't tell me you can't make it?'

There were some things Luke just couldn't hide. All those years in Special Forces successfully giving his interrogators the blank poker face on escape-and-evasion exercises. Name, rank and number, that was all. Anything else: 'I'm sorry, I cannot answer that question.' Yet here he was now, transparent as a pane of glass when it came to Elise. He knew that a week hence he could be anywhere. In fact, the chances were he probably would be somewhere else, given what they had learned today. Would they have found the device by then? What if the patient had been bluffing and London, not Manchester, was the real target?

His brain racing, Luke found it hard to picture himself skipping off to an Ellie Goulding concert when he was one of the very few people who knew that a radioactive bomb could go off anywhere in

Britain at any moment. 'It's fine,' he lied. 'I thought I had something on then.'

But Elise knew him too well. 'Bollocks,' she said calmly. 'It's me you're talking to. I'm not one of your squaddies, remember? If you don't want to tell me, that's fine, I get it. Just don't give me any BS. I thought we'd agreed on that.'

'You're right, and I'm sorry.' Luke ran his hands through his sandy hair and let out a deep sigh. He had so much on his mind he wondered if now was the time to break protocol and let her in on some of it. But how many other couples were in the same situation? He was damned if he'd be the first to break the circle of trust and leak.

'Luke,' said Elise, pulling him closer and kissing him again on the lips. 'Luke, I love you – I hope you know that – but some things have got to change. Things haven't been right between us these past few weeks. It's OK, I'm not about to accuse you of anything, but you have to admit you've been quite distant, haven't you?'

Luke could hardly deny she had a point. But where was all this leading?

'So I've been thinking,' she continued. 'Now would be a really good time to consider moving to something . . . a little more . . . stable?'

Luke met her eye. 'Elise, I have a stable job. I work for the Foreign Office. Well, let's call it a branch of government anyway. They pay me a monthly salary. Remember?'

'Yes, I know that and I don't want to stop you doing what you like. It's just that you're hardly ever here, are you?'

'I'm here now,' he replied, and she shot him a look.

'Sorry,' he added, 'that was crass. Where are you going with this?'

'Well,' she said, brightening, 'you remember Hugo? At Goldman Sachs?'

Luke groaned. 'Oh, God! What's the golden boy up to now?'

'I know you don't like him,' continued Elise. 'A lot of men don't. But hear me out. Hugo's brother, Jackson, runs the family investment business.'

'Of course he does.'

She ignored his interjection. 'Well, Jackson wants to meet you. He's looking to hire someone with your skills.'

'My skills?' Whoever Jackson was, he couldn't have the faintest idea of the sort of thing Luke had spent the last few years doing. If he did, it would probably give him nightmares. 'And what kind of a name is Jackson? Is he in entertainment?' Almost as soon as he'd said it Luke regretted it. He was coming across as an arse.

'I'm sorry,' he told her. 'I'm just out on my feet here. If that's what you'd like then, sure, I'll meet him.' Go through the motions, thought Luke. At least you can say you've made the effort. Listen to what he's got to say, pretend to consider it, then make your excuses and leave.

'Great.' Elise smiled. 'I'll set it up.'

She forgot to mention the mystery woman at the art gallery.

Chapter 70

WHILE LUKE SLEPT fitfully, the wheels of government machinery were rolling through the night, unseen by the public. The single word 'Manchester', uttered by a sick man in a London hospital, had triggered a national response. The Prime Minister and senior members of the National Security Council were alerted; authorization was quickly given for full preventative measures to be taken. One of the first calls made from the task force operations room in Thames House was to the Police National CBRNE Centre at Ryton, in Warwickshire. Located south of Coventry, and 130 kilometres down the M6 from Manchester, it was judged the most suitable base to respond to the new information. All leave was cancelled: officers were called at home, brought back on duty, then organized into four-strong search teams, equipped with FH40 radiation detector pagers: grey devices that resembled a bulky mobile phone. Every available scientific detector van was mobilized, with two being diverted from East Midlands airport and sent up to Manchester. Under Operation Cyclamen, the joint venture between the UK Border Agency and the Home Office to prevent radioactive materials entering the country, a light aircraft with detection equipment was put up to criss-cross the night skies over Greater Manchester.

Of course, one awkward question was troubling those directing the operation. What if 'Manchester' was just a red herring to distract everyone from the real target?

'We can't take any chances on this one,' said Alwyn Hughes, the national security adviser. It was one a.m., a full five hours since Luke and Jenny had reported in from the hospital, and he was speaking on a secure line to the director general of MI5. 'The advice the Home Secretary and I have given the PM,' he said, 'is that we maintain those assets up at Manchester but be prepared for this device to crop up in any of our cities. Especially London.'

'We've put out feelers with all our CHISes around the country,' replied the MI5 boss, 'and the Greater Manchester Police Counter-terrorism Unit is working its sources now. Kelly's gone straight up there to oversee it.' There was a brief buzzing on the line.

'Sorry, I didn't catch that,' said the national security adviser. 'Who?'

'Kelly Little. The national coordinator for CT.'

'Of course, good. Look, I don't think we can maintain this level of activity for very long, so the pressure is on your people to find this thing, and it's only going to get worse.'

'You think I don't know that?' said the director general.

'Of course you do. Forgive me,' said the Welshman. 'It's just that sitting where I am right now is bringing this whole thing into focus. I've just signed an order to break open the strategic reserve of casualty bags. Three hundred.'

Chapter 71

ANA MARÍA ACOSTA was not an impatient woman. But the journey from 94 Ashburnham Gardens to the house in Twickenham took her nearly an hour, during which time she used the horn no less than seven times. Driving her beloved midnight-blue Audi RS 5 convertible through the lurching late-afternoon traffic of south-west London, she went over the priorities. Suárez had been quite explicit on the phone. Drop everything, get over to the safe house where the hired muscle were staying and sort things out. Use your discretion, he had told her. From the sound of it, something had gone very wrong in that house and things were unravelling fast. They couldn't have that, not at this late stage in the operation. It needed to be dealt with immediately. Her plan for the English spy's girlfriend had to be put on hold.

She parked in the quiet suburban street and reached onto the back seat for her outsize tan leather handbag. She locked the car, walked up to the door and pressed a manicured finger to the entry phone for the ground-floor flat. Ana María grimaced. The buzzer was smeared black with over-use and slightly sticky to the touch. She wiped the tip of her finger on her jeans. '*Sí?*' came a disembodied voice from inside.

'Final,' she replied. It was the simplest of prearranged code words and she was buzzed in.

The room stank. That was the first thing she noticed. That and the unmade beds, the empty beer cans, the discarded fast-food containers and the scattered porn mags they had made little attempt to hide. Ana María stood there in her dark denim skinny jeans, her immaculate leather shoes, her tailored jacket and her crisp white shirt, which revealed only a hint of cleavage, and took it all in at a glance. Five men, sitting, squatting, sprawling among all this detritus. Three were smoking, drawing long gasps on those coarse Pielrojas black-tobacco cigarettes from South America. Another was cramming the last of a takeaway doner kebab into his mouth, absent-mindedly wiping his greasy fingers on the thin yellow bedspread beside him. Then he licked them. These men disgusted her.

'Qué barbaridad,' she remarked, curling her lip in contempt. 'Which of you wants to speak up?' They looked from one to another in silence. 'Fine.' She pointed at the man who had just finished eating his kebab. 'You!' she commanded. 'Tell me, in your own words – and please take your time – what in hell has gone wrong here? You were given a simple task. Collect the merchandise, bring it to London, store it somewhere safe. Other people, smarter than you, will take over. But no. We've lost two people. They're in hospital and the alarm has been raised. This *bastardo* government knows what is coming now. The net will be closing in on us. So?'

'Señora . . .' He was a big man with big fists, but spoke meekly. Ana María Acosta had acquired a certain reputation within the underworld. 'We followed our instructions. We did exactly as you ordered. The pick-up in Cornwall went without any problems. We covered our tracks on the beach, we made the rendezvous at . . . *Cómo se llama?* What was it called, that place?' He turned to the others behind him.

'Jamaica Inn,' they chorused.

'Yes, Jamaica Inn. We made the switch there, then drove up here to Londres. We came off the M4 at the junction as planned, and took that road on the map. And now, *mira,* we are here, in Twicken Ham.' He stopped, catching his breath.

'So what went wrong?' she pressed.

'At first everything was to plan. We have housed the cargo at the address they gave us. It's in a lock-up, not far from here and—'

'Take me there.' She cut him off in mid-sentence. 'I need to see it.'

'Señora, please, we cannot go in there. Not now. Not after what has happened. You see, they called us, the two *submarinistas.* They called us from Plymouth when they began to feel sick. They warned us. This – this *instrumento* we have been transporting, it makes anyone who goes near it fall sick. It is not safe to be around it.'

Ana María scanned their faces. Was anyone here going to man up and finish the job? Apparently not. 'So does this mean,' she spoke slowly and deliberately, 'that you will not be completing the job you have been asked to do?'

All five men looked down at the carpet, too embarrassed to speak.

'That's OK,' she said gently. 'I understand. Just do me this one favour. Write down the address of the lock-up and you can all go back to your lives. You will be taken care of, don't worry.' The men brightened. She took out a pen and a small notebook and passed them to the man still squatting there. She waited patiently, still close to the door, as he scribbled down the address and returned the notebook to her.

'And now I must pay you all your farewell bonuses,' she said. Her back to them, she reached into her handbag.

Later, safely buckled into the Audi, she reflected on their expressions when she had turned to face them. Priceless, something she would always treasure. It was the look of despair, the acknowledgement of failure, the acceptance of punishment. The silenced Czech-made Skorpion machine-pistol had bucked and trembled in her hand as she emptied the entire magazine into the room, sweeping it from side to side, slicing through the worthless trash who had let her and *El Patrón* down. Thirty rounds should do it. When the shooting stopped she had sniffed and smiled, the weapon still warm in her hands, savouring the familiar smell of cordite smoke from the spent cartridge cases that littered the floor at her feet. God, how she missed killing: there were so few opportunities now in this job.

Ana María punched a number into her phone. In another part of London a man with slicked-back hair and a ponytail answered the call. '*Hola*,' she said. 'It's me. It's done. Send someone to clean it up.'

Chapter 72

'IS THAT IT? All that fuss for this? *Madre de Dios*, it's nothing special, is it?'

For a long time they just stood there, staring at it, keeping their distance but fascinated by its latent power, by what it could do, the damage it could cause. Behind them, the heavy metal door of the lock-up had been bolted shut. The instructions had been clear. It was paramount that nobody should see what was inside. Outside, just beyond the industrial park, the residents and workers in the shops, the off-licences and law-abiding businesses of Twickenham went about their daily lives, oblivious to what was hidden in their midst. The 'pig', the cylindrical object that had been conveyed halfway across the world to them, was unremarkable to look at. True, it was an unusual shape, like a giant metal Thermos or a miniature milk churn. Its only distinguishing features were its two metal handles and the small yellow and black sign near the top with the triangles. But to Ana María, standing at a respectful distance, it was all about what it could do. To her, it was beautiful.

'This isn't going to be a problem, is it?' said Silvio, the man with the slicked-back hair.

'What? The drivers?' she replied, surprised. 'Of

course not. They've played their part and now no one is to know. Suárez is already choosing the replacements for the next phase.'

'And the welder?'

'He's ready. He's been working hard for us.'

Silvio nodded. Then a frown creased his forehead as he remembered something important. 'You know, *El Patrón* is concerned about this contamination issue. He's not worried about the two submariners. They, too, have played their part. But he wants to know if this is going to affect the operation.'

Ana María composed her thoughts. How much should she tell him? Perhaps not everything, Silvio could be jumpy at times. Now was clearly the time to offer some reassurance. 'I consulted our expert, that head of department at the university. He tells me there is a reason behind it. They got sick because they were exposed for too long, that's all. They spent days with it at sea. He says as long as you keep your distance you're fine.'

Instinctively, Silvio took several paces back, moving away from the device. 'But how do we know that it's not leaking now? We could be contaminated ourselves without knowing it, no?'

Ana María laughed. 'You shouldn't worry,' she said, staying exactly where she was. 'If there was a risk of contamination, all those idiots I disposed of in the flat would have been sick.'

'And?'

'They all looked fine, believe me. Just scared. And useless. The operation is better off without them.'

'How much did they know?' asked Silvio. 'Isn't there a chance they could lead the police here, to this place?'

'Those goons? None at all. I checked the flat. There's nothing to reveal where this place is. That piece of information died with them.'

'And the *submarinistas*? What if they're telling everything they know to the medics in hospital?'

Ana María had suddenly had enough of his questions and his worrying. *'Escúchame,'* she told him. 'Listen to me. You need to have more confidence in Señor Suárez. He thinks of everything. The two submariners were fed a cover story. Some city up north. If they tell anything it will lead the *gringos* to look in the wrong place. Those pilots were useful fools, that's all.'

Silvio took a cautious pace forward, still wary of the shiny metal container that stood inside the suburban lock-up. 'So when do we begin the next phase? Has the other material been sourced?'

Ana María glanced at her watch to check the date. 'You mean the explosives? Yes. We're on schedule. We have time. The party is still days away.'

As they spoke, the welder was hard at work, goggles and gloves in place, in a windowless basement not three kilometres away. Keith Gammon loved his work. Ever since he was a boy he had worked with metal, cutting it, crafting it, welding and shaping it. And this was his biggest challenge yet. Ten years ago he wouldn't have touched a job like this. But since then, his life had taken a different course. It had started well, with a stint in the Royal Engineers, learning explosives and demolitions, but when he'd left the Army he'd fallen in with a bad lot. He'd made his choices, been caught and convicted. They'd done him for theft of copper signal cabling, resisting arrest and causing grievous bodily harm to a British Transport Police officer.

Keith Gammon had come out of Wandsworth Prison an angry and bitter man. In his last six months inside he had made certain connections, people with good contacts on the outside. When the legitimate job offers did not come knocking at his door, he had made the call to the number they had slipped him just before his release date. It was small stuff at first, modifications to vehicles and equipment, erasing registration stamps, putting decommissioned firearms back into service, nothing too taxing for a man of his skills.

Later, when the big offer had come from the man with the ponytail, he hadn't had to think too hard about it. The welder was under no illusions, of course. Even though they gave him only a vague outline of what the job entailed he knew it would be highly illegal, and not without risk to himself. He certainly didn't fancy going back inside, but what they were offering in return almost made his eyes water. A quarter of a million in cash, half up front. Well, he could do a lot with that money, and he knew exactly where he was going to put it. The welder had his eye on a down payment for a nice little place in the sun, a gated compound near Marbella. After this, Keith Gammon was going straight, it would be *Adiós, Inglaterra* once this job was over.

The Colombians were being more than generous, he reckoned. He had given them a shopping list of what he needed for the task and they had come good, even got him a brand-new Miller 625 Extreme Plasma Cutter, fresh in from the US. He held it now, admiring its clean lines and latent power. Metalwork had come a long way since he was a lad. He shook his head and laughed as he went back to work with the cutter. Practise, practise and practise again. The job had to be done to perfection. Keith Gammon saw himself as so much more than a welder: he was a top-level metallurgist and nothing if not a consummate professional.

Chapter 73

IN THE ROLLING hills of Colombia's Antioquia province it was raining again. Great, drifting skeins that moved like grey ghosts across the verdant landscape. Valentina gripped her umbrella and picked her way carefully down the potholed road, trying not to ruin her shoes. Behind her lay the road that led up to the planter's villa, El Pobrecito's current safe house, where she had nodded goodbye to the guards on the gate and set off for the long weekend to see her family. Everyone across the country was getting ready for the Fiesta Nacional, and as she approached her village, she felt its relaxed, party mood. Children were tying ribbons to balloons in doorways, and coloured lights hung outside the low, thatched huts that lined the road, connected to the generators that hummed and shuddered in their aluminium frames.

Valentina was not in a relaxed party mood. In fact, she felt far from it. The information she had overheard in the last twenty-four hours was burning a hole in her conscience. She had to pass it on, first chance she got. So she did not go straight home that day. Stopping eight hundred metres short of her parents' house, she turned off the road down a narrow, overgrown track that wound through the forest. Good. There were no recent footprints and the broken branches she had placed across the track were still in place. She stopped twice, pretending to take shelter from the incessant drizzle, scanning the track behind her in case anyone was following, the way the Englishman had taught her. Three hundred metres in, she turned off the track and picked her way through the wet foliage until she found the tree stump. She reached into her bag and took out a metal comb. It was an unremarkable object – García's guards had not given it a second glance when they searched her bag – but now she turned it sideways and drove it into the ground.

Valentina began to dig and scrape. The soft, wet earth gave way easily, and as she removed the mud with her bare hands the hole soon turned wet and slick with rain. But she persevered, using the metal comb to probe the earth until it met a hard edge. She had found what she'd come for. Valentina was already soaked but she didn't care. She pulled out the flat stainless-steel box, about the size of a laptop case and still sealed airtight, just as she had left it. She used her sleeve to wipe the mud off it.

Valentina was not, by profession, an acupuncturist. That was pretty much the last piece of training she had received, some months earlier at the embassy safe house outside Bogotá, along with several other cover professions. A student drop-out from Colombia's Universidad Javeriana, she had been a sore disappointment to her family. They had had such high hopes when she had won the coveted place to read Latin American literature at the prestigious university, the first person from her district to go there. It was in her second semester that she had started to hang out with a different crowd, a bad crowd. There were whispers that they had connections to the *narcotrafi-cantes.* Not that her family were any the wiser, being five hundred kilometres away on the other side of Medellín. But the university had its own security people, all ex-cops and military, and they were not blind. The raid on the accommodation block had swept up Valentina and three of her classmates: 850 grams of 90 per cent pure cocaine in a canvas book bag, with several hundred tiny plastic sachets ready for sale, all made for pretty incriminating evidence. Pleas of 'It was for personal use' fell on deaf ears. Her expulsion was never in doubt: it was a clear case of commercial distribution on campus. But the dean was in two minds as to whether or not to turn her and the others over to the police. The university could do without the embarrassing questions, the publicity, the unwelcome media attention. He had raised the subject at dinner that evening with his good friend the diplomat from the British Embassy, a certain Señor Benton. The dean was surprised and delighted to hear that the embassy ran its own re-education programme for gifted individuals who had taken a wrong turning in life. Señor Benton, he learned, would be delighted to meet the troubled Valentina with a view to taking over her education and offering her a second chance in life.

After that things had fallen into place quickly. With the promise of a British passport and a place at a London college in a year's time, Valentina had proved herself more than willing to switch allegiance. She had never really liked the narcos she had met anyway. And she had something unusual to offer. Her family lived just outside Ituango, less than eight kilometres from the operations base of one of

Colombia's most dangerous drug-lords. Her family knew people who worked for him. She was young, attractive and intelligent. Placing her inside the man's favourite refuge had turned out to be surprisingly easy. Nelson García was rumoured to have health problems and she was uniquely positioned to offer him a remedy.

When she returned to her village, now a qualified acupuncturist with the certificate to prove it, it was only a matter of days before she was summoned to meet him. Her first treatment session with El Pobrecito had followed the next morning. She was in.

Valentina looked up at the tree canopy and held out her hands, palms turned upwards. It had stopped raining. The storm over the hills had passed and there was no more static in the atmosphere. It was time. She released the hasps on the sealed box, which opened with a quiet hiss, breaking the airtight seal. Carefully, she took out the waterproofed black iPad, switched it on and waited for it to boot up. Then she removed the other object in the box: a black Fiio X1 high-resolution music player. At least, that was what it looked like to the outside world. When Benton had given it to her in Bogotá he had explained, almost apologetically, that it did not play music. It was a CD, a 'concealed device'. Hidden inside was a Inmarsat Mini C terminal, a compact transceiver that would allow her to transmit and receive messages. Valentina connected the two devices, then stared at the keyboard on the iPad, trying to recall the mnemonic she had memorized. She needed it to give her the line of code that would get her through the first security gateway embedded in the machine's hard drive. She closed her eyes and it came to her, her favourite line from 'In the

Glad Hours of the Morning' by the Mexican poet Homero Aridjis:

Todo es calido en los cerros pintados de oro viejo
(All is warm along the hills painted old gold)

She typed in T-E-C-E-L-C-P-D-O-V, the first letter of each Spanish word in the verse. The effect was instantaneous. The screen went blank, then turned a rich dark green, a similar colour, although she didn't know it, to the building at Vauxhall Cross. In the centre was a small rectangular box, with a blinking prompt bar waiting for her to fill in the next line of code. Valentina typed in her mother's birthday, followed by her postal zip code when she was living in Bogotá. The screen changed again, to reveal a coat of arms, a black motif she recognized. It was a lion, a unicorn and a shield beneath a crown and a motto: *Dieu et mon droit*. She was through security and into the encrypted SIS program.

Valentina was about to prepare her message for transmission when there was a sudden crash in the foliage not far behind her. She whirled round. Had she been followed from the villa? She had checked behind her several times as she walked down the road and there had been nobody. She waited, frozen to the spot. If one of García's men saw her now she had no chance. Then she relaxed: a white-faced monkey loped past, giving her a cursory glance before bounding off into the trees.

She returned to her equipment, moving the Inmarsat transceiver to left and right, as she had been shown, angling it towards the closest satellite, the Atlantic Ocean Region-West, at 54'W. Finally, when the satellite signal was strong enough, she pressed send. In a fraction of a second her message was beamed skywards in a 'burst transmission', reaching a satellite whose existence was known only to a very few people at Vauxhall Cross, then bounced back to earth to be decoded in a small room just south of the Thames riverbank.

Tradewind had made contact.

Chapter 74

THREE DAYS HAD passed since the Manchester tip-off and the investigations were yielding precious little. Leads and clues had dribbled away into nothing, like water into sand. The search was still being discreetly conducted on the streets of Manchester but a sudden 'find', a strange metal object left outside the Victoria Baths, had turned out to be a false alarm. It was an old milk churn left there by some drunken students the night before. In the skies above, the city detector planes patrolled in vain. Of the rogue isotope and its handlers there was no sign. Despite the threat they knew to be hanging over the country there was a determination among senior officials in Whitehall that life had to go on. Remembrance Sunday was fast approaching.

Sir Adam Keeling, the MI6 Chief, had decided, on balance, not to cancel his private dinner with his visiting French counterpart from the General Directorate for External Security in Paris. They had met up earlier in the day at his office but there was still so much to discuss that they would make it a working dinner at his home. Eight o'clock that evening found him in his detached house at the end of a gravelled drive in Kingston-upon-Thames, brandishing an extremely sharp knife and calling over his shoulder to his wife, 'Darling, I'm carving now.' On the dinner table there were candles, fine bone china and a bottle of 2001 Monbousquet claret from St Émilion, brought up from the family cellar. His wife, Margaret, had cooked the leg of lamb to perfection: crisp, brittle skin, punctured with sprigs of rosemary and garlic, the meat pink and juicy inside. Sir Adam carried the wooden board bearing the joint into the dining room and proposed a toast. The four of them stood, raising their glasses: the Keelings, the GDSE director and his chief of staff. 'The Queen,' they murmured in unison.

The doorbell rang. Sir Adam checked his mobile phone and saw there had been a missed call and an SMS from Khan: *Need to see u urgently. Coming over now. Sorry re short notice.* He knew his director of Counter-terrorism too well to question why he was disturbing him at home on a Friday evening. Jobs like theirs inevitably came with certain intrusions.

The armed policeman from the Met's Diplomatic Protection Group checked Khan's ID and showed him in. 'Mr Khan to see you, sir. He says you were expecting him?'

Sid Khan made rather an elaborate show of wiping his feet on the bristly doormat as Sir Adam took his coat.

'Will you stay for dinner?' asked the Chief. 'I'm sure there's enough to go round.'

'Very kind, C,' replied Khan, 'but I've had my tea already.' He turned to the other three. 'Apologies, one and all, for interrupting you.'

'I think you may know Yves Moreau, my opposite number in Paris?' said Sir Adam, making the introductions. 'Director, this is Syed Khan, my director of Counter-terrorism.'

'My pleasure,' said the Frenchman. 'Yes, we met when you came to Paris.'

Khan followed the Chief into his study next door, adding over his shoulder, 'I'll try not to keep him too long.'

The Chief closed the door behind them and motioned Khan to one of the two heavy leather armchairs. 'Drink? Can I pour you a whisky?'

Khan gave him a quizzical look and the Chief slapped his forehead. 'Sorry, I always forget. Of course. Something soft then – lime cordial?' He walked over to the sideboard, his limp as pronounced as ever, and spoke with his back to his guest: 'Is this about the Estonia incursion?' He handed Khan a tall glass of cordial, tinkling with ice.

'No, it's a bit more serious. It's the other matter,' said Khan. 'We've heard from Tradewind.'

The Chief faced him, still standing. Khan had his full attention now. 'When was this?'

'Agent Comms called me just over an hour ago. As soon as I read the printout I came straight over. Thought you'd want to see it for yourself.' Khan passed him a single sheet of paper.

The head of MI6 put on his glasses and spent a full minute reading and rereading it. He was emitting a low humming sound, the giveaway signal that he was less than satisfied. He turned it over in his hand, as if expecting more information on the other side, but there was none. 'This changes everything,' he said, sweeping his spectacles off his face and placing them on the bookcase. 'If García is making preparations to pack up and leave the country it can mean only one thing.'

'That he's moving into the endgame?' said Khan.

'Precisely. That would certainly be my assessment. He knows what's coming down the line once this thing goes off and he's getting out while he can . . . Panama, she reckons?' Sir Adam looked across at Khan, one eyebrow raised.

'That's what she says in her transmission,' said Khan, waving at the paper still in the Chief's hand.

'Can we intercept him?' asked Sir Adam. 'Get the Colombians to grab him before he leaves the country?'

There was a soft knock on the door and Margaret popped her head in to give Sir Adam a meaningful look. She was wearing a simple but elegant black dress beneath a necklace of blue lapis lazuli from Afghanistan, almost the sole benefit she had derived from her husband's Kabul posting. 'Darling, your guests. They haven't come here to see me, you know!'

He lowered his head and raised a hand in submission. 'I know, I know. I'm sorry. Can you tell them I'll be out very shortly? This is rather important what we're discussing here.'

'I'm sure it is, but I think Monsieur le Directeur next door has heard about as much as he ever wants to about my grape-picking days in Provence. It's your turn now.' She left the room, closing the door behind her.

'It's risky,' said Khan, picking up their conversation from where they had left off. 'If we can even get a trace on where he's flying out from, lifting him now might bounce his people into detonating this thing early. The Security Service and the Met are working flat out to track it down before they do. They need every day they've got.'

Khan hadn't touched his lime cordial, the Chief noticed.

'Or,' said Sir Adam, 'if we can take their principal player out of operation it could just decapitate their whole operation.' He paused. 'I think we need Langley to step up their game on this one. After all, Latin America is more their backyard than ours.'

'Well, there's always the JSOC option,' said Khan. 'Joint Special Operations could finish the job our man Luke started. Go for the full takedown of García's operation, with assistance from the Colombians. But I'm not sure that's the right route to go down.'

'No,' replied the Chief. 'Neither am I. We need a subtler approach. How close is Tradewind now to the main player? Can she discover where they've hidden the weapon? I'm talking about over here. Because that, more than anything else in the world, is where our Service could deliver a difference. We started this thing. We should be the ones to finish it.'

Khan looked down at the glass of lime cordial in his hand, as if suddenly remembering it was there. He took a swig. 'Tradewind is in a good place,' he said. 'We've placed her about as far upstream in that organization as we can hope to get, without turning one of his most trusted people. But even if she can find that information for us, there's no knowing when she'll next have a chance to transmit. We don't even know if García is planning to take her with him.'

'How's he getting out of Colombia?' asked Sir Adam.

'Probably flying below radar cover at treetop height across the Darien Gap. It'll be from one jungle airstrip to another. Then he'll want to disappear with a new identity to sit back and watch his work here unfold on CNN or BBC Mundo.'

'All right. So what do you propose?' said the Chief.

He knew that Khan would not have come to his home bearing problems without solutions.

'García still has an exploitable weakness,' replied Khan. 'His health. That's how we got Tradewind in. So I've given this a lot of thought, and I can't really see any way round it. It has to be Operation Sicarius.'

The Chief gave a heavy sigh. 'We'll need sign-off from the PM for that. And from the attorney general. I'm seeing the PM first thing in the morning. He's going to ask what the chances are that it will work. So, what are the percentages?' Sir Adam's jaw was set firm.

'Tradewind is the only agent we have in place who could do it,' replied Khan. 'She's had minimal training for something like this and we'd still need to get the material to her. But it's all we've got left in the toolbox at this stage. I'd give it about a seventy-five per cent chance of success.'

'Do it.' He was moving towards the door and back to his guests. 'Execute.'

Chapter 75

NO ONE COULD accuse Luke Carlton of being superstitious. By the time of his seventh birthday he had rumbled his dad for dressing up as Santa Claus. Even before he'd lost his parents on that terrible afternoon in Colombia his enquiring mind had already decided there were no such things as ghosts. But Luke did sometimes wonder if he possessed a sort of sixth sense, an antenna that alerted him to trouble just ahead of time. It had kicked in more than once on those Special Forces night raids back in Afghanistan, made him look twice at his plans, his routes in and out, prompting the minute adjustments that ended up saving lives. On his own side, not the enemy's.

That morning was one of those moments. Four days had passed since his visit to the isolation ward and he had already had Groves at MI5 asking him, twice now, if he was absolutely certain the patient had said 'Manchester'. If Jenny Li hadn't been there to hear it too, he might have started to doubt his ears. The preventative measures and the non-stop searches put in place around Greater Manchester were costing millions of pounds and questions were being asked about how long this could go on.

Yet Luke now had a deeply uncomfortable feeling

that forces beyond his control were shifting into gear and that he was about to be affected in some way. It had started the night before, when he'd got back from work at Thames House. He was surprised, to put it mildly, to open the door to his home and see two expensively dressed young men lounging on the sofa as if they owned the place. Brothers, he guessed, but not twins. One was vaguely familiar.

'Hiya, babes,' said Elise, greeting him with a kiss and steering him into the room. 'Did you get my text?'

Luke hadn't looked at his phone since that morning. It had remained switched off while he was working inside MI5's main building and he had forgotten to turn it back on when he left for the day. 'I didn't, but that's my fault,' he replied. 'Hi, I'm Luke,' he said, reaching out a hand to the two unknowns.

'Yah, I know. I'm Hugo Squires,' said the nearest of the two, returning the handshake. 'We've met before. And this is my bro, Jackson.'

I don't believe it, thought Luke. I've let myself get ambushed in my own bloody flat. He had to hand it to Elise, this was smart work. She had moved fast after their late-night chat about his career, which he had pushed to the back of his mind. But he didn't let his smile falter. 'Can I get you both a drink?' he asked.

'Nah, we're good, thanks,' said Hugo.

'How was work today?' Elise asked Luke, joining them as she sat on the edge of the sofa.

He had the distinct impression he was coming in on the tail end of a conversation that might well have involved him. 'So-so.' For a second he wondered what would happen if he gave them an honest answer, if he shouted across the room, 'You want the truth? Work is going fucking abysmally! There's a radioactive dirty bomb somewhere in this country and we can't find it! Why, how was work for you today?'

Instead he shrugged, then spoke quietly to Elise. 'Can you give me a hand with something next door?'

As soon as they were in the bedroom he shut the door abruptly and turned to her. 'Elise – what the hell?'

'Easy, tiger. I sent you a text – I'm sorry you didn't get a chance to read it. You remember the conversation we had a few nights ago? About a possible career change?'

'I do. I just didn't expect you to move this quickly.'

'Well, the boys were free tonight so I thought, Why not? Look, I'm only trying to do what's best for us here. And you did say you'd hear him out – Jackson, that is. Well, he's here now and he was keen to meet you.'

Luke regarded her for a long moment. She was so beautiful, with her long, graceful neck, that sparkle in her eyes and those full lips. He was on to a good thing and he knew it. For the second time, he found himself saying, yes, he would hear out what Jackson had to say. 'Any thoughts on supper, though? We could always pop in to the Woodman just down the road?' He was playing for time but she was ahead of him.

'No need,' said Elise. 'I've put a lasagne in the oven and Hugo's made a salad.'

'Hugo's made a *salad*? Who *are* these guys, Lise?'

'Don't be a caveman. Just come next door and be nice.'

To everyone's relief, the evening passed off peacefully. Luke, it had to be said, couldn't quite bring himself to like Hugo Squires but he thanked him for looking after Elise on the dreadful evening of the phone call in the restaurant. He did, though, warm to Jackson. Everyone knew the meeting was all about seeing if Luke would consider shifting careers, yet they avoided talking about anything to do with investment management. When the two brothers departed in a cab Luke agreed to meet Jackson in a week's time. He knew he couldn't keep putting things off indefinitely. Sooner or later it was going to come down to him having to make a choice – Elise or the Service – and it would be a tough one. But he also had a feeling that bigger events were about to intervene.

Chapter 76

AT SEVEN FORTY-FIVE the next morning a black BMW X1 with tinted windows, the MI6 Chief in the back, pulled into Horse Guards Road. At the police checkpoint that guards the discreet rear entrance to 10 Downing Street the car turned right and slowed but didn't stop. Certain cars in Whitehall have revolving numberplates and this was one of them. Inside the police post the officers on duty recognized the registration number they'd been given and lowered the cylindrical barriers, allowing the BMW to sweep into the forecourt and park in the far left-hand corner.

By eight thirty C's meeting with the Prime Minister had ended. He left the room, grim-faced, with the PM's signature on a document, countersigned by the attorney general, tucked into the inside pocket of his suit jacket. Operation Sicarius had been authorized from the top.

Sir Adam Keeling walked briskly along Tudor Passage, the corridor connecting Number 10 to the nearby Cabinet Office. Now he had to brief a hastily convened meeting of the senior members of the National Security Council. Taking his place beside Sid Khan, he faced the room. 'We are holding this meeting,' he began, 'because a situation has arisen with our principal player in Colombia which leaves us little choice. We've looked at all the options but I'm afraid we're going to have to go for a termination.'

No one at the table said a word. The way things were going or, rather, were not going, with no breakthroughs in locating the ticking bomb, everyone had expected something like this.

'Let's not delude ourselves here,' continued Sir Adam. 'This still doesn't give us any guarantee we can stop the detonation. But with the principal eliminated it is our assessment –' he coughed – 'it is our assessment that his other operators will lose their incentive to go through with the attack. If anything, we expect it to set off an internal leadership battle within the cartel.'

While the Chief was speaking, a balding man in a dark, pinstripe suit had let himself quietly into the room and taken his place at the other end of the table. 'I would just like to add a word here,' interjected the newcomer. 'As Attorney General, I have looked long and hard at this. Is it legal? Is it proportionate? Does it comply with international law? Well, Sir Adam and I have gone over every angle with the PM. I need hardly say that it would be infinitely preferable if our Colombian friends could capture the man alive and bring him to justice.'

Several figures round the table nodded, although the Home Secretary remained noticeably impassive. 'But we understand,' continued the attorney general, 'that that is next to impossible. We've seen what happened when the Colombian police tried to close in on him. They lost nearly a dozen men and García got clean away.'

'What about a drone strike?' asked the Defence

Secretary. 'The Americans ought to be able to deploy a Reaper from Florida, surely.'

'Let me answer that one, if you don't mind,' said Sir Adam. 'Getting a drone into theatre isn't the issue. It carries with it a certain risk.'

'I'm sorry?' The Defence Secretary leaned forward. 'I'm not following you.'

The Chief hesitated before answering. 'You'll appreciate,' he said, 'that this is highly sensitive. But we have an agent in place close to the target. A drone strike on García would be a death sentence for that agent. Plus we don't have an exact fix on where he is right now.'

'Can't you extract him?' asked the Defence Secretary. 'The agent, I mean.'

'Not at present, no. We have no means of contacting them. Plus what they're providing us with, when they can be in contact, is Grade A intelligence.'

There was a silence, broken after a few seconds by the attorney general.

'Now, it has long been this country's policy,' he resumed, 'that we don't do assassinations. Obviously things changed in late 2015 with Syria, where those drone strikes were judged as legitimate self-defence under Article Fifty-one of the UN Charter. The situation we're facing today is a little more complex.'

'Which is why,' interjected Sir Adam, 'this will not be our operation.'

'It won't? Then whose will it be?' asked Sir William Orgrave, Cabinet Secretary, the ultimate Whitehall warrior. He knew full well that if this came washing back in their faces, he would be the one left sorting it out.

'Washington's,' replied the Chief, regarding the

Whitehall mandarin with an unwavering gaze. 'Officially, this will have a CIA signature. Just with a little input from us.'

'And the Americans are onboard with this?' questioned Orgrave.

'Completely,' replied Sir Adam. 'We had an early conference call today with their National Security Adviser. The CIA already have a substantial presence in-country and they're working up an insertion plan as we speak.' His tone carried a note of finality. 'Now, if there are no more questions I must be on my way. We have a rather busy day ahead of us.' It was not yet nine thirty a.m.

The meeting broke up and Khan caught a lift back to VX with the Chief. He had stayed silent throughout the meeting in the Cabinet Office. Nearly twenty years younger than Sir Adam, he was in no hurry to stick his neck out on an operation he considered to be right on the cusp of legality. But if Sir Adam Keeling was happy to put his name to it, then that was fine by Khan.

As the car swept westwards down Millbank, ignoring the speed limit and the yellow box cameras that flashed in impotent disapproval, both men stared out across the Thames in the weak early-November sunlight.

'Dangerous times, Sid,' remarked the Chief, 'dangerous times.' It was a comment that could have applied equally to the national threat situation or to their own careers. Heads were going to roll if they messed this one up. As they sped past Tate Britain, home to some of London's finest art treasures, the Chief broached the subject he and Khan had been mulling over. 'Who did you have in mind?' he asked. 'Who's going to deliver the goods?'

Sid Khan suspected the Chief already knew the answer, just wanted to hear him say it out loud. 'Well, it has to be Luke Carlton, doesn't it? There's no one with a better skill set.'

'I concur,' said Sir Adam. 'We'll need to pull him off that task force at Thames and get him into the lab at VX right away. I want him back in Bogotá by this time tomorrow.'

They had reached the junction with Vauxhall Bridge Road, the lights were changing to amber and they were swinging left onto the bridge, hugging the left-hand lane.

'That said,' cautioned Khan, 'we do have a duty of care here, Chief, given that he nearly got himself wiped out on the last assignment.'

'On a scale of one to ten, how dangerous would you estimate this mission to be?'

At first Khan didn't answer. He peered out of the window at the grey expanse of the river beneath them. 'I'd look at it another way,' said Khan. 'On a scale of one to ten, how much danger is this country in right now?'

Sir Adam grunted, reaching to unbuckle his seat-belt as the gate opened to let them through. 'Fair point,' he said. 'Send in Carlton.'

Chapter 77

THE FRISSON, THE buzz, the elixir of excitement that Luke had experienced on that earlier mission to Colombia was now spent. He felt inert. This was a job, an assignment, nothing more, not a calling. Now heading west once more over the Atlantic, no fretting lawyer in tow this time, he gazed at his reflection on the in-flight entertainment screen. He had not yet got round to switching it on. His face stared back at him: he looked tired, even before the mission. Luke rubbed the knuckle of his partly missing middle finger and considered the last twenty hours, pursing his lips. He didn't want to think about Elise's reaction when he had given her the good news that, yes, he was off again.

First had come the call from Angela, pulling him out of the ops room at Thames House. A car was waiting outside, she told him, to whisk him across the river. Time was tight if they were going to get him on the 12.50 flight but first he needed to come into Vauxhall Cross. Luke had known from her sympathetic tone that someone higher up the chain was about to shovel a load of metaphorical manure in his direction.

'You absolutely have the right to refuse this one,'

she told him, as she met him by the lifts in the circular lobby on the ground floor of the MI6 building.

'And you think I should be saying no?'

'I didn't say that.'

'But that's what you're implying?'

'Listen, Luke.' Without knowing she was doing it, she squeezed his arm, then immediately let go. 'You – you're already proving yourself here. You're starting to think like a case officer. You're on the point of making the grade.' Angela stopped as two colleagues passed, nodding at her but saying nothing. 'You really don't need to take on this mission,' she said, in a hushed voice. 'They can always find someone else.'

'But someone who doesn't speak Spanish, right? Or know the Colombian cartels? Or how to handle themselves in a fire fight?'

'It's conceivable,' she said, picking her words carefully, 'that we don't have anyone else in the Service with all three of those skills. We could hand it to the Americans. They've certainly got the resources. But then we relinquish control and, of course, we are the target here.'

'Well, that settles it,' he said, giving her an easy smile. His safety seemed to trouble Angela more than it did him. 'I don't really have a choice, do I? Given the threat that's hanging over this country right now.'

Four floors up and five minutes later, in Sid Khan's office, it had been a very different conversation. No room for wavering there, it was straight down to business.

'You'll be going in with the Americans,' announced Khan. 'So, as you know, we're putting you on the twelve-fifty BA flight non-stop to Tampa.' He glanced at the clock on his wall. 'That's just under three hours away so we don't have a lot of time to prep you for this. You're due to land at seventeen forty local time and someone from Langley will meet you and take you straight to MacDill. I expect you know it.'

'MacDill Airforce Base?' said Luke. 'For my sins, yes. Home of SOCOM – US Special Operations Command. I did a course there once.' His mind flashed back to days and nights of gruelling, bone-breaking training alongside the operators of Delta Force and Naval Special Warfare. His muscles ached just thinking about it.

'You'll be going in with a mixed team,' said Khan, 'CIA and Special Ops. You'll have a complete security envelope around you at all times. There'll be no repeat of what happened last time.'

'That's reassuring,' replied Luke.

Khan shot him a look, which reminded Luke that he still had questions to answer about going off-piste on his last mission. Apparently today was not the day for a reprimand.

'I cannot emphasize enough,' said Khan, speaking with unaccustomed gravitas, 'how critical this mission is.'

'Got it.'

'It's your task, Luke Carlton, to make contact with Tradewind, deliver the package, show her how to administer it, then stay on location long enough only to make sure the job is done.' Khan stood up, came round to Luke's side of the desk and sat on its edge, looking directly at him, as if searching for reassurance that the proven warrior they had selected really was up to the task.

'García,' he continued, 'has to be terminated before he can flee Colombia. Why? Because once he gets to

Panama he's immune. At least, he'll think he is. The moment he decides he's somewhere safe he'll execute his plan. *Bang!* Then we're too late. He's already moving towards the end phase now.'

'Tradewind is someone you've had in place for some time? An agent recruited by Benton before he was murdered by the narcos?' Khan said nothing. 'Why wasn't I told this the last time you sent me over there?'

Sitting just a few centimetres away from Khan, Luke could see that his words were making the other man uncomfortable, but he didn't care. If they were about to send him back into the jaws of Hell then he deserved to know the full picture.

'I'm going to level with you, Luke,' said Khan. 'I may have misjudged you at first. I didn't let you in on Tradewind because I didn't think you were ready. Right now, that agent is *the* most valuable HUMINT source we have in the whole of Latin America. There are only six people in this building who even know she exists. Now there are seven. By the time you've read your assignment brief you'll know as much as I do.' Khan glanced up again at the ornate clock on the wall, a gift long ago from the Lahore Cricket Club. 'Time is running short, and the boys and girls in Tech Division are waiting downstairs to give you a crash course in the dark arts.' He stood up and held out his hand. 'For the second time in a few weeks I'm finding myself saying this to you. Good luck. Execute the task and please come back in one piece.'

Chapter 78

IN A DARKENED room at Vauxhall Cross, Luke sat waiting as the screen in front of him jumped to life. It was a 2002 news clip from Moscow. Black-clad Russian Special Forces were bringing a violent end to a stand-off with Chechen terrorists who had taken around a thousand people hostage in a theatre.

'Fentanyl,' said the biochemist sitting beside him. 'They used a form of fentanyl to end that siege. Remember?'

'Think I was still at uni at the time.'

'Fentanyl is an opiate, a narcotic analgesic that's eighty times more powerful than morphine. In tiny doses it can be perfectly benign. You've probably heard of people using a fentanyl patch as an analgesic?' Luke nodded. 'It's also used in substance abuse, combined with other ingredients. As a chemist, I have to say I dislike the term "designer drug", but that's what they call it. It's got other names too, like China White, Perc-o-Pops and Dance Fever. It's led to a lot of sudden deaths.'

The video playing on the screen was now showing a procession of bodies being carried out to ambulances. A light flurry of Moscow snow was swirling around them.

'Used as a gas, as they did inside the theatre there,' continued the chemist, 'it can be lethal. It shuts down the body's respiratory system, leading to asphyxiation, cardiac arrest and death. The Russians basically got their sums wrong, and around a hundred and thirty people ended up dead in that place. We never did discover the exact formula they used.' The chemist held up his hand as a signal and the image on the screen changed. 'Know who this guy is?' he asked. A bearded man, silvery grey hair, intense eyes, open collar.

'Looks familiar,' said Luke. 'But no. Sorry.'

'Khaled Meshaal. The political leader of Hamas. In 1997 Israel's Mossad sent a hit team into Amman to kill him. Their weapon of choice?'

'Fentanyl?' offered Luke.

'Close. Levofentanyl. A derivative. The plan was to distract his attention then spray it into his ears and for him to expire quietly forty-eight hours later. But it didn't quite work out like that. They got caught, Meshaal went into a coma and there was an almighty diplomatic row, Clinton on the phone to Jordan's King Hussein and so on. In the end the Israelis had to hand over the antidote and he lived. Major embarrassment for the Israelis.'

Luke could see where this was going. 'And you're going to ask me to do the same thing to our player in South America?'

'Not exactly. Things have moved on quite a bit since then. Come with me.'

Luke followed him into an adjoining room. It had fluorescent strip lights and a clean, almost aseptic feel. Men and women hunched over their workstations or conferred quietly while pointing to streams of data on screens. Even to Luke, still only in his thirties, they all seemed incredibly young.

'Not quite the Gadget Palace you see in those Bond films,' said the chemist, leading him to a table. 'And no silver Aston Martin lurking behind the curtain, I'm afraid! But we do have this . . .' The chemist turned and nodded, just once. A young man hurried over with a small green plastic box marked 'Travellers' First Aid'.

'Jed,' he said, 'I'd like you to show Mr Carlton the toolkit.'

Carefully, the assistant opened the lid of the box and laid its contents on the Formica table. Luke leaned in for a closer look. He saw a set of needles, a syringe and a pair of thin transparent phials, each filled with a clear liquid tinged slightly yellow. 'It's an acupuncture set,' announced the chemist, 'but with a twist.' He sounded as though he were describing a kitchen blender with more than one speed setting.

'Your agent,' said the chemist, indicating the row of needles, 'will need to administer these ordinary needles first. They're harmless. But these . . .' he indicated a row set apart, noticeably thicker than the others '. . . are hollow, like a hypodermic. They deliver the poison. It's a form of fentanyl citrate. Just two milligrams is more than enough to kill a man.'

Luke had to resist the urge to move away from the display on the table. One slip-up, and his mission would be over before it had begun. He watched as the chemist completed the demonstration.

'The needles fit like so into the syringe. All you need to do is draw out the liquid so that it fills the needle, point it away from you and give it a squirt. Then you detach the syringe and leave the needle in place.' He saw Luke's expression. 'I know what you're thinking. Surely I need to press down on the syringe to inject it, right? Well, no. This stuff is so potent that to work it just needs to break through the epidermal layer – sorry, puncture the skin. Until then it's held inside the needle by surface tension. When that's broken and the needle enters the subcutaneous tissue, hey presto, it's check-out time for your man. Want to have a practice?'

'Not really, no,' said Luke. 'I imagine the same applies if I or our agent sticks themselves by mistake?'

'It does, and we've taken that into account.' The chemist lifted the base of the box to reveal a further phial and syringe. 'Under here you'll find the antidote. Naloxone. But I really wouldn't advise going down that route if you can avoid it. It, um, hasn't always been a hundred per cent successful.'

'Thanks,' said Luke, as the two chemists packed away the contents and presented him with the green box. 'I'll bear that in mind.'

Chapter 79

THE WARMTH OF the Florida afternoon wrapped itself round him the moment Luke stepped out of the terminal building. Late afternoon, still twenty-six degrees, and he could just make out the high-rise skyline of the city shimmering in the heat haze. After nearly ten hours cooped up in the plane, he took a deep breath of the balmy air. This was a pleasant change from the wet winds and single-digit temperatures of London in early November.

'Welcome to Tampa. You've just missed the tail-end of hurricane season,' said the man from Langley, who had met him off his flight.

Their conversation had dried up on the short, straight drive along Route 589, then the 600, from the international airport to the South Tampa Peninsula that ended in a high-security gatepost and a sign saying simply 'MacDill Airforce Base'.

Through security and driving along the North Boundary Boulevard with the windows down, Luke felt a moist breeze blowing in off Hillsborough Bay. He ducked as something large and unseen roared very low overhead.

'Ah, don't worry about those,' said his escort, breaking his silence at last. 'That'll be the KC-135s comin' in to land. Air-to-air refuelling tankers. Gotta bear in mind, this is first and foremost an airforce base.'

And a lot of other things too, Luke noticed, as they passed a pair of large red-roofed buildings with a sign announcing the headquarters of Centcom, US Central Command, the division of the US military that runs all its operations from the Middle East and beyond, into Afghanistan and Central Asia. He wondered how much thought had gone into that, as they drove past a road signposted 'Centcom Avenue'. They pulled up at the officers' quarters and the escort checked Luke in for the night. Clean bedding, a washbasin and a wardrobe. Frugal but functional – Elise would probably approve. He had once made the mortal mistake of telling her about some five-star suite he had been put up in on an assignment in Dubai. 'That's it,' she had told him. 'You're bloody well taking me with you next time.'

American breakfasts, Luke reflected, are one of life's guilty pleasures. You know they can be spectacularly bad for you, all those deliciously crisp rashers of oak-smoked bacon saturated in cooking fat, jam with every ounce of natural goodness purged out of it, waffles piled high with the bottle of maple syrup within easy reach. Yet it all tasted so good.

He had taken his tray and sat down at a crowded table in the Special Ops canteen, wedged between large men with bushy beards, bunching, load-carrying shoulders and straggly hair. Most, he noticed, had crows' feet around the eyes and the thin white tan lines below the temples that came from wearing wraparound shades on operations in hot countries. They didn't talk much, not even to each other. The man next to him reached over and silently passed him the salt and pepper without being asked. One look at the men told Luke they had spent an unhealthy amount of time in the most dangerous corners of Afghanistan, Iraq, Yemen and Somalia, seeing and doing things they could probably never talk about.

'Luke Carlton?' A large figure loomed above him. 'Todd Miller.' He flashed a perfect white smile and held out a tanned hand the size of a joint of gammon. 'Glad you got in all right. I'm the mission commander. Hey, no rush, take your time. I'll run you over to the briefing room when you're done. Then you can meet the team.'

'Cheers,' said Luke, wiping his mouth with a paper napkin and rising to his feet. 'I'm good to go, thanks. Let's head off now.' The guy was huge. Probably a college quarterback in his younger days. Luke wondered what had driven him to join this death-or-glory outfit. Patriotism? Ambition? A passion for extreme sports? If it had been ten or fifteen years earlier he would have put it down to the 9/11 effect, all those thousands of outraged young Americans signing up to serve their country as best they could in the wake of the worst terrorist attack it had ever known. But Todd Miller looked too young for that – he would still have been at school when the Twin Towers fell.

There were fourteen of them in the briefing room, keeping themselves to the edges by the framed pictures, sipping coffee – black, no sugar, Luke felt sure – talking quietly. It was a mixed bag, just as Khan had said. Part CIA, part JSOC Special Ops, only two women, probably from Langley. An unusual insignia on the wall caught his eye: a large blue, red and yellow emblem featuring a spear surrounded by what appeared to be flames. Emblazoned across the top were two words, *Molon Labe*.

'It's Ancient Greek,' said Miller, handing Luke a coffee. '*Molon Labe* means "Come and take them." It's our motto here at Special Operations Command. It's supposed to be what King Leonidas said to the Persians when they demanded his three hundred men lay down their weapons at Thermopylae.'

'Nice one,' said Luke. 'A sort of ancient version of "Fuck you"?'

'You got it,' replied Miller, giving him a firm slap on the back.

A short, squat man with ginger sideburns came into the briefing room and clapped his hands just once. 'OK, listen up,' he announced. 'Captain Miller's gonna start the briefing.' No uniform but everyone seemed to know who he was. Luke put him down as the unit warrant officer. Everyone took their places as Todd Miller stood by the wall screen at the far end of the room. He was dressed, as most of the men were, in beige cargo trousers with capacious pockets, dark brown mountain boots, a skin-tight polo shirt and a baseball cap with the brim curved over, shielding his eyes. Miller signalled for the first image to come up on the screen and Luke nearly sent his coffee hurtling across the table.

It was Nelson García, El Pobrecito to his people, and someone had helpfully labelled him 'Principal Player'. Well, of course they'd all need to see what he looked like, but still . . . Looking across the room now into those cruel, sadistic eyes and remembering what the bastard had done to him, and what he had nearly had done to him, sent a chill down Luke's spine. He thought back to those hours in the Chop House where García's thugs had been preparing to lop off his limbs, one by one. Christ, was he insane to have taken on this mission? Undoubtedly. And to think that Angela had offered him an out – what, only yesterday? But it was a bit late to change his mind now.

Miller had stopped talking and the image on the screen suddenly changed. A headshot of a Hispanic girl appeared. Early twenties. Lightly tanned face framed by a neat bob of dark hair, haloed by a beam of sunlight against a whitewashed wall. She looked almost beatific. Luke couldn't help but smile as he heard the rumble of approval come from the assembled men.

'Valentina Gómez, ladies and gentlemen,' said Miller, tapping the screen with a telescopic aerial snapped off a discarded transistor radio. 'Our asset in theatre. And, note, she is a friendly. This lady is a UK intel asset. I say again, she is a friendly intel asset.' Luke looked down at the thin A4-sized classified file he had brought with him and riffled through it until he found what he was looking for. Vauxhall Cross's blurred file photo of Tradewind did not do her justice. Benton's skills as an agent-runner had clearly not extended to photography.

'The Brits have codenamed her Tradewind,' continued Miller, 'so we'll use the same nomenclature. She's co-located with the principal player who frequently moves location, mostly in Antioquia province, here.' Valentina's face vanished to be replaced by a satellite map of Colombia that zoomed in on a province north-west of Bogotá. 'She has no means of contacting London unless she leaves the estate and visits her folks in the village,' said Miller. 'The last transmission she made was just forty-eight hours ago. It was marked "Top Urgent" and alerted her controllers in London that García is packing up and preparing to ship out in the next few days. She thinks it's to Panama. We have no means of contacting her but we do know she's with her family right now. And they live . . . here.' The satellite image tracked smoothly across the terrain and zoomed in on a row of basic houses. It did not escape Luke's attention that US optics were a whole lot slicker than the ones he was used to back home.

'I have a question, Chief.' It was one of the JSOC guys. He had stopped chewing gum just long enough to ask his question. 'Any reason we don't just call in a drone strike and flatten the place? Save us all a lot of trouble.'

'Hoo-ar,' echoed someone next to him, and the two knocked fists with an audible clunk of bone on bone.

'There are plenty of good reasons,' replied Miller, 'and I'll let our British guest here address them. Mr Carlton?'

Luke grimaced. 'Mr Carlton' reminded him of all those PT instructors on the All Arms Commando course in Devon, their 'Mr' dripping with sarcasm. He put down his coffee and got to his feet, nodding his thanks to Miller. 'Morning, everyone,' he began. 'As some of you may know, we have a very delicate situation in play over in the UK right now. A CT situation.' He noticed the CIA guys from Langley all looked down at their coffee. They knew. 'The action we're undertaking in Colombia has to be finessed so we can achieve a specific aim.' Oh, for God's sake, he was starting to sound like a management consultant.

'OK, let me put it another way. There are two reasons we can't use a drone. One is that it would likely take out Tradewind along with the target. And the other is that we don't know where García is right now. She is the only asset we have inside his inner circle. She's the one with access to him, so that means . . .' Luke sensed from looking round the room that they had all got it, but he completed his sentence anyway '. . . we have to get to her village, hand over the goods, give her a crash course in how to use them and then she has to execute the task, the first chance she gets. Todd?'

Miller thanked him and took over. The briefing moved to logistics, routes in and out, extraction plans, call signs, back-up contingencies. 'So to sum up,' he concluded, 'wheels up at thirteen hundred hours. Four hours' flight time into the base at Medellín. Insertion by road. In position by nineteen hundred hours local. Any questions?'

As the meeting broke up Luke saw a man and a woman making their way towards him, waiting patiently for their chance to squeeze past some of the hulking Special Ops men. They were civilians, he guessed. They didn't have the military mannerisms of the others in the room.

'Hi, there!' the woman said brightly, when they reached him. 'We're from OTS.' She looked at him expectantly.

'OTS?'

'You know, OTS. The Office of Technical Service. Part of DS and T?'

Luke looked from one to the other blankly. Was this a test? 'I'm sorry,' he said, 'I'm not familiar with that. I thought you were from Langley.'

'Oh, we are,' she replied. 'We work at the Directorate of Science and Technology. We do the gizmos for the Agency.'

'Ah,' said Luke. Why hadn't someone told him? Once again he had the feeling he was being sent into action without the full knowledge set.

'We'd like to show you something,' said the woman, 'something you'll need to hand on to Tradewind. If now is convenient for you?' She and her companion pulled up chairs next to his. The man still hadn't said a word, but now he reached into the satchel he was carrying and silently placed a woman's compact on the table. He flipped it open to reveal a circular mirror and flat powder puff.

'Looks kinda normal, right?' remarked the woman. 'But you'll see we've made some modifications.' She peeled back the powder puff and put it to one side on the table. Beneath it, inside the compact, lay a tiny keyboard and a miniature eyeliner pencil, sharpened at one end to a fine point.

'It's a communicator.' The man broke his silence. 'It's only short-range – about ten kilometres max – but it does the job. The SIGINT guy on your team will be able to pick up her messages on his receiver. You tap the keys using this,' he indicated the sharp end of the eyeliner pencil, 'and it's powered by a tiny lithium battery at the back here.'

Luke was lucky enough to have good eyesight but he had no idea if Valentina would be able to cope with such a tiny keyboard. 'What if she can't make out the keys? If they're too small for her?'

'We've taken care of that,' said the woman. 'If you look at the mirror you'll see it's magnifying. Oh, and all the keys are printed in reverse so they show up the right way in the mirror.'

'Not bad,' said Luke.

'Yeah, we think so too,' she replied, with a smile. As they got up to leave, she added, 'Just one thing: it is super-fragile so no hard landings, huh?'

'Roger that,' said Luke, and tucked it into his breast pocket.

Back in his room in the officers' quarters, Luke took out the green plastic Travellers' First Aid box and snapped it open. He took a long look at the needles that would inject the poison into the man who was wreaking such havoc in Britain. Now would be the moment to look forward to García's end. But Luke felt nothing. He just needed to be sure he knew exactly what to tell Valentina when he showed her what to do. He snapped the box shut, lay back on his bed and phoned Elise.

Chapter 80

IN THE PLANTER'S villa in the hills of Antioquia there was a bustle of impending departure. Only the tight inner circle around El Pobrecito knew either the reason behind it or his real destination. But everyone who worked for him was aware that the big man was moving out. Something major was going down and he obviously had no intention of being around when it happened. The rumours were rife, especially among his more junior employees, like the men who washed his fleet of jeeps, maintained his extensive armoury or brought in the pineapples he so enjoyed. Some said he was planning a hit on Señor Margoles, the mayor of Medellín, or on one of the rival cartels to the north. There was even some wild gossip that he was retiring. But the word on everyone's lips was that Nelson García was moving his base up to Panama and taking only a handful of his most trusted people with him.

Amid the packing cases and the designer suitcases, El Pobrecito was focused on the task in hand. With just days to go, he wanted nothing left to chance. He called Suárez to join him on the balcony, gesturing for him to take a seat on one of the flimsy cane chairs that had seen better days.

'That Englishman, Carlton, the soldier spy,' began

García, 'the one those idiots in Buenaventura let escape. Where is he now?'

'Back in London, Patrón. One of our people at El Dorado airport saw him board the flight.'

'I think it's time we made life uncomfortable for him, don't you? Is Ana María ready?'

'She is,' replied Suárez, brushing a mould stain from the chair off his linen trousers. 'She's had a little matter to take care of, but that's done now.'

'Then it's time to put the pressure on. Tell her to go ahead. Hide the Englishwoman somewhere safe and start sending demands to keep him guessing. I want him to lose his mind.'

'Of course, Patrón. Right away.'

In London, the evening was already drawing in when Elise left work for the day. She could feel and see the difference now, the shorter, darker days as the impending British winter announced itself with lights coming on at 3.30 p.m. and squalls of fallen leaves swirling up from the pavements. Leaving the Stratford Gallery and the well-lit streets of Piccadilly behind her, she caught the bus south of the river, as she often did when the wind was turning the Thames choppy and she didn't fancy commuting home by river taxi.

Deep in thought, she walked the last few hundred yards to their flat in Battersea. Except that Luke would not be home tonight, or the next night, or the one after that. He was off on yet another of his bloody assignments. And just when she thought they were making progress, that second meeting with Jackson all set up, the prospect of a more stable life for them both so tantalizingly close.

It was as she was passing beneath the arch of the railway bridge that it happened. A blind spot where, if there was no other traffic on the road, no one would see what was taking place. The white van sped past her, then slammed on its brakes, slewing to a stop just ahead. It happened so incredibly fast she had no time to react. The doors flew open and before she knew it she was being dragged into the back, a cloth was crammed into her mouth and a black hood pulled over her head. In less than thirty seconds the van had moved off.

Jolting around in the back of the windowless vehicle, her arms tied roughly behind her back, Elise's mind was in turmoil. Who were these people? Why her? It must be a case of mistaken identity. But as the shock of capture began to wear off and she took stock of her situation, she realized she knew exactly who was behind it. And if they were the same people who had happily drilled a hole in her boyfriend's foot, she was in deep trouble.

Chapter 81

ANA MARÍA ACOSTA had thought hard about what she would do with Elise when they brought her in. Should she keep her in comfort, or deprive her of sleep and starve her? Have her bound hand and foot and chained to a radiator, or let her pace around, scared and confused, in a locked room? Maybe she could even have a bit of fun with her, play with her, like an orca tossing a seal into the air before the kill. After all, the bosses seemed indifferent to what she did to her, whether she lived or died, just as long as her continued captivity proved a distraction to the interfering Englishman Luke Carlton.

But Ana María was nothing if not thorough when it came to preparation. She was not a woman who left anything to chance, a quality that had marked her out for great responsibility within the cartel. By the time Elise was being snatched that evening, Ana María had already chosen a succession of different hiding places where they would hold her. Some were cartel safe houses, secure addresses all over London with well-established covers where the rent was always paid on time, in cash, and nobody asked awkward questions. Just one aspect of the massive, multi-billion-dollar global cocaine trade that had oiled and corrupted its way into so many hidden corners of the economy. Others were out in the Home Counties, a discreet rural garage or a disused stables on a farm tucked well away from the road and prying eyes. It was vital that they kept moving the girl around, never let her stay in one place for too long.

Which was why Ana María was so apoplectically angry when they phoned her to tell her where they had initially taken Elise. 'How stupid can you people be?' she shouted. Unbelievable! The idiots had driven her to a garage in a Twickenham cul-de-sac just two streets away from the lock-up containing the device. Apparently the van was sitting in there now, engine off, with Elise in the back. Ana María heaved a sigh of exasperation. She made a snap decision.

'Move her,' she told them. 'I'll text you the address. And don't ever take her back there, do you understand?' Then a thought occurred to her. No, surely they couldn't have overlooked that. It was in the instructions. But she'd better make sure.

'*Y muchachos*,' she added. 'And, guys, please tell me you took her phone off her straight away?'

There was a long pause before the reply came.

'The phone is not with her.'

'You mean she has no phone?' pressed Ana María. 'Or you took it off her?'

'We took it off her.'

'When?'

'A while back.'

'And you've thrown it away?'

Again, a pause before the answer.

'It's thrown away.'

It was like dealing with primary-school children. Ana María was far from happy with the responses she was getting: it was blindingly obvious that they had forgotten to take Elise's phone. But she knew she would never get a straight answer out of the people the cartel had sent for this job. She would have to work with what they had given her. At least the phone was gone; now they needed to move the prisoner to a new location.

Inside the van the air was thick with tobacco smoke and expletives. The men who had snatched Elise were an eclectic bunch: two Colombians, two Spaniards and a Bolivian, a taciturn South American Indian the others rudely called Indio – 'native'. As they waited for the address to come through, they had some colourful names for the bossy woman from Madrid with her *elegante* language and her condescending tone. They grumbled about her and the fuss she was making.

None of them paused to wonder whether their prisoner might understand Spanish. Silent and motionless beneath her black hood, Elise was tuning in to every word, learning to recognize each separate voice, noting their disapproval of Ana María and running through the possibilities of how she could exploit this. Curiously, she was not scared. She felt alive and alert, poised like a predatory cat. She would wait for her moment.

A few kilometres away and in another borough of Greater London, the woman they cursed was working on the message to be delivered that night. Over the past few weeks, Ana María had tried gently to argue against the kidnapping. It was not that she felt compassion for Elise, far from it, more that she had a fine sense of operational security. Why jeopardize the main event? she had asked. Why risk leading the *inglés* to where the device was hidden? Or to the arrest of a main team member? She had a strong sense that Suárez shared her misgivings. But El Pobrecito was adamant: he wanted to taunt Carlton and his government. That was his vindictive nature. And he was the boss, the *patrón*, so Ana María did as she was told and drafted the message she would give them. She read it back. 'We have your Elise Mayhew. We know about her. She is your spy's girlfriend. So you have forty-eight hours. Send home all of your spies from our country. Or she disappears. For ever.'

No, that didn't sound right. She crossed out the last four words and replaced them with something more cryptic. 'Or you will see the consequences.' Now, how best to communicate it? It was a choice between a cyber café or a phone box. Ana María decided to go for the traditional approach. Just why, she wondered, as she pulled on her coat and hunched her shoulders against the damp night breeze, does anyone use phone boxes any more when everyone has a mobile? Call girls and criminals, she decided, glad that a few phone boxes had survived. Ideally, of course, she would have sent someone else to deliver the message over the phone – she had not kept her name off every criminal database for so long without being extremely cautious. But Ana María had had enough of others making crass mistakes and she remembered the advice her mother had given her all those years ago in their kitchen in Madrid. 'You want a job done properly? You do it yourself.' How very true.

She heaved open the heavy door of the red public phone box, ignoring the gaudy calling cards of the prostitutes and the rank smell of urine that wafted up from the stone floor. She took a small black box, about the size of a cigarette packet, from her bag. The VC-300 portable voice changer had been Suárez's idea and she was glad of it now. A length of wire extended from the box to an 'acoustic coupler', which resembled a single cushioned headphone and had to be placed next to the phone's receiver. Then she dialled 999. When the call connected she asked to be put through to the police. Ana María spoke clearly and without fear, delivering her scripted message in exactly ten seconds, then hung up. Precisely forty-seven seconds later she was in a car heading west, putting some distance between her and the phone box. She had kept her mobile switched off.

Chapter 82

SID KHAN WAS working late in his Vauxhall Cross office when he took the call from the Met. It was from Central Communications Command in Lambeth and a phone call from them at nearly ten o'clock at night was unlikely to be good news.

The Metropolitan Police receive an average of twenty-one thousand 999 calls every day. Some are genuine emergencies, most are not. The one they had received at 2012 hours that night had sounded like another prank, but the call handler wasn't so sure. She logged the call, recorded its contents, mapped its source on the geolocator – a phone box in Shepherd's Bush – and alerted her supervisor, pointing out that the caller had hung up after just ten seconds. The supervisor had wasted no time. She had rung SCO19, Specialist and Crime Ops, in Cobalt Square, just south of Vauxhall station. She relayed the message that a man with a thick Glaswegian accent had rung in from a phone box, claiming to be holding hostage one Elise Mayhew. In Cobalt Square they had run a quick data check on the name and 'Luke Carlton' had flashed up alongside it, with instructions to alert the switchboard at SIS in case of any suspicious incident.

'Sorry to bother you so late,' said the voice in Sid Khan's ear, as he took the call in his office, nursing a cup of Tetley's tea, one of the few comforts left to him during all the extra hours he had put in, night after night, since the crisis had erupted. 'It's Superintendent Chris Worlock here. I'm the senior investigating officer on a potential hostage case, which might involve one of your people . . .'

When the call ended Khan put down the phone and held his head in his hands. This could not be happening. But it was, and while the police would do their thing, acting on what little they had to go on, he needed to take certain measures at his end. They had a duty of care towards Luke, who would expect to be told at once, but Khan also had a live operation running. He reached for the phone and started to punch in Angela's number, then stopped, his finger poised over the buttons. Slowly he put down the receiver. Quietly, Khan tidied his desk, turned out the lights and left for the night.

Chapter 83

THE COLOMBIAN CITY of Medellín is served by a large and busy airport, José María Córdova International, the second biggest in the country. But the flight coming in from MacDill Airforce Base in Tampa, Florida, did not land there. Instead, under a discreet agreement between Washington and Bogotá, clearance was given by the Colombian government for the grey-painted US Commando II transport plane to touch down at the lesser-known regional airport of Olaya Herrera. Out of sight of anyone passing through the passenger terminal, the military flight from MacDill taxied to a stop inside one of the large hangars to the south. Onboard, Luke stretched, yawned and unbuckled his seatbelt. Anticipating a long night ahead, when he would need to stay fully alert, he had slept for most of the four-hour flight. The operatives from Langley were checking the signals on their mobile phones while the Special Ops guys were knocking gloved fists together, a silent gesture of good luck before a mission.

When the ramp went down, the team filed out to a waiting fleet of three mud-spattered civilian minivans. All three, Luke noted, had little curtains pulled across the back windows, ostensibly against the sun.

A man was standing in front of them, with his hands on his hips and a cigar clamped in his mouth. He seemed vaguely familiar to Luke, yet at first he couldn't place him. He knew he didn't particularly like him, but he couldn't recall why. As soon as the man opened his mouth he remembered. It was Sergio Ramirez, the laconic CIA officer he had encountered in Tumaco, the one he had initially mistaken for an OAP playing draughts. So much had happened since then, but Luke remembered two things about Ramirez: that he had refused to give him anything useful on El Pobrecito, and that he had warned him to stay well away from the drug lord. This could be awkward.

Ramirez was shaking hands with the people from Langley and directing them to their vehicles but when he spotted Luke he came over and gave him a bear hug. 'Glad you made it through, buddy,' he said. 'That must have been some ordeal in the Chop House.'

'Thanks,' Luke replied warily.

'But, hey,' added Ramirez, disengaging himself and raising an admonishing finger. 'Don't go solo on us again. We're here to support you Brits on this mission, so stick with us. Are we on the same page here?'

'We are.'

'Good. Then let's go to work.'

Each vehicle had a Colombian driver and passenger seated up front, fully vetted and paid-up individuals run by the CIA station in Bogotá. Born and raised in Medellín, they knew the best routes around the city. They also knew which of the roads leading out of the valley and into the hills of Antioquia would be watched by García's people and should be avoided.

The journey from the airport to Valentina's village, normally a four-hour drive, would take closer to six.

It was just past 1630 hours when they moved off in convoy, nosing out of the airfield through a service gate and merging into the traffic on Carrera 81. Back in this country for the first time since his narrow escape in Buenaventura, Luke was having distinctly mixed feelings. This was all happening a lot sooner than he would have liked, given the grisly ending García and his men had had in mind for him. But the professional in him wanted to see it through. He needed to get García out of his life once and for all. It wouldn't be easy, given the graffiti he had spotted on the urinal wall at the airport. *'Fuera gringos!'* it read, 'Foreigners get out!' and *'Muerte a los americanos!'* 'Death to the Americans!' He had seen similar, many times, painted on peeling walls in Ciudad Juarez up on the US–Mexican border, but Luke realized that whoever had written it at the airport had had access airside. For all he knew, they had even watched them land and leave. And that did not give him a good feeling about the mission.

Chapter 84

'WE HAVE SOMETHING of a dilemma here,' announced Sid Khan. He looked around the faces assembled in the windowless room on the sixth floor at Vauxhall Cross. They were in the 'SitCen', one of SIS's situation centres, designed for exactly the kind of emergency that faced them now. It was the morning after Elise's kidnap and Khan had called the meeting so early in the day that outside, in the grey half-light of a November dawn, many of the cars along Vauxhall Bridge still had their lights on.

'Do we do the decent thing,' he continued, 'and inform Luke Carlton that his girlfriend's been kidnapped – which could jeopardize the whole Medellín operation? Or do we quietly let him get on with it and leave the Met to try to resolve it before he gets back?'

Hands and fingers shot up around the table as several people jostled to have their say, but Khan held up a restraining hand, palm outwards, tilting his head to one side. 'Before you make up your minds, I'd like you to hear what Superintendent Worlock has to tell us. He's the SIO on the case and he's come across the road from Cobalt Square to brief us. Chris . . .'

The policeman buttoned his jacket and half rose out of his chair, then thought better of it and sat back down. 'Thank you.' He looked around the room as he spoke. 'As of now, we do not, as such, have an exact location for the hostage, Ms Elise Mayhew. But I do have some details I'd like to share with you from the Green Team at Cobalt.'

'Excuse me, Green Team?' interrupted Greg Sanderson, head of Latin America. 'What does that mean?'

'Sorry. Police jargon. Whenever we have a kidnap situation – and around half the UK's kidnappings occur in London – we divvy up into three teams. Green handles intelligence, Blue does surveillance, and Red the negotiating.'

'I see. Thanks.'

'So here's what we know,' continued Worlock. 'The individual concerned left her office in central London at seventeen forty-five hours yesterday. She travelled by bus to her home in Battersea. At precisely twenty twelve hours one of her captors made the 999 call that Lambeth passed on to us. We estimate she was lifted off the street some time between eighteen thirty and twenty hundred hours.'

'Genius,' muttered a voice down the table. It was Carl Mayne, Operations director. A fiercely ambitious man nearing the end of his career in the Service, everyone knew he saw Khan as his rival.

'Carl, please,' admonished Khan. 'Just hear him out.'

Worlock looked from one man to the other, as if to say, When you two have quite finished . . . Then he went on, 'So we're hoping to do the comms exploitation on Ms Mayhew's mobile, if we can recover it. We've accessed her service provider and we've built up a clear digital map of where she was taken. For the first twenty minutes.'

'And?' said Mayne, a touch impatiently.

'And here it is.' Worlock handed round a single sheet printed with a grid map of west London. A thick green line traced a route from Battersea, westwards through Richmond and out to Hanworth, a suburb near the M3 in Middlesex.

'Well, shouldn't you be there now?' suggested Mayne.

The policeman had volunteered to leave the ops room at Cobalt Square to brief these people at Vauxhall Cross, but now he was having second thoughts. They seemed an ungrateful bunch to him. 'We've already sent a team to Hanworth,' he replied patiently. 'They're going through the bins now and knocking on doors. We see this a lot with kidnaps, believe me.'

'See a lot of what?' Mayne again.

'The kidnappers suddenly find a mobile phone on their captive so they rip out the SIM card and chuck it away, then they move off fast. I'm not holding out a great deal of hope we'll find anything at that location, but we're going through all the CCTVs in the area, looking for any vehicle passing through in that time frame that's big enough to hide someone in the back.'

'But the bottom line, Chris . . .' Khan wanted to remind everyone why they were there '. . . is that you're broadly confident you can find her, yes?'

'No, I didn't say that exactly. What I said was that historically most kidnaps end peacefully within twelve hours to three days. Usually it's money they want. But this one is different. They're asking you to close down whatever you've got going in whichever country it is these people are from.'

'Colombia,' said Khan. He didn't think there was much point in hiding it: they were all supposed to be on the same side. 'Anyway, we've still got a decision to make,' he added. 'Do we tell Luke Carlton?'

Angela Scott let out a strangled snort. 'I'm sorry,' she said, her voice rising. 'Did I hear you right? We're actually debating whether or not we inform Luke Carlton that his girlfriend has just been kidnapped? Are we really having this conversation? Of course we need to tell him! It's a duty of care!'

'Angela, please,' interjected Carl Mayne. 'It's a legitimate question. No one's suggesting we don't tell him, just that we delay it by, say, twenty-four hours. Do I need to remind everyone we're running an extremely sensitive op that has a major impact on the current national security threat? And Luke is integral to the success of this op.'

There was a short, awkward silence until Sanderson asked, 'Do we know exactly where he is right now?'

'We do,' replied Khan. 'He landed in Medellín a few hours ago. He's with the team from Langley. He should have made contact with Tradewind by now. So, whatever he does is mission critical.'

'For heaven's sake!' exclaimed Angela. 'He has a right to know! It's not too late to tell him.'

'Whoa, whoa, whoa!' said Mayne, making a vertical slicing motion through the air with his hand, a legacy of his Army days in the Household Cavalry Mounted Regiment. 'No one's calling anyone until we've thrashed this out. Let's say we tell him right away. What effect do you think that's going to have on his operational capability?'

'I know what the answer would be if it were my wife,' said the head of HR.

'Precisely,' said Mayne. 'Which is why I don't think

we can possibly tell him until the operation is concluded. There is simply too much at stake. Sid? Any thoughts?'

Khan took his time answering, but it was fairly obvious to anyone in the room that he had made up his mind some time ago. 'I concur,' he said. 'I've got the national security adviser ringing me practically every hour to check where we are on this. I don't think it's feasible for me to say, Sorry, we've pulled the op on compassionate grounds. We're letting the main player get away.'

But Angela was not giving up without a fight. 'Is it out of the question,' she asked, 'for someone else to fill in on this job instead of Luke? Are we really saying the whole of JSOC and Langley between them have got no one else who fits the bill? Because I find that rather hard to swallow.'

'OK,' said Mayne, suddenly standing up and ignoring her question. He, too, had made up his mind. 'I'm going to take an executive decision here. Wherever anyone's moral compass happens to lie on this one – and, Angela, for the record, your concerns are duly noted – I'm afraid that the national interest takes priority. We are not informing Carlton until the mission is over. And that . . .' he paused to look everyone present in the eye '. . . is final.'

Chapter 85

POTHOLES. THEY HAD been travelling for just over two hours and already Luke was sick of them. Along with everyone else in the convoy, he was being pitched forward without warning or thrown sideways, banging the side of his skull against the window, every time they drove over one. Which seemed to be about every twenty metres. Luke pulled back the frilly curtain to peer out through the tinted glass at the darkened scene flashing past outside. There were long stretches of black nothingness as they drove past thick vegetation. Then there would be a kaleidoscope of colours, filtered through the raindrops that splashed against the windowpane, as they passed through tiny village night markets lit by yellow hurricane lamps that hung from rickety wooden stalls. He caught glimpses of pyramids of fruit he didn't recognize and large, squat women in flowery dresses, fanning smoky braziers or turning over chicken wings spliced on sticks of singed bamboo. Absently, he pulled out a half-melted Snickers bar from the ration sacks they had brought with them and started to eat it. When they went over another pothole he bit his tongue.

His earpiece crackled into life. 'Stand by, stand by. RV point five hundred metres ahead.' It was Todd Miller in the lead vehicle. Luke was surprised to find he had been asleep. It was past ten and he rubbed the side of his head where it had banged against the window. Some of the other operatives had wedged folded scarves between themselves and the glass.

They stepped out into the damp cool of the Antioquia night, a perfect ambient temperature at fifteen hundred metres above sea level. No wonder García had made this province his main operating base. All around Luke people were stretching their legs, some doing lunges to wake numbed limbs, and there was a steady hiss as men relieved themselves into the bushes. They were in a deserted, darkened side road off the main track that led to the village of Naranjo. Two Colombian operatives had guided the convoy in with red-filtered torches and Miller now approached Luke with them in tow.

'Here's how it's going down from here,' he said. 'Our Special Ops guys will push forward in a moment to recce the village from a distance. When they give me the signal, these guys here' – he gestured to the two Colombians, but did not introduce them – 'will escort you in. Still reckon you can be in and out in under thirty?'

'I'm aiming to be out in twenty,' replied Luke. It seemed a world away now, but he had spent most of that morning back at MacDill rehearsing exactly how he would train Valentina to use the specialized acupuncture kit in as short a time as possible.

When Miller moved off to brief the men going forward, Luke squatted on his haunches, adjusting his senses to the night. The cicadas had started up in the trees, and from somewhere inside the tangle of undergrowth an owl was calling softly. Briefly, he closed his eyes and thought about the mission. This was not the same as squeezing the trigger when someone came running towards you intent on ending your life. It wasn't even the same as killing a man in cold blood. It was teaching somebody else to carry out the job he could not get close enough to do himself. She was certainly brave, Agent Tradewind. He wondered what made her want to risk everything for the mission. Was it the chance of a new life in Britain? Or did she harbour a hidden loathing for the drug lord whose empire was infecting her country?

'OK, Carlton, you're up.' Miller was back, his great quarterback's frame materializing silently in the dark. 'Coast is clear. The boys will lead you in. She knows you're coming.' He clapped Luke lightly on the back, then spoke quietly into his mike. 'Beefeater moving now. Over.'

Beefeater? Who had dreamed that one up, he wondered, as they started off down the track, the Travellers' First Aid box taped to his waist.

They approached Naranjo from behind, moving quietly along the edge of the forest where the foliage crowded in on the village. Just short of their objective one of Luke's two Colombian guides tapped his arm, pointed up to his own eyes with two fingers spread, then indicated the undergrowth at their feet. It took Luke a second or two to spot him in the darkness: it was one of their own team, a Special Ops sniper with a telescopic nightsight and a long rifle resting on a bipod. Todd Miller certainly had his back covered tonight.

Valentina's family home looked very much like all the others in the same row. A single-storey brick-built bungalow with pink walls and a corrugated-iron roof. Modest, but not impoverished. Luke could see there was a veranda with chairs at the back, lit by a light on the wall, and flowers climbing up the pillars. Baskets of more flowers hung from the rafters with a set of wind chimes. He took all of this in as he moved forward, but he was focused on the girl sitting on the back patio, wearing a white cotton dress. He recognized her immediately as Valentina. An old transistor radio stood on the table beside her playing salsa music, turned down low. This was not ideal. He would have preferred to get her well away from her parents' place and the village, but they were working against the clock: García and his henchmen could flee the country at any moment, and Luke needed enough light to show her what had to be done. He checked his watch: 2225 hours. Hopefully her family would be asleep by now.

When Luke closed the distance between them, Valentina's head jerked up, like that of a deer startled by a predator, alert and expectant. He pointed towards the house, questioning. She put her head on one side, resting on her hands, her hair hanging down in dark tresses. Good.

'Aguapanela?' she asked, in a whisper, as Luke pulled up a chair, careful not to scrape it on the veranda's bare concrete floor. It was the first word spoken between them, and the irony didn't escape him. Here they were, about to plan a murder, and she was offering him sugarcane water. Valentina was pointing to a cup of what looked like tea with a half-lime resting on the saucer. He remembered *aguapanela* from earlier visits – it was a strong drink, a bit like coffee – and declined: he was buzzing enough already. There was

no time for introductions or small-talk: Luke had set a mental stopwatch from the moment he had stepped out of the shadows and thirty seconds had already passed.

He began with the compact communicator. That was the easy part, just plain tradecraft, nothing too far from the comms training she had received after she was first recruited to the Service. Then he untaped the Travellers' First Aid box from its hiding place and opened it on the table, facing the box towards her. Quietly he talked her through the different needles, the phials of fentanyl citrate and how to attach them.

Then came the moment, a wobble, when she realized exactly what she was being asked to do. Valentina looked up at him and he saw fear in those brown doe eyes. He put his hands on her shoulders. 'I know,' he said. 'This is so much more than you agreed to do but it's incredibly important for us and for your country, for your people.' She held his eyes, waiting for him to say more, to convince her that taking such an immense risk was really necessary. 'But you know that Nelson García *es un hombre muy malo,*' Luke continued. 'He has killed so many people, ruined so many lives. Valentina, his thugs murdered Jerry Benton, remember? The man who gave you a second chance in life?' It was a cheap shot, but the clock was ticking and Luke needed to be sure she would go through with it. Eventually she nodded her assent and looked down again at the box of poison. As a trained acupuncturist, Valentina knew her job, and when it came to handling the needles she was way ahead of him. The handover was starting to look easier than he had expected. He glanced at his watch. Fourteen minutes. Not bad.

Luke held out his hand and smiled. *'Buena suerte.'* He wished her luck and started to rise from his chair.

And that was when they heard her mother call from inside the house. *'Tina, mi hija.* You have visitors. It's your employers. I've sent them round the back to find you.'

Chapter 86

IN A FRACTION of a second, Luke and Valentina exchanged glances. He had known her for less than fifteen minutes and he had no idea how she would react. There was no time to make a plan, no time for him to escape: they would have to wing it. The Travellers' First Aid kit lay open on the table, its lethal contents on display for anyone to see. The sniper, he knew, would have him covered: a couple of rapid squeezes on the trigger would drop García's men before they could present a threat. But if it came to that the whole plan would unravel. There would be no chance of getting to García and the mission would fail.

Luke dropped to the floor of the patio, flattening himself against the concrete while reaching for his personal weapon, strapped to his side ever since they had left the base in Tampa that morning. Valentina moved fast: she skipped down the steps into the garden at the back of the house and intercepted the two men just as they rounded the corner. Luke could hear her greeting them enthusiastically – she obviously knew them. Then she called, loudly enough for him to hear: 'I'll just go and get my things, then join you at the front. Please, wait for me there.'

They were taking her back to García.

Luke waited a full minute, then lifted himself off the patio floor, walked into the garden at the back and vanished into the foliage, entering the forest exactly where he had left it. Fifteen minutes later he was back with Todd Miller and the vehicles. He hefted himself into the second row of seats in the lead minivan and brushed a few twigs off his clothes as he sat behind Miller. 'It's done,' he said. 'Garcia's people came to take her back. A little close for comfort, I have to say.'

'So I heard.' Miller tapped his earpiece: he'd been getting constant updates. 'We had no intel they'd be coming for her so soon.' He held up a hand. 'Excuse me, I have to notify MacDill.' To the base in Florida, Miller spoke just a single word: 'Nexus.' It meant the delivery had been made, the package handed over. Tradewind was on her way back to García.

Luke, Miller and the SIGINT operator with the receiver sat in the minivan waiting for Valentina to confirm she was with García. It was after midnight when the small device buzzed into life. As the message came through, the comms operator scanned it onto his monitor, then passed the device to Miller without a word.

It was not what he was expecting.

Chapter 87

IN A NONDESCRIPT basement beneath a nondescript building in a street that looked exactly like the one next to it, Elise Mayhew sat bound to a wooden chair. The only other person in the room was Ana María and she was standing just two metres away from her, arms folded, head on one side, considering her.

That bitch! I knew it. Elise had suspected there was something not quite right about her when the elegant Spanish woman had wafted into the Stratford Gallery to enquire, ever so politely, about an artist who had never existed. Now she knew. Ana María was clearly part of some horrendous criminal underworld. What the hell did she want? Was Elise about to be trafficked? No. This was tied up with Luke and his work. It had to be. Elise was scared but she willed herself to stay calm, her eyes following Ana María as the Spanish woman started to pace about the room.

She was behind her now. Elise couldn't see her but she sensed her standing very close. She felt a manicured hand reach down and stroke her cheek as Ana María spoke for the first time since their encounter in the art gallery. 'What shall I do with you?' she whispered, her face so close that Elise could smell her perfume. She recognized it as J'Adore by Dior. 'I have an idea,' continued Ana María, walking in front to face her square-on, her heels clicking on the wooden floor. Elise watched her smooth the creases in her skirt with both hands. She looked, at a pinch, almost like some of the people Elise knew from her job at the gallery: elegant, sophisticated, well dressed. So what on earth was a woman like her doing mixed up with the underworld? Someone had to be paying her a lot of money and that, she reckoned, probably meant drugs. Oh, God, how was she going to get out of this?

'I'm going to ask my partner to keep watch over you,' announced Ana María. 'You do exactly as she tells you and you will be fine. Is that understood?' Elise nodded and mumbled behind the gag.

'You want me to remove that thing? Well, it's a little too soon for that, don't you think? You've only just arrived. Why don't we let my partner decide? Hmm?' And with that Ana María was gone.

Alone in the room, Elise considered her situation. Breathing slowly and evenly, she was under control and thinking clearly. All those hard hours in the martial-arts *dojo* had taught her qualities she could now draw on: resilience, tenacity and the ability to withstand a few knocks. Up to a point. It depended on what they had in mind for her. That was the big unknown. She knew one thing, though: if she ever got the chance she could take the Spanish woman down. Sweep her off her feet and lay her out cold in two moves. But then what? These people, whoever they were, were hardly going to leave her an open exit to the street. And where the hell were the police? Surely someone must have seen her being snatched and raised the alarm. Elise struggled ineffectually to release her arms but they remained tightly bound. She stopped: she should save her energy for when she needed it.

Chapter 88

'WHAT WE NEED,' said Alwyn Hughes, the National Security Adviser, 'is a multi-layered approach. It needs to start at the Cenotaph and work outwards. We'll need to put a ring of steel around all the royals and VIPs. And I want a counter-terrorism piece written into the public order safety plan for the day.'

With three days to go before the annual Remembrance Sunday parade, preparations were in full swing. On the wide expanse of Wellington Barracks next to St James's Park the band of the Grenadier Guards had been rehearsing for days, belting out such martial tunes as 'Heart of Oak' and the sombre strains of Elgar's 'Nimrod'. Horse Guards Parade had been swept clean, every item of litter gathered up, and extra security cameras were being installed. Police leave had been cancelled. The national terrorist threat level was still at its highest, although there was little outward sign of anything different. The newspapers and broadcasters had exhausted every possible scenario for what had prompted the government to raise the level to Critical. Most were sourcing it to threats emanating from Syria, Libya or Yemen. None had traced it back to South America.

But in the high-security confines of the Cabinet

Office in the heart of Whitehall, where the country's key decision-makers met on the National Security Council, one question kept coming back to haunt them, with ever greater urgency. Given the catastrophic threat of a radioactive dirty bomb, should the Remembrance Sunday parade be going ahead? All the searches around Greater Manchester had drawn a blank, the ports had turned up nothing, the human informants run by the Metropolitan Police and MI5 had failed to produce any meaningful leads. Increasingly the NSC was veering towards the view that London was bound to be the target.

'If we cancel Remembrance Sunday in London,' cautioned Sir William Orgrave, the Cabinet Secretary, 'we might as well tell the public what's really going on and press the panic button. The PM will have to go before the nation and people will expect answers that we simply don't have. No, I wouldn't advise it.'

'But by going ahead,' argued Hughes, 'surely we're offering ourselves as a great barrage balloon of a target. The Sovereign will be there, obviously, along with half the royal family, prime ministers past and present – well, you know the score.' From somewhere down in the street a siren rose in pitch as it passed their building, then faded away as it moved off towards Trafalgar Square.

'Let me remind everyone what we're talking about here,' resumed Hughes. 'If a dirty bomb were to go off in central London, you're looking at thousands of square metres getting showered with radioactive particles. There'll be people with first-degree burns, people with skin peeling off, not to mention all the thyroid cancer and other after-effects down the line. Whole streets, whole blocks would have to be evacuated. It could take weeks to decontaminate.' His eyebrows arched as he spoke. The Doomsday scenario he described had clearly been playing on his mind.

'Are you saying we should cancel?' asked Alan Reynolds, the Home Secretary, his neat black hair as immaculate as ever. His eyes darted around the room, keen as a kingfisher's, sussing out his other colleagues to see where they stood on the matter.

'No,' replied Hughes, in his calming Welsh tones. 'At least, not yet.'

'Well, we're cutting it a bit fine, aren't we?' chipped in the Met's national coordinator for counter-terrorism, a seasoned deputy assistant commissioner. 'There's just three days to go and we're no closer to locating the device and defusing it. If we can't find it, surely the public's safety has to come first.'

'No one's arguing with that,' said the Cabinet Secretary. 'But can anyone here recall the last time the Remembrance Sunday parade in London was cancelled?' There was silence. 'No?' continued Orgrave. 'Nor can I. It's a national bloody institution, part of our calendar. So if we pull the plug, you can be absolutely certain the media are going to get wind of what's behind it, and then what?' Again he looked round the room as if to emphasize his point.

The Home Secretary twirled his pen between his fingers but said nothing, averting his gaze.

'I'll tell you exactly what,' continued Orgrave. 'You're looking at a mass egress out of London. Every road, every motorway clogged and backed up for miles. And where will they go? Hmm? We simply aren't set up to deal with a crisis of that magnitude. We've had nothing like it since 1940 and the Blitz.'

After forty-five minutes the meeting broke up without consensus. But in the most time-honoured of all Whitehall traditions, a decision was taken: to delay making any decision until there was more information to hand.

Chapter 89

ELISE JOLTED AWAKE. She could hear footsteps approaching. How long had she been asleep? An hour? Two? Longer? Instinctively, she glanced down at her wrist to check the time, but her watch had gone. Of course it had. They had taken it from her when they'd thrown away her mobile phone. A dull, monochrome light was seeping into the room, the colour of November, so it must be morning. Elise's arms hurt from where she was bound and she had pins and needles in all her limbs. She tensed and relaxed her muscles as much as she could, flexing her fingers and trying to work her circulation. With a shock she realized that the gag was gone – that at least was a plus. They must have removed it while she slept in case she choked on it. Which meant they planned to keep her alive, at least for now.

When the door opened she braced herself. Would it be one of the underworld thugs who had bundled her into the minivan yesterday? No. It was a woman, but a very different one from the fragrant Ana María. She was shorter than average, a little broad in the beam, and wearing a faded red polo shirt above stonewashed jeans. No jewellery, no make-up, no ring, and Elise detected a faint smell of stale cigarettes.

'Good morning.' Elise broke the silence. She was remembering something Luke had told her when they were idling away an afternoon on holiday. 'If you're ever taken prisoner,' he had said – she had laughed at that – 'try to establish a rapport with whoever's guarding you. Break the ice, get them talking, get them thinking of you as a fellow human instead of a nameless prisoner. That way you'll get better treatment, and when the time comes, they may just help you by looking the other way.' Good advice, she reflected now, but this one appeared a hard case, not exactly a talker.

'I really need to use the bathroom,' she said. '*El baño?* Please?'

The woman took a step forward and put her face very close to Elise's, examining her critically as if she were a suspicious package. Elise did not like what she saw in those eyes: hardness, cruelty, a total absence of compassion.

'You be quiet,' hissed the woman, 'or I put your eyes out.'

The words shocked Elise to the core. It was a blunt and horrible reminder of her predicament: these people could do anything they liked to her and apparently no one was coming to save her. She would keep quiet from now on.

The woman turned round to look at the door as it opened. It was Ana María, as immaculate as ever, come to inspect her prisoner.

'Is she behaving?' she asked in English.

The other woman didn't answer, but Elise spoke up.

'Please. Why are you holding me? I don't know who you are or what you want. This has to be a mistake. Come on,' she implored, 'just let me go and I'll tell no one about this, and—'

The back-handed slap was so hard it rocked Elise in her chair, cutting her off in mid-sentence. It left her gasping, her eyes stinging and tears welling. She could taste blood at the corner of her mouth where the blow had split her lip. The shorter of the two women had delivered it and now stood hissing at her like a venomous reptile. She raised her arm, ready to hit Elise a second time, but Ana María placed a restraining hand on her. '*Paciencia*,' she said, as she moved closer to Elise.

'We're offering your government a choice. A simple exchange. You for him.'

Elise looked at the two women, so very different yet partners in the same crime. There was no longer any doubt in her mind. They were from the gang who had kidnapped Luke in South America. And they were cruel. They had already shown that, phoning her while they tortured him with an electric drill. Human life clearly meant little to them. Her spirits sank.

Elise could feel a bruise coming up on her cheek where the woman had hit her, but now Ana María was speaking to her once more.

'And this is my friend.' She laid a hand on the other woman's arm. 'This is Linda. I have things to take care of now so she will look after you.' What the hell did that mean? Elise had known the woman less than five minutes and already she had threatened to blind her, then hit her. This wasn't good news. Ana María was sinister, but Elise suspected she was in for a rough ride at the hands of this woman from the *barrios*. Linda was coming towards her now, holding something. She recognized it as the gag in the last moment before it was tied over her mouth. It was so tight that it bit into her cheeks, stretching her lips. Linda looked at her work, grunted in satisfaction, and then the pair left. If Elise could have breathed normally she would have heaved a sigh of relief. Every minute spent away from them was time away from imminent danger. But she was under no illusion: they would be back, and when they came she had to be ready.

Chapter 90

IN THE MET'S specialist operations room, upstairs in Cobalt Square, there was a buzz of excitement. Nearly twenty-four hours after she had been kidnapped the team assigned to the Elise Mayhew case reckoned they might be looking at a breakthrough. Under the direction of Superintendent Worlock and two chief inspectors, they had pulled in every last frame of CCTV footage from every camera on every street within a five-hundred-metre radius of the last-known location of her mobile phone. Trawling through the jerky, monochrome footage, they focused on activity filmed between 1830 and 2000 hours the previous evening. While Elise's handset had yet to be recovered, the CCTV material had yielded clear images of three vans with enough covered rear-window space to conceal a prisoner. Two vehicles had been traced to their owners, who had been questioned extensively. One turned out to belong to a garden nursery in Cheam, the other to a furniture upholstering company in Staines. But the third vehicle had been bought recently, paid for in cash and, according to the DVLA database, was registered to a Mr Hernando González of 58 Woodlock Avenue, Isleworth.

Superintendent Worlock sat on the corner of a desk

in the ops room and peered at a computer monitor, studying the image of a van parked outside a lock-up garage in south-west London. One of the Met's most experienced hostage-case handlers, his once-neat sideburns had turned to unruly grey wisps in recent years. He wore reading glasses, these days, and adjusted them now, pushing them further up the bridge of his nose. The Kidnap Unit's Green team, assigned to exploit the intelligence, was gathered behind him.

'ANPR?' asked Worlock.

'Already done,' replied a detective sergeant. Following standard protocol, he had run the numberplate through the national automatic numberplate recognition system, a network of at least seven thousand cameras, many of them hidden, that allows police to track the movement of suspect vehicles around the country.

'And?' Worlock asked.

'It didn't spend long at that address in Hanworth. It drove out thirty minutes later. We've clocked it passing a camera in Walton-on-Thames, then moving on to an address in Weybridge, just south of where the M3 meets the M25.' The DS sat back, scanning his boss's face for a reaction.

'When was this?' asked Worlock.

'Well, the vehicle movements were last night. But we've just received the data now.'

'Get Blue team onto all three of these addresses. I want to know every single movement in and out of each of them.'

'Will do, Boss.'

Superintendent Chris Worlock returned to his glass-walled office, mulling over two decisions he needed to make, and very soon. Should he contact SIS and give them the latest developments, or wait till he had something more concrete to tell them? Was Elise Mayhew in such imminent danger – a Grade 1 situation – that he needed to call in a tactical firearms officer to advise the teams on the options available to them? But something else was also nagging at the back of his mind.

There was no return address, not even a digital one, for him to reply to the hostage-takers' demands, even if he chose to. That meant he could not deploy Red team, his negotiators. But it also meant the hostage-takers didn't want to be contacted. They're jacking us around, he thought. His mind made up, he reached for the phone to call the tactical firearms officer.

Chapter 91

SOMETHING HAD CHANGED. She could sense it the moment they pulled up at the gates of the planter's villa. Valentina had sat patiently in the back of the jeep as García's henchmen drove her along the darkened forest roads at what seemed to her an unnecessary speed. They had given her no reason for this late-night summons, but she was used to that. García kept unpredictable hours. But she had an inkling of what it meant, given all the preparations to leave: he must want her to accompany them. Finally she had earned her passport into his inner circle.

The guard on the villa gates was drunk. It was obvious, in fact he was making no attempt to hide it. Wearing a faded American combat jacket, a chequered Arab scarf round his neck and a flat green Mao cap, he held his Galil assault rifle in one hand and a half-empty bottle of *aguardiente* in the other.

'They left without you, *chica*,' he sneered, resting his arms on the open passenger window of the jeep. 'They clearly don't give a damn about you.' It was Luis Fernando, Valentina's least favourite security man on García's payroll. She would never forget what had happened on her first day, his scrawny hands all over her, pawing at her breasts as he pretended to pat her down for weapons. Now he appeared to be almost triumphant. Valentina might have won the confidence of El Pobrecito but, clearly, she was not so special that he had thought to take her with him. This now left her exposed, and she knew it. The guard craned his head inside the vehicle, addressing her in the back. She found his breath intoxicating, and not in a good way.

'Señor Suárez left instructions for us,' he told her. 'He said we were to take extra care of you.' He erupted into laughter, playfully punching the driver's shoulder and winking at him.

Valentina was no fool. She knew exactly what was going on. Without her patron, her protector, she was now at the mercy of others at the villa who had always resented her. This was their payback time. She was going to have to fight for survival. 'I need the toilet,' she said. 'Urgently.'

'Of course,' replied Luis Fernando. 'I will escort you myself.' He led the way towards the gatehouse, his feet shuffling, but the assault rifle still firmly in his grasp.

It was a basic room attached to the hut, sealed with a flimsy wooden door. He made a half-hearted attempt to follow her inside, but she pushed him gently back as she closed the door behind her and bolted it. The room whined with mosquitoes and she noticed one of the men had scrawled his name on the wall. Using his own excrement. These people were barbarians, she thought. But now she had just seconds to make a plan. All too aware of the enormity of the task entrusted to her, Valentina took out the compact transmitter Luke had given her less than an hour ago. She had to get word to them about García. The light inside the cubicle was dreadful, just a single weak bulb dangling on a flex, but she held up the compact to it so she could make out the keys and typed in a single sentence: *'Se ha ido al extranjero.* He's gone abroad.' She pressed transmit, replaced the powder puff and snapped the compact shut.

There was a sharp rap on the door. That sleazy bastard Fernando again, growing impatient. 'Come on out, *chiquitita,*' he called. 'It's time to play with the boys.'

She could almost see the leer on his face.

Valentina yanked the flush to play for time, then a thought occurred to her. The Travellers' First Aid kit. It was her only weapon, and since García was gone what was there to lose? She might as well put it to use. The rapping on the door was growing insistent. 'If you don't come out,' shouted the guard, 'I'm gonna come in there and wipe your pretty little arse myself.'

Valentina grimaced. Was it possible to despise this creep any more than she did already? She shook her head in disgust and took a deep breath. She was ready.

When she unlocked the door Fernando pushed it open and barged into the tiny cubicle. He seized her roughly by the shoulders but she wriggled free and wrapped her right arm around his neck, as if in a lover's embrace. The needle must have stung when it went in because he leaped back and howled in pain, clapping his hand to where she had stabbed him. *'Puta!'* he hissed. Incensed, he raised his arm to smash his fist into her face then held it poised in mid-air, as he fought for breath. He didn't know it but his respiratory system was failing. He had absorbed a lethal dose. As he collapsed in the doorway, his torso heaving, Valentina stepped over him and started to run, aiming to cover the shortest distance between the gatehouse and the edge of the forest.

Perhaps, if she had been wearing different clothes, something more practical, she might have stood a chance. But her white dress and mid-heel court shoes were working against her that night: she was lit up like a beacon as she raced across the courtyard towards the safety of the trees. The first three bullets hit her in the small of the back, pitching her onto the gravel. Her bag hit the ground a split second later, spilling out a small green rectangular box. Valentina was still breathing when García's men emptied the rest of the magazine into her. They checked her pulse, then reached under her armpits and dragged her lifeless body into the forest for the dogs to find. Valentina Gómez, Agent Tradewind, would never see England.

Chapter 92

IN HIS TEMPORARY office in the Grade 1 listed building overlooking Horse Guards Parade, Major General Rupert Milton (retired) put on his spectacles and studied the document in his hand. It read well, he concluded, because he had written almost every word himself. General Milton took his responsibilities extremely seriously. He had been planning this for nearly twelve months and now, with just three days to go before the event, he wanted every *t* crossed, every *i* dotted. That, he told himself, was why they had put a Guards officer in charge. You want something like this to go by the book? Then you call on someone like him from the Household Division. It isn't every Tom, Dick and Harry who gets asked to take charge of organizing Britain's Remembrance Sunday parade in Whitehall.

'This,' read the report, 'is a supporting detail page of the main policy document.' How those Whitehall types loved expressions like that. 'At 1100 hours on Sunday, 13 November, the National Service of Remembrance will be held at the Cenotaph on Whitehall to commemorate the contribution of British and Commonwealth servicemen and -women in the two World Wars and later conflicts.'

So far, so good. The retired general read on, searching for errors. A heading in bold print announced who would be attending and taking part.

- 0845: Royal British Legion (RBL) detachments form up on Horse Guards Parade and in Whitehall
- 0945: All detachments march out from Wellington Barracks
- 1100: Two minutes' silence marked by the firing of guns from King's Troop, on Horse Guards Parade. Cenotaph Service commences
- 1120: Cenotaph Service concludes and RBL detachments disperse past the Cenotaph

'Members of the public,' it continued, 'may observe the ceremony from the pavements along Whitehall and Parliament Street. Orders of Service will be distributed to the public by Scouts. Whitehall was to be opened to the public at precisely 0800. Those attending are advised not to bring large bags. Security in the area remains tight and the Metropolitan Police have powers to remove obstacles (such as camera tripods) where they obstruct public access.'

General Milton put down the paper. He realized he was grinding his teeth again, a habit he had acquired all those years ago as a fresh-faced young cadet at Sandhurst. 'Security in the area remains tight.' Ha! That was an understatement if ever there was one. Milton was one of the few 'in the know'. Only the week before he had been summoned to the MoD across the road and briefed by the Defence Secretary herself, no less. Yes, there was an ongoing threat, she had told him, but the situation was contained. There was no hard intelligence to indicate that London was the target, although units were poised to move anywhere in the city the moment they got a lead. No need for alarm, she told him, just thought he ought to be aware.

General Milton got up and walked over to the window that looked westwards, down onto the equestrian statue of Viscount Wolseley and out onto the wide expanse of Horse Guards Parade. Now long retired, he still liked to imagine himself reviewing his troops there, taking the salute while standing stiff as a board on a raised wooden dais, surveying the massed lines of crimson uniforms, the wind ruffling the black bearskins and the sun glinting off bayonets. Well that was all in the past now, this was his main effort now, the parade this coming Sunday. And if General Rupert Milton had anything to do with it, it was bloody well going to go off like clockwork.

Chapter 93

KEITH GAMMON HAD woken up late that morning, alone as always, in his one-bedroom flat in Hounslow. Living on his own didn't bother him – in fact, he had had quite enough unwanted company in prison to last him a lifetime. His wife, Pauline, had left him soon after he was sent down, as he'd known she would. Taken the kids with her, she had, and moved somewhere up north. Gutted at the time, Gammon had gone through some dark days coping with the depression that followed. He had emerged so much stronger, or so he believed, but he was bitter to the core. It was not just the government, the establishment, that he hated, not just the people who had put him away for so long: it was society as a whole. It had dealt him a rubbish hand, Gammon concluded, and now it was payback time, a chance to even the score. His welding skills were being called upon by people willing to pay him a small fortune. He felt valued and appreciated. And if some bad things had to happen to some people as a result of his work, well, so be it. That simply wasn't his problem. If Keith Gammon had ever had a conscience, he had discarded it long ago, flushed down the drains of a Category B men's prison in south-west London.

He had taken the call the day before. It was the Spanish woman, Ana somebody, who had rung him to tell him quietly that it was on. Now he towelled off after his shower, pulled on the clothes that lay flung across the back of a chair, let himself out of the flat and went down the road for a full English. Aldo's Star Café was his local greasy spoon. They knew him in there and he didn't even need to order, just a look and a nod as he pushed through the door and the fryer was on. Got to go to work on a full stomach and all that, he told himself. Begin it in style and you can cope with whatever the day throws at you.

Later, seated at the Formica table, splattered with the detritus of his fry-up, Keith Gammon got to thinking about the job. Much of it he had already done: the modifications to the floor of the Nissan Primastar van they would use and the basic shape of the moulded 'coffin' that would contain the device. They had planned it all in stages, him, Ana María and that bloke Silvio with the ponytail whom he didn't much care for. Long hours spent poring over sketch maps, street maps and satellite images, all in the smoky back room of a South American restaurant in Bayswater. Cigarette stubbed out as someone emphasized a point, another lit almost at once. On the wall he could see a lurid painting of an overweight woman sitting beneath a palm tree on a beach, and the shelves were lined with empty wine bottles. There was too much talk in Spanish for Keith Gammon's liking – he couldn't follow a word of it – but Ana María had paused frequently to translate for his benefit.

They had reached an understanding the first time they'd met. She'd promised to make him well off if he did the job they asked of him, and he promised to ask no questions and tell no tales. She also promised him, in her sweet and gentle voice, that if he ever betrayed them to the police the cartel would hunt down his children and post him their severed hands.

'Rising bollards,' Gammon had told them, when it had been his turn to offer advice in that Bayswater back room.

'Excuse me?' It was not an expression familiar to the South American criminal underworld in London.

'You've got to get past the rising bollards,' he continued. 'It's what they're called, those black pillars blocking the access to Horse Guards Parade. All hundred and twenty-six of them. I've counted. They're about a metre high, made of steel, and we're going to need to cut through three if you want to get the van through.'

Ana María had shaken her head emphatically. 'No,' she told them. 'We do it a different way, a more subtle way. I will arrange the paperwork and they will let us through. Leave it with me.'

'*Y entonces?*' said Ponytail. 'And then?'

'And then,' answered Ana María, 'we do what we discussed.' She turned to the welder. 'North-west corner of the parade ground. There is a big brown building like a fortress, covered in some red plant. There is a camera on top, but don't trouble yourself about this. It faces out across the square. If we stay close in by the wall it will be, how you say, a blind spot. Here, let me show you on the map.'

That had all been weeks ago. Since that meeting they had bought the Nissan Primastar van second-hand, touched up the paintwork, made the modifications, and purchased the JCB mini-digger they would need on the day. They had done the drive-pasts, the dress rehearsals, practised the cover story and printed the documents to back it up. Today it would be for real.

At twelve noon precisely, the light blue Nissan Primastar with the British Gas logo stopped on the corner of Keith Gammon's street in Hounslow. 'You can't miss it,' he had told Ana María. 'It's right by the junction of the Twickenham Road and the Mogden Sewage Treatment Works.' He had clambered in, clutching a large holdall, and settled himself in the passenger seat. Silently, she had handed him a forged laminated ID card. Everyone in the van had been issued with one. 'British Gas. Looking after your world,' it said, and there was his picture next to a data box.

My name is
MR JOHN BLANE
This card expires on: **31/12/2017**
ID Number: **654337**
If you want to check my identity please call
0800 612 77660

Ana María was incredibly thorough, he had to give her that. She had thought of everything. Anyone calling that number would be put through to what sounded like a twenty-four-hour British Gas switchboard. Yes, they would be told, after a pause to check an imaginary computer database. We do have a Mr John Blane on our books. He's a qualified engineer. Been with us for years. Thank you for calling British Gas.

As they drove east along Great Chertsey Road, heading to a suburban car park to collect the digger, then on into town towards Whitehall, Ana María had given them all one final briefing. They had two hours, and no more, in which to complete the job. That was from the time they appeared on site to the time they would drive away. Any longer and too many questions would be asked. There was also the risk that secondary probing checks could be made. She and Ponytail had briefly debated whether to mount the operation by day or by night. In the end, they had opted for daylight. 'Hiding in plain sight,' Ana María called it. Night time would seem too suspicious.

At 1305 hours, as Major General (retired) Rupert Milton was enjoying a Cheddar cheese and pickle sandwich at his desk in Horse Guards, the blue van with the British Gas livery pulled up at the north-west corner of the parade ground two hundred metres away, towing a canary-yellow mechanical digger. It stopped at the exact point where the line of black metal rising bollards met the walls of Lenin's Tomb, which were covered with the autumnal red leaves of Virginia creeper. Since the Home Secretary had raised the terrorism threat level to Critical, the whole of Whitehall, known as the Government Secure Zone, now had a discreet but reinforced police presence.

Parked on Horse Guards Road with the engine running, beside the Guards Division Memorial on the edge of St James's Park just a hundred metres away, the two police officers in the patrol car watched the Nissan Primastar and the digger pull up. They reacted immediately. While one called it in to his superior, an inspector at the back of Downing Street, the other got out to investigate.

WPC Granger approached the driver's side of the van. The day was unusually mild for November and she was wearing only a black stab vest over her white uniform shirt. Politely but firmly, she told the driver he must move along: this was a secure area; he could not park there.

'Sorry, ma'am. We've been told this is a priority. Looks like there's a gas leak in the pipes below here. The Gas Board thinks one of the old mains has cracked. Got a letter from the council. We need to dig down and investigate.'

The driver of the Primastar, wearing a black jumpsuit with blue stripes and a British Gas logo, reached into the glove compartment and produced the letter.

'Can I see some ID, please?' she asked, then looked at the letter. He handed her his British Gas card, and WPC Granger looked from one to the other. 'Wait here, please,' she told him. She moved away a couple of metres and radioed in the names and phone numbers printed on the ID card and the letter.

It took her colleague in the patrol car less than ten minutes to call back. The man at 'Westminster City Council' who had answered the phone had been more than helpful. Yes, he confirmed, they had had reports of a gas leak in that location, and proceeded to go into far more detail than the policeman had asked for.

'You see, this is a City Gate problem,' he had told him. 'It's part of the local gas distribution system for Westminster. It's where our system accepts gas from another transmission system. So the transfer price under the ground at that point is what we call a City Gate price. That's why we've sent a team over to Whitehall to sort it out before we get into a pricing row with First Utility, and we don't want that!' Satisfied, the policeman had rung the British Gas number and that, too, had checked out. The blue van was cleared to proceed.

Inside the police post at the back entrance to Downing Street, another policeman pressed two switches simultaneously. At the opposite end of the parade ground three of the black rising bollards were retracted into the ground, allowing the Nissan Primastar and its digger to drive slowly onto Horse Guards Parade.

Chapter 94

ANA MARÍA AND her team worked with practised speed. It was 13.20 when the bollards were lowered. They had been on-site for precisely fifteen minutes and she wanted them away and dispersed inside the next hour and three-quarters. There was no need to venture far into the parade ground: they had already selected the spot where the trench would be dug. Just fifty metres in was enough to bring them to that out-of-the-way corner where the CCTV camera mounted on the wall above could not angle down far enough to film them.

They parked the van and the digger just short of the Gallipoli Naval Memorial, beside half a dozen faded poppy wreaths, placed there the previous year. In this secluded spot, where the sombre walls of Lenin's Tomb met the magnificent Grade II façade of Lutyens's Admiralty House, they went to work. Just as they had rehearsed, out on the disused airfield in Surrey, the men, in their black-and-blue British Gas overalls and white hard hats, threw up a cordon of orange plastic cones around the Primastar. Nobody wanted a nosy member of the public getting too close to what was going on.

Keith Gammon remained inside the van. After all

the modifications he'd made to it with the extreme plasma cutter, he liked to think of the second-hand Nissan Primastar as his own. The vehicle now had a removable sliding panel where the floor had been. Outside, the black-clad 'engineers' got to work with the JCB HM25 Hydraulic Breaker, attacking the surface of the parade square with the hand-held power tool. By 13.35 they had broken through the hard upper surface and marked out a rectangular trench to be dug. It took a further fourteen minutes to manoeuvre the mini-digger into position and then, at the exact moment that the mechanical claw was raised and they were poised to begin digging, WPC Granger was back. And this time she had an inspector with her.

'Who's in charge here?' he asked.

Ana María stepped forward. 'I am,' she said, and smiled at him from beneath her hard hat.

'Right. We've had a complaint from the people in Horse Guards over there.' He pointed. 'Apparently no one told them you'd be digging up half the parade ground. Can I see that letter of authorization, please?'

'Of course,' she replied, handing him the letter from Westminster Council. The words 'URGENT INVESTIGATION WORK' were printed in capitals and underlined. Further down the page the phrase 'Risk of Gas Explosion' caught his eye. 'There's a job number and a phone number on there, Inspector,' added Ana María. She stood her ground, relaxed and calm, one hand on her hip. Anyone who had known Ana María Acosta in her university days in Segovia would have remembered her as a highly skilled poker player, a consummate bluffer. It was a talent that continued to serve her well.

'We can pack up and leave now, if you like,' she said casually, 'and come back another day. But I must ask you to sign here. I will need your badge number. If there is an accident here tomorrow because we were prevented from doing our job . . . then I cannot be held responsible.'

It helped, of course, that Ana María had devised a back-up plan. It was not ideal: the secondary target was less iconic, and placing the device behind a rhododendron hedge in St James's Park would probably delay them by a day. But knowing they had a Plan B gave her the confidence to brazen this one out.

The inspector looked from one face to another. Her point was well made. He certainly didn't fancy seeing his photo on the front page of the papers above some caption like 'The Man Who Blew It'.

'How much longer is it going to take?' he asked.

Ana María squinted up at the gold hands on the clock in the eighteenth-century tower on Horse Guards. It was just coming up to two.

'We should be done within the hour,' she told the policeman. 'But we'll do our best to be away before then.'

The inspector handed back the letter from 'Westminster Council' and turned on his heel, WPC Granger at his side. He called over his shoulder as he walked away: 'Not a minute longer, mind.'

Inside the blue van, Keith Gammon had been listening to the exchange with mounting concern. He didn't like being around uniforms. He certainly didn't like the police, and the thought of what might have ensued if the officers had decided to search the back of the Primastar caused his hands to tremble. That wasn't good, with what he was about to do. Peering out of the vehicle, he watched the mini-digger at work. They had already excavated the first metre.

By 14.35 the trench was finished. One of Ana María's team of five jumped down into it to check it. It had been dug to meet exact specifications measured in advance: one and a half metres deep by two metres long by one metre wide. The man stood up and flashed a thumbs-up to Ana María. She walked over to the van and tapped on the window. Gammon wound it down.

'Now it's your turn,' she told him.

The most delicate phase of the operation was about to begin.

It was now essential that neither the police nor anyone else came anywhere near the trench. Ana María had delegated one of the team to keep watch while the driver climbed back into the van. Carefully he repositioned it in two moves, shifting it just a couple of metres to the left so that now it covered the hole. Two of the team joined Gammon in the back. Together they pulled back the retractable floor, revealing a rectangular gap of much the same dimensions as the trench. Next, they dragged the heavy coffin-shaped box from the back and positioned it over the hole. There were three handles on it, attached to ropes, and, under Gammon's instruction, they each held on, bracing themselves with their legs apart as they took the weight and lowered the box into the trench.

When it was done, and they were satisfied that it was settled on the bottom, Gammon switched on the head torch on his hard hat and dropped through the open floor of the van, balancing himself on the edges of the 'coffin', then standing inside it, next to the heavy cylindrical canister. He was less than a metre away from 750 grams of radioactive caesium chloride. He called for someone to pass him his toolbag.

The cartel had not chosen Keith Gammon for his welding skills alone, although that was a vital part of the contract. His military experience in handling high-explosive charges and detonators had piqued their interest, the result of a casual conversation during prisoners' association at Wandsworth. If they could source the explosives, they asked, could Gammon put together a viable device? He could, he had assured them. Now it was time to prove it, with the clock ticking and two uniformed police officers just a hundred metres away.

From a cellophane wrapper inside his toolbag he slowly withdrew a long lump of what looked like orange putty. It was 250 grams of Semtex 1A, sourced by the cartel from their underworld contacts in Eastern Europe the month before. Kneading it with his hands, he moulded it around the base of the canister, positioning it in such a way that, when it exploded, the force of the blast would split the canister in two and drive its toxic contents high into the air. Keith Gammon had some idea of what was in the canister. He had done basic NBC training – nuclear, biological and chemical – during his time in the Army, before it had been rebranded as CBRNE. But if someone had asked him about the properties of caesium chloride, its half-life, and how long it would take to remove from an area the size of Whitehall, he could not have told them. He was also unaware of what had become of the two Colombian submariners who had fallen ill with acute radiation sickness after transporting the material in a tiny confined space across the English Channel in a storm.

Blocking everything else from his mind, Keith Gammon concentrated on inserting first the master detonator into the Semtex, then a second as back-up. He took hold of the wires trailing from the detonators and inserted them into the homemade switch device, an object about the size of a refillable cigarette lighter, which he had built and tested at the disused airfield.

'Everything all right down there?' called one of the men above, breaking Gammon's concentration and almost causing him to drop the switch. 'Ana María says can you get a move on.'

'Ana María can sod off,' said Gammon, under his breath, then added, louder, 'It's fine. Just five more minutes.'

He felt along the edge of the switch until he located two further wires leading out of it, the positive and the negative. He inserted the other ends into what would look to many people like a chef's professional timer. It was a magnetic countdown timer but he had doctored it to Ana María's specifications. She had been most precise about this. Instead of running to just twenty-four hours, this one could be set to go off at any time over the next five days.

The next bit always scared him, even now, all these years after leaving the Army. He checked his watch, calculated the number of hours and minutes remaining till the time she had chosen for the device to be detonated, then programmed it into the timer. Finally, and this was the true heart-in-mouth moment, he moved the switch to 'on'. Nothing happened. He was still alive.

'Coming up,' he called. 'You can fill it in now.'

*

Ana María had promised the police they would be off the parade ground within an hour, and they were. At 14.55 they drove to the edge of the square where they had entered it less than two hours earlier. She waved to the police patrol car and waited patiently for the retractable bollards to be lowered. At 15.01 the blue Nissan Primastar van, with its distinctive logo and the yellow JCB mini-digger in tow drove off Horse Guards Parade and turned right, then right again, merging into the traffic on Trafalgar Square.

They were leaving behind something that had travelled more than twenty-two thousand kilometres across two oceans from the Pang Sang Un People's Defence Unit on the outskirts of Pyongyang to the heart of London. They were leaving behind Nelson García's gift to the people of Britain: his Palomita, his Little Dove. Ticking away unseen beneath the earth and gravel of Horse Guards Parade, a device was primed to send a cone-shaped plume of lethal radioactive debris high over Whitehall. The timing was important to all of them – to Ana María, to Suárez and, most of all, to García. He wanted this to be symbolic. He wanted what followed to be something that twisted the bayonet of pain in the conscience of a nation. You mess up my operations? You pay the price. That was his message to Britain.

The time of detonation had been chosen some weeks ago. It would take place the following Sunday, as the country was marking the most solemn moment in the national calendar. The moment when Big Ben would strike eleven times, and when broadcasters would remind Britons of a time long ago, in 1918, when 'at the eleventh hour, of the eleventh day, of the eleventh month . . . the guns fell silent.'

Chapter 95

DRIVING IN CONVOY down a rutted road, swerving at potholes and touching the brakes each time some nocturnal forest animal scuttled in front of them, the pair of GMC Suburbans moved north through the night. Nelson García was seated in the rear vehicle, cushioned by the suspension and his own considerable bulk. Uncomfortable as the journey was, he felt buoyed up and elated. Everything was coming together nicely. The London plan was about to go into operation, and when it did, they could search for him all they liked but he would be a hard man to find: Suárez had seen to that.

There had never been a Panama plan, of course – that had always been a decoy, a red herring, something to set the staff gossiping. They had a chuckle about that now, him and Suárez, as they made their escape through the darkened back roads of Antioquia province. If they had known that a heavily armed, highly trained and extremely frustrated US Special Ops team was squatting in a forest layby just a few kilometres to the south, well, García would have laughed even louder.

Ninety minutes out from the old planter's villa, the lead vehicle's headlights lit up a gap in the trees where the forest thinned out, and García's party swung off the road into a field. They had reached the airstrip. Beneath a canopy of camouflage netting, a Cessna 206 single-engine turboprop was being readied for departure, its three fat rubber tyres glistening with rainwater, reflecting the beams of the torches. Bags were rapidly stowed in the back of the plane while the flight plan was checked but never filed. Someone handed García a Thermos of iced lemon juice as Suárez stood, his hands on his hips, keeping an eagle eye on proceedings.

'Alfonso!' García called to him, and waved him over. El Pobrecito liked to get people to come to him. 'I know you think of everything,' he said, 'but indulge me, please. Reassure me one more time. *La Colección* is safe, is it not?'

Suárez tipped his head to one side and smiled, as if to say, Do you honestly think I'd let you down on something as important as that?

'The Collection is safe, Patrón. They will be arriving in San Salvador any minute now. All the arrangements have been made.'

García reached out an arm and hugged him. '*Buen trabajo*,' he told him. 'Great work. I knew I could count on you. Because, you know, if anything happened to—'

'Patrón!' Suárez cut him short. 'The Collection is all safe. Trust me on this.'

The Cessna 206, known sometimes as the Super Skywagon, has a cruising speed of just 280 kilometres per hour and only six seats, enough for the pilot to take García, Suárez, Vicente Morales and his favourite bodyguard, a bull-headed man known only as Animal. The last seat was piled with their effects, which included at least six hundred rounds of ammunition. The Cessna 206 was a small, discreet plane, especially when its fuselage and wings were painted a dull brown, as this one's were. A perfect aircraft, in fact, for flying very low across a darkened South America when you didn't want to be seen. Little wonder that the jungle valleys of Bolivia and of Peru's Apurímac region were littered with craft that hadn't made it.

After a lurching trundle across the field, the pilot made some final checks of his instruments, then opened the throttle and accelerated into the darkness. Squeezed behind him, García and Suárez locked hands as the Cessna became airborne, a silent gesture of self-congratulation amid the rasping roar of the Continental engine. It was 01.45.

Levelling out at low altitude, the Cessna headed almost due east. This, like the Panama rumour, was also a deception. Twenty minutes into the flight the pilot veered sharp right, taking them on a dog-leg flightpath south. Beneath massing thunderclouds they flew just below radar cover for another three hours straight, at times the plane almost kissing the treetops.

'La selva amazónica!' shouted the pilot above the engine noise, pointing down to the darkness below. He turned in his seat to see his passengers' reaction, but they were fast asleep. No one heard him announce that they had crossed into the vast region known as the Amazon Basin, where up to an hour's flying time can pass with no sign of human life. They were still in Colombian airspace but drawing close to the borders of three countries.

Preparations on the ground to receive García's flight had begun some months back. Once again, Suárez had sent people to see to that. Part of an old timber loggers' access road had been cut in a dead straight line through the jungle. The cartel had had it upgraded and resurfaced. At half a kilometre long before it turned a bend, it was more than adequate to accommodate the 430-metre landing distance needed for a Cessna 206.

And down on the banks of the Rio San Miguel, where the muddy river tributary twisted and coiled its way through the jungle, there was a large tin-roofed ranch that looked no different from a hundred others scattered across the area. Built high enough to escape the Amazon's rising floodwaters during the rainy season, it was comfortable but not luxurious. It was close to a national park, the Cuyabeno, so it was not unusual to see boats chugging up the river and dropping off visitors, mostly eco-tourists. It was true that the ranch had rather more communications equipment than was usual, but the large, rotating satellite dish and the plethora of aerials were artfully hidden at the back, out of sight of anyone coming up the river. It had one other key advantage. It was, in theory, beyond the reach of Colombia's powerful counter-narcotics police: the ranch, 'La Machana', was across the border in Ecuador.

Chapter 96

THE CONTRAST COULD not have been greater between the upbeat, ebullient mood of García's party as they soared off into the night in the Cessna and the despondency of Luke, Todd Miller and all the others in their team who were left behind. Their quarry had eluded them, their mission had failed, and Tradewind had dropped out of contact. All in all, reflected Luke, a truly crap day.

There was nothing for it but to return to the same Medellín airbase, Olaya Herrera, whence they had set out, and wait for further instructions from London, Tampa and Langley. The driver resumed his place while Luke and Todd Miller regarded each other in the dim green glow from the vehicle's dashboard, both thinking the same thing. We've just flown 2,200 kilometres across the entire span of the Caribbean, mounted a complex, well-planned operation, done everything by the book, and still we've failed.

For Luke, the prospect of returning empty-handed from South America for a second time in as many months was utterly galling. After what he had gone through at the Chop House in Buenaventura he had had serious misgivings about venturing back to Colombia and poking the hornets' nest that was

García's cartel. But he had put aside his own fears to get the job done and finish with El Pobrecito once and for all. That, plainly, hadn't happened.

When his encrypted phone vibrated in his pocket and he saw it was a call from VX, he was half expecting to get his marching orders. Perhaps Fate was telling him to listen to Elise and take the investment job after all. No. He wasn't ready for that.

He answered the call. There was a slight delay due to the encryption.

'Luke?' said a middle-aged voice, stern and authoritative.

He didn't recognize it. He angled his body away from the others and cupped his hand to the mouthpiece. 'Speaking. Who's this?'

'It's Carl Mayne, director of Ops. We haven't met – at least, not face to face.'

Here we go, thought Luke. Flight home, cattle class, and thanks for the work you've done but we won't be needing your services any more, Mr Carlton. 'He's gone,' said Luke abruptly. He might as well get it out there straight away. 'García's taken off. Possibly to Panama. We did everything—'

'I know,' interrupted Mayne. 'Langley already told us. Don't beat yourself up, it couldn't be helped. Listen, there's been a development. The mission's still on.'

'It is?'

Todd Miller was looking at him questioningly so Luke mouthed: 'SIS in London.' Miller nodded and went back to studying an illuminated, rolling map on his handset. It was now close to 0330 hours, and most of the other passengers in the minivan were asleep.

'Yes,' continued Mayne. 'You need to listen very carefully. NSA have been in contact and they've passed something to us through GCHQ. Seems they intercepted a call on a satphone a few hours ago.' Luke hunched forward, trying to shut out the noise of the journey so he could listen.

'NSA managed to geolocate it to an unregistered airstrip north of where you just were and voice-matched it to one of the known players. Alfonso Suárez. I believe he oversees all of García's security. Anyway, he made a second call mid-flight. They're still in the air now and we're tracking them.'

Luke felt like he'd been given a new lease of life. 'So they're heading north to Panama?' he asked. 'Can we intercept them?'

'Opposite direction. They're heading south, towards the tripartite border, the point where Colombia, Peru and Ecuador all meet. I've got it on the screen in front of me now. They're just about coming up to the equator as we speak.'

'Well, we're totally good to go here,' said Luke. 'What's the plan?'

At that moment there was a screech of tyres and Luke felt the seatbelt bite hard into his shoulder as the vehicle braked sharply and swerved to avoid a goat that had wandered onto the road. It stared dumbly back at them.

'Motherfocka!' shouted someone in the back. 'Next time run it over, why don't you?'

'Just the hazards of driving at night in this country,' said Luke, into his phone.

'Colourful language,' said Mayne. 'Now listen, we're still going for a takedown of García but we can't do it without the full cooperation of the Colombians.

We're setting up now for them to take you in to wherever García's plane puts down.'

'Even into Peru or Ecuador?' questioned Luke. 'You mean a cross-border op?'

'That would be deniable!' snapped Mayne, then added, in a more conciliatory tone, 'It's been done before, mind you. In 2008. The Colombians took out the FARC number two and seized a whole load of insurgent laptops. Some incriminating stuff on there and we helped them sort through it, so they owe us one. Hold on, someone's telling me something . . .'

Luke strained to catch what was being said in London as they passed through a town where salsa music was spilling out onto the street from an all-night bar. Other people, thought Luke. Normal people, just going about their daily lives. Then Mayne was back. It would be coming up to nine in the morning in London, he realized. No wonder the man sounded so fresh.

'So here's what's happening,' said Mayne. 'You should get back to the airbase at Medellín around first light.'

But Luke was distracted. Over in his seat Todd Miller was on the phone, clearly trying to get his attention. When Luke looked straight at him, Miller gave him an emphatic thumbs-up. So he was getting the good news at the same time.

'There'll be a plane waiting to take you and the team down to a place called Puerto Leguízamo,' continued Carl Mayne. 'It's a Colombian naval base on the river, slap bang on the equator. That's your launch point. We'll have more info for you when you get there. Miller's being told the same thing now. Stay in touch.' Mayne rang off.

Luke was running short on sleep and had had little chance to shake off his jetlag from London. But none of that seemed to matter now. They were back in the game. A tightly wound ball of tension inside him seemed to dissipate and for the first time since he'd left Florida his thoughts turned to Elise. It felt good to know that while he was hot on the trail of the bad guys in South America his girlfriend would be heading off to work about now. He imagined her in their Battersea flat, making the bed, checking herself in the mirror and heading out of the door. Perhaps she had slept in one of his T-shirts.

Chapter 97

ELISE MAYHEW WAS despondent. She was still wearing the clothes they had kidnapped her in, a navy-blue business skirt and sheer tights. She was dressed for her real life, working in a West End art gallery, valuing paintings, negotiating sales, putting together catalogues and exhibitions. Yet she was bound to a chair in a bare, windowless basement, begging to be taken to the lavatory next door, her every move observed by a woman with a violent, unpredictable temper.

Linda had provided her with precious little sustenance since her capture: a plastic bottle of tap water, a packet of savoury biscuits and a single apple. Whether this was designed to weaken her or whether it was just out of laziness, Elise wasn't sure. But she certainly wasn't going to repeat the mistake of asking again for something more substantial: last time, her guardian and tormentor had flown into a rage, leaving the room in a rush then returning with something in her hand. It had looked like a primitive mobile phone and, for a moment, Elise had thought she was going to be ordered to call someone. But the object had two metallic prongs. No sooner had Elise worked out what it was than Linda jabbed it into her thigh. There was a crackling sound and a searing red-hot jolt of pain tore through her as she jerked backwards in the chair, letting out a high-pitched scream as the electric charge pulsed through her body. Never had Elise experienced pain like it. And now the woman was holding the electric cattle prod in front of her face, waving it from side to side. 'You eat what I give to you,' she hissed. 'You don't ask.'

In the evening they arrived to move her again, Linda and two of the men who had snatched her in Battersea. She was making a careful note of their features now. One was a little overweight, with a florid, blotchy nose and receding hair. Every time she saw him he was wearing the same tan jacket with the grease stain and the tear in the sleeve. Maybe Ana María wasn't paying them very much. The other was short and wiry, but he had striking blue eyes, unusual for a Latino. His face had a bronzed glow, and in other circumstances she might almost have thought him good-looking. Elise guessed he had been on a late-autumn holiday or had recently arrived from South America. The men were careful not to address each other by name in front of her but she once overheard Linda call him León. She would remember that name.

It was her third journey as a captive and this time she sensed she was in a car, not a van. Wordlessly, they had thrown a blanket over her head, then forced her down into the back of the vehicle behind the front seats. Linda had sat practically on top of her and, just to make a point, she had briefly switched on the electric prod so Elise could hear the terrible static crackle, just in case she had any ideas of trying to make a run for it.

When they stopped, some forty-five minutes later,

and brought her out of the vehicle, her head still covered, she knew they had left the city behind. The air was cooler, fresher, and she could hear the distant rush of traffic from somewhere over the horizon. They guided her down a flight of wooden steps into a cellar, sat her on a wooden crate, removed the cover from her head and left her alone with the door locked. Her arms remained bound behind her back.

Elise fought rising despair. What was it that her *sensei*, her karate instructor, used to tell her? 'The greater the wind, the stronger the tree'; 'Engage your mind and body'; 'Focus on mastering your internal environment.' That had all sounded so eminently clever, so full of Eastern wisdom in the clean and ordered confines of the *dojo*. But somehow she couldn't bring herself to apply it to her present situation. What would Luke do? Did he know of her predicament? The worst of it was, she had no idea if the police were even aware that she was missing.

Chapter 98

THERE WAS SOMETHING not right, Luke reckoned, about a place that called itself a port when it was at least five hundred kilometres from the nearest ocean. Puerto Leguízamo was a riverside port on the Rio Putumayo, right on the border with Peru. He had looked it up on Google Maps on his phone, waiting, with the rest of the Special Ops team, at the Medellín airbase for their Colombian Airforce flight south. Switching his phone to Google Earth, he stared down at a sea of green: the Amazon rainforest. A mud-brown river coiled across the page and an interactive hyperlink indicated their destination, the Base Naval, the Colombian military's remote outpost just two hundred metres from the Peruvian border. He scrolled westwards and there, barely fifty kilometres distant, was Ecuador and the tripartite junction of the three countries. From the short time he had spent at Vauxhall Cross, Luke knew this was serious bandit country, a place where weapons, drugs, money and people criss-crossed borders illegally, blending into the jungle or hiding themselves among the impoverished communities that eked out a living on the banks of the rivers. He scrolled eastwards, following the course of the Rio Putumayo deep into Brazil, until it joined forces with the mighty Rio Amazonas at Manaus, over sixteen hundred kilometres away. It made him realize just how vast this jungle was, and how it dwarfed the tiny base they were heading to.

As they filed onto the C130 transport plane, Luke reached into his breast pocket and took out a pair of yellow foam earplugs for the night flight. He never went on operations without them. Strapped into his seat, he and most of the rest of the team were asleep even before the four-engined transport plane soared into the night sky above the twinkling lights of Medellín.

The Colombian Navy's base at Puerto Leguízamo felt curiously like home to Luke. Not proper home, of course; not like his and Elise's flat in Battersea, or the bleak Northumberland farm where he had passed his teens. No, more like what he remembered from his Colombian childhood: the heat, the humidity, the smell of lush vegetation, fresh with rainwater, and flies turning lazy circles about his head. It also reminded him of the SBS base back at Poole. There was the main camp, with the accommodation blocks, the parade ground, helipad, armoury and offices, the equivalent of North Camp on the Dorset coast. Then there was the boatyard, not quite the well-oiled ship-shape operation they ran down at Poole, known as the Hard, with all the immaculately maintained RIBs and other assorted assault craft, but a boatyard all the same. The difference was that here in Colombia, the mission was operational 24/7. The bad guys were out there in that jungle and swamp, just across the river, day in, day out. And he knew this because Carl Mayne had told him so. García and his senior lieutenants had landed just a couple of hours ahead of them. The net was closing.

Two hours after dawn broke Luke stood with the rest of the team on the quayside of the naval-base boatyard, trying to hear what was being said over the deafening screech of parrots in the trees above them. He stood with his legs braced slightly apart and his sleeves rolled up, watching. The Colombian Marines had a new weapon in their armoury and their commanding officer was extolling its virtues. '*Este aparato es innovador!*' he announced proudly, pausing for the interpreter to translate. 'He says, "This equipment is a game-changer." '

Luke and the Americans looked from the officer to the machines behind him, parked up on the sloping mud of the jetty, ready to be deployed.

'The Griffon 2000 assault hovercraft has changed the nature of our operations,' continued the Colombian colonel. 'In the dry season, which we're coming into, it allows us to pursue our enemies across the mudbanks and reach places we could not reach before. There is no hiding place now for the *narcoterroristas*. Gentlemen, we are pleased to offer you our help.'

Luke was back in his element: an ex-commando dropped into a jungle naval base, looking down at these giant beasts of the river. The assault hovercraft were just over eleven metres long with a single massive turbofan at the back. Painted a dark grey-green, they each had a powerful .50-calibre machine-gun mounted on top, while their rear canopies bristled with antennae.

'It has a top speed of thirty-five knots,' added the Colombian officer, 'and it can carry fourteen fully equipped Marines. These craft just arrived here from Britain!'

The hovercraft, Luke knew, were just one element of a complex plan they would need to put together to close in on García and finish him. They would require input from the NSA to fix his exact location, then maps had to be drawn up, insertion routes chosen, forming-up points, radio frequencies, a medevac plan. They were walking into the briefing hut when Luke's mobile vibrated again in his pocket. He thought about ignoring it but saw it was from Angela, in Vauxhall Cross.

'Give me two minutes and I'll catch you up,' he called out to Todd Miller.

'You got it.' The American's giant frame towered over the Colombian officers beside him.

Luke stopped beneath the spreading branches of some tropical flowering fruit tree. The parrots had dispersed and he had no difficulty in hearing Angela's voice cutting crisply across the eight thousand kilometres that separated them. 'I hesitate to ring you at this time,' she said. 'I know you're right in the middle of things.'

Oh, God, don't tell me they're calling it off.

'But there's something you need to know.' Her voice sounded unusually strained.

'Go on,' he said.

'It's Elise. 'She . . . she's been kidnapped . . . by García's people. I'm not supposed to tell you but I believe you have a right to know.'

For several seconds he didn't say a word.

'Luke? Are you still there?'

He was silent at first, but the questions were crowding in thick and fast. 'I'm still here,' he said eventually.

'When did this happen? And where? Have they said what they want?'

'It was two days ago, in Battersea, near your flat,' said Angela. 'The Met are handling it.'

'What the hell does that mean?'

'It means they're working as fast as they can to get her back. Look . . . the people who've got her, they want to trade. You for her.' She let that sink in, then added, 'Obviously it's out of the question.'

A figure appeared in the doorway. It was Todd Miller, and he was growing impatient. 'Hey, Carlton. Time to wrap up the romantic phone call. I need you fully focussed here.'

Chapter 99

IN A SPARSE basement room beneath an ordinary house, in a quiet residential cul-de-sac near the junction of the M3 and M25, Elise Mayhew was undergoing a metamorphosis. Suddenly, inexplicably, she no longer felt afraid – not of Linda or of the South Americans who kept bundling her in and out of the backs of vehicles to move her from one hiding place to the next. She was still alive, still largely unharmed, and she had reached a conclusion: she was going to get through this in one piece. In fact, she was going to do more than that. She was going to escape.

Ana María might be an accomplished poker player but she wasn't the only one who could put on an act. Each time Linda had come into the room to check on her or escort her to the bathroom, Elise had taken care to cultivate an air of weakness, helplessness and despair. With bogus tears welling in her eyes, she had pleaded with Linda to untie her bonds. 'I'm not going anywhere,' she gasped, pointing to the locked door, 'and you still have the key.' Eventually Linda had agreed. 'Give me your shoes,' she had ordered, almost as an afterthought.

Alone in the basement, once Linda had left, Elise resolved to wake up her aching limbs. With no one around to watch her, she began some basic stretching exercises. At first it was a tremendous effort – the last two days had taken a lot out of her – but she persevered. Twice, she went to the door to listen in case anyone was coming. Silence. She moved back into the centre of the room, savouring the simple pleasure of walking after all the hours she had spent tied to a chair. She seemed to have been abandoned, which was infinitely preferable, she reflected, to having to cope with Linda and her electric cattle prod. Now she felt light on her feet, alert and alive. And then she heard the key turn in the door.

After that things could have gone either way. Elise could have sat down on the crate in the middle of the room, apparently weak and despondent, cowed into submission by the bleakness of her situation. But when the door opened and Linda walked in, unaccompanied, something clicked in her head. It was as if a voice were saying to her, You're only going to get one chance, and this is it. Take it.

And it was true: Linda had clearly changed her mind about untying her prisoner because she was holding the electric prod in one hand and a length of cord in the other. 'Sit down,' she snarled.

Elise moved towards the crate, judging the distance between herself and the other woman. Three metres, two metres, one metre . . . When Linda was within range Elise erupted into an explosive *mae geri jodan*, a devastating karate front kick that caught the Colombian woman completely off-guard. It was as if all the pent-up terror Elise had experienced since the moment they had snatched her was concentrated in that single controlled kick. Back in the training *dojo,* Elise was capable of landing a kick to the head of a man as tall as her, if not taller, but Linda was a good fifteen centimetres shorter and her head made an easy target. The hard heel of her right foot caught Linda right beneath the chin, knocking it upwards and snapping it backwards with a sickening crunch that shocked even Elise. The Colombian collapsed onto the floor, motionless. She was out cold. Elise braced herself for the next person to come through the door, but no one followed. It seemed they were alone in the house.

So, what now? Elise stood there, balanced on the balls of her feet, breathing heavily, heart racing. Her instinct was to run outside and wave down the first car she encountered. But what about Linda? These people already knew where she and Luke lived, and where she worked. They were bound to be back.

Elise stood over the Colombian, legs poised, fists clenched, ready to put her back on the floor if she made a move. Linda's eyes opened but she wasn't moving. At all.

'No puedo moverme,' she murmured, a note of rising panic in her voice. 'I can't move.'

A trick? Elise kicked the woman's leg, not hard but enough to hurt, testing her reaction. It was unresponsive. Elise reached down and shook her arm, expecting that at any moment Linda would grab her. But she didn't. She lay there, slack and listless, repeating over and over that she couldn't move.

It took several seconds for the enormity of what had happened to register with Elise. Had her kick knocked the woman's head back with such force it had ruptured her spinal column? If her nervous system was now disconnected from the neck down, then that meant that Linda must have lost control of nearly all her body.

Elise was in turmoil. In all her years of practising *Shotokan* karate she had never hurt anyone like this. It was one thing to knock the woman down so she could escape, quite another to condemn a fellow human being to a largely lifeless body. Despite everything that Linda had done to her, Elise felt a surge of guilt, remorse and even pity. She bent down so her face was close to the stricken Colombian's and patted her shoulder gently. 'Someone,' she told her, 'will be back to help you.'

And now she needed to get away from this place before anyone returned. If the narcos came through the door and found this scene she dreaded to think what they would do to her. Elise moved quickly, out through the door of the basement, quietly up the steps, pushed open another door and felt cool November air. It was getting dark – or was it getting light? She couldn't tell. It seemed to be between day and night. There was a short stretch of open ground between her and the cover offered by the nearest hedge. She looked around, saw no one and sprinted to it, barefoot. She crouched, her body hard up against waxy laurel leaves, her breath coming in short gasps. She waited to see if anyone was in pursuit. No. She was free.

Chapter 100

'I MUST APOLOGIZE,' said the Colombian Special Forces colonel. He spoke in a strong American accent. 'These pictures are not so clear.' They were sitting round a briefing table in the shed, the corrugated-iron-roofed shack on the sprawling Amazon naval base at Puerto Leguizamo where his unit planned their offensive operations against criminal traffickers running guns, drugs, people and money on this tense stretch of Colombia's southern border.

'These were taken at oh six hundred this morning. On an overflight by one of our surveillance planes.' He was handing round a sheaf of freshly laminated A4-sized photographs to the US team from MacDill and to a number of his own subordinates. Luke was doing his best to focus. This was important. No, it was more than that: it was crucial. This should be the op that finished García once and for all. Yet inside he was seething. And desperately worried about Elise. In the short time between ending his phone call with Angela and walking into the briefing shed he had abandoned the idea of flying home to search for her. He could do nothing in London that the police weren't already doing. In any case, his mission was here and he needed to see it through.

He held the aerial surveillance photograph in his hand. As far as he could see, it showed little more than cloud and jungle canopy, a blur of greens and greys that made him think of something a struggling French impressionist might have knocked out on a bad day.

'If you look carefully, gentlemen,' continued the Colombian officer, 'you will see the objective on the left at the bottom of the frame, right on the riverbank, past the ox-bow bend. Thanks to our friends at Langley . . .' he paused to smile at the two CIA men in their beige fishing jackets and expensive designer spectacles '. . . we have the exact coordinates from the SIGINT intercepts. So, that is the ranch. That is our objective.'

Luke stared at the photograph. In Special Forces he had spent a fair bit of time on satellite and image interpretation. IMINT, they called it. He had even done a course on it at the Defence Intelligence and Security Centre at Chicksands in Bedfordshire. But he was damned if he could make out any useful detail. 'Any video?' he asked. 'Any moving pictures from ground level?'

'It's coming,' replied the colonel, looking around to see who had spoken. 'Matter of fact, it's being filmed right now. We got two local guys going past in a canoe. Fishermen. At least, that's what they look like. Don't worry, we'll get the video to your team ASAP.'

Todd Miller stood up and thanked the Colombian colonel, who stepped neatly aside to give him room.

'OK, gentlemen, time is pressing. The J2 intel is that García and his party touched down on the Ecuadorian side of the border at precisely . . .' He stopped to check his watch. 'Four hours ago.' He held up four fingers. 'The good news is that he thinks he's safe over there. So, the predictive intel assessment is that he's going to stay put. Which means we've got him cornered, like a rat in a box.'

Privately, Luke did not share his optimism. As the only person in the room to have come face to face with Nelson García – and live to tell – he thought it unwise to underestimate the man's ability to wriggle away and pop up somewhere else. García was a survivor, and finishing him off was like dealing with an ever-mutating virus.

'Let's move this on,' said Miller, in his Texan drawl. He walked over to the whiteboard, marked up with coloured arrows, circles and acronyms. He was about to say something important when he was interrupted by a cacophony from above. The parrots were back in their tree above the briefing shed, announcing their return with a cacophony of squawking and trilling. Miller simply raised his voice a notch until they calmed down. 'OK. What we're mounting tonight is a combined US–Colombian operation,' he shouted, above the birds. 'And, Colonel, we're truly grateful for your cooperation in this matter, especially given the sensitivity of crossing borders.'

'Don't mention it.' The Colombian grinned.

'This operation,' continued Miller, 'has been designated highly classified and has been given the codename Operación Anaconda.' He looked across at the Americans, sitting mostly on the left of the room. 'That's Op Anaconda for you folks from Stateside.' There were a few grunts of acknowledgement but people were dead tired: quite a few of the team from MacDill were rubbing their eyes and stifling yawns and Luke was doing the same. They had been travelling almost non-stop for twenty-four hours since leaving the base in Florida. In an ideal world, they would rest up, plan the op, carry out rehearsals and go in, firing on all cylinders, in a few days' time. But they didn't have that luxury. García had to be found, fixed and eliminated. Now. Washington and London were in total agreement there.

'We will deploy in three teams,' announced Miller, speaking in a normal voice now the parrots had settled down. 'First in will be the cut-off group, the screen. This will be inserted covertly, tonight, here . . .' He indicated a point marked on the whiteboard and everyone leaned forward to get a better view. 'They'll be dropped in two kilometres south of the objective, then proceed on foot to go firm at a point approximately three hundred metres from the ranch.'

The Texan gauged his audience's reaction, then continued.

'The second group, comprising the main force, will deploy along the River Putumayo, then up the San Miguel tributary into Ecuador.' Some vigorous gum-chewing was going on among the Special Ops guys as he said this. Yet their faces betrayed nothing. If anyone in that room was nervous, they were not showing it.

'The main force will be mounted in the Griffons, the assault hovercraft,' continued Miller. 'Their task will be to carry out a full-frontal assault on the ranch. We expect some pushback from the narcos, but not a lot. They don't have the firepower and they'll be hoping to get away. Which is where the cut-off group comes in.' He made a slicing motion with his hand towards one of his own team. 'Captain Dietermeyer? This will be your tasking.'

'Boss.'

'Your mission is to capture Nelson García alive and let Luke Carlton here interrogate him. The Brits have a lot at stake in this. He is not – I repeat – he is not to be allowed to get away. Questions?'

'Reserve force?' asked someone at the front, an operator with a broad, flat face framed by a ginger beard. For a second, he reminded Luke of Henry VIII.

'I was just coming to that,' replied Miller. 'The third group is our reserve force, positioned just here.' Again he pointed to the sketch map on the whiteboard. 'Our Colombian partners have a helicopter landing site on their side of the border. Medevac will be based there, in case we run into problems.'

Problems. Luke recognized that word as a euphemism for a whole world of pain, like getting ambushed almost before the op had started, or finding that the people you're after have twice the firepower you expected. Deep in thought, he chewed the inside of his cheek and watched Todd Miller take a swig from a canteen on the table then swat away a fly.

'OK,' Miller went on. 'Aviation. As from midnight tonight we'll have one of the new AC130J Ghostriders flying in close air support out of Tres Esquinas airbase north-west of here. Think airborne artillery, folks. Those things carry a 105mm cannon. That's enough to ruin the narcos' entire day.'

Miller stopped talking and suddenly punched his arm through the air. He looked as if he was taking a swing at an invisible opponent. In fact, he was checking his watch. 'Local time now is ten fifteen hours. Next briefing will be back here at sixteen hundred hours. Before then I suggest you get your heads down. And remember,' he faced the Americans, 'the only easy day was . . . ?'

'Yesterday!' they chorused, knocked fists and filed out into the suffocating heat of an Amazon morning.

Chapter 101

LESS THAN A hundred and fifty kilometres away upriver, Nelson García, billionaire, transcontinental cocaine trafficker, was not enjoying his new life across the border in Ecuador. For him, the euphoria of their night flight to safety out of Colombia had quickly worn off. Now everything about these temporary jungle quarters that Suárez had chosen for them was starting to annoy him. The third-rate food, the dank, close climate, the incessant mosquitoes. It was as if they were conspiring to spoil his mood. Already he missed the cool hills of the Colombian highlands, his horses and his women.

'*La Machana!*' He spat out the ranch's name with contempt as he and Suárez sat on the veranda above the riverbank, smoking. It was the afternoon after their arrival from Colombia and the big man was still complaining of a bruise on his thigh, sustained early that morning when the pilot had brought down the Cessna a little too steeply onto the log-cutters' road between the trees. Suárez had hit his head on the flimsy ceiling as they landed, but he chose to keep his complaints to himself.

The two men looked at the remains of their lunch, which lay beside them on a rattan table. The plates were already crawling with ants.

'What is she trying to do to me, this simpleton of a cook?' grumbled García. 'Cassava bread and yoghurt? Tell me, do I look like a vegetarian to you?'

They regarded the Rio San Miguel that flowed beneath them in silence, its dark, placid surface broken occasionally by a liquid splash as a fish leaped, then vanished.

'Pirañas,' remarked Suárez, examining the tip of his cigar. 'Now there's a fish that knows how to hunt. You know what they do, Patrón? When they find their prey in the water they swarm all over it and use their teeth, like this.' Suárez made a gnashing motion with his jaws. 'They don't eat straight away. They just chew bits off their victim and let them fall to the bottom, then go back and eat them when it's stripped bare.'

'Yes, I've heard that story,' answered García, turning to look at his closest and most trusted confidant.

Suárez laughed. 'How do I know?' he continued. 'I saw it on a nature programme once. Perhaps that's what we should have done with that *bastardo* Englishman, Carlton. Let's just hope he gets contaminated with the rest of them.'

'Ah, yes. *La contaminación.*' Colombia's fugitive drug lord cheered up considerably at the thought of it. 'How much longer now?' he asked. 'I can never understand these time-zone differences.'

Suárez went to his phone and checked the countdown function. 'Less than twenty-four hours, Patrón. That *española,* the Spanish woman, Ana María, will send us the signal when it's done. She has already proved herself. She is reliable.'

'Don't patronize me, Alfonso!' snapped his boss. 'Tell me exactly how long to go?'

'Just under sixteen hours. And we are in a good place for when it happens.'

'And then how long?' persisted García. 'How much more time do we have to spend in this malarial shit-hole? Hmm? You know what I saw this morning in my *baño*? A tarantula! Just sitting there all black and hairy. He was as ugly as you. *Madre de Dios* . . . I have to leave this place soon.'

'Be patient, Patrón. It won't be for long.'

'And what's wrong with the communications here, hmm? I want news of La Colección. Have they landed safely? I want to speak to them tonight. Please arrange it.'

'Sí, Patrón.'

Their conversation tailed off and Suárez went off to check the guard detail he had organized. García, weary and irritable, slouched indoors for a siesta. The air-conditioning units on the wall rattled and wheezed. In his room, his temporary quarters in this godforsaken swamp, he lay back on his bed, which sagged in the middle. Yet another annoyance. He folded his arms behind his head on the pillow. As the air-con did its job and cooled him, the sweat from the humid afternoon evaporating off his forehead, he felt a familiar longing. He needed something to distract him. He needed the company of a woman, despite the problems he had been experiencing in that department. Again and again, his thoughts kept returning to that acupuncture girl, Valentina. Yes, it had probably been a mistake to leave her behind. He wanted her now. His mind was made up. In the morning he would send for her. And with that reassuring thought, El Pobrecito drifted off to sleep. He was out of Colombia, he was beyond the reach of the DIRAN *anti-narcóticos,* he was secure.

Chapter 102

IF NELSON GARCÍA could have seen what was being prepared for him downriver at the naval base, he might have thought twice about taking that siesta.

The roar was like nothing Luke had ever heard. It filled his ears and shook the damp, marshy ground on the banks of the Rio Putumayo where he stood, watching in awe. It was late afternoon at the equatorial base on the edge of the Amazon jungle, and the Griffon 2000 assault hovercraft were being taken out for a rehearsal and weapons check. The noise from the Deutz 350hp engine and the three-bladed propeller was so loud that most of the Americans were clamping their hands over their ears. In a riverine landscape more used to dugout canoes, with tiny hand-held outboards, this was the Amazon version of a shock-and-awe weapon.

'I want these things to put the fear of God into García and his narcos,' Miller had said in the briefing shed. 'They think they're safe across the border in Ecuador? Wrong. We're comin' for them.'

The noise of the hovercraft did not seem to bother the Colombian Marines, who were used to them by now. As the giant green turbofans reached full pitch the men clambered over the inflated black rubber skirts of the hovercraft and hauled themselves aboard. Up on the roof the gunner loaded a gleaming belt of ammunition into the .50-calibre Browning heavy machine-gun, a Second World War vintage weapon that could still lay down a devastating rain of fire on any battlefield. With bullets the size of a man's thumb, it was said that one of them had only to pass within a few millimetres of you for the shockwave alone to smash your arm or take it off altogether.

Luke felt a twinge of regret that he would not be going into action on one of these river beasts. But as MI6's man on the operation, his was a subtle and far more important role. The Griffon 2000s would be the hammer. He would be right in the centre of the anvil. By agreement with Miller, Luke would join the screen force, inserted after dark by stealth helicopters, dropped into position behind the objective, ready to kill or capture García and his command team.

When the hovercraft moved off downriver towards the Brazilian frontier, throttles opening in a fountain of spray, they left behind a sudden stillness on the riverbank. Luke was aware that something was biting the underside of his arms. Sandflies. They were swarming up into the air from the mudbank and attacking any exposed flesh they could find. He rolled down his sleeves and tried not to think of visceral leishmaniasis, the debilitating tropical disease transmitted to humans by dogs via sandflies.

But biting insects were the least of his worries. While others had slept ahead of tonight's mission, Luke had worried about Elise. If this was García's attempt to unsettle him, it was working. He had called Sid Khan, he had called Angela, and had even called a mate in the police, in the vain hope that someone, anyone, might have some leads. And then, as he was leaving the riverbank to sort out his weapons, his phone buzzed once more.

'Luke? It's Angela. Good news. She's been found.'

'Is she OK? Can I speak to her? Where is she?' Relief was flooding over him like a wave but he still had so many questions.

'She's being debriefed down at Wilton Park,' replied Angela. 'She's shaken, but physically she's OK. She's a brave girl, Luke. I'm going to insist you take some serious time off together when this is over.'

'Thanks. Jesus, what a relief.'

'I'm sure,' said Angela. 'But things are getting very tense here. There's been talk of cancelling the Remembrance Sunday service at the Cenotaph. It's going ahead, for the moment . . . Look, d'you have everything you need out there?'

'Pretty much,' replied Luke. 'The Americans seem to have all the right kit. As ever.'

'Good. So go in there and close down García's operation once and for all and stop this nightmare for all of us. It has to end.'

Chapter 103

THE REHEARSALS WITH the Griffons on the Rio Putumayo were not the only ones under way that Saturday. Eight thousand kilometres away, on a parade square next to St James's Park in London, the band of the Grenadier Guards had been putting in their final practice for Remembrance Sunday the next morning. The drum major had shouted himself hoarse as he made them go over the anthems time and again until he was satisfied. Anyone on Birdcage Walk, the road running from Buckingham Palace to Parliament Square, would have been treated to the stirring strains of 'Heart of Oak', 'The Skye Boat Song' and 'Nimrod' from Elgar's Enigma Variations. The parade square at Wellington Barracks was a swirl of marching grey greatcoats and black bearskins.

Major General Rupert Milton (retired) was not in the habit of going into town on a Saturday. It was a day more usually reserved for shopping with Mrs Milton in the farmers' market where they lived in Gloucestershire. But he took his duties exceptionally seriously, sometimes rather too seriously, according to her. And when it came to tomorrow's parade he wanted nothing left to chance. He would stay up in town until it was over, he decided. In fact, he had booked himself a room at his club, the Cavalry and Guards on Piccadilly. Since early that morning he had been in his office at Horse Guards, going over the final details, running his finger down the list of VIPs who would be laying wreaths the next day. The Duke of Kent . . . The Earl of Wessex . . . Prince Harry . . . then the politicians, PMs past and present. Blair, Brown, Major. Good, they'd all be there.

By early afternoon he could stand it no longer. The sound of the band rehearsing less than a kilometre away was drawing him in, like a moth to the flame. They were playing 'Men of Harlech'. As a former Grenadier he was particularly proud that they would be performing this year. The band of the Grenadier Guards was the oldest in the British Army, dating back more than three hundred and fifty years, and he was damned well going to let everyone know it. It was time for an impromptu inspection, he decided. He would go and see how they were getting on right this minute. He put away his notes, locked them in a drawer, took his coat off the hook on the back of the door, the beige one with the velvet collar and the tiny hole in the breast where his clasp of medals was pinned, when, and only when, occasion demanded. His bowler hat was there too, but he would leave that for tomorrow's parade.

Milton marched briskly down Birdcage Walk and presented himself at the gate with his pass. The young Guardsman on duty, stiffening to attention, was probably no more than a third of his age. And had probably already seen an operational tour in Afghanistan. Good man, he mused, good man.

Milton's timing was perfect. He arrived on the parade square just as the band was taking a breather.

'Drum Major! Glad I caught you,' he barked, the red blood corpuscles in his cheeks standing out on this fine autumn afternoon.

'Sir!' replied the drum major.

'All going well? Any problems? Got everything you need?'

'All good, thank you, sir.'

'I don't suppose you've noticed that bit of building work on Horse Guards Parade, have you?'

'Can't say I have, General. Why?'

'Well, it's damned unsightly, all that disturbed earth and a row of orange cones. Not what we want to see on Remembrance Sunday.'

'No, sir.'

'Still,' said Milton, 'you won't have any problems marching round it, will you?'

The drum major looked surprised. 'If it's on Horse Guards, that's where we'll end up once we've marched down Whitehall. I'm sure we'll manage. Now, if you'll excuse me, sir, we need to crack on one more time with "Rule Britannia".'

Chapter 104

IT WAS THE waiting that always killed him. You train hard, thought Luke, you push yourself to the limit, you draw up your plan, you rehearse it, and then you sit around and wait. In this case, for darkness.

At 1745 hours, Luke's phone rang, just as the tropical dusk was closing in around the naval base and the worst of the heat was draining from the day. It was Carl Mayne, at Vauxhall Cross – Luke seemed to be hearing more and more from him, these days. Had he replaced Sid Khan in the pecking order? He put that thought out of his mind. Right now, office politics were the last thing he needed to be thinking about.

'Carlton? It's Carl Mayne here at VX. Glad to hear your other half made it.'

Luke was pretty certain that wasn't what the man had called him to talk about so he waited for him to go on.

'Listen, there's been a development. Rather a good one, as it turns out. Wait – what's all that squawking?'

'Oh, that? That's the local birdlife. It's the parrots coming home to roost. It's nearly dark here on the equator.'

'Right. As I was saying, we've got some traction on

the García front. You may not need to go for a termination after all.'

'I won't?' *So why am I here?*

'Not if you can get him in front of you. We've got some information we'd like you to use.'

'OK . . .'

'It's his extended family. He calls them his *Colección*.' Luke hadn't given a thought to García's family – he'd been so busy going after the man himself. But yes, of course, El Pobrecito was bound to have cousins, siblings, other relatives. Maybe none were connected to his business, or maybe they all were, but he would certainly care what happened to them. Family was strong in Colombia.

'Go on,' said Luke.

'We've got them. All of them,' said Mayne, somewhat triumphantly.

'Sorry, I'm not following you. You grabbed them in Colombia?'

'No, in El Salvador. They landed this morning by executive jet at a place called El Papalon. It's in the south-east. Tegucigalpa station picked up word they were coming in so we got the Salvadoreans to lift them when they landed. They're being held now at the Intelligence Directorate in San Salvador.'

'Does García know this?' Luke was already thinking ahead as to how he could use this information. No doubt Mayne was going to lay it out for him anyway.

'Not yet,' replied Mayne. 'But NSA have picked up several attempts by him to call them. He's going to be worried about them, which is exactly where we want him. So you need to use this, Luke, but use it carefully. Remember what we're going for here. Stopping the bomb. Nothing else matters. Put whatever pressure you can on him.'

'Then I have a suggestion,' said Luke.

'I'm listening.'

Luke checked around him to see that he was alone, then began to speak. By the time he had finished, Mayne was almost lost for words. 'That's dark, Carlton. Oh, that is dark. I like it. Where the hell did you think that up from? OK, I don't want to know. Fine, well we've got the software for that, we'll make it happen at our end.'

Chapter 105

THERE WERE NO lights to illuminate the helipad, and there was no noise other than the low thrum of the muffled rotors as they waited for the off. In the darkness, the Sikorsky UH-60 Blackhawks looked exactly like any other Blackhawk helicopter in a dozen countries around the world. But these were stealth variants, their Special Forces pilots part of the Night Stalkers Unit out of Fort Campbell, Kentucky. Using advanced composite materials and unusual angles on the airframe, they were designed to be almost invisible to radar.

At one minute past midnight they lifted off in a pair, fully laden, carrying twenty-one troops, Colombian and American. And Luke. This was the advance screen, the cut-off group to be dropped into the jungle two kilometres behind García's ranch. They flew low, as Todd Miller had said they would, so low their fuselages were almost brushing the tops of the trees, but there was a good reason for this. The Ecuadorean Airforce had an air-defence unit at Nueva Loja, less than a hundred kilometres away from García's place. They flew west, following the line of Colombia's jungle border with Peru, then south, heading deeper into the Amazon rainforest. At 0020 hours they crossed the border into Ecuador, entering Colombia's neighbour without permission, and flew on over the mostly uninhabited Cuyabeno National Park.

They approached from the south, a few kilometres short of the Rio San Miguel and far enough away from García's ranch not to be heard. In the cockpits the US pilots had switched to infrared, using all their concentration as they held their craft at the hover just above the jungle canopy. One wrong move now and their rotors might collide with the foliage, bringing the whole craft crashing down in a fireball. There would probably be no survivors. At forty metres above the ground the two Blackhawks disgorged their passengers over the side. In quick succession they fast-roped down through the open hatches, dropping silently through gaps in the trees to land on the damp jungle floor with a soft thud. Adjusting their eyes and senses to the trees around them, the patrol regrouped. Captain Dietermeyer did a quick head count and they set off, heading due north for the river.

Even in the darkness Luke could feel they were making faster progress than expected. This was primary jungle, pristine in some ways, because where they now walked the towering hardwoods had never been cut down. In secondary jungle you had to contend with all the smaller plants, the shrubs and the twisting, tangled foliage that grew up and blocked your path. But here they were able to move swiftly between the soaring trees, their night-vision goggles locked into place beneath the rim of their helmets, their canvas-sided boots picking their way across the leaf litter, alert to the threat of tripwires and Claymore mines.

By 0145 hours they were in position, spaced out at

intervals in a wide arc, three hundred metres south of La Machana, García's refuge on the riverbank. Luke was right in the centre of the arc, within whispering distance of Captain Dietermeyer and his signals guy. They had a good clear signal back to Todd Miller on the base at Puerto Leguízamo but they were keeping comms to a minimum. Squatting close to the ground, Luke peered intently through his goggles, looking for movement ahead. Nothing. Here I am again, he thought, back in this sodding jungle, and for a moment his mind flashed back to that day in his childhood. A ten-year-old boy straying way out of his comfort zone, exploring a dark, dank and dripping world that held mysteries beyond his imagination. A day that had ended in tragedy. A day that, quite possibly, had shaped him into the person he was today. And there was another memory, equally unwelcome, of a Colombian patrol of police commandos, the elite Jungla, perched above García's lair in the hills. They were all gone now, those ten men, all murdered in cold blood that morning outside the farm, betrayed by the bent Tumaco police chief and his treacherous insiders. There were certainly scores to settle here.

0340 hours. Another twenty minutes to go before the Griffon assault hovercraft were due to go in. Luke massaged the space where his middle finger should have been. Sleep had been out of the question in the jungle. He felt wired, tuned to every croak of a tree frog, every rustle of the leaf litter as men adjusted their firing positions, watching and waiting. Then he heard it. A low, distant drone, just audible above the cacophony of natural sounds around him, along with the persistent whine of mosquitoes. But there it was, the Ghostrider, the 'Death Angel', as some people called it, the US Airforce's gunship flying top cover just across the border inside Colombia. Onboard, there was a massive 105mm howitzer and enough high-explosive shells to obliterate a small village. He just hoped they had been fed the right coordinates.

Luke and the others in the cut-off group were not the only ones to hear that sound. Standing in the shadows on a wooden jetty above the banks of the Rio San Miguel, three hundred metres away, a pair of García's bodyguards on night watch heard it too. They exchanged a few nervous words and strained their eyes in the darkness to try to spot the unseen aircraft. Few planes came straying over this empty part of the Amazon so anything that close had to be suspicious. Should they wake Suárez? Probably a good idea. The security chief would expect to be told, even if it turned out to be nothing. They might even get rewarded for their vigilance.

But now there was another sound, a deeper throbbing roar that seemed to be building. The two guards looked towards the east: it was definitely coming from downstream. Both men unshouldered their assault rifles. Nothing good could possibly be coming up the river at this time of night.

They had left it too late to alert Suárez. Because just then a burst of white light seemed to explode in their faces as a high-powered beam swept over the water and up onto the wooden jetty where they stood, frozen with indecision, their assault rifles dangling uselessly in their hands, their night vision temporarily blinded. The roar was deafening as two giant hovercraft came powering up the river. From behind the guards on the jetty, a door to the ranch flew open and Suárez appeared, a ghostly apparition caught in the searchlight in his white T-shirt and surf shorts, a gold crucifix round his neck glinting in the reflected light. '*Hijos de puta!*' he yelled at the guards. 'What's wrong with you two? Shoot the fucking lights out!' He ducked back inside to look for García and get him out. If this was an Ecuadorean police raid, then someone would be held accountable. Suárez had seen to it weeks ago that the right people had been paid off, and handsomely. García's cartel did not take kindly to being double-crossed. Later someone would lose their balls but right now he needed to get his boss to safety.

From where the cut-off group lay concealed, Luke was hearing all of this and feeling like a racehorse in a starting stall. The action was kicking off and he wanted a part of it, but his time was yet to come. Now another noise was erupting from down on the river. It was the .50-calibre machine-gun mounted on the hovercraft. Luke recognized its heavy, rhythmic thump from his time in Helmand and he could envisage the massive bullets tearing into the wooden jetty and splintering it like a balsawood toy. The gunners had orders to hit the riverbank, not the house, but Luke could hear long, uncontrolled bursts splitting the night air. This was getting out of hand.

In his bedroom Nelson García knew they had come for him. Was it the Ecuadorean police? The DEA? MI6? A rival cartel? It didn't matter. Someone had betrayed him and now his only thought was of self-preservation. His heart pounding, he rolled off the sagging mattress and slithered awkwardly under the bed. It sounded like World War Three had erupted outside.

'Suárez!' he called, as he groped around for a weapon to defend himself when they came through the door. 'Suárez!' he called again, louder this time, an unfamiliar tone creeping into his voice. The sound of fear. Had his loyal lieutenant abandoned him? García's scrabbling fingers closed around a familiar object. It was the metal grip of a MAC-10 machine pistol. And – thank you, God – there was a thirty-two-round magazine already inserted into it.

Nelson García rolled onto his side, brought the gun up into a firing position and cocked it. The safety was off. With the animal cunning that had propelled him to the top of his dangerous trade, he was working out his next move. He remembered that there was a door at the back of his room that opened onto a wooden staircase at the rear of the building. From there, it was only one floor down into the forest and they wouldn't look for him there. All he had to do was fire a holding burst when they came through the door, which should give him time to get away. Nelson, *amigo*, you've got through tighter jams than this.

When the bedroom door crashed open García was ready. From his floor-level firing position he squeezed off a long burst at the first man through, tightening his index finger on the trigger of the MAC-10 as it bucked in his hand, spewing out a stream of 9mm bullets at almost point-blank range. But only one man had come in: there was no one behind him. In the split second before the man fell, sent reeling backwards by the force of the bullets as they tore into his intestines, García caught the look of surprise on Alfonso Suárez's face. In his panic, El Pobrecito had just ended the life of his most trusted partner.

Chapter 106

REMEMBRANCE SUNDAY, AND Major General Rupert Milton (retired) was up early. He believed a chap needed no more than six hours' sleep at the most. When commanding his regiment on an emergency tour in Northern Ireland in the 1980s, he had frequently had to make do with a good deal less than half of that. It was a fact about which he frequently reminded his wife. 'I know, dear. So you've told me,' she had said, more times than she cared to remember. Now he was completing his rounds of what he liked to think of as his 'Whitehall Area of Responsibility', his final tour of inspection ahead of the VIP arrivals.

As the man in overall charge of today's solemn ceremonials, he expected everything to be in place. And it was. The serried ranks of Army, Navy, Air Force and Marines were already arrayed three deep, flanking the broad strip of tarmac that was Whitehall. The crowd barriers were up on either side of the Cenotaph, the white stone monolith to The Glorious Dead in the centre of Whitehall, midway between the black gates of Downing Street and the Department of Health across the road. The police cordons were in place, officers checking passes as the crowds of military families and well-wishers filtered in to take their places behind the barriers. The royal reviewing stand was there too, protected by an extra cordon of armed police this year. For the third time that morning, Milton looked at his watch. Not long now until the Queen and the royal party would appear, flanked by their protection officers, ready to lay their own wreaths at the foot of the Cenotaph, as they did every year. Milton glanced up into the skies above the capital, where a small black-and-yellow police helicopter hovered on station. It was, perhaps, one of the few indicators that Britain was still at threat level Critical, the highest on the national scale. Milton knew it to be a Eurocopter EC-145 from the Met's Air Support Unit. He knew this because the Home Secretary had told him so, part of his not-to-worry-it's-all-in-hand speech ahead of the ceremony. Apparently the Eurocopter possessed something called an electro-optical turret that could beam back images in real time to Gold Command on the ground at Lambeth police station. Well, it could play Beethoven's Fifth for all he cared, as long as it didn't interfere with his parade.

The weather was playing a blinder this morning – he certainly had no complaints there. The second Sunday in November had dawned bright and clear and looked like staying that way. It was as if London had been given a lick of fresh paint. As General Milton walked briskly past the mounted ceremonial guard and through the arched tunnel beneath Horse Guards he was pleased to note his breath frosting in the chill morning air. It reminded him of his first hunt with the Avon Vale Foxhounds and of damp morning manoeuvres on the North German Plain, digging trenches on Luneberg Heath against the great Warsaw Pact invasion that never came. That, reflected

Milton, was when we had a proper-sized army, not like today. He quite missed the Cold War.

Ah, that was more like it. He paused at the eastern entrance to Horse Guards Parade, surveying the myriad cap badges as veterans of several regiments, some long disbanded or merged, gathered under the banner of the Royal British Legion. There was the Suffolk Regiment. Ha! And there were the Royal Green Jackets, now part of the Rifles, the largest regiment in the British Army and fast marchers. Clever chaps those – the Black Mafia, they called them, with their black buttons and their uncanny ability to get their people into the top slots of the Army. But Rupert Milton was a Guardsman and he had never regretted for one minute being anything else.

There were thousands of veterans and reservists too, men in suits, berets and bowlers, women as well, he was pleased to note. General Milton liked to think of himself as something of a progressive: there was nothing wrong in his book with a few fillies showing up on the parade ground, if that was what it took to move with the times. But he could see now that so many reservists and veterans had volunteered to march down Whitehall this morning that their ranks were spreading right out to the limits of the parade ground, as far as the Gallipoli Memorial where all those unsightly orange cones were. He still hadn't had a satisfactory answer as to what that had been about. Nobody seemed to know who had authorized it. Still, he had more important things on his mind today.

General Milton's ruddy features creased into a smile as he watched the King's Troop, Royal Horse Artillery, arrive with their ceremonial field gun, all polished brass gleaming in the pale November sun. It would be their job, when the chimes of eleven o'clock struck, to fire the single cannon shot to announce the start of the two-minute silence. Royal Marines buglers would follow it up by sounding the Last Post. Everything was falling into place nicely, he concluded. They would remember this, he told himself, as the best organized Remembrance Parade for many years.

Chapter 107

NELSON GARCÍA WAS a proud man reduced to blind terror. There was no time to mourn the death of his closest confidant, Alfonso Suárez. Heavy, gut-shredding bullets were smashing into La Machana, the place that was supposed to have been his safe refuge while his petty act of revenge was meted out on a distant enemy. Thumb-sized projectiles were tearing into the flimsy woodwork above and beside him, showering him with vicious splinters. Designed to fire on targets up to two thousand metres distant, the Griffon hovercrafts' Browning .50-calibre heavy machine-guns were bringing a hail of devastation raining down on the building from less than a hundred metres away. And as the gunners on the roofs of the assault craft switched their ammunition to armour-piercing incendiary, small fires were igniting all around him. He had to get out.

Shuffling and squirming across the floor of what had been, only minutes earlier, his bedroom, García wriggled to the door at the back of the ranch. The cacophony of incoming fire was deafening. Any second now he expected to be cut down by the bullet that would end his life. But El Pobrecito was a survivor. He had always known that one day something like this would come, and despite the fear that filled him he was utterly focused on saving himself.

Half rising from the floor, he punched open the door and rolled onto the wooden landing at the back of the ranch. The bullets were still cutting through the night air all around him and there was no time now to take the steps. He launched himself over the side, falling the three metres through the air to land heavily on the grass. A sharp pain tore through his solar plexus. A broken rib? Probably. He didn't care. He was the hunted quarry and he had to get away from the pack. Ducking low, he ran at a crouch towards the cover of the trees. The firing had stopped abruptly and he could see helmeted figures silhouetted against the flickering flames at the back of the ranch. They were swarming up the steps like rats, those pieces of *mierda*, seeking him out.

By nature, El Pobrecito was a man of the city slums. He had never felt comfortable in the wild – he distrusted it – but now, in the darkest hour before dawn, the jungle would be the blanket that masked his escape. He trod carefully, moving with surprising lightness for a man of his size, putting as much distance as possible between himself and the blazing ranch. The fools who came for him, they wouldn't think to look behind them in the forest where he was, and when they did he would be long gone. Maybe he would go to ground in Ecuador for a few weeks. Let it all settle. Or maybe he would join his family – *La Colección* – in El Salvador. Spend a bit of time fishing on the Pacific, lie about in hammocks, eat some prawns, yes, that would be good.

García moved on, feeling his way through the

darkened forest, then stopped dead in his tracks. Something had appeared on his right thigh, wobbling and wavering. Now it was creeping up his body to settle on the centre of his chest.

It was the bright red dot of a laser.

Chapter 108

LUKE HAD BEEN observing his prey through his night-vision goggles for a full minute before he lit him up with the laser sight. He wanted Nelson García to come close enough to realize there could be no way out, no possible escape. His guards were all dead – they had had word on the radio from the team going through the ruins of the ranch. Apparently the body of Suárez, the cartel's head of security, had been found too. They said it was cut to ribbons.

As soon as Luke had got a visual on the man, watching him feel his way in the dark past the hanging vines and feathery ferns, he pulled out his encrypted phone and dialled Carl Mayne in London. Then he kept the line open, plugging an earpiece into his left ear and clipping a throat mike to his collar, leaving his hands free.

'We're all set at our end,' said Mayne. 'We're listening in. Just give us the word when you're ready and we'll patch you through to San Salvador.'

Nelson García was fewer than fifty metres away from Luke and Captain Dietermeyer's group when he spotted the red dot of the laser playing on his thigh. Silently, using well-practised hand signals, the US

Special Ops officer had sent three of his men to encircle García from behind. As the Colombian drug-lord stood motionless, considering his options, Dietermeyer clicked the pressel switch on his VHF radio, connecting to Todd Miller at the Puerto Leguízamo naval base. He kept his words to a minimum.

'Bravo One is under our control,' he told the mission commander. 'I say again, Bravo One is under control. We're extracting.' The American peeled back the green Velcro covering on his waterproof watch and checked the time: 0455 hours. Already a rising chorus of birdsong was building in the canopy above their heads. Dawn was coming and they were still in Ecuador. Illegally.

'Ten minutes, Carlton. That's all I can give you,' said Dietermeyer. 'Then we need to haul ass double-quick back across the border. Miller wants us out ASAP. If the Ecuadorean military catches on to us being here, we're in a whole world of pain. We'll be extracting by hovercraft and taking García with us.'

Ten minutes. That was all the time he had to carry out one of the hardest tasks of his career. Luke was acutely aware of the enormity of what now rested on his shoulders. Finding a way to get García to call off the bombing and reveal the whereabouts of the weapon would be a massive task at the best of times. Perhaps with their prisoner safely under lock and key on a military base in Colombia, his resistance eroded by lack of sleep and days spent contemplating the next forty years in a rat-infested jail, Luke could work a persuasive case on him. But they were ten kilometres inside a hostile country with no authorization, far from the nearest safe base and time was against them. Luke was looking at a ruthless, unpredictable psychopath, a man more likely to go to his grave with a smile on his face than offer his enemies the means to head off the planned explosion. But he had one card up his sleeve and he intended to use it.

He lifted himself from his crouch and nodded to Dietermeyer.

'Nine minutes fifty seconds,' the American reminded him. 'Then we're out of here.'

Luke was already gone, moving quickly, closing the remaining distance between himself and García in seconds, keeping his Diemaco assault rifle trained on the Colombian's chest as he strode through the trees.

When Luke got within spitting distance of him, he could see that Nelson García presented a pathetic sight. The now former drugs lord was on his knees on the jungle floor, both hands clasped behind his back while two US Special Ops men kept him covered with their weapons, one with the muzzle touching García's shoulder blade. Lit by the grey light of dawn, his thinning hair was plastered with sweat across his brow, his clothes were torn and dishevelled and his hairy belly was sagging over the waistband of his trousers. Yet pity was the last thing on Luke's mind. This was the man who had dispatched a dirty bomb to Britain, who had murdered ten police commandos in cold blood, who had sent Luke to the Chop House in Buenaventura to be slowly dismembered alive. It was time to go to work on him.

Luke squatted on his haunches and saw the spark of recognition in García's face. The man remembered him. And now El Pobrecito was smiling, his lips curling upwards in a fleshy-lipped sneer that Luke found both repulsive and surprising.

'So you lost, Carlton,' he said. 'Because my little Palomita is hidden in your city and your people can't find it!' He broke into a weak laugh, then clutched his side in pain from his broken rib.

Luke answered him calmly, despite the seconds ticking dangerously by.

'Did I? So where's your family today, Nelson? Where is *La Colección* now?' García looked up sharply, cold eyes squinting at Luke's face. The sneer had vanished. He seemed unused to anyone addressing him as Nelson.

'If you touch one hair of their heads!' he roared, flecks of his spittle landing on Luke's cheek.

'Oh, we're going to do a lot more than that,' replied Luke, without flinching. 'Do you remember what your people did to my foot with that electric drill back in Colombia?' He leaned forward as if about to share a great confidence with the man. 'Let me tell you a secret,' Luke whispered. 'That drill? It really, really hurts.'

He shifted back so he could look García in the face. 'But you know what? I'm going to let you choose which one gets the drill first. How about Luisa, your sister? Hmm? D'you think she could take it? Or maybe your two fat cousins, Alejandro and Jaime? We could do them together. Maybe if they're lucky they'll pass out with the pain.'

He was speaking with an almost unnatural calm but in his head Luke was all too aware he was running out of time. How much did he have left? Six minutes at the most. Six minutes before they had to pile onto the hovercraft and hand García over to the Colombian government. Then his chance would be lost.

'Hijo de puta!' García swore at him. 'I don't believe a word of this shit. You don't have my family. You don't have anything. You think I'm falling for your stupid games?'

Luke shrugged then spoke a single phrase into his mobile phone, loud enough for García to hear. 'Begin the treatment.' He passed the Colombian his phone.

The sound that followed nearly made García drop the phone. First came the high-pitched whine of a handheld drill. That noise alone, screeching from Luke's mobile, could be heard by almost everyone in the cut-off group as they packed up their kit and prepared to move down to the riverbank. But what followed was worse. It was a woman's scream of terror and García recognized the voice.

'Luisa!' he shouted, clamping the phone to his ear. The sound of the drill went on for a further ten seconds and left García trembling with a rage he could barely control. One of the US operators had to dig the muzzle of his weapon hard into the man's back to stop him launching himself at Luke.

'I'm going to count to five,' said Luke, very calmly. He reckoned he had about three minutes left. 'If you don't tell me exactly where the bomb is and when it's timed to go off, we'll move on to the rest of your family. One—'

'I don't know where it's hidden, I swear! It's in England, that's all I know!'

'Two—'

'OK, OK, it's in London. Near the palace,' he hissed.

'What palace?'

'The Queen's palace.'

'Not good enough,' replied Luke. 'Three—'

'*Chocha!* I don't know the name of the place. White Hill or something. Suárez chose it.'

'When? When's it timed to go off?' Luke was unable to keep the urgency out of his voice. Because that one frantic conversation, down there in the mulch of the Amazon jungle at dawn, was the culmination of everything he had been working on for weeks. 'Nelson!' he yelled, shaking him by the shoulders. 'When's it going off?'

But García was spent. His shoulders slumped and he turned his head away to one side, refusing to cooperate any further.

'Four!' shouted Luke grimly. 'When I count five the drilling starts again. I'm not pissing about.'

Out of the corner of his eye, Luke could see Captain Dietermeyer trying to attract his attention. He was pointing frantically at his wrist and making a cutting motion with the flat of his palm. They were out of time.

'Eleven,' mumbled García. 'It's going off at eleven this morning in London. Now let my family go.'

'Oh, Christ,' said Luke. He had just worked out the time difference. If it was 0508 hours now in Colombia, it must be 1008 hours in London. That left fifty-two minutes. Fifty-two minutes to find the bomb and defuse it before a shower of radioactive debris erupted over the thousands of people packed into Whitehall. On Remembrance Sunday.

Chapter 109

IN PARLIAMENT SQUARE a light breeze swirled through the half-bare plane trees, then gusted along the wide boulevard leading to Trafalgar Square, the street known as Whitehall. Picking up strength, it ruffled the coats and hats of the families crowding behind the barriers and rippled through the ranks of servicemen and -women as they stood to attention, a crimson poppy pinned to every lapel or behind every cap badge. Guardsmen in their black bearskins and Athol grey greatcoats towered motionless over almost everyone else as the band of the Grenadier Guards played 'O Valiant Hearts', a hymn composed to commemorate the fallen of the First World War.

By 1008 hours Horse Guards Parade nearby had been packed solid with men and women in uniform. Exactly as the late Alfonso Suárez had known it would be. The reservists and former soldiers, sailors, airmen and Marines were all waiting their turn to march down Whitehall in formation, to salute the Cenotaph, paying homage to the fallen. Young men barely into their twenties, some bloodied by combat in Afghanistan, mingled with veterans from long-gone campaigns in Aden, Malaya and Borneo. A reviewing stand had been erected opposite the Guards Division Memorial, where Prince William, the Duke of Cambridge, would shortly take the salute.

Suárez had known the parade ground would be filled to capacity because the year before he had stood beside Ana María on the edge of St James's Park, observing it all from a discreet distance. Together they had noted where the CCTV cameras were positioned, where the blind spots were, where the troops would concentrate. Together they had selected the spot where the device would be buried, and together they had devised the cover story.

Exactly one thousand metres away, SIS's director of Operations looked as if he might be having a heart attack. Normally known for his crisp, military manner, his face had turned ashen and his forehead was covered with a light sheen of sweat. Those in the room with him that morning had noticed he was breathing in short, slightly laboured gasps. Carl Mayne was not having a heart attack, but what he had just heard over the phone from Ecuador had left him shaken. Fifty-two minutes. That was all the time they had to prevent Britain's first ever dirty-bomb attack, somewhere in the streets beyond Thames House. The investigations team were gathered around the Polycom SoundStation, listening on speakerphone to Luke's exchange with García as it had come in live from the Ecuadorean Amazon, with a two-second delay. They were in the operations room at Thames House, the central node of all the government's efforts to locate and disarm the device.

Damian Groves spoke first. Ecuador might have been an SIS operation but as the MI5 senior investigating officer on the case it was down to him to set the wheels in motion. And his reaction, in those first hollow seconds, was to say exactly what they were all thinking: 'Fuck.' Groves knew instinctively, the moment the phone call ended, that intelligence had run its course.

'Get Grimshaw on the line – NOW!' he shouted. 'He's got to get his EXPO teams out there this second!'

From Thames House the call went straight through to the Counter-terrorism pod inside the control room at Lambeth police headquarters, a vast warehouse-like room where the Gold and Silver commanders were already flat out running the policing for Remembrance Sunday. Andy Grimshaw, commander of the Met's SO15, the Counter-terrorism Unit, had just crammed a Rich Tea biscuit into his mouth while taking a slurp from a mug of lukewarm tea. Already that morning he had had to deal with two false alarms and one hoax bomb scare.

'Grimshaw,' he said tersely into the handset, sending a shower of biscuit crumbs over his workstation. He listened, tapping his fingers on the desk, for just thirty seconds. 'OK. We're on it,' he said, and slammed down the phone.

At 1013 hours, from the forecourt of Curtis Green, on the site of the old Whitehall police station, a pair of dark blue Range Rovers drove out onto Victoria Embankment, past the tourists taking selfies by the Thames, and turned right towards Big Ben. If anyone had been watching them, on that bright and breezy November morning, they might have noticed how low their chassis were to the ground. Both vehicles were heavily armoured to withstand an explosive blast and both were driven by a class-one police driver, trained to swerve through built-up areas at high speed.

Beside and behind the drivers sat six explosives officers, the EXPOs, still known to many as the Bomb Squad, wearing full CBRNE protective gear: black Pro-Tec helmets, ballistic goggles, boots and black charcoal-impregnated suits designed to offer some protection against chemical, biological and radiological agents. As part of the public-safety plan for the day, they had already been forward deployed to central London from their base near Euston station. Close behind them came a lorry, a large box-like vehicle known as the Beast. It contained all their heavy equipment, including the caterpillar-tracked bomb-disposal robot dubbed Felix for its nine lives.

Kate Bladon rode in the front vehicle. Twenty-nine years old, a former British Army captain in Explosive Ordnance Disposal with several tours in Afghanistan under her belt, she was now a police inspector with SO15. She had made the 'lonely walk' to defuse a device many times. 'You can pull in all the hardware you like,' she would say to friends, 'all the electronic counter-measures, all the remotely controlled robots, but at the end of the day it takes an operator on two legs to go in there and make a device safe.' On the seat behind her lay a protective suit made up of more than fifty kilos of Kevlar body armour, plastic and foam, and a helmet with visor shield, her dubious defence for the task ahead. If and when they found the device, it would be Kate Bladon's job to defuse it.

'Pull over here!' she commanded. 'Beside the statue. Yes, right here.' They pulled up abruptly beside the imposing bronze sculpture of Sir Winston Churchill on Parliament Square. With the streets already sealed off by the police for the parade, there was no other traffic. She spoke quickly into her radio, briefing the team in the vehicle behind.

'Number two team – you deploy on foot from here with the dosimeters and start making a sweep to get a signal. Number one team will stay with me and head to Buckingham Palace. We'll proceed up the Mall from there and converge at the back entrance to Downing Street.'

'And the Beast, ma'am?' prompted an EXPO in the seat behind her.

'The Beast stays right here. Keep the engine running.'

From a hundred metres away on Whitehall came the sound of the band playing 'Flowers of the Forest'. The order to evacuate had not yet come through. It was 1018 hours.

Behind Kate and her team, a whirlwind of activity was spinning ever faster. In the Lambeth control room, Commander Andy Grimshaw had gone straight over to brief the Gold commander. His reaction was similar to Damian Groves's at MI5. 'Jesus bloody Christ!' he said. 'So we've got under fifty minutes to evacuate over five thousand people from Whitehall?'

He was already thinking it through as he spoke. As an experienced counter-terrorism detective, he had been involved in countless national security exercises, many involving Special Forces, rehearsing for countless imaginary scenarios. Wembley, Twickenham, Old Trafford, they had often planned for something big, with the shadow of the 7/7 and 21/7 bomb plots hanging over every exercise. But this, today, was of a whole different magnitude.

'OK.' He spoke to his Silver commander, the next level down from him. 'We need to move the royals and the VIPs out first or they'll be swamped in the stampede. Tell SO14 Royal Protection to get them out now. Same goes for SO1 Specialist Protection. The PM and the Cabinet need to be pulled out at the same time.' He looked at his watch. 'They've got seven minutes. Then we're alerting the public. We stop the band and make the announcement. We'll need to corral the public across Westminster and Lambeth Bridges. And we'll need holding pens. Get the emergency services primed, and SO15 will tell Aldermaston what's going on.'

The Atomic Weapons Establishment at Aldermaston in Berkshire, better known for its design and maintenance of Britain's Trident nuclear missile warheads, had been on high alert from the moment the COBRA committee concluded that a radiological device was heading for Britain. Its scientists, deeply immersed in the unpleasant effects of radioactive fallout, had been briefing government departments constantly. They now had people permanently embedded in Counter-terrorism Command at New Scotland Yard. As Inspector Bladon and her team raced down Birdcage Walk to begin the search from the Buckingham Palace end of St James's Park, she called them. 'Listen,' she said, 'I need you here now. We're just two streets away – or we're about to be. Grab your kit, get in a vehicle and get yourselves down to the big statue in front of Buckingham Palace and we'll meet you there . . . What? . . . No, I've no idea what it's called. It's painted gold, that's all. Just be there.'

At 1019 hours the band on Whitehall stopped playing. And from all around rose the sound of sirens.

Chapter 110

WHEN THE BAND of the Grenadier Guards stopped playing and put down their instruments halfway through Elgar's 'Nimrod', those standing closest to the royals had already noticed something was up. In the last few minutes they had seen the Queen, dressed entirely in black with a double row of pearls and a florette of poppies pinned with a brooch, hurried off the stand, escorted by worried-looking plainclothes police officers in dark suits. There was no time to bring up one of the fleet of claret-coloured Bentleys or Rolls-Royce Phantoms. Instead, a pair of Range Rovers had nudged their way through the crowd, their doors had been flung open and the entire royal party had been unceremoniously bundled inside, then driven off at high speed out of London towards Windsor Castle.

It took a little longer for SO1, the Met's Specialist Protection Group, to herd the Prime Minister and senior members of his Cabinet through the gates of Downing Street and down to the car park at the rear. From there they dispersed towards Chequers, the PM's country retreat at the foot of the Chiltern Hills, and to two other country-house addresses outside London, known only to a very few in government. A third group, the foreign dignitaries, was rounded up by SO16, the Diplomatic Protection Group, and taken to an underground room beneath the Cabinet Office. Several heads of state protested vigorously, believing it to be an exercise, but they got no explanations from the police, who were insistent that this was for their own safety.

Kate Bladon's number two team reached the junction of Great George Street and Horse Guards Road on foot, only a few metres west of Parliament Square, just as all hell broke loose behind them. Police vehicles, fire engines and ambulances were converging on both entrances to Whitehall from several directions. A chief superintendent was on the raised stand, addressing the crowd through a megaphone.

'This . . . is a civil emergency. Please move calmly towards the exits to Whitehall. Do not run. Police officers will guide you towards the exits.' He was doing his best to remain calm but everyone in the crowd could hear the tension in his voice.

'It's a bomb!' somebody screamed. 'There's a bomb!'

Like the spark that ignites a forest fire, the rumour spread. Somebody tripped and fell, then another, and suddenly the stampede began, as people clambered over discarded brass instruments, bearskins and drums. The troops that had stood in such perfect formation only minutes earlier joined the public in the blind rush to get off the packed street. Those at the northern end ran towards Trafalgar Square, those at the south towards Parliament Square and Westminster Abbey. Many of the carers who had patiently wheeled their ageing and infirm charges to the parade stayed with them, struggling to push them to safety as others poured past them. Several veterans were abandoned in their wheelchairs where they sat, utterly bewildered by what was going on around them. One man closed his eyes, pressed his mottled hands together and began to pray.

The Gold commander's ambition to herd everyone calmly over the bridges to the South Bank remained just that, an ambition. There simply wasn't time to set up barriers and cordons as hundreds poured past the police and ran blindly away from Whitehall. On Horse Guards Parade, word quickly reached the reservists and veterans waiting their turn to march. Those standing closest to the Guards Division Memorial had seen Prince William whisked away in a Range Rover without taking the salute, and now police were appearing with megaphones ordering everyone to clear the area. The beautifully polished field gun, brought in to fire the eleven o'clock salute, lay abandoned on its chassis as police hurried everyone off the square and out onto the Mall and Birdcage Walk.

At 1035 hours Kate Bladon and her team were still in their vehicle, driving slowly up the Mall from Buckingham Palace, checking their radiation dosimeters, followed by a pair from Aldermaston, when they saw a solid wall of people streaming towards them. Their faces told of fear and panic.

'Lock us in,' she commanded the driver, as men and women rushed past, some stopping to bang on the doors and wave frantically at them to turn back.

At 1037 hours Kate's radio buzzed. It was Sergeant Murray Bamford, from the second team of EXPOs, whom she had deployed on foot in Parliament Square.

'Ma'am, we're getting a reading,' he told her over

the radio. 'The dosimeters are registering.' As he spoke he was holding an FH40 digital gamma survey meter, a silver-and-black oblong box with an LED display window. The black numerals were blinking and rising as he walked.

'It's increasing the closer we get to Horse Guards Parade,' he told her.

'Right. Get there as fast as you can and meet me on the square,' she told him, and ordered the driver to step on the accelerator, scattering the crowds still streaming away from the parade ground. In the few seconds it took to cover the remaining four hundred metres and turn the corner into Horse Guards, Kate ordered the Beast to be brought up on station from Parliament Square.

At 1039 hours Kate Bladon and her team reached the north-west corner of Horse Guards Parade to find Sergeant Bamford and his team of four already there. They were spaced at intervals of a few metres, holding their radiation dosimeters out in front of them, like divining rods searching for underground water. As she leaped out of the armoured vehicle and joined them, she could see clearly where their sweep was leading them.

'Stop!' she shouted. 'Only one person goes forward from here and that's me.' She was facing the orange-and-white cones and the taped-off area of disturbed gravel next to the Gallipoli Memorial. The last few disabled ex-servicemen were being helped off the parade ground, hurried along by police. A helicopter was hovering directly overhead, beaming live pictures back to the Gold commander at Lambeth. The Beast was parked next to the abandoned ceremonial field gun.

At 1041 hours, Kate Bladon approached the suspect area of gravel, then stopped dead in her tracks. Her FH40 dosimeter was telling her all she needed to know. Whatever device was emitting the gamma rays was buried beneath her feet, below the surface of the parade ground. But now she faced a massive problem. If they couldn't see what they were dealing with, there was no point in deploying the caterpillar robot: it would have nothing to make contact with. Dig it up? She looked at her watch for the umpteenth time and bit her lip. With eighteen minutes before detonation she realized she needed to refer upwards and radioed the Bronze commander at Lambeth.

'We're out of options,' she told him bluntly. 'There's no time left to uncover the device, which could set it off if they've got it rigged. We have to go for attenuation. I need your OK on this one.'

'You want to contain it? You sure you can't make it safe? Because, strictly speaking, this has to go up to a COBRA.'

Kate Bladon respected authority and she was respected in turn by her subordinates. But at that moment, standing there in her black protective suit, metres away from a ticking dirty bomb, she lost it. *'Are you fucking kidding?'* she screamed into the radio. 'In seventeen minutes this thing is going to go off and contaminate half of central London. We need to go for mitigation – now! Do I have your permission?'

'Wait one,' he replied.

Kate squeezed her eyes shut in frustration and looked up to the sky as five seconds passed, then ten. Then a different voice came over the radio.

'Gold commander here. Do whatever you have to do to contain the blast.'

'Thank you, sir.'

Kate turned towards the Beast and gesticulated wildly for it to be brought over.

'Get the igloo out,' she ordered, as the lorry drew up, 'and place it on top of that disturbed earth over there.'

But the police driver leaned out of his window and shook his head. 'Sorry, ma'am. We haven't got it. It was sent up to Manchester, remember?'

'Oh, for fuck's sake!' Kate shouted. It was 1044 hours.

'Hang on, though,' yelled the driver, his face lighting up. 'We've still got the dome in the back.'

Oh, you beautiful man, thought Kate. 'Get it down here now!'

'It's bloody heavy.'

'Sergeant Bamford!' yelled Kate. 'Get everyone over here, put the dome in place, then move everyone back to behind the Guards Memorial over there.' She pointed to the nearest solid structure that could provide any cover at all.

The sirens were still wailing as the six EXPOs manhandled a large metal-and-plastic dome out of the back of the truck and staggered over to the cordoned-off area, knocking over orange cones as they went. On Kate's command, they lowered it to the surface of the gravel, looked at her for the nod and sprinted for the shelter of the memorial. At 1057 hours her team were crouched behind the stone pillar when one of the two scientists from Aldermaston spoke up.

'When this thing goes off,' she told them, 'we've got to move away fast. Even with the dome there could be seepage out of the sides. This area is going to take days to clean up, maybe weeks. You do realize,' she added grimly, 'we're all going to have to be checked for radiation after this?'

For Kate Bladon's team of EXPOs, crouched behind the Guards Division Memorial that day, those three minutes were perhaps the longest of their lives. They were the only people left on Horse Guards. Downing Street had been evacuated, Whitehall had been cleared – even the police helicopter had moved off. To all of them down there, squatting just ninety metres from a buried and primed dirty bomb, it seemed an incredibly lonely moment, as if they were the sole survivors left in London. At five seconds before the hour Kate looked down at her feet and said quietly: 'Stand by. Here we go.'

The detonation, when it came, would have been a gigantic disappointment to Nelson García. It was the very antithesis of the toxic fireball he imagined enveloping his enemy's capital. To the nine men and women close enough to hear it that morning it sounded like a muffled thud, almost a dud explosion, which, in a way, was what it was. Instead of jetting upwards in a vertical shower of radioactive isotopes, coating hundreds of buildings and streets all over Westminster, the blast reverberated ineffectively against the heavy composite underside of the Dome, almost completely containing and absorbing it.

Three seconds after the explosion they were about to pull back into St James's Park when Kate turned to Sergeant Bamford in amazement. He was holding something above his head.

'I don't bloody believe it!' she said. 'Were you filming all that on your phone, Sergeant?'

'I was, ma'am. Got to have something to show the grandkids one day.'

'I've got a better idea,' she replied, smiling. 'Send it to my phone and I'll make sure it gets to the operator who discovered the intel just in time. He sounds like one hell of a guy.'

Epilogue

'PLEASE, BABES,' SHE purred, putting a finger to his lips, 'just don't answer it.'

Luke rolled over in bed, glanced at the incoming call and winced. 'Sorry, I think I'd better take this one,' he said.

Elise sat up, pulled her knees to her chest and pouted at him, feigning disapproval. 'You promised,' she whispered, scowling.

As he hesitated, he reached behind her and gently massaged the back of her neck with the tips of his fingers. Elise closed her eyes, tilted her head and smiled. My God, she looked beautiful, even with the traces of a bruise where the Colombian woman had hit her. Right now, Luke felt he wanted never to leave her again. Yet he still picked up the phone. 'Luke speaking . . . Oh, right . . . What? In forty minutes? That doesn't give me a whole lot of time . . . OK, I'll be there.'

'It seems,' he said, leaning over to kiss Elise on the lips, 'that I've been summoned. To see the Chief.'

'Is that a good thing or a bad thing?' she murmured, her eyes still closed as he massaged her shoulders.

'You know what? With these people, I have no bloody idea. They're probably going to keep me guessing right up until the moment I walk into his office.'

He moved to get up off the bed but Elise opened her eyes, reached out and held him, suddenly serious. 'Listen,' she said. 'I want you to know something important.'

'Go on,' he said.

'I did a lot of thinking while I was being held by those people.'

Luke looked at her warily. 'Elise, I promise you. You don't need to worry about them ever again. They're all behind bars now, every one of them. And that's partly thanks to what you offered up in the debrief.' He smiled as he remembered something. 'You know what my mate Jorge at the Colombian Embassy tells me?'

'What?'

'That García will never again see the light of day. They're holding him in solitary at a jail just outside Bogotá. But once the legal paperwork comes through from DC the Americans will ship him to a Supermax prison in Colorado.'

Elise had released her grip on his shoulders and Luke was up and pulling on a pair of trousers, then walking over to the wardrobe to choose a shirt and tie.

'Still can't believe that Ana María woman tripped up like that,' he said, selecting a woven navy tie. 'Getting traced back through her mobile phone. From what you said, it sounded like she was smarter than that. Anyway, sorry, Lise, I interrupted you. You were about to tell me something?'

'Well, what we've both been through these last few weeks has changed the way I look at things,' she said. 'Call it a one-eighty, if you like. But I think I understand now what it's all about, and what it is you do, and I suppose what I'm trying to say is . . . I'm proud of you, I really am.'

Luke stopped buttoning his shirt and for a moment, just a moment, he felt quite emotional. He loved her so much. 'Good to know,' he said lightly, 'but remember I'm still only on contract to them.'

Luke was right. The Service was not going to tell him anything before he got to the Chief's private office. Not even Angela had given him the heads-up this time. Travelling in the lift to the sixth floor, he caught sight of his reflection in the mirror, and as he straightened his tie he thought that the face looking back at him had aged since they had first sent him to Colombia. It seemed as if years had passed since that fateful morning meeting in October. Yet what had it been? Four weeks? Five? Barely that. And already in that short time he had added another unwelcome scar to his growing collection, a dark red weal on his foot where it had encountered that electric drill.

'This way, Mr Carlton.' Sir Adam Keeling's PA pointed to the door, gestured for him to go through it, then closed it quietly behind him. Luke took in the scene at a glance: the spectacular picture window looking across the river to Millbank, the modern Azerbaijani carpet, the portrait of the Queen, and all those unsolicited gifts from around the world, balanced on the windowsill. A curved dagger from Bahrain, an incense burner from Oman and, bizarrely, a life-size replica of a seagull.

But it was the people assembled in the room who caught his attention. 'Ah, Carlton,' said the Chief, limping towards him and holding out his hand. 'Well rested,

I hope. So, I think you know everyone here?' He swept an arm towards the others. 'Carl Mayne, our director of Ops, Sid Khan, director of CT, Angela Scott, your line manager, of course.' He nodded to each of them in turn, exchanging his warmest smile with Angela. 'And, last, because you can never have too many lawyers present, I've asked John Friend to join us.'

For a second Luke saw a man in his pyjamas, framed in the doorway of a Colombian hotel room, his eyes wide with horror as he took in the scene of carnage on the floor in front of him. Then he shook his hand. 'Hi, John.'

'Hello, Luke.'

'Before I say what I want to say,' said Sir Adam, 'I believe you had some concerns regarding how we dealt with García's family in El Salvador.'

Luke had another image in his mind now: the look on García's face when he heard his own sister's scream down the phone and the noise of that electric drill somewhere in the background. 'That's true, Chief.' Luke looked pointedly at Carl Mayne. 'I was assured they wouldn't be harmed.'

'And nor were they,' replied Sir Adam. 'And I'm pleased you did have those concerns, because I want you to know that not a hair on her head was touched. The same goes for all his extended family.'

Luke relaxed a little, but he wanted to know more.

'We actually used the Vortex programme that Sid Khan helped develop when he was in Tech Division,' said the Chief. Luke glanced across at Khan, who gave a slight bow. 'We took a sample of his sister's voice, recorded while she was in custody after they landed, and morphed it into a scream. Then we simply added in the effects of the drill and played it down the line from San Salvador. I think we can agree it did the trick, don't you?'

'You mean she was never under any duress at all?'

'Luisa García,' said the Chief, with a mischievous smile, 'does not even know her brother was on the end of that phone call. No, she's fine. They're out of custody now. They'll be back in Colombia by the end of the week. Now . . .' Sir Adam Keeling cleared his throat and looked knowingly at the others gathered in his office. 'We've asked you here today,' he said, 'because you've done an outstandingly good job for us. This country, and my Service in particular, owes you a debt of gratitude.'

'Thank you, Chief.' Luke was surprised to find he was blushing.

'As you know, because of our line of business,' continued Sir Adam, 'you won't get any public recognition for it. That's not our way. But we do have something else to offer you. Angela?'

The Chief turned to his right as she passed him a crisp white envelope. 'Please open it,' he said, as he leaned against the corner of his desk.

Luke took the envelope and pulled out a single sheet of vellum, folded into three. It was addressed to him and signed in green ink.

'It's your letter of engagement,' said Sir Adam, quietly, 'should you choose to accept it, of course.' He held out his hand again. 'You've made the grade, Carlton. We'd like to offer you a permanent job here as a case officer in the Secret Intelligence Service. Oh, and Carlton? Just one more thing. We've got an interesting situation developing . . . somewhere that might appeal to you. We'd like you to take a look at it. If you're up for it, that is?'

Acknowledgements

My thanks go to my ever-loyal publishers, Transworld, for backing this book, and in particular to my brilliant editor, Simon Taylor. Annoyingly, it was hard to argue with any of your suggestions. I am extremely grateful to my agent (publishing agent, that is), Julian Alexander from LAW, for believing in this whole project from Day One. Thank you to those of you I consulted who drew on your many years of experience in dark and dangerous places (notably Whitehall). To James, Mal and Chris for your input on the Royal Marines and the SBS, to Richard, John, EG, Admiral Lord West and others for your advice on intelligence and security matters. To Steve Johnson for sharing some of your profound scientific knowledge and to Brett Lovegrove for your hard-earned expertise on counter-terrorism policing. To Sir Tim Berners-Lee for your help on digital technology and to Matt and G for advice on IEDs. To Linda Davies and Mike Ridpath, for passing on some of their bestselling novelists' tricks of the trade, and to Rupert Wise, Linda, Tina and Charles Blackmore for hosting your anti-social guest when he typed away in your homes. To Penelope Coate and the Spanish department at Putney High School for their help with my Spanish. To

Sasha Gardner for helping out on the Cornwall recce. Last, thank you to the people of Colombia. Yours is a wonderful country. May the years ahead be peaceful.

No input was asked for from, or offered by, any arm of Her Majesty's Government.

And Luke Carlton returns in Frank Gardner's blistering new thriller

ULTIMATUM

Turn the page for a taster of what's in store . . .

Prologue

'*Salaam, Ali jaan*. It's me.' The voice, unmistakable, hoarse and crackly over the encrypted line. 'So. It's all in place?'

'It's all in place.'

'No changes?'

The man didn't answer straight away. He removed his earpiece, tipped his head back, closed his eyes and wiped the palm of his hand over the stubble that covered half his face. Still in his thirties and already the coarse hairs that crept up his cheek were flecked with grey. He sighed. *How many times had they been over this?* He replaced the earpiece and spoke into the mike.

'No,' he replied patiently, 'there are no changes. Everything is exactly as we discussed.'

'Good. Because you know—'

'Yes, yes, I know. So much is riding on this.'

'So much? SO MUCH? Are you playing with me, Ali *jaan*? Have you forgotten all the meetings in Qom? The sermons? The instructions? This is everything! Everything we have ever worked for. Remember, we are just the facilitators here, nothing more.'

The man waited for him to finish. He closed his eyes once more and pinched the ridge of flesh between his eyebrows. So many months of planning, so many contingencies to think of. So many what-ifs. By God, he was tired. But the man on the other end of the line was not done yet.

'So, Ali *jaan*. I am counting on you. WE . . . are all counting on you. No mistakes. Nothing left to chance.' It was part question, part order. 'Are you certain you can do this?'

'Yes,' said the man abruptly, just a hint of irritation creeping in now. 'I am certain.'

'Then do it.' There was a click and the line went dead.

Chapter 1

The pitch. The proposal. The moment of truth. That split second in time when the man or woman in front of you realizes with a start just exactly what it is you're suggesting. That they should risk everything, maybe even their lives, their families, to betray their own organization, their own country, to steal a secret and hand it over to British intelligence. Get it right and you might get to reel in a big fish, some Grade A source that keeps on giving, propelling you into the upper echelons of MI6, perhaps retiring gracefully to the shires with a knighthood, a valedictory lunch with the PM and some quiet recognition from your peers. Get it wrong and you're toast.

When Luke Carlton arrived for the rendezvous that morning he had just four words reverberating in his head, over and over again. 'Don't fuck it up.' His contact was nervous as hell, that much was obvious. The man was sitting there at a table in the corner, visibly sweating, perched half off his chair, twitching like a bird, glancing repeatedly behind him at the door, as if expecting trouble to come flying through it any second. A television set, mounted on the wall, was tuned to a football match with the sound turned down. Luke held out his hand and gave him what he hoped was a reassuring smile. The hand he gripped was damp and slippery, their half-hearted handshake slid quickly apart.

'I shouldn't be here,' said the contact. Luke could see that his shirt collar was frayed in several places and his suit jacket was old and stained. He definitely needed the money, or he probably wouldn't have turned up.

'Well thanks for coming anyway,' said Luke breezily. 'Can I get you something to drink?'

The man shook his head, waving away the suggestion. 'I haven't much time,' he said.

'No, of course,' said Luke, sitting down. 'So, er, have you had a chance to think about what we discussed, the last time we met?'

'I'm not clear on what you're proposing?' the other man replied, shuffling his chair closer to Luke's. 'Please. Tell me exactly what it is you want from me.'

Here we go. Deep breath. Take the plunge. This was the watershed moment when Luke would shift from one dimension to another, from legit to illicit. Luke reached into the inside left pocket of his jacket and drew out an unmarked envelope and put it on the table, keeping it covered with his hand.

'I'd like to offer you a job,' he said. No reaction. OK, keep it going. 'A job that pays good money.'

The man's eyes flicked down towards the unopened envelope. Luke kept it covered.

'In here,' he continued, tapping the envelope with his fingertips, 'is something to get you started. Think of it as a welcome present from my employers.'

The man looked perplexed, his eyebrows furrowed. 'But I still don't understand,' he protested. 'What is it you want me to do?'

Enough. Surely we've been through this already. It was time to stop beating about the bush. Luke needed to lay his cards on the table.

'I need you to . . .' Luke hesitated. He had to phrase this just right, there could be no misunderstanding. The contact was watching him intently now, waiting to hear how he would finish the sentence. His eyes, keen as a hawk's, met Luke's.

'I need you to get me the passcode for the State Security datafiles.' There. He had blurted it out in one breath, as if expelling some toxic, unwanted object from his system.

What happened next took place in a dizzying blur. Before Luke had a chance to react he saw the contact reach beneath the table where he must have triggered some kind of signal. Suddenly there was a high-pitched alarm going off and the door came crashing in. Two bulky figures dressed in uniforms he didn't recognize came barrelling through the open doorway and lifted Luke bodily out of his chair then pinned him hard up against the wall. It was too late to resist: one of them already had his hand clenched around his balls while the other held a Taser to his throat.

The 'contact' sighed and rose slowly from his chair, took out a handkerchief and wiped a layer of shiny theatrical grease off his face then folded it away, tucking it neatly back into his pocket. He sauntered over to where Luke stood, restrained by both arms, and smiled affably.

'Better luck next time, Carlton. I'm afraid that was a failed pass. You revealed your hand too early.' He patted Luke on the shoulder and nodded to the two 'guards' to let him go.

'Oh, there's tea and biscuits in the debriefing room

when you're ready. They'll play back the tapes to everyone in there.'

Luke's shoulders slumped. He was not used to failure.

'Listen,' the 'contact' consoled him, 'practically everyone fails this part of the course the first time round. Don't worry, you'll get another shot tomorrow.'

He left with a wink then stopped and called out over his shoulder. 'Remember, nobody said Agent-Running was easy.'

. . . to be continued

BLOOD AND SAND
Frank Gardner

On 6 June 2004, in a quiet suburb of Riyadh, BBC security correspondent Frank Gardner and cameraman Simon Cumbers were ambushed by Islamist gunmen. Simon was killed outright. Frank was hit in the shoulder and leg. As he lay in the road, pleading for his life, a figure stood over him and pumped four more bullets into his body at point-blank range . . .

Against all the odds, Frank Gardner survived, and this is his remarkable account of the agonizing journey he's taken – from being shot and left for dead to where he is today, partly paralysed but alive.

It is a journey that began twenty-five years earlier, when a chance meeting with explorer Wilfred Thesiger inspired in the young Frank what would become a lifelong passion for the Arab world – an abiding interest that would take him throughout the Middle East and lead to his becoming a BBC journalist. And this same passion would, in the wake of 9/11, send Frank on another journey that came to dominate – and nearly end – his life: his coverage of Al-Qaeda.

Honest, moving and inspiring, *Blood and Sand* reveals a deep understanding of the Islamic world and offers an insider's compelling analysis of the ongoing 'War on Terror' and what it means in these uncertain times.

'Chilling, graphic and admirably unsentimental'
GUARDIAN

'What makes Gardner's moving, often humorous, deeply personal story so important is the fact that he has woven into it a brilliantly dispassionate, clear-eyed account of the Islamic world'
SCOTSMAN

'A superb reporter . . . his terrible experience only makes his analysis all the more telling'
EVENING STANDARD

FAR HORIZONS
Frank Gardner

Lost on a Sumatran volcano ... pursued through Tokyo by a Japanese gangster ... picnicking with the French Foreign Legion in Africa ...

Ever since his student days, BBC Security Correspondent Frank Gardner has travelled in many of the world's most out of the way places. Then, in June 2004, his life – never mind his ability to travel – was nearly brought to a violent end by Islamist gunmen. Incredibly he survived and, against all the odds, is again looking towards far horizons. Recent adventures have included skiing in the Alps, scuba diving in the Red Sea, exploring the jungles of Thailand and once more reporting from far-flung destinations like Colombia and Afghanistan. And this is a man who no longer has the use of his legs ...

Far Horizons is Frank Gardner's compelling account of the travels that made him the man he was on that fateful day in June – and of the journeys he's made since, and how they have helped him become the remarkable and inspiring individual he is today.

'Gardner is a good storyteller ... Always revealing, often riotous and sometimes very moving'
TIME OUT

'His adventures fly off the page ... entertaining and charmingly self-deprecating'
NEWS OF THE WORLD

'A bold, life-affirming read'
GQ